CV

THE FIRST TIME . . .

"No, I do not want another beer. Just you, Maggie. All I want is you," J.D. had said.

Neither of them had moved, held by the moment and by the intensity of each other's gaze.

"Tell me now, Maggie, if you don't want this to go any further. Because if I so much as touch you now, there'll be no turning back . . . no way to stop it. Do you understand what I'm saying?"

Her nod was barely perceptible.

He touched her neck with the back of his hand, his fingers slowly tracing a path, following the V of her blouse. When he reached the top button, he caressed the skin underneath. Still looking directly into his eyes, she reached her hands up slightly and began to unbutton his shirt. He brought her close and held her, found her face and kissed it, then her waiting lips. The powerful heat that had sparked when he'd kissed her the night before ignited full blast. . . .

For orders other than by individual consumers, Pocket Books grants a discount on the purchase of **10 or more** copies of single titles for special markets or premium use. For further details, please write to the Vice-President of Special Markets, Pocket Books, 1230 Avenue of the Americas, New York, NY 10020.

For information on how individual consumers can place orders, please write to Mail Order Department, Paramount Publishing, 200 Old Tappan Road, Old Tappan, NJ 07675.

MOMENTS IN TIME

MARIAH STEWART

POCKET BOOKS
New York   London   Toronto   Sydney   Tokyo   Singapore

This book is a work of fiction. Names, characters, places and incidents are products of the author's imagination or are used fictitiously. Any resemblance to actual events or locales or persons, living or dead, is entirely coincidental.

An *Original* Publication of POCKET BOOKS

POCKET BOOKS, a division of Simon & Schuster Inc.
1230 Avenue of the Americas, New York, NY 10020

Copyright © 1995 by Marti Robb

ISBN: 0-671-86854-3

First Pocket Books printing March 1995

10 9 8 7 6 5 4 3 2 1

POCKET and colophon are registered trademarks of Simon & Schuster Inc.

Cover art by Franco Accornero

Printed in the U.S.A.

With Deepest Gratitude to . . .

Loretta Barrett, my agent, whose kind words of encouragement gave me reason to believe in myself,

and

Linda Marrow, editor extraordinaire, whose wit, style and sensitivity took the pain out of the rewrites and made this all seem so easy.

Every author should be so blessed.

M.S.

Grateful Acknowledgments to . . .

Wendy Wyant, who with patience and good humor brought me kicking and screaming into the computer age.

Warren Bell—my "twin"—who helped me to understand what the process of making music means to a musician, and in doing so helped bring definition to a character or two.

Helen Egner, who has earned the right to say "I told you so."

Carole Spayd, who made the trek from Bucks County on countless hot summer Sundays to read the latest chapter, and whose enthusiasm kept me going.

Joan Sanger, whose magic helped transform a manuscript into a book.

And, of course, my family: my parents; my husband, Bill; and the two characters of whom I'm most proud, Kate and Rebecca.

1

MARGARET SUSANNAH CALLAHAN AVERY BORDERS SHIFTED UN-comfortably on the sofa cushion, wishing for all she was worth that she could be someplace—anyplace—other than here in her mother-in-law's living room at this particular moment in time. Inches away to her left sat her husband, J. D. Borders, singer and songwriter, a longtime favorite on the British pop music scene. And right now, in his wife's opinion, the world's biggest son of a bitch.

He tried to steal a seemingly casual glance in her direction to see if he could gauge what exactly was going on behind those big green eyes. He studied the set of her jaw, the immobile expression on her face, and knew without doubt he was in big trouble.

He ran his left hand nervously through his hair. Why in the world had he ever consented to this damned interview? He had a general dislike of the whole routine, avoided it whenever possible, not being particularly comfortable in speaking about himself under the best of conditions. He knew this interview—to be televised live to the entire U.K.—would be worse than most. He had reluctantly agreed only because his mother, a longtime fan of Hilary Gates's, had caught him in a very weak moment. J.D. had been amused that though his had been a well-known name in the music business for better than twenty-five years, he hadn't "made it" in his mother's eyes until he'd been asked to be a guest on Hilary's show. He knew the only acceptable excuse for canceling, at least as far as his mother was concerned, would have been major surgery. Had it not been for his mother and the fact that his children were all upstairs with their grandmother eagerly awaiting the start of the show, he'd have gladly stayed in London and skipped the whole episode.

He wished he could think of something to say that would elicit a response from his wife, who, he suspected, would rather be back home in the States conferring with her lawyer. There had been so many times throughout their fifteen years together when they'd been so much on the same wavelength that speech had been unnecessary between them. This was not one of those times.

Maggie had completely shut him out and retreated behind a placid mask, totally detached from him and the situation. He knew that she was anything but calm, knew that inside she was seething and for less than two cents she'd happily break the nearest lamp over his head. He had absolutely no clue as to what she would say or do once the cameras started to roll tonight and Hilary began her assault.

Maggie had not spoken a word to him in three days, nor would she listen to anything he'd tried to say to her since their concurrent arrival in separate cars almost an hour ago. His heart had leapt expectantly when he'd pulled into his mother's driveway just seconds after Maggie had emerged from her car. But she turned away when he approached her, walking past him as if he was invisible. She'd gone directly upstairs to see their children and had just moments earlier joined the group gathered in the living room prior to the start of the show.

Now he was seated so close to her that his hands began to shake and beads of sweat formed on his brow at the sight of her. He suspected that Maggie had worn her hair in precisely the style he liked best—pulled back off her face, held high on each side by tortoise shell combs, the long dark auburn ringlets cascading down her back, deep bangs framing her eyes—simply to torture him. She was wearing a simple black dress, a particular favorite of his, long sleeves that started at the very edge of her shoulders, cut low front and back, long bare neck, no jewelry other than large rectangular gold earrings and her wide gold wedding ring. The massive diamond solitaire with which he'd surprised her on their tenth anniversary was conspicuously absent from her hand.

He sighed with frustration. She clearly wanted nothing to do with him, had no interest in any explanation he'd tried to offer since she'd walked into their hotel suite in London on Friday morning and found him getting out of the shower and Glory Fielding, his former lover, standing there wrapped in a towel.

He had to admit it had looked bad.

Maggie had simply looked at him with the most devastated eyes, turned heel, and walked out before he'd been able to tell her that things weren't exactly as they seemed. He wasn't sure who'd been more surprised, he or Maggie.

No one, as far as he knew, had any inkling of the tempest that had so recently shattered their lives. *So, Maggie,* he thought, *what will you do? Will you give Hilary the big scoop she's after, the scandal she'd so dearly love, blow away fifteen years of marriage by announcing that you're leaving me?* He could not discount that possibility, judging by the look on her face. Anything she did at this point would not surprise him.

On the opposite side of the room, Hilary was absorbed in her last-minute primping, assuring herself that her light blond hair was perfect, her silk dress smoothed over her tall, angular frame. Though in her midfifties, in her mind's eye she was a twenty-five-year-old femme fatale, her mirrored self fifteen pounds lighter than she really was. She checked her makeup to ensure it was doing its job, suitably denying both reality and gravity. Crow's-feet? No, no, there's a bad reflection. Sagging jaw line? Of course not, the lighting's bad. One of her close friends had confided to another that someday Hilary would wake up, take an honest look in the glass, and break a leg as she tripped over herself rushing to the nearest plastic surgeon.

The show was about to begin, but tonight Hilary could not muster the usual buzz of excitement. The anticipation simply was not there. Usually she was in an inward frenzy, turned on by the knowledge she'd been able to dig up something with which she'd be able to shock her viewers. Most often, it was the one thing her guests would least like to be publicly revealed. It was this talent that had earned her the title in which she took the greatest pleasure: "Bitch of the BBC."

Hilary's monthly televised interview show was the highest-rated program in the U.K., a must-watch simply by virtue of her uncanny ability to bring out the absolute worst in her guests. She had an uncanny instinct to find the soft spot in the armor and to sniff out those areas the interviewees least wanted to discuss. It was said that if Hilary went through your laundry, she'd immediately find that one article that somehow was overlooked in the wash.

The show was eagerly awaited by a gossip-hungry public who stopped everything from nine till eleven P.M. every fourth Sunday to watch her operate. Hilary believed in her soul that she was more popular than the queen, and for two hours every fourth Sunday, she most definitely was.

Tonight, she feared, would be one of those rare occasions when no bombshell would be dropped, nor would there be anything that would titillate or intrigue her waiting viewers. She anticipated absolutely nothing noteworthy from these two. J. D. Borders—appealing though he was—and that little American wife of his would have been her dead last choices for a show, but her producer, a longtime fan of J.D.'s music, had run into them at some charity function and become totally smitten with Maggie, for reasons that were simply beyond Hilary's comprehension. Oh, she was attractive enough in her own way, Hilary gave her that. Maggie had dark hair (which she has *got* to be coloring, since she must be fortysomething) and that cute little body (which only God knows how she's managed to keep after all those children) and that pretty but hardly spectacular face that showed barely a line (perhaps a nip here and a tuck there?).

J.D., however, was another story, she thought as she dodged one of the cameras being moved into position and snapped on her microphone. He was one of those men who actually got better looking with each passing year. Forty-three years old now, with hardly a gray hair and still a great body and that wonderfully rugged face, that heavenly smile, that incredible trademark voice. Even the most "in" of insiders swore he'd been one hundred percent faithful to Maggie over all the years (*which is,* thought Hilary, *absolutely criminal if it's true—I'd love a tumble with him myself*). Hilary had tried from every possible angle to uncover some dirt, even old dirt, along those lines and had come up dry at every source. It was inconceivable to her that this woman had managed to hold his attention for fifteen years with never an indiscretion.

Hilary's mind was racing. God knows she had done her best to ferret something out. She was scrupulous about her research, rarely, if ever, permitting anyone to assist her in this most important aspect of her preparation for each show. She knew that no one else had her ability for reading between the lines in old magazine articles or newspaper clippings or casual conversations with family members and friends. No one could shine the light into the dark corners like Hilary.

Even the prep for this show had been excruciatingly dull, she recalled as she checked her face for the last time. This will be one of the longest, most boring . . . she snapped the mirrored case shut and looked around the room.

Maggie had been adamant that the interview be conducted here, in the family living room, rather than in the more formal parlor across the hall. When Hilary had made her preshow visit, the room had been washed in the soft light of a late afternoon sun, the pale rose of the walls a gentle background to the lush floral chintz of the furniture and the plush carpet of dark green beneath her feet. The

5

French doors had been open then, framing a vista of the garden beyond which had appeared as a living work of art, the colors blending into an impressionist backdrop. Now in the harsh light of the television cameras, the earlier charm of the room faded somewhat, and the glorious view had been eliminated by the darkness of the evening hour.

Even her guests seemed to have lost some of their previous sparkle. She'd turned to look at the couple seated on the sofa, gazed long and hard. What was it that seemed out of sync?

J.D.'s elbow rested on the back of the sofa, his chin in his hand as he stared blankly into space, obviously deep in thought, his expression impossible to decipher. Anxiety? Confusion? At the very least, he appeared ill at ease.

Hilary turned her scrutiny on the wife, whose head was bent forward as a technician attempted to untangle several strands of long hair from the microphone wires. That task completed, Maggie repositioned herself, very definitely, Hilary observed, leaning away from J.D. as if determined to put as much distance as possible between them, even though they sat less than a foot apart. They had not spoken, Hilary suddenly realized, since Maggie had entered the room a good twenty minutes after everyone else had assembled. Something was definitely amiss. She could smell it now.

The couple had been warm and loving, clowning affectionately, when they'd met with Hilary a few weeks earlier to go over the show's format. Now there was a definite frost in the air. Something about the set of Maggie's shoulders, the way she was pointedly not looking at him, was a distinct contrast to their last meeting. And there was something else, something about their very physical appearance. Gone was the glowing, animated pair who'd greeted her when she'd arrived for her previous visit. In their places sat two lackluster strangers, their faces gray and their bloodshot eyes underscored by dark rings, as if they'd been on a month-long binge and decided only this morning to sober up. If they were prone to alcoholic excesses, she would have heard. That type of thing could not be covered up easily

6

these days. Yet there had not been an inkling of any such indulgence.

Yes indeed, Hilary's instincts were aroused now. Something is most assuredly out of whack between these two, and she, Hilary, would only have the length of the show to find out what it was and wrench it from its hiding place.

"So . . . are we all set here? Two minutes till show time," she said sprightly, her enthusiasm renewed. *This might be fun after all,* she thought; *it's been forever since I've had to work blind, without having my plan of attack formulated in advance. This could be a real challenge.* To Maggie she cooed, "You look lovely, Maggie. That dress is stunning on you. Don't you agree, J.D.? Your wife looks positively adorable."

"God, yes, she always does." He bit his lower lip to stop its tremble. *I know exactly how she looks, know every inch of that face as well as I know my own. I could sketch her in the dark and not miss a freckle. She always looks good to me, always has and always will. If we both live to be a hundred, I'd still think she was the only woman in the world worth having. That is what is making this whole damn situation so crazy. I have never really wanted anyone but Maggie. Since the very beginning, there has never been anyone else.*

His frustration was becoming unbearable. Maggie hadn't so much as looked at him. He knew he had to get his thoughts collected in the next forty-five seconds to somehow get through to her during the course of the show and find a way to make her understand what had happened, make her listen. *All I have to do,* he reasoned, *is find the right angle.* His heart sank with an all but audible thud. He would have but two hours—the length of the interview—to get her attention, to put his life back together again.

Maggie turned her body slightly to face Hilary more directly, knowing that in order to maintain her composure or some semblance of it, she would have to be attentive so that Hilary could not catch her off guard. She was smart enough to know Hilary would not have been oblivious to the coolness between her and J.D.—an eight-year-old could pick that up, let alone someone with Hilary's experience.

She reminded herself that her children were watching and willed herself to be as pleasant as she could under these damnable circumstances. There would be time enough in the morning to tell them they'd be returning to their home in the States—without their father. She vowed to say nothing, do nothing, that would lead to a public revelation before she'd told them herself, then said a hasty prayer that she would be able to exercise enough control to get through this night without having a breakdown or generally making a fool out of herself. Her best bet, she reasoned, was to keep her mouth closed as much as possible and only speak when she could not avoid a response.

She looked over at her husband, knew he, too, was anxious and miserable. *Good. It serves the son of a bitch right.*

The burning anger returned as she again saw in her mind the scene she'd walked into three days earlier . . .

On Thursday morning they had left the children with J.D.'s mother and had checked into their favorite hotel in London. J.D. had promised an old friend that he'd join him in recording one song on a new album that afternoon, and Maggie had accompanied him for two days of shopping and some quiet time together. On Friday the sound of the rain had awakened her before dawn, and she had rolled over to watch him as he slept. Lax in slumber, his face appeared as youthful as it had when they had first met, and she smiled to herself as she inched toward him on her elbows. Kissing his chin, then his cheek, then his lips, she coaxed him awake and into her arms. By the time their lovemaking had concluded, so had the rain, the sun peaking through the drapes, tiny shards of light crawling across the dark red carpet.

"This is the single best reason to leave the children with my mother and come into the city at least once a week," he observed, "and certainly blows a hole in that magazine article I read a few days back."

"And what article was that?" she asked, nuzzling his chest, eyes closed.

"The one expounding on the notion that women lose their inclination once they pass forty," he grinned, anticipating her response. He felt her eyelashes flutter on his skin as her eyes flashed open.

"And have you noticed a decline in inclination over the years?" she asked archly.

"Absolutely none," he assured her, his hand caressing the small of her back, "I was merely repeating the theory. I thought perhaps I'd write a rebuttal."

"Do so anonymously, please," she yawned, "or the tabloids will have a field day."

He laughed and moved his arm to permit her to turn onto her stomach.

"And what have you planned for today?" he inquired into the tangle of dark hair.

"I thought I'd do some shopping," she replied, "since school will be starting soon, and I'd like to buy some school clothes for the kids while we're over here. Everything's always so hectic by the time we get back to the States. And I want to get something very special for your mother's birthday. She'll be sixty-five this year, you know. Anything ending in a zero or a five is a big birthday."

They called room service and enjoyed the luxury of breakfast in bed, no small children bouncing on the mattress, no tiny faces begging for a bite of this or a sip of that. She dressed casually and by nine-thirty was ready to begin her errands.

"And what will you be doing while I'm out spending the bulk of the proceeds from your last album?" she asked.

"I will finish reading the paper and take a shower. Maybe pop down to the local bookstore and look over the selection. I'm in the mood for a good, challenging mystery. Come back in time to have tea with me downstairs," he suggested, "and you can tell me what wonderful surprise you found for my mom."

She leaned down to kiss him and in doing so spilled coffee onto the tray that she'd knocked with her elbow. Frowning, she sopped up the dark liquid with several napkins, grumbling, "I'd say I'm getting off to a good start today."

He pulled her down to him and kissed her.

"I'd say you got off to a very good start today," he reminded her.

She laughed and headed out the door.

Once out onto the street, she stopped, debating whether to take a cab or to walk. It was a pleasant enough morning, she decided, and paused to get her bearings, considered her errands, and crossed the street. She strolled along for several blocks, enjoying her solitary excursion, though her normally brisk pace was impeded by the crowds that were rapidly filling the sidewalks. Following first one side street, then another, she stopped several times to peer into the shop windows at items that caught her eye.

The city bustled, as it always seemed to do in summer. The first morning rush of cars and buses hurrying folks to work had eased, their places on the streets now taken by the red double-decker buses jammed with tourists. She stopped to give directions to a group of Japanese tourists seeking Buckingham Palace, reminding them the guard changed at eleven-thirty and encouraging them not to miss the gardens as she pointed out the way. As they moved on by, the storefront that had been obscured by the throng came into view. The small antique shop was just opening for the day, and a quick glance at the window revealed a diminutive writing desk tucked into the display.

She leaned closer for a better look. It was perfect, she thought, for that short wall in the front hallway of the home they shared with J.D.'s mother during summers and vacations. They had expanded the old house several times over the past few years as their family had grown, the last time enlarging the entry as they added a library and a sunroom to the left of the main stairway. She went inside the antique shop and carefully looked over the desk. It was just the thing. She asked the dealer to hold it for her while she ran back to the hotel to fetch her husband in hopes that he would like it as much as she did.

She had entered the suite and gone directly to the bedroom, then seeing the bathroom door partially open and hearing the water from the shower, she called his name just as the sound of water ceased.

She would never, she knew, forget the way it had all appeared to her as she opened the bathroom door. The scene replayed itself in slow motion every time she closed her eyes: J.D.'s look of surprise and confusion, Glory's smug little smile as she turned to face Maggie.

The pain and shock had knocked the breath from her lungs, numbed her mind.

"Oh, Jamey, no . . ." she had heard herself whisper, then had turned and stumbled blindly from the room, out into the hallway, where she had leaned against the wall awaiting the elevator, a fist pressed tightly into the excruciating pain exploding in her abdomen. Her mind had been frozen, and she later recalled having prayed that she would not scream or throw up in the elevator as she descended to the lobby and sought a cab.

It had never occurred to her that J.D. would be unfaithful to her. Maggie had honestly believed she knew him to the depths of his soul. Yet, hidden deep in her heart had always been the fear that Glory, who never seemed willing to abandon a desire to rekindle that old flame, would someday succeed at taking him from her, as she'd so often taunted she would.

Glory Fielding was every wife's nightmare. Even now, in her midthirties, she was still a most spectacular-looking woman with long golden hair and the face of a beautiful, innocent child. Three days ago, on Friday morning in a London hotel suite, Maggie's nightmare had become reality.

She had fled to the sanctity of Rick Daily's country home some twenty miles north, grateful to find that Rick had gone to the city with his daughter for a few days. The housekeeper, well acquainted with the entire Border crew—Rick, J.D., and Maggie having been friends for years—permitted her to stay without asking any questions and had, upon Maggie's instructions, denied her presence when J.D. had called. The message that had been relayed to Maggie was that he needed desparately to speak to her, that she must give him a chance to explain.

He'd been caught with another woman under the most incriminating circumstances, she had indignantly scoffed. What on earth could there be to explain?

Swallowing the lump that had risen in her throat in response to the memory, Maggie raised her chin resolutely, blinking away the burning in her eyes. All she wanted right now was to conclude this ordeal with her dignity intact. She commanded herself to somehow manage to keep her hostility toward him cloaked for the next two hours, then she could slam the door in his face. By this time tomorrow she would be on her way back to the States with her children. *Just two more hours and I will never have to be in the same room with him again. Just two more hours . . .*

"Well, we're all set. Camera one," Hilary gestured behind her, "will be rolling first . . . Watch for the lights, there's the cue . . . Smile, you two," she commanded her guests as the lights glared and Hilary's recorded theme song signaled the start of the show.

2

"TONIGHT, FRIENDS, WE'RE PRIVILEGED TO HAVE AS OUR GUESTS one of the mainstays of the pop music scene, J. D. Borders, and his wife, Maggie. We're pleased you both could join us this evening. J.D., you've given us better than twenty-five years of popular music. So many of your contemporaries have come and gone and come back again. Yet you, for the most part, managed to remain something of a permanent prescence in the business all this time. Why do you suppose that's so?"

"Well, I'm not sure that I've done anything that's quite that notable," he began with characteristic modesty, trying to control his quivering voice, forcing himself to speak slowly and to concentrate—no easy task with his life falling apart. "There are any number of very excellent musicians who started out back in the sixties who have been very successful, much more successful than I. Maybe at times I remained more visible than others because I never stopped recording. Maybe I've felt somewhat more pressure to keep working all these years simply due to the fact that I have so many children to support." He turned to look at Maggie and

13

recognized her "we-are-not-amused" expression. His mild attempt at light humor having failed, he cleared his throat and continued.

"And many of the others from that time never went away at all. Some of the best performers from the early sixties through the seventies moved around a great deal within different bands. You could start out with just about any of the well-known groups from that period and trace different members into other bands that would lead you to still others. A lot of us did that, you know, went from one band to another."

"How would you describe the changes in your music over the years?" She shuffled a small stack of note cards.

"I don't know that it's changed remarkably. There's been some evolution, of course, as I've matured—keep in mind that I was barely seventeen years old when I started, so the songs I wrote back then would reflect a seventeen-year-old's perspective. In general, though, I don't think my style has changed dramatically. The same influences are there."

"Those influences being . . ."

"A real hodge-podge, actually. Blues, jazz, rock—particularly American rock and roll—and I'd studied piano for many years, from the time I was five or six years old, so I had a classical background."

"How did an aspiring classical pianist end up in a rock-and-roll band?" Hilary asked with mild curiosity.

"Rick Daily," he answered simply, as if the name was explanation enough.

"You hooked up with him at a fairly young age, as I recall. How did all that come about?"

"My cousin, Robby, had told me about this great band he'd seen at a pub in a town down the road. One night he talked me into going with him—I was only sixteen and Robby had to sneak me in. Rick was already something of a local celebrity by then. Watching him perform was like nothing I'd ever seen or heard—there simply wasn't anyone like him and still isn't, by the way. I was starting to fancy myself a pretty decent musician about the same time I heard

Rick was looking to start up his own group. I gathered all my courage to ask him if he would listen to me play. We hit it off, and that was how I picked up with Rick and formed our first band: Daily Times."

"It sounds like Rick was quite an inspiration to you back then," noted Hilary.

"He still is." J.D. nodded. "He's still the best."

"What caused your eventual split with him?"

"Nothing dramatic, I assure you. And the split was strictly professional," he explained. "Over the years, we simply developed differently—musically—as our individual styles matured somewhat. We'd tried working around that for a few years, but neither of us have the ability to compromise gracefully. So, when the split came, it was very natural, very much inevitable. And when Monkshood's last tour concluded, we simply went our separate ways, though we've remained the best of friends."

"And that last tour was back in, let's see, 1976?"

"Close." He nodded. "It was in '75. And of course, that was the year I met Maggie."

He shifted slightly to face his wife, but if she noticed, she gave no sign. She had been silent since the show had begun, had declined to participate, as if she were no more than a fixture in the room. Though she shared the same sofa, in her mind, she was clearly thousands of miles away. No doubt rehearsing, he thought grimly, what she'd say to her lawyer when she got back home.

He ached knowing how deeply she was hurt, could not bear the thought that he had caused her such pain. If only he could get through to her long enough to make her listen to the truth, she would understand, he was sure of it, but she had removed herself from the scene so totally that she seemed not a part of it.

A few lines from a song he'd written years ago hummed in his ears like a pesky mosquito he was unable to swat. He tried to concentrate on what Hilary was saying, but the words and tune went around and around in his head, an insistent, melodic ferris wheel that would not stop.

Every tomorrow holds a little bit of yesterday.
Night's still with us come the morning, though the
   darkness fades away.
The years, long past, still hold us fast
And beckon us to stay.
The key to tomorrow lies lost in yesterday.

How long had it been since he'd written those words?
Fifteen years? Sixteen? He could not recall.

The key to tomorrow lies lost in yesterday.
The key to tomorrow . . .

The smallest of smiles played on his lips, then spread
slowly as it occurred to him that his only hope of weaving
her back into his life would be to somehow use what
remained of the show to remind her of all they'd been
through together, all they'd meant to each other over the
years. He would have to take control of the conversation,
parade their memories before her, and convince her beyond
doubt that she could not live without him.

To Hilary, he said congenially, as if relating a tale to his
best friend, "Nineteen seventy-five was a year of both
endings and beginnings. It was, as you mentioned, Hilary,
my last tour as part of a band, though I didn't realize it at the
time. The way things happened, with Maggie coming into
my life so unexpectedly, always made me feel somehow that
it was all meant to be."

"Kismet," suggested Hilary.

"Yes. Exactly. At least, that's how I always think of it, the
day I met Maggie." His boyish smile drew their hostess
unwittingly into his scheme.

"Sounds romantic." Hilary met his smile with her own.
He certainly has a disarming sort of charm, she mused.

J.D. laughed. "The circumstances were hardly romantic,
but it is an interesting story."

Hilary was not oblivious to the tension that was building
in Maggie's face. She had half turned in her husband's

direction, then glanced toward the door, as if fighting an urge to leave the room. *This is a most peculiar scene,* Hilary thought. *It may be amusing to let them play it out.* She decided to encourage him to pursue this nostalgic path.

"Sounds like fun. Tell us about it."

Maggie met her husband's eyes for the first time in three days, and in spite of the distance she'd chosen to put between them, silently pleaded, *Please don't do this.* He acknowledged how much it would hurt her—hurt them both—to look back but hoped that by the time the show had ended, she'd understand that it was only desperation that permitted him to knowingly inflict any further wounds to her heart. It could mean the difference between losing her and winning her back. He had no choice but to continue.

"The band was on a bus, coming into Philadelphia . . ." he began, and in spite of her best efforts to block him out, it all came back to her as her husband recounted the events of that day a long fifteen years ago . . .

It had been an unusually warm day for so early in March, the record high temperatures more like early summer, with clear blue skies and warm breezes and that feel of the sun that normally doesn't arrive until mid-May. A real teaser of a day, sandwiched in between the blustery gray gloom of late winter, which seems to last forever in eastern Pennsylvania, and the first true touch of early spring.

J.D. had been asleep on the back of the bus that had carried the band from Pittsburgh, where they'd played for two consecutive nights, into Philadelphia where they would appear for two more at the city's largest arena. The U.S. leg of the tour was barely a month old, and already J.D. couldn't wait till it was over. He hated touring after the exhilaration of the first few weeks on the road wore off. The monotony of the hours spent actually traveling made him crazy. There had to be a better way to live.

As the bus's road rhythm ceased, he sat up, somewhat disoriented, and looked around to find the other members of the band and the better part of their traveling entourage stoned. The heavy, sweet smell of marijuana thick in the air.

"Where are we?" he called out to no one in particular.

From the front of the bus came the reply "Philadelphia."

"Why are we just sitting here?"

"Accident up ahead. Looks like a bad one, too. We ain't goin' no where for a while, so get comfortable, boys," the driver called back to his passengers.

The parklike area along the river was alive with people, as if every jogger and biker in the city had emerged to take advantage of what would most likely be the best day they'd have for at least another month. That would account for the heavy traffic. Four o'clock on a Sunday afternoon in March was probably not normally a happening time in this city.

Rounding a slight bend in the river, along a path about twenty feet in from the road, came a jogger, long strides for such short legs, he'd thought at the time, watching the white shorts and red sweatshirt move closer. Cute little body that moved with an even, rhythmic gait. Cute little face, rigid with concentration as she ran. He found himself wondering what was on her mind that absorbed her so deeply, then smiled unconsciously at the sight of her. Definitely a cutie, not a knockout, but she definitely deserved a second look. He amused himself momentarily wondering if she'd be among the scores of girls who'd be waiting outside the doors of the arena come Tuesday night after the concert. His instincts told him not to waste his time looking for her face in that crowd.

A discordant motion from the jogger caught his eye. She was almost parallel to the bus when she began to stumble, both hands reaching out in front of her to break the coming fall. Her left foot twisted slightly under her as she appeared to go down in slow motion. He watched to see if she would get up. She made a wobbly attempt but could not stand.

Pain reflected in her face as her small body crumbled back to the ground, and she banged a fist into the dirt in frustration. Over on the path closer to the river ran another group of joggers. A row of hedges obscured her from their view, and they did not notice her. He waited another minute to see if someone would stop and help her. No one did.

Oh, what the hell, he thought, *I could use a stretch right about now.* He walked to the front of the bus, motioned to the driver to open the door, and hopped down.

As he approached her, he noticed she was holding her left ankle in both hands. She looked up at him, tears sliding slowly onto her cheeks, and it struck him that her eyes were the oddest shade of green he'd ever seen, like deep bright emeralds, the color almost unnatural. They held him for a very long moment.

"I saw you fall," he said awkwardly, hoping to break their spell.

"You and everyone else on the drive." She swallowed hard, wiping her wet face with the back of her right hand.

"What can I do?" He felt unexpectantly stupid.

"Got any ice?" she asked with just a hint of sarcasm, stripping the white wool sock gingerly from her foot and tossing it toward the running shoe that lay on the ground.

"Got the next best thing." He headed for the bus. "Be right back."

He bounded onto the bus and grabbed a T-shirt that someone had tossed onto the front seat, then opened the beer cooler. Not too much ice remained, but the water was frigid. He soaked the shirt and headed back to her.

"Maybe this will help," he offered.

She sat with her forehead resting on her raised right knee, her left leg stretched out before her in a straight line, bare toes pointing skyward. His first impression had been correct. She had nice legs, a nice little body.

"Ahh . . . What should I do with this?" he asked, holding the dripping T-shirt in his hand.

"Wrap it around my ankle. Here. Give it here, I can do it." She was grateful for his help, and her face softened.

"I'll do it. Just put your leg up a little if you can . . ."

He wrapped the cold wet shirt holding what was left of the ice around her ankle several times. The swelling was more visible now.

"Oh, God, that's cold." Her mouth twisted, and she punched the ground as he had seen her do earlier, but she motioned him to continue.

"I don't know if I'm doing this right," he said, hesitating somewhat apologetically.

"No, no, you're doing fine," she replied.

He could feel her eyes studying his face. Well aware that he was far from handsome, he knew most of his success with the opposite sex rested upon his status as lead singer with a rock band. She gave no indication she knew who he was. Would it make a difference to her if she did?

"What next?" He looked up to find her still watching his face. He wondered if she liked what she saw as much as he did.

"Nothing. That's great, thank you." She graced him with the sweetest smile he'd ever seen.

Sunlight on the waters, he thought, looking into her face.

Aloud he said, "What will you do now?"

"Well, I have a friend who's running down here somewhere. Hopefully, he'll be passing by soon enough so that I can get a ride home."

As if on cue, a lone male jogger came into view. She raised a hand to him, and he quickened his pace as he ran to her.

"Maggie, what happened?" he called out, his voice full of concern.

"I guess I missed a stride. I'm not really sure. Maybe I hit a stone or something," she called back.

I should have known this one would have a boyfriend, J.D. thought. *The best ones always do. What the hell, I'll never see her again anyway.*

"How bad is it?" The boyfriend knelt over her anxiously.

"It doesn't hurt quite so much, now that the cold's gotten to it." She looked up at J.D. and smiled that wonderful smile again, and he felt his stomach tighten. "This Good Samaritan here appeared out of nowhere, Jake, and wrapped it for me."

J.D. and Jake took stock of each other, as men have a tendency to do. Jake looked unimpressed with what he saw.

"Come on, Maggie, I'll carry you back to the car." Jake stood up.

He was very tall and very handsome, his size and movie-star good looks intimidating. His casually possessive manner toward the woman irritated J.D., who felt suddenly intruded upon, though he knew full well he had no rights to her. He felt himself fading insignificantly into the background with the stopped cars, the river, and the passing joggers.

"Look, you go finish your lap. I'll be okay. Maybe just help me over to that bench and . . ." She gestured toward a small picnic area.

"Don't be ridiculous. I want to get you home and take a closer look at that leg." The big man lifted her effortlessly from the ground in one motion.

"I have to admit it does hurt some," she said with a grimace.

"You might want to have a doctor take a look at that for you sometime soon," J.D. said as they turned to walk away.

"Jake's a doctor," she replied.

Jake grinned somewhat smugly in J.D.'s direction.

She stretched her hand out to J.D., leaning over one of Jake's immense shoulders to do so. "Thanks for everything. You've no idea how much I appreciate your help. And your company. Oh . . . your shirt." She looked down at the black and purple fabric that was tied around her ankle.

"Keep it," he said, taking a step forward to take the offered hand. She smiled and for a brief moment looked him squarely in the eyes. Something deep inside told him this woman wasn't like anyone he'd ever met before, and he acknowledged reluctantly he wasn't likely to come across her again. His brief involvement with her was over, and so he turned and walked toward the bus.

"She was cute, J.D. You invite her to the hotel later?" Rick Daily, the band's lead guitar player and a notorious womanizer, assaulted him the minute he'd reboarded. "Wouldn't mind getting a closer look at her myself. Will you send her to my room when you're done with her?"

"Go to hell." J.D. was unusually testy.

"Yeah, you're right, I never much cared for that healthy, wholesome, athletic type." Rick stretched luxuriously in his seat as J.D. passed him without a glance.

"Rick likes his women loose and lazy, J.D., you know that," one of the other band members chimed in.

"Who was she anyway?" the guitarist called over his shoulder.

"Just some jogger" was the mumbled reply. J.D. returned to his seat and leaned back, looking out the window. He could see the big man's form moving down the path, seemingly unburdened by the weight of the small woman with the big green eyes. He stretched his legs across the seat and looked out the window again. They were no longer in view.

3

"MAGGIE," HILARY ADDRESSED HER FOR THE FIRST TIME SINCE the show began and reached out to touch Maggie's knee to get her attention. The younger woman seemed momentarily disoriented. "I said, were you as smitten at that first meeting as J.D. obviously was?"

"Oh." Maggie'd been lost in thought. Her attempts to ignore the sound of his voice had been futile. She'd heard every word, seen it all just as it had happened. She'd hated being transported back to that time against her will. "No. Not really."

"You simply went on your way with your boyfriend and forgot about him?" Hilary asked, an eyebrow raised, studying the younger woman's demeanor, trying to get a handle on what was really going on here.

"Jake wasn't my boyfriend," Maggie said with some vexation. "He was a good friend, but it was hardly a romantic relationship."

"Bullshit," J.D. muttered under his breath.

"Excuse me?" Maggie turned slowly toward him, one eyebrow raised in annoyance.

"Jake was in love with you," he replied calmly.

"It was not that kind of relationship," she insisted.

"Maggie, I saw how that man looked at you. It wasn't as buddy-buddy as you care to recall."

Hilary leaned back, hoping some sparks would fly or, with any real luck, a good argument.

"I recall perfectly well. I was never in love with him," she protested.

"That well may be, but he most definitely was in love with you." He relaxed slightly, delighted to have gotten her to speak to him, even if it was in anger.

Maggie glared at him. Neither spoke for a minute. The fireworks Hilary'd hoped for fizzled into a wisp.

"Had you simply dismissed J.D. then? No interest? No spark? No impression?" She had to reel Maggie back into the conversation.

"Well, I can't honestly say he hadn't made an impression . . ." Maggie grudgingly admitted. He'd made an impression, all right . . .

As Jake had helped Maggie into the passenger seat of his car, he asked a bit too casually, "Who was that?"

"Who was who?" Maggie knew exactly who.

"The long hair. The scruffy-looking guy who . . ."

"He wasn't really scruffy looking. And he was a really nice guy. He just showed up out of nowhere and lent a hand. I've no idea who he was." Maggie wondered why she felt the need to be so defensive of a man she'd never met before and would never see again.

Jake frowned as he slammed the door.

When they'd gotten to her apartment, Jake unwrapped the T-shirt and dropped it on the coffee table as Maggie eased herself onto the sofa. He had stopped at his office and picked up some Ace bandages and some painkillers.

"Actually, it doesn't look as bad as I had thought, though you know that orthopedics is not my specialty. Maybe getting the cold to it as quickly as you did helped. If it's bad tomorrow, though," he added as he wrapped her leg with the heavy bandage, "I'll want you to stop in for an X ray."

"I think it will be okay," she said, "but maybe I'll take a

24

few of those little white pills of yours. It is throbbing unmercifully right now."

"I'm sure it is, Maggie, but I'd recommend that you go easy on the little white pills. What did you eat today anyway?"

Reluctantly she admitted she hadn't eaten much of anything since breakfast.

He went into the kitchen and returned with a banana, a glass of milk, and two pain pills, which he placed on the table next to the sofa.

"You don't take this medication on an empty stomach, so eat the banana and drink the milk and then you can have your pills."

"Okay, doc." She smiled wearily.

"Want me to run out and get you something more substantial, a sandwich or dinner?" he offered.

"No, no, I'm fine with this. I'm really more tired than hungry all of a sudden. But thanks anyway."

He went into the bedroom and brought the phone into the living room, stretching the cord as far as it would go.

"Just in case you need it." He placed the phone on the floor nearby. "Look, I'll let you get some sleep. And I'll leave you with enough pain pills for tomorrow in case you need them. It looks like it's only a mild sprain. You should be fine in a day or two. Don't hesitate for a second, though, if you need anything to call me, okay?"

"Yes, thank you. Thanks for everything."

He leaned down and kissed the top of her head. She watched as he walked through the door and listened to his footsteps as he bounded down the stairs.

She leaned back onto the pillow Jake had placed behind her head. *I should feel guilty. I know Jake really cares about me and that he is a truly fine and good person. But I can't help it. There's no fire in him, and God help me, I won't make that mistake again. Mace was the world's sweetest guy, but I had no business marrying him.*

She felt a little groggy from the medication, the pain in her ankle having eased into a dull ache, and she closed her eyes, snuggling down under the afghan Jake had tucked over her. She thought of the stranger who'd come to her aid this afternoon—the odd clothes and the British accent and the long hair, the hazel eyes slightly too small for his face and the mouth, slightly too large, that so easily drifted into that crooked smile. *Now he,* she thought as she fell asleep, *had fire . . .*

When Maggie awoke, the room was in total darkness save for the hazy glow of the street light outside the window. She sat up slowly and dragged several strands of hair back from her face. From the center of town she could hear the church bells. It was nine o'clock. She sat up and turned on the lamp next to the sofa, then stood to test her ankle cautiously. The pain wasn't as acute as it had been earlier.

She glanced at the table in front of the sofa, at the heap of purple and black fabric that had, hours before, been wrapped around her leg. She pulled it to her, spread it out flat, and leaned over to read the one-word inscription across it's front: Monkshood.

Maggie blinked. She could see it as clearly as if the shirt now lay before her eyes.

"Well, then, how did we go from a casual meeting wherein neither of you identified yourselves to fifteen years of marriage and five children?" Hilary asked.

"It's seven children, Hilary, and that's the point where fate stepped in." J.D. realized the effect the conversation was beginning to have on his wife was exactly what he'd hoped for. Oh, she was fighting it, all right, but he knew if he could keep it going, sooner or later she'd surely crack. With any luck, he would hit upon that one memory she'd be unable to resist. The key to tomorrow . . .

She was still sitting far apart from him, had not looked at him when she spoke. But his hopes were high. They'd been too deeply in love for far too long for him to quit now.

"As I'd said earlier, Hilary, the band—Monkshood, that is—was booked into the local arena for two nights, Tuesday and Wednesday of that week, so ordinarily, we'd have had Monday off. But as it happened, our stage manager had gotten ill and remained in Pittsburgh, and as I was concerned about the spots and outlets and so on, we went into the arena on Monday to make certain that everything was lined up for Tuesday's show . . ."

J.D. had become embroiled in an argument with the arena's stage manager over the placement of the spotlights and the outlets when he and the other members of the band arrived around eleven-thirty the next morning. Nothing seemed to be where he wanted it, and the stagehands didn't seem to be in any hurry to work things out to his satisfaction.

The stage manager was irritated, too. He called the front office to complain that one of the performers was giving him a hard time. They promised to have someone from the promoter's office down there to straighten out any misunderstandings. When the promotion assistant arrived and saw how agitated J.D. was, he quickly resolved the situation to J.D.'s satisfaction, then invited the band down to the in-house restaurant for some lunch and a few beers while the agreed-upon changes were made.

They entered the restaurant, which was also a bar that served as a dinner and after-event drinking spot, through a door that opened from the oval-shaped hallway following the curve of the arena's main concourse directly overhead. Since it was also a private club, it was almost deserted at the lunch hour, it's patrons being mostly arena employees. They took a large round table opposite the bar and gave their orders to the waitress. She returned in minutes with a tray of frosted mugs of beer.

The promoter was talking in a monotone, telling them how he'd heard from his contacts in other cities how well their tour was going, what a hit they'd been this time around. J.D. was barely listening. Out of the corner of one eye he saw the door through which he'd passed moments before swing open and watched as a dark-haired woman slowly entered the room. She was wearing dark blue slacks and a fuzzy white sweater, a colorful scarf draping her neck.

She was limping ever so slightly, favoring her left ankle. Mesmerized, J.D. watched as she slid onto a barstool, turning herself sideways in her seat to wave a greeting to the thin, gray-haired man behind the bar. She hadn't turned around, hadn't seen him there. The waitress walked over, exchanged a few words with her, and returned to the kitchen. The bartender placed a bottle of soda and an ice-filled glass in front of her.

Three enormously tall black men in sweatpants entered the room and, spying the woman at the bar, joined her. J.D. couldn't hear their conversation but could hear her laughter, lighthearted and unaffected. "Who's the girl?" J.D. asked quietly, unable to take his eyes from her.

The promoter, hunched over his lunch, looked across his sandwich, which was dripping large clots of cole slaw onto the plate in messy globs. "Maggie Callahan. Works for the arena. One of the accountants in the finance office." It was then that he clearly read the look on J.D.'s face and added, "Forget it, pal. She's not your type."

"How do you know what's my type?" He lowered his voice even more, controlling a sudden surge of dislike for this fellow.

Realizing the unintended affront, he attempted to placate J.D. "I'll rephrase that. You're not her type."

"What is that supposed to mean?"

"Maggie dates strictly button-downs, understand? Professional types. Not rock singers." J.D. was glaring at him, so he continued, trying to smooth the feathers he'd ruffled. "Anyway, she's not the sort of girl you'd be interested in, trust me. She's very straight, J.D. When you say *joint,* Maggie thinks elbow or knee, get the picture? And besides, she wouldn't be caught dead with a guy whose hair is longer than hers."

Rick turned in his seat to take a look at the object of the discussion, now seated at the table where the waitress had placed her lunch. Rick turned back to J.D. with a wide grin on his face.

"Hey, that looks like—"

"It certainly does . . ." J.D. got up from the table and walked over to where she sat. He pulled out a chair, turned it around, and straddled the seat in one motion.

She looked up at him in utter astonishment.

"You!" Her smile told him she was as pleased as she was surprised at his sudden appearance. "For God's sake, this is unbelievable."

"That's exactly what I was thinking." He reached his right hand to her. "We never did get introduced yesterday. I'm J. D. Borders. You're Maggie Callahan."

"How do you know my name?" she asked, puzzled.

He cocked his head toward the table where he'd been sitting, indicating the promoter. "I asked."

"What are you doing here?" she asked bluntly, then flushed dark pink, adding, "I mean, people don't normally just walk in here off the street for lunch . . ."

"Looking over the stage. I'm playing here with my band tomorrow night and Wednesday."

She paused, trying to recall the acts scheduled that week, then suddenly remembered the T-shirt.

"Monkshood," she said aloud.

He nodded.

"Are you any good?" she asked.

"Come and find out for yourself." His grin was a casual invitation.

She smiled slightly. "I just might do that."

He asked about her ankle, and she told him it was better. They made some small talk for a few minutes. He was running out of things to say but wasn't willing to leave now that Fate had allowed him the good fortune to unexpectedly cross her path again.

He liked looking at her face. Pretty skin that he knew would be soft to touch, heart-shaped mouth that would be warm and sweet to kiss, those eyes that drew him in and made him oblivious to everything else . . .

He pulled a piece of paper from his pocket and slid it across the table. "Do you know where this place is?"

"Sure," she said, glancing at the scrap, "it's a club in town. Mostly jazz. They get some fine musicians there from time to time. I used to go there a lot."

"Well, one of the finest is playing there tonight. Hobie Narood. Know who he is?"

"Of course," she said with a nod, "anyone who's listened to a jazz station on the radio for more than ten minutes knows who Hobie Narood is. I've seen him play several times. He is the very best of the young sax players. Or, at least, he was. He's in Philadelphia? I hadn't heard. I thought he'd retired or something . . ."

"'Or something' is closer to truth," he told her. "He's taken a few years off to get himself together. More or less."

"Drugs?" she asked.

"No," he replied slowly. "Hobie's a product of two cultures. His mother was of Jamaican descent, raised in England—hence his name, Hobie, as in Hobart—and his father was African. From Anjjoli. His father was the minister of justice. Under Kashad, the former president. Both of them were assassinated in the coup two years back." He looked at her blank expression and asked with just a touch of humor, "Don't you keep up with international politics here?"

"Of course," she said. "I just didn't know that about him. And I was wondering how you knew so much."

"Hobie and I go way back. We played in a band together for six years. Daily Times. Ever hear of it?"

"Yeah." She obviously had, judging by the look on her face. "Daily Times was very big when I was in college. You were in that band?"

He nodded to indicate he had been.

"What did you do?" she asked directly.

"Played the piano and sang and wrote most of the songs." He couldn't help but lay it on, hoping to impress her.

"Son of a gun," she said, grinning, "and here I was thinking my Good Samaritan was some indigent back-packer from the Isles 'doing the States' on a lark."

"Well, I suppose I must have appeared that way," he conceded with a somewhat sheepish laugh. "I'd been sleeping on the bus all day, and I guess I was a bit rumpled."

She picked up her empty glass and leaned her head back, allowing some of the ice to fall into her mouth.

"I'd lost track of Hobie for a while. He has spent the past several years coming to terms with his roots is, I guess, the best way to describe it." J.D. was thoughtful for a moment, wondering how much of the story to tell. "His mother refused to live with his father in Anjjoli, since they permit—encourage, really—the men of position there to have more than one wife. Saline, Hobie's mother, was not impressed with the fact that her husband's four subsequent wives were a mark of honor of his wealth and his significance within the government. After his father's assassination, Hobie went to Anjjoli, made contact with his other family, and sort of immersed himself in it. He's married an Anjjolan girl—only one, I might add—and is sort of a folk hero there, you know. The Anjjolans welcomed him with open arms, son of a slain hero and an internationally known musician, to boot." He stopped himself suddenly and looked to her apologetically. "I can't imagine why I rattled on like that. I'm sorry . . ."

"Don't be." She tapped a finger gently on his arm, which was stretched along the side of the table, his hand just inches from her own. "I've been fascinated. Narood is one of my all-time favorite sax players. I'm just glad to know it wasn't drugs or something that took him out, happy to hear all that talent hasn't gone to waste."

"You know, I'd asked him to call me when he was ready to get back out again. Maybe he couldn't catch up with me, maybe he thought I wasn't serious about it, I don't know. He never did get in touch."

"Let me guess—you're going to pop in on him and surprise him tonight."

He nodded.

"I'll bet he'll be really glad to see you." She smiled, and he was again transfixed by the color of her eyes.

On impulse, he asked, "Would you like to go?"

She put her glass down and looked across the table. "Truthfully, yes, I'd love to go. I'm very partial to good jazz. And I'd love to see Narood play again. But I have plans to meet a friend for dinner."

"Ah, yes, good old Dr. Jake, no doubt." He rested his chin on the back of the chair, attempting to look as dejected and forlorn as possible.

"No, no," she laughed, "an old friend. A gal I went to college with. Actually, though, we'll be in the city, not far from the club. Maybe we'll stop in for a drink when we're done, if it's not too late and if I can talk Caroline into going."

"Great." Maggie with a chaperone was better than no Maggie at all. "Well, I suppose I should let you finish your lunch, and it looks like I'll have to get back to work. I see my band is packing up on me."

Rick was walking toward the table.

"How's the wounded jogger today?" he inquired.

Maggie looked blankly at J.D.

"This is Rick Daily. Maggie Callahan." He turned to her and explained, "Rick's our guitar player. He was on the bus yesterday, watching out the window while I tended to your injury."

"I'm sorry now that I didn't get off the bus myself." Rick leaned a hand on the back of her chair. "You look even better close up."

J.D. watched as Maggie leaned back in her chair to take in Rick's six-feet five-inch form, the long black hair, the exceptionally handsome face, the laughing eyes. There was no question—Rick was a most spectacular-looking man. There wasn't a woman alive who could resist his charm if she thought for one moment that Rick was interested. Yet Maggie seemed undaunted.

"Well," she said, "I'm just lucky that J.D. came to my rescue. Otherwise I might not have been able to walk at all today."

Rick straightened up, sensing that she'd dismissed him. "Yes, well, glad to see you're okay. We've got to get moving, J.D."

"I'll be right with you."

Rick rejoined his group, which was preparing to leave the table.

"Well, I'll look for you tonight." J.D. got up and turned the chair around and pushed it under the table. "I hope you can make it."

"If not, I'm glad we ran into each other today. I really did

32

want to thank you again for helping me yesterday." She looked up and smiled, and he noted the light sprinkling of freckles across the bridge of her nose. Fairy kisses, someone had told him once. It seemed appropriate.

He wished he had the nerve to beg her to cancel her dinner plans and go with him instead. He sighed inwardly, telling himself he had done the best he could do to see her again. The rest would be up to her.

"By the way," she called to him as he turned to go, "what's the J.D. stand for?"

"James David," he responded over his shoulder, grinning, pleased that she'd been interested enough to ask.

Catching up with the others as they passed through the doorway into the hall, he asked the promoter, "Where can I get a haircut?"

4

"And did you, in fact," Hilary inquired, "manage a haircut?"

"Absolutely," he laughed. "Immediately upon leaving the arena, I went back to the hotel and sought the barber. Not the best haircut I ever had, mind you, but it served the purpose."

"And I take it you were suitably impressed with his efforts, Maggie?"

"I don't recall," she replied flatly, attempting to add as little as possible to the conversation.

J.D. knew she was lying through her teeth. It was a good sign.

"Well, I recall perfectly," he told Hilary. "It seemed I'd waited hours that night, wondering if she'd show up. My eyes never left the door, watching for her. I can't tell you how relieved I was to see her walk in. She was dressed in a sort of long sweater, like a sweater, but it was a dress, dark green it was, like her eyes. We had to wait a bit for the show to begin, and there was recorded music playing," he reminisced, his voice slowing slightly as he described the scene.

"I asked her to dance, just to have an excuse to touch her. I was the world's worst dancer . . ."

"You still are," Maggie jabbed with neither emotion nor a glance in his direction. Her eyes remained fixed on a painting across the room.

"No question." He laughed good-naturedly. "But you were as soft and warm as I'd knew you'd be. And you smelled of honeysuckle. Even today, that scent brings back that evening in vivid detail. You, Hobie, the wonderful music . . ."

He watched with a sinking heart as she turned her face to the garden. The image had not been strong enough, he told himself. It had not been the memory that would open the door.

"And Narood played that night? Wasn't that the first leg of his big comeback?" Hobie Narood was a topic Hilary'd very much like to discuss.

"Yes," J.D. stammered slightly, tripping over his own memories, finding himself suddenly tangled in something he wanted desperately to avoid. He heard a voice speaking rapidly, then realized it was his own. "God, but he was great that night. He was always great . . ." His voice faded momentarily, and Hilary was afraid he'd refuse to go on, but go on he did in a rush of words that seemed to pour out on their own, as if they, not he, had control of his mouth.

"Rick and I joined him onstage. We just plain jammed— the three of us—for better than an hour. Just like old times. He was very definitely the best sax player I've ever heard. We tried to talk him into coming with us on tour. We'd missed him terribly—Rick and I—since Daily Times had broken up. It had been more than four years since we'd played together. But he had commitments, you know. He had a new agent and had bookings for the next eighteen months. Then he was off to Europe for that big tour, and of course, after that, his career really took off. It was a while before we caught up with him again."

"Not until 1988 . . ." Hilary leaned closer, her eyes narrowing. J.D. had never publicly spoken of the incident. This was definitely worth pursuing. She all but salivated at the thought of being the one to get him to make a statement, to break his mysterious silence about what had happened that night in Anjjoli.

In spite of the loathing she felt toward her husband, Maggie glanced at him out of the corner of one eye, as habit forced her almost against her will to note his reaction. He sat immobile, sweat beading on his lip.

Years of playing backup for one another caused her to speak without making a conscious decision to do so.

"That's not quite true, Hilary. We saw Hobie and his family from time to time over the years. And his wife, Aden, is still a close friend," she heard herself say, then forced the discussion in another direction. "But that was the first time I'd heard J.D. sing and the first time I'd heard Rick play. I'd been totally unprepared for how good they were."

"And what rock had you been hiding under during the sixties?" Hilary asked sarcastically, annoyed that her efforts to delve into the horrific events in Anjjoli had been thwarted. "Daily Times was one of the premier bands of its day."

"Of course, I'd heard their records, but it wasn't the same as being there live. And I hadn't realized that Rick was that Rick Daily. He hadn't made a very good impression on me. The first time I met him I figured he probably played mediocre guitar, but the band kept him on to attract the girls. He was just too good-looking and a bit of a Neanderthal in those days." She smiled slightly at the memory.

The sound of her voice—she'd been rambling a bit, as she had a tendency to do when she was nervous or upset—intruded through J.D.'s dark thoughts of Narood. *I kissed Maggie for the first time that night,* he thought, recalling the jolt that had passed through him when he'd put his arms around her, there in the parking lot. He'd leaned back against her car and kissed her. It had shaken him, all but bringing him to his knees. And so he had kissed her again, all the while hoping with all his heart that she had never kissed Jake that way.

He looked at her, so close to him, yet so distant, sadness in every line in his face. He loved this woman so much. *What will it take?*

Had she jumped into the conversation to take the focus off him, knowing he could not discuss Narood, or had she merely been protecting herself from the memory of that terrible night in Anjjoli? Was she softening just a little? He decided to keep the momentum going, just in case.

"Maggie's friend had spent the entire evening avoiding Rick's advances. He's always had an eye for the ladies, you know, and Caroline was quite lovely. They've become good friends over the years, but that first night, I distinctly recall Caro mumbling that she'd never met a man with a bigger ego or a smaller brain." He chuckled. "And I'd all but fallen flat on my face over Maggie, so before rehearsal the next day, I found her office in the arena and popped in and asked her to meet me for a drink after the show that night."

"That must have been a pleasant surprise," Hilary commented, trying to think of a way to steer the conversation toward something more newsworthy or controversial than their courtship.

"Not really," Maggie replied bluntly.

"You must have been a very confident young lady," Hilary observed. *And hopefully more personable than you've been tonight.*

"He had made his intentions clear enough," Maggie said flatly.

"Maggie means I'd sent her flowers that morning. Roses. Three dozen white roses," he said softly.

"How romantic." Hilary shuffled through her notes, looking for something she could use to change the subject. "That would certainly get my attention."

"It was a nice touch," Maggie replied dryly, deftly securing a hair comb that had slid from it's web of dark curls.

"It was more than a nice touch," he told her, playfully poking her on the arm, but she pulled away and seemed to withdraw again. He returned his attention to Hilary. "And it did get her attention. I couldn't wait to get off stage and be alone with her . . ."

* * *

The welcome in her eyes as she watched him approach through the crowded bar had warmed his heart. He pulled out a chair and sat down next to her. They sat and looked at each other for a few moments. Her green silk blouse was a perfect match to her eyes.

"Like the show?" he asked to break the silence.

"It was," she drew her words out slowly as if searching for just the right ones, "it was, well, pretty good."

"Pretty good!" J.D. exclaimed indignantly. "Pretty good! That was the best goddamned band you ever heard and you bloody well know it."

"You're right, of course, it was the best," she laughed. With simple sincerity, she said, "Even after hearing you and Rick last night, I wasn't prepared for how good the band would be. I don't think I'd ever heard but three or four of the songs before."

"Old Daily Times songs," he offered. "For some reason, Daily Times got more airplay on your radio stations than Monkshood has had. We've done a lot better in Europe than we've done here."

"Why's that?"

"Heavier promotion there. Don't ask, Maggie. The record companies make those decisions. This is our first tour here that's attracted any kind of widespread attention. And the publicity's been better this time around."

He took her hand and absentmindedly played with her fingers for a moment.

"So you thought we were pretty good, did you?" He was enjoying looking at her. Her dark hair curled behind her ears, and her eyes shone in the faint light.

"Actually, I was impressed," she told him.

"Thank you. I wanted you to be," he quietly admitted.

"Another drink, Maggie?" The waitress was passing the table.

"Yes and a . . ." She looked at J.D.

He provided his order: "Scotch and water."

"Actually," she said after the waitress had departed, "I probably don't need another drink."

She told him she'd had two drinks upstairs and another while she was waiting for him.

"You're right," he agreed. "Lightweight that I suspect you to be, you absolutely do not need another drink. The last thing in the world I want tonight is to have you pass out on me."

There was no mistaking the look on his face nor the meaning behind his words.

She tried to make light of it. "And if I passed out, I suppose you'd take advantage of me."

He shook his head slowly and looked directly into her eyes.

"No, Maggie, I want you to be wide awake."

They both knew there was no joke intended.

She tried to make small talk for a few minutes to ease the tension. Finally, he said, "It's getting late, Maggie."

"What time is it?" she asked.

"Almost eleven. Come on, Maggie. It's time for us to go."

J.D. was stopped several times for an autograph, and he smiled and wrote his name on whatever was offered to him, somehow managing to hide his impatience to leave, to be alone with her. Finally, they were outside, headed toward Maggie's car, which was parked in the employee's lot directly behind the arena. He was stopped four more times between the building and the car.

"Let's move it, Maggie, before someone else waves a cocktail napkin in my face." He took her by the elbow, following her lead.

"Well," she said as they got to the car, "isn't that the price of stardom, the loss of your privacy?"

"I never wanted to be a star," he replied quietly.

They were in the car now, Maggie starting it up and looking across the console at him. "Then why do you do it? Why aren't you a teacher or a pharmacist or something like that?"

"Because music is a very big part of me. I love the whole process, writing, singing, putting all the pieces of a song together, playing around with different instruments to get a different sound, performing. I love it all. It's what I do best, the only thing I've ever done. Remember that I've been doing this for the past ten years, since I was seventeen, eighteen years old. Why did you become an accountant?"

"Because I like numbers," she told him. "I like the way they always make sense and I like the logic of it all, the consistency of numerical patterns."

"Well, they're not so very different, you know, numbers and music. The same key on the piano always plays the same note," he mused, "just like adding the same two numbers will always give you the same sum."

He turned the radio on, suddenly deep in thought. Tonight's show had been a stunner. He was still coming down from it in spite of the laid-back attitude he outwardly displayed. He looked at Maggie, hoping the best part of the evening was still to come. He wanted her so badly and wondered if she was aware of how he felt.

He knew that once he started to come down off the adrenaline, he'd crash and sleep for twelve or fourteen hours. He always did. Of course, he'd always been stoned for the better part of the night after each concert, unlike tonight. He had taken the promoter's words literally and left the joints behind. He was taking no chances.

He cast a sidelong peek at Maggie, who'd stopped at a red light and was biting her lower lip, staring ahead. He was having trouble reading her. She wasn't like most of the women he met in his travels.

She pulled the car into a parking lot and turned off the engine.

"We're here," she said simply.

As they got out of the car, he asked, "Do you live alone?"

"Yes."

They walked across the lot, and he followed her up the steps of a large brick house. She rummaged in her purse for the key to the outside door, then swung it open, and they went through the dimly lit foyer and up to the second floor.

The phone was ringing in her apartment as she unlocked the door. She went through the doorway on the right, turned on the light, and picked up the phone. J.D. could see into the room from the hallway. Maggie's bedroom was all blue and white, neat and feminine but not fussy, with two dressers, a desk, a large overstuffed chair, a fireplace, a bedside table, and a double bed. He wondered how much action the latter had seen.

"Oh, Mitch, I'm so sorry. I'm so embarrassed," he heard her say. "I completely forgot. I hope you didn't wait there for too long. No, really, you don't have to do that . . . Fine . . . Yes, that would be fine . . . I'll talk to you then . . . Thanks, Mitch . . ."

As she hung up, she saw J.D., arms folded across his chest, leaning against the door frame, wearing an amused expression.

"I, ah, I blew a previous commitment for tonight," she explained self-consciously.

"You mean you stood up some poor guy." He was pleased that she had overlooked someone else to be with him.

"Yes," she replied, lowering her eyes and walking past him into the living room. The walls were darkly paneled, the curtains drawn, giving the room a closed and dreary look. She turned the lights on as she passed through, bringing some bit of life to the space.

"Want a beer?" she asked.

"Sure," he sighed, following her into the kitchen, where she found a cold bottle of beer for him and a diet soda for herself. *This girl really knows how to party,* he thought wryly as he leaned back against the sink on the opposite side of the room from where she stood. *This has all the makings of a really big night.*

They stood and made small talk for a while, long minutes passing awkwardly. The sound of the phone ringing startled them both. She excused herself and went into the bedroom to answer it. As she reached for it and raised the receiver, she became aware that J.D. had followed her into the room, and she met his eyes as she turned around. He took the phone from her hand and replaced it on the base. Their eyes still locked, they stood still as stones.

"Ah, do you want another beer?" she whispered hesitantly, mild panic and indecision clear in her face.

The tiniest of smiles played across his lips.

"No, I do not want another beer. Just you, Maggie. All I want is you."

Neither of them had moved, held by the moment and by the intensity of each other's gaze.

"Tell me now, Maggie, if you don't want this to go any further. Because if I so much as touch you now, there'll be no turning back . . . no way to stop it. Do you understand what I'm saying?"

Her nod was barely perceptible.

He touched her neck with the back of his hand, his fingers slowly tracing a path along the V of her blouse. When he reached the top button, he caressed the skin underneath. Still looking directly into his eyes, she reached her hands up slightly and began to unbutton his shirt. He brought her close to him and held her, found her face and kissed it, cheek to chin, then moved to her lips, which were waiting for his. The powerful heat that had sparked when he'd kissed her the night before ignited full blast, and it was unbearable.

Later, they both lay in silence for a long time, J.D. cradling her, stroking her hair wordlessly, drinking in her sweet scent. Neither of them could think of a thing to say, both so stunned by the depth of what had passed between them. J.D. was thinking he'd never had a rush like that in his life, had never had a high better than the one he was coming down from now.

After what seemed like hours, she cleared her throat. "Jamey?"

He smiled in the darkness, moving his hand up and down her arm, savoring the feel of her skin.

"You are only the second person who ever called me that."

"I'm sorry. It just came out. I don't even know why I said it," she apologized, embarrassed.

"You don't have to be sorry. I like it," he told her.

"Who was the first?" she asked after a few minutes had passed.

"My grandmother. Everyone else in the family calls me

J.D. I imagine she'd have a few other names for me right about now, since it's been so long since I've paid her a visit. Come to think of it, I haven't seen my mother in a while either. Or my sister, for that matter." He lay back against the pillow and exhaled deeply. "It's too easy to lose track when you're moving about so much of the time."

"Don't you like it? You're living a life most guys only fantasize about."

"The truth is, after a few months, it's not as much fun as you thought it would be. I don't even know where I am most of the time. And after a while, I don't even care, because it doesn't matter. It's all the same, every day. It all goes into a blur in my head. The hotels are different, but they all look the same, the crowds look the same, the scenery starts to all look the same. There's no connection to anyone or anything. Except the band. That's why you become closer than brothers. They're the only constant in your life."

"Why do you do it then?"

"Because it's my job. Look, you want to make records, you sign a contract with a record company. You agree to do certain things after they let you make your record. One of those things usually is to do so many live appearances, to tour to promote the record, to get people familiar with your music so that they will want to buy your record. And if enough people hear you and like you and buy your record, then your record company is happy and you get to go back and make another record so that you can go on another tour. It's like a big wheel, Maggie, it just keeps turning your life around and around. Albums turn into tours that lead to the next album that turns into the next tour . . ." His voice trailed off.

"Somehow I have to think there's more to it than that."

"Well, obviously I've oversimplified things a bit, but that's the bottom line. It's a business like any other business."

"How long is this tour?"

"Twenty U.S. cities. We started in Europe, toured there for two months. Then three months here, a few dates in Canada, then home for however long."

"So you've been traveling since, what, December, January?"

"Late December."

"Did you travel a lot last year, too?"

"Not quite as much. We did the album we're promoting now. Before that I got tied up helping a friend do an album." He thought back to the six months he'd spent working with Glory Fielding on that atrocity of hers. Where had his brain been when he was getting roped into that? Somewhere between his waist and his knees, he suspected, in a portion of his anatomy that lacked the ability to think. "The year before we toured almost constantly."

"I couldn't live that way," she noted. "I'm too focused. I take too much comfort from the familiar. I like going to work in the same place every day, seeing the same faces, coming home to the same place every night, seeing my family whenever I want."

They lay in silence again. He thought back to the many women he'd slept with over the years—seldom the same woman more than once, none of whom had made a lasting impression on him. Even his affair with Glory had been marked with a certain detachment; he'd never really been close to her, had never been in love with her the way the press had played it up. For all her beauty and wildness, she'd never really touched him. No one ever had until he'd met this woman who now lay so close beside him.

She stirred in his arms, and he looked down at her. Something about her made him feel so good, so together.

"Jamey?"

"Hmmmmmm?"

"Kiss me good night."

He bent his head down to kiss her and was surprised to find her wanting more than just one kiss. He was extremely happy to accommodate her.

The next morning he awoke and reached for her instinctively. She wasn't there. He half panicked. Had he dreamed what he had thought to be the best night of his life?

The sound of the hair dryer from the bathroom assured him that all was as he remembered. He lay back on the pillow, glad that he had followed his instincts and stayed with her, despite a few early awkward moments. She emerged from the bathroom, fresh from the shower, looking squeaky clean and fresh-faced. It took every bit of his self-control not to reach out and pull her to him.

"Good morning. Sleep okay?" Her sunny smile dazzled him.

"Fine," he replied, though he'd hardly slept at all. He wasn't used to going to bed so early, and besides, he'd never had feelings for anyone like the ones she brought out in him. They kept him awake all night, terrifying him and making him blissfully happy at the same time. "How 'bout you?"

"Great."

She probably had. She looked rested and terrific.

"What time is it?" he asked.

"Almost seven."

He groaned. "Middle of the night for some folks."

She laughed. "Actually, this is a late morning for me. I'm usually up before six to run, which I obviously can't do until I get a little more strength back in my ankle."

"I have never understood why anyone would want to get up at the crack of dawn, use a full day's worth of energy in the first hour, and then be exhausted for the rest of the day," he said flatly.

"It doesn't exhaust me. Actually, I have much more energy when I run in the morning. It feels good. And it gives me time to sort out problems, think things over. It more or less pumps me up for the day, gets my mind and body in gear."

"Well, if last night was any indication of your body being in gear, then I say, don't mess with success."

She laughed and moved to the closet to select her clothes for work, on the way picking up discarded items from the night before. He went into the bathroom.

When he came out, she was sitting on the bed, chin resting on her knees, which were drawn up to her chest. Her robe had partially opened to expose her leg. He hesitated for a second, then sat down slightly behind her and rubbed her shoulders. He wanted to be near to her, to touch her.

"Penny for them," he inquired.

She shook her head. He continued to massage her shoulders and felt the tension there begin to slip away. He could barely stand it, being so close to her. He felt the roller coaster take off inside him again and struggled to contain it. Finally, she turned herself around, put one hand on either side of his face, and drew his face to hers. *Sweet Jesus,* he thought, *thank you for giving her the ability to read my mind . . .*

"Oh, my God, look at the time. I have to be out of here in ten minutes."

His eyes opened slowly, his peaceful near slumber disturbed. "Don't go to work. Stay here with me."

"Can't do it. I have a ton of things to do today." She got up quickly, grabbed the clothes she'd earlier removed from the closet, and disappeared into the bathroom. Five minutes later, she was sitting on the edge of the bed, shaking him.

"Jamey, you have to get up now if you want a ride to the hotel. Would you please acknowledge that you hear my voice?"

"Yes. I hear you. I just don't want to get up."

"Do you want to sleep for a while? I can drive back and pick you up at lunchtime."

"At least until lunchtime."

She laughed. "What time do you need to be back?"

"Before we go on stage," he mumbled into the pillow, and they both laughed.

"Do you want me to call around four or five? I can pick you up after I'm done, at six. You'll get back before the show, although it will be close."

"Make it five. That'll give me enough time to get myself together. If you're sure you don't mind, I would very much like to stay and go back to sleep." He pulled her close to him again. "Sweet Maggie. I don't know what it is that's happening here, but God, Maggie, it's so good."

She smoothed his hair back from his face and kissed him and stood up. Reluctantly, he let her go.

He listened as her footsteps faded on the steps, heard the

downstairs door close behind her. He got up and went to the window and watched as she crossed the street and got into her car. He wondered if she had looked back before she pulled out of the lot. He turned back to the room and got back into Maggie's bed. He wished she was still there, curled up next to him.

It was a long time before he was able to sleep, tired as he was. There was too much to think about this morning, and the faint scent of honeysuckle on the pillow distracted him. Before falling asleep, he found the phone book and placed a call to the florist he'd called the day before.

Funny, the way things go, he thought, *you get into a routine and you just float along with it. Then in the blink of an eye, something changes, and everything looks different, feels different. The music's good, the tour has been more successful than anyone could have predicted. And now there's Maggie . . .* He tried to remember the last time he'd felt this good about himself. Maybe the day Daily Times got it's first recording contract. Maybe the day their first album charted. Nothing else had given him the satisfied feeling he had deep inside. For the first time in his life, all the pieces were there. He hoped he could put them together.

5

MAGGIE HAD BEEN TOYING WITH A PHOTOGRAPH SHE'D ABSENT-
mindedly picked up from the table to her right, pretending
not to listen, though it had been impossible not to hear his
voice. She glanced down at the framed image in her hand.
She and Lindy. They sat on the beach at Cape May, New
Jersey, back to back, Lindy's long, white-blond hair
wrapped around her by the wind, her expression cocky,
sassy. Maggie was squinting from the sun, which pierced
through the dark glasses she wore. The summer of 1974. The
year before she'd met J.D.—and, of course, the year before
Lindy had met Rick and the craziness had started. Maggie
had always harbored a secret guilt, that had she not introduced them, if they'd never met, maybe Lindy's life would
have taken a different turn. And yet she knew with absolute
certainty that disaster would have found Lindy one way or
another. The woman was marked for tragedy just as surely
as the beginning of every new day was marked by the dawn.

And who could have foreseen it, back then when they
were young and still awaiting something that would define
their lives? Maggie was on cloud nine, caught up in a
romance that had seemed to come from nowhere and to

blossom overnight. Lindy had been there with her practically from the start of it . . .

"Maggie, you have to be the most difficult person in the world to catch up with. I've been calling you for days." Lindy's voice on the phone was half teasing, half concerned. "You're not avoiding me, are you?"

"No, of course not," Maggie reassured her, absent-mindedly shuffling through a file that lay open on the top of her desk. "And it hasn't been 'days.' I spoke to you on Sunday morning."

"And have been unreachable since. I called your apartment last night about four times. The last time the phone seemed to be picked up and hung up at about the same time. It worried me."

"No need to worry." Maggie yawned, then laughed. "Excuse me."

"Oh, I see," laughed Lindy knowingly, "sounds like a big night. Dare I be so presumptuous to ask if there was some action at the Callahan hacienda last night?"

"No, you may not." Maggie knew that Elena, whose desk was immediately behind Maggie's and who had seen her leave the bar the night before with J.D., was hanging on every word.

"Hmmmm, let's see, I know it wasn't Jake—I saw him this afternoon on Pine Street and he asked me if I'd spoken to you over the past few days. He's been trying to call you, too. Let me think, who's a likely candidate . . . Mitch? Not Mitch, Maggie . . ."

"What's wrong with Mitch?"

"Nothing, except he's just so serious all the time. Dull and dry and no sense of humor. He's not a fun person, Maggie." Lindy dismissed him.

"Well, actually, I did have a date with him last night, but it slipped my mind," Maggie admitted.

"Then who was it?"

"Someone I met over the weekend. On Sunday. I'll tell you about it later . . ."

"Wait a minute. Jake told me he was with you on Sunday,

jogging down on the drive . . . said you had some sort of accident . . . Oh, your foot. How's your foot?"

"It's fine. A little weak and sore, but okay."

". . . and that he found you on the ground and carried you back to the car . . ." Maggie could tell Lindy was replaying Jake's conversation in her mind. ". . . and took you home . . . When did you have time to meet someone on Sunday?"

"Lindy, give it a rest. I can't really talk right now." Maggie tapped her pencil on the desk.

Elena was rummaging in a drawer of files immediately to her left. Maggie's silence over her date the night before and the way she had tucked away the card from the florist's delivery of another huge bunch of flowers that morning—a dreamy look on her face—was driving everyone in the office crazy.

"I haven't given up. I'll get it out of you one way or another," Lindy assured her. "Before I forget, can you get me a ticket for the concert tonight? I know you won't want to go, but I'm dying to see this group. Monkshood. A bunch of the girls from my office went down last night, and all they could talk about all day was this incredible band and this unbelievably hunky guitar player. And can I have your parking spot?"

"Yes to the ticket, but you're on your own as far as the parking place is concerned. I'll be using it."

"You're kidding. Do you have to work late?"

"No."

"Don't tell me you're staying for the show . . . Oh, I guess you heard about the guitar player, too?" she teased, knowing that other than dealing with the contracts and the reports regarding box office receipts, Maggie, whose taste in music was limited to jazz, rarely gave a second thought to who was performing.

"Something like that. I'll get you the seat next to mine if it's available."

"Great," Lindy replied, wondering why she hadn't had to twist her arm as she usually did.

"I'll meet you for dinner, how's that? Probably around seven, so we won't have too much time."

"Sounds great. I'll stop into your office . . ."

"No, don't do that. Go in and get a table, and I'll meet you. Gotta run." Maggie hung up abruptly, not wanting to have to explain that she would most likely just be arriving back at the arena herself around seven after driving back to her apartment to pick up J.D.

She turned her attention to the file on her desk, and by the time she'd completed what she needed to do, it was 6:05. She cleared her desk and locked it, grabbed her jacket, and sped out the door, leaving a few startled co-workers puzzled by her quick departure without so much as a good-bye.

J.D. was outside sitting on the front porch steps, his jacket folded across his lap. He walked across the lawn when he saw her pull around the corner, got into the passenger side, and leaned over, kissing her once, twice, three times.

"My neighbors will be talking about me," she protested but only minimally.

"No doubt." He leaned back into the seat, grinning, and rolled down the window.

They made some small talk in the car, but she could tell he was distracted, keyed up. He tapped on the console, and the expression on his face told her he was a million miles away. She wondered if he was always this nervous before a performance.

She pulled into the already jammed parking lot, the attendant waving her into the employees' section, and she parked as close to the building as she could. They walked through the doors and were past the guard's desk behind the glass partition before anyone in the crowded ticket lobby realized who had just walked by.

"Will you wait for me in the bar?" he asked, and she nodded. He leaned over and kissed the tip of her nose before following the hallway toward the dressing room area.

Maggie opened the door to her office and turned on the light. She hung her jacket on the back of her chair and sat down for a minute to compose herself. She'd been like this all day, everytime she thought of him. No man had ever affected her the way he had. Not Jake, not Steven, whom she'd almost thought she was in love with back in September. Not Mace, her former husband. It bothered her to feel this way. Tomorrow he'd be gone. She fingered the petals of a rose. How could he have known she'd preferred white to red, the usual rose of choice?

Seven-fifteen. Not much time for dinner. Maggie hurried down the hall and into the bar and found Lindy seated at a table.

"Why so late? Where have you been?" Lindy asked.

"I got tied up."

"Here's your dinner. I ordered for you since we're running out of time. Good thing you showed up. I couldn't eat two of these myself."

The waitress placed a plate of chicken salad in front of each woman.

"So, Margaret," Lindy said, grinning, "let's hear it. And don't leave out any of the good parts."

"Well, you know I fell on Sunday. Flat on my face. There I was, jogging along, then the next thing I knew, my ankle went out from under me, and I was headed toward the ground. It was so odd, I still can't figure out what happened—"

"Maggie, while God knows I'm sympathetic that you got hurt, this is not really the recent history I'm interested in hearing about, you know? I mean, I already heard all this from Jake, and right now, the part I want to hear about is—"

"What exactly did Jake tell you?"

Lindy put her fork down, sighed, and recited the salient points of the conversation.

"You went jogging with him down by the river. He took the long trail, you took the four-mile trail. You fell. He found you on the ground. You hurt your ankle. He came down the path and you were sitting there, and some scruffy guy with long hair was—"

"Well, he's far from scruffy, and he doesn't have long hair anymore." Maggie laughed at Jake's description of J.D. She should have guessed that, had Jake mentioned him, it wouldn't have been in complimentary terms.

Lindy's jaw dropped. "What are you saying?"

"He got a haircut," Maggie said matter-of-factly.

"Who got a haircut?" Lindy's eyes sparkled with curiosity.

"J.D." Maggie continued to eat, barely looking up at her companion.

"Who is J.D.?" Lindy leaned halfway across the table.

"The guy I met on Sunday." Maggie's deliberate nonchalance was driving Lindy crazy.

"Let me get this straight. J.D. is the scruffy long-hair who came out of nowhere on Sunday and—?"

"He didn't come out of nowhere. He came off a bus. Though I didn't notice it at the time, I mean, I don't remember seeing the bus, he just told me later—"

"What'd you do, give this guy your number while you were sitting there on the ground and—"

"No, he just sort of walked away." Maggie looked at Lindy whose eyes were now saucer-sized. Maggie had enjoyed teasing her, but the lateness of the hour prevented her from carrying it any farther. She briefly related how she'd unexpectedly run into J.D. on Monday, how she'd seen him Monday night and then last night.

"Who'd ever believe it. Maggie Callahan, shacked up with the singer from a rock-and-roll band." Lindy's expression was sheer incredulity.

Maggie laughed and pushed her chair back. "It does sound a bit unlikely, I admit."

"Unlikely isn't even the word, Maggie. It's the craziest thing I've ever heard of. He must be some guy."

"He is."

They walked back into the hallway and turned toward the steps. Hearing the opening drum solo and the wild response from the crowd, Maggie knew the band was onstage and beginning its performance. She half dragged Lindy, moving as quickly as she could through the congested concourse to the doorway to the box. They took their seats as J.D. began to play.

"That him?" Lindy whispered.

Maggie nodded.

"He looks short," she observed, assessing the figure behind the keyboard.

"He's not real tall," Maggie nodded.

Lindy looked around the barely lit area. "Anyone here have binoculars, do you think? I want to get a good look at this guy."

"You'll see him later. Do not humiliate me by asking if anyone has binoculars, please." Maggie giggled. "Just shut up and listen."

J.D. was singing now, and Lindy raised her eyebrows to signal she liked what she heard.

"Guy's really good," whispered Lindy, "I mean, really good."

"Yes. Now be quiet."

They sat and listened, then stood and applauded with the rest of the audience when the ninety-minute set had concluded. The enthusiastic crowd was loath to let the band leave the stage, and they played two more songs, then stood at center stage one last time to acknowledge the screaming ovation they received.

"The band is great, Maggie. And the girls at work were right. The guitar player is stunning."

Maggie laughed. "Rick Daily. He's a real character. And just about your speed."

"Let's go get a drink, Maggie. I am positively dying to hear the rest of this story."

Maggie was deep in conversation with Lindy when J.D. entered the bar, his hair still wet from the shower he'd taken hastily in an effort to waste as little of his last night in Philadelphia as possible.

"Hi," Lindy said as he sat down, "I'm Lindy Burton."

"J.D. Borders." He smiled and turned his attention to Maggie, whispering, "How long do we have to stay here?"

She shook her head, seeing the light in his eyes and replied, "Not long."

He ordered a drink, and Maggie watched as he furtively admired Lindy from across the table. When his eyes strayed back to Maggie, she'd raised an eyebrow to let him know she'd caught him giving her friend the once-over.

"She's Daily's type, not mine," he confided into her ear, "lean, mean, and flashy. And frankly, I'm wondering how we'll get rid of her."

Before Maggie could respond, Rick appeared out of nowhere, and J.D. grinned broadly, knowing that he need not be concerned about having Lindy on his hands for the rest of the evening.

"Can I get one of those?" Rick asked the waitress as she put J.D.'s drink on the table and he pulled up a chair and sat down. "I've been sent as a one-man delegation to talk you two into joining us back at the hotel. The rest of the guys think it's criminal that you've kept Maggie to yourself these past few days. You're welcome to come, too, of course," he added to Lindy, not for a second oblivious to the beautiful blonde with the million-dollar smile and the big blue eyes seated next to Maggie.

They sat and talked but were constantly interrupted by fans passing the table who could not resist stopping and telling them how great the show had been. After a long fifteen minutes, J.D. turned to Maggie and said, "Let's go home."

"Oh, Maggie . . ." Lindy pleaded with her.

"Doesn't mean you have to leave, Lindy. You want to come over to the hotel with me?" Rick flashed his best smile.

He didn't have to ask her twice. With a wink in Maggie's direction, Lindy rose and draped her jacket over her shoulder. Rick appeared bewitched as all five feet ten inches of the perfectly proportioned leggy blonde emerged from the chair.

"Last chance, J.D." Still mesmerized by the incredible legs barely covered by Lindy's short skirt, Rick obviously couldn't have cared less at that point what J.D. would do with the rest of the evening.

"Thanks anyway." J.D. shook his head. "Ready, Maggie?"

Traffic was heavier than she'd anticipated. The long line of cars waiting for the bridge seemed to take forever to move, the river of headlights flowing slowly to the roadway below. They stopped at a light, and J.D. put his hand on the back of her neck, tracing little circles on her skin with his fingers. She felt the heat from him in even the small touch and wished the light would turn. That dizziness he always made her feel washed over her, her body responding down to her toes.

"Are we almost there?" he asked, the twinkle in his eyes clearly indicating what was on his mind.

She cleared her throat. "A few more blocks."

"Good."

By the time she'd unlocked the apartment door, the anticipation was unbearable.

They were half in the hallway, half in the doorway to her bedroom. The hall light was on, the rest of the apartment in darkness. He pushed her jacket off over her shoulders, and she left it on the floor where it landed. He reached for her, and they held each other.

"I do not want a beer, just in case you were about to ask," he teased, then kissed her neck, starting under one ear and moving around her throat to the other, then kissed lower on her neck, then lower. She thought she'd die from the ache that was growing rapidly inside her. She moved backward into the room, backed up to the bed, and he took every step with her, still kissing her, his hands undressing her and hers undressing him. She prayed she would not black out, as she feared she might, from the unbelievable rush that was overtaking her.

Afterward, they lay in the darkness with only the light from the street lamp outside the window to illumine the room, listening to each other's breathing, still holding on to each other. Neither could let go.

"Shazzam," he said finally, and she laughed. He rubbed the side of her face with his and murmured, "That was so good, Maggie, so good."

She ran her fingers through his hair, trying to find her voice.

"Ah, Maggie, this is how I want to spend my life. Sing for a few hours every night, come back here, and make love to you, just like this." He nuzzled her face.

"Jamey, do all the guys in your band use drugs?" she asked unexpectantly.

Startled, he looked down at her. "What? Well, yes, I suppose they do to one degree or another."

"Do you?"

"Yes," he admitted, wondering what had caused her to ask.

"To what degree?"

"Sometimes to a very high degree."

"Why?" she ignored his play on words.

He pondered the question for a moment. "I don't know, I never really gave it much thought. I guess because sometimes there's nothing else to do. Because sometimes the whole thing gets to me, and the loneliness is more than I can deal with and nothing else makes it go away."

"You could kill yourself."

"I don't use things that could kill me."

"What do you use?"

"Mostly hashish."

"I don't understand why someone like you needs to do that."

"Maggie, it's so easy for you to sit there and say that, so easy for you to pass judgment. You have a pretty nice life, you know? A good job, your apartment, friends who are always there for you. Look, you have no concept of what it's like to be on the road for eight, ten months in a row. It takes me weeks to recover from it every time. It is the loneliest life you could imagine. You never have the time to establish any relationship that can last, because you're never in one place long enough to really get to know someone well enough to develop any kind of connection that—"

He stopped in midsentence as she tensed slightly.

"Oh, no, Maggie, no, no, I didn't mean this time. This time is different. You're different. I've never met anyone who's made me feel the way you do. I don't understand it, and I don't know why it's happened, but I swear it's never happened to me before. All these years, it's never happened like this."

"Jamey, you don't have to say things that . . ."

"Maggie, it's the truth. And the real truth is that it scares me to death. I don't know what to do about you."

He ran his fingers up and down her arm absentmindedly, the silence building with the tension that spread through her. She'd tried to find words to ease the situation, not wanting to hear him utter some stock line, but she could not think of one intelligent thing to say, and so she lay in his arms, fighting a sudden, unexplainable urge to cry.

"Maggie," he said after a time, "over the past ten years I've been with dozens of women, some whose names I didn't even know, and I never gave a damn if I ever saw any of them again. Being with you is different . . . I don't think I ever made love with anyone in my life until last night. Do you know what I mean?"

"Yes," she said softly.

"It won't end with tonight, you know that, don't you?"

She nodded slowly and, without a word, drew him to her again. When they both fell asleep, much later that night, they were both at peace.

"Jesus!" J.D. woke with a jolt. "What the hell was that?"

Maggie had gotten out of bed and accidently knocked over the table holding the lamp and phone, all of which crashed to the floor. J.D. put his pillow over his head.

"Sorry." She giggled as she retrieved the fallen items. "I'm so sorry."

"What time is it, dare I ask?" The voice from under the pillow was muffled.

"It's six-thirty."

"Why are we up so early?" he grumbled, emerging from beneath the pink-and-blue-flowered pillow to look at her.

"I can't help it. My body is just used to getting up at an early hour."

"I think a bit of reprogramming is in order," he muttered somewhat crankily.

Laughing, she went into the bathroom and, when she

came out, found him watching the doorway for her. She smiled and walked into the room.

"Want some coffee?"

"Too early," he shook his head. "I don't want to wake up yet."

"You have to wake up. You have to come with me when I leave today, you know. I'll drop you off at the hotel. Do you know what time the bus is leaving?"

"No, but they won't go without me."

"Come on." She poked him. "You have to get up, Jamey."

"Why don't you come back to bed for a while? We have plenty of time." He reached out and grabbed her arm and pulled her down to him.

"Maybe for ten minutes . . ."

"Don't put that kind of pressure on me, Maggie. Ten minutes isn't quite enough . . ."

The ride to the hotel was a bleak one, neither he nor she could think of anything to say. He kept his hand on her shoulder the whole way, memorizing her face and all its expressions. Before they knew it, they were in the hotel parking lot, and she had pulled up near to the entrance to the building.

He made no move to get out of the car, simply rubbed her shoulder as if his touch could tell her the things that eluded words.

"Jamey, I have to get to work." She did not meet his eyes. Her voice was low and a little shaky.

"Maggie, I'll call you . . ."

She tried to smile good-naturedly.

"Don't look at me like that. It's not a line, Maggie," he protested. "Do you really think I could walk away from you and never come back?"

He leaned over and held her face, studied it, kissed it.

"Come on, lover boy. The bus is leaving. We were wondering when you'd show up." Rick tapped on the window. "Good morning, Maggie."

She smiled and waved a half-hearted greeting. Rick motioned to J.D. to roll the window down.

59

"Ah, such sweet sorrow," he said as he leaned in the window.

J.D. wordlessly raised the window, effectively shutting out the intruder, who laughed as he walked toward the waiting bus.

"Look, maybe it won't be too bad." J.D. played with the fingers of her right hand. "Let me look over the schedule and see where we're going to be."

"Don't you know where you're going?"

"Someplace south, I think, I'm not sure. I don't pay that much attention to it, you know. It usually doesn't matter." He kissed her. "And besides, I'm the one who should be worried, leaving you here with Jake and Mitch, and God knows who else is hot on your trail. Not that I blame them. If I had the chance, I'd be parked on your doorstep twenty-four hours a day. And I'd never take no for an answer."

"You never had to," she said, trying to smile, "and you never will."

"Reason enough to come back at the earliest opportunity. And I will, Maggie. I swear I will. We'll be together again before you know it."

She watched from the car as he boarded the bus, a nagging uncertainty filling some huge space inside her. In spite of his protests, she had no way of knowing if she'd ever see him again. She swallowed the enormous lump in her throat and stepped on the gas pedal, heading toward the road that would take her to work. She could not bear to watch the bus pull away.

6

MAGGIE'S HEAD WAS BEGINNING TO POUND. THE LAST THING SHE needed right now was a stroll down memory lane. *He's doing this on purpose,* she fumed silently. *Making me remember. As if it could make a difference. The son of a bitch has no excuse for what he's done, and he thinks if he muddies the water with the good old days, I'll overlook his little fling for the sake of auld lang syne. Well, it won't work. That was then and this is now.*

When I think of the angst I suffered over him, wondering if I'd been just another roadstop, jumping every time the phone rang . . . If I'd known then what I know now, would I have been so anxious, more so with each day that passed, not hearing from him? Would I have been able to have passed him off as a bad experience, poor judgment on my part, and just gone about my life? It hadn't seemed so then, she reminded herself. *I walked around with a knot in my stomach for five days, praying he'd call. What was that old expression, Be careful what you pray for, your prayers might be answered?*

* * *

Three nights after J.D. had left Philadelphia, Maggie sat on the floor in her living room, her back propped against the sofa, her legs stretched out straight and crossed at the ankles, a half-empty pizza box in front of her on the coffee table.

"Look, Maggie, it's only been a couple of days, for heaven's sake. You'll hear from him," Lindy said in an attempt to reassure her.

"I don't know." Maggie was pensive, toying with the pepperoni absentmindedly. "On the one hand, I really believed he was sincere, that there really was something between us. Like we tuned in to each other right from the start, and it felt like the best thing that ever happened to me . . ." She nibbled slowly, trying to explain it as much to herself as to her friend.

"Then, on the other hand, I think, this guy's really slick, you know? Has his lines down pat, like maybe it's his angle. Goes into a new city every couple of days, finds a girl, goes into this sincere routine, and bingo, he has a home for the next forty-eight hours or so. It's hard not to fall for it, Lind. He's good-looking in his own way, funny, talented, sweet, intelligent, sexy—any woman would fall for him." She grimaced. "I did . . . a testimony to his acting abilities."

"I'm still not so sure it was all an act, Mags. No, seriously, it wouldn't add up." She waved away Maggie's look of skepticism.

"What wouldn't?"

"Well, for one thing, the haircut," she noted with a grin. "Think about it. He only did it to get your attention. He didn't have to—there's any number of women who wouldn't have cared if he had three noses. There are girls who think rock singers are very sexy, you know? They don't care that some of these guys are dog meat."

"So what's that got to do with it?" Maggie stood up, hands on her hips, waiting for Lindy to make her point.

"Everything. J.D. knows it. Knows he can waltz in just about anywhere and score."

"Want any more of this?" Maggie nodded toward the remaining slice of pizza.

Lindy shook her head, and Maggie took the carton into the kitchen, folded it up, and put it into the trash. She came back into the living room with the wine bottle, refilled both their glasses, and sat down Indian style on the carpeted floor.

"Well, if nothing else, your association with J.D. has certainly made a lot of other guys sit up and take notice."

"Attention like that I can do without." Maggie grimaced. "It's been a steady stream into the office, guys from the ticket office, the promoter's office, even the guy who handles the concert commercials for one of the radio stations. You wouldn't believe it."

"Honey, everyone always had you pegged as such a straight little arrow, sweet and serious-minded. Now they're all taking a second look."

"The only reason for the line at the door is the general assumption that I was sleeping with a rock singer."

"Which you were." Lindy could not resist the obvious.

"Which I was," Maggie conceded wryly.

"That's what it is, isn't it?" Lindy leaned forward, her glass tilted in Maggie's direction. "That's what's bothering you. It's not the gossip or the guys hanging around."

"Then what?"

"Guilt."

"Lindy, give me a break," Maggie grumbled.

"Your Catholic conscience is acting up, honey."

"I'm not really a Catholic anymore." She waved a hand, attempting to lightly dismiss Lindy's theory.

"Come on, Maggie, you can take the girl out of the church, but you can't take the church out of the girl."

"What's your point?" an exasperated Maggie demanded.

"Callahan, you are Catholic to the bone. And you're feeling guilty because you spent a lot of time last week in bed with a man you hardly know. And there's no guilt like Catholic guilt when it comes to sex."

"That's silly. I'm twenty-eight years old . . ."

"Chronologically. Mentally, you're sixteen." Maggie started to protest, and Lindy cut her off. "All of you are, all you unmarried Catholic girls think the same way. You've been told all your lives not to do it, then when you finally do, you have trouble looking yourself in the face. Unless, of course, you're going to marry the guy. That's okay, because you can confess it before the wedding, then start your married life with a clean slate. So that doesn't count."

Maggie laughed heartily in spite of herself, acknowledging a small element of truth in Lindy's flippant observation.

"How many guys have you slept with since you and Mace got divorced?" Lindy persisted.

"Not a whole lot." Maggie shrugged.

"Ever have a one-night stand?"

"Of course not, Lindy, but—"

"Ever sleep with someone you weren't having a relationship with?" Lindy continued her probe.

"Lindy . . ." Maggie sighed with resignation.

"And how long has it been since you slept with anyone? Before J.D. Who was the last guy?"

"None of your business."

"My guess would be Stephen, last winter," Lindy ventured with a sly grin.

Maggie responded by rolling her napkin into a ball and pitching it toward Lindy's face.

"That's what I thought." A smug Lindy ducked and poured herself another glass of wine.

"Okay, so what's that prove? That I'm selective, that I'm discriminate, that I like to know the person I wake up next to . . ." Maggie presented her rebuttal calmly.

"How long did you know J.D.?"

"Oh, all of maybe seventy-two hours," Maggie admitted with a wry smile. "It seemed longer than that, seemed like I'd known him for a long time."

"And now you're wondering if you knew him at all?"

Maggie did not respond.

"It's okay to have a relationship that's based strictly on physical attraction, Maggie. It happens all the time," Lindy said softly.

"Not to me it doesn't. And it was more than that," insisted Maggie.

"Are you sure? Or are you just trying to justify the whole thing to yourself?"

"You're a pain in the ass, you know that?"

"Hey, look, I don't really care who you sleep with or how often. I just know how you are about things, particularly men. I've never seen you lose your head over anyone. All I'm saying is that you shouldn't feel guilty because this one time, you did."

"What makes you so smart?" Maggie asked grudgingly.

"All those years I spent in clinics, I was under observation almost all the time," Lindy shrugged. "People talk a lot around mentally ill children. They think you can't hear or understand what they say. I learned a lot about how people think. I may not have talked for a long time, but I didn't miss too much of what went on around me. Right now, you are second-guessing yourself, berating yourself, doubting yourself. And all I'm trying to tell you is that you don't have to."

"Thanks." Maggie silently pondered the irony that she, solid, sensible Maggie Callahan, was being analyzed by a bona fide manic-depressive. What, she asked herself ruefully, is wrong with this picture?

"I might add that a lot of people I've been in group therapy with over the years have been guilty Catholics. That's how I recognize it in you." Lindy grinned. "And as far as the office gossip is concerned, keep in mind that there's probably a bit of jealousy involved there. I'll bet there's not a woman in that building who didn't wish she was you last week."

"Maybe so, but it's tiresome. I walk into the room, and conversations stop. I know everyone is talking about how I lost my head and then got dumped on my ass."

"Maggie . . ."

"It's true. I did. It just serves as a reminder to me of why I've always kept my mouth shut where my personal life is concerned. Why I've never broadcasted who I see or what I do," she said grimly, once again chiding herself for her less than discrete behavior the previous week.

"I don't know how you could have kept it from everyone. God, Maggie, he popped into your office whenever he felt like it, sent you flowers every day, and had them delivered to your desk. You were in the bar together . . ."

"I might just as well have had it posted on the marquee outside the building," Maggie lamented, then added, "and the flowers stopped when he left."

"Look, by next week, everyone will have found something else to talk about. Just ignore it. And the guys will back off, you'll see, as soon as the novelty wears off and they realize that you're not interested in the game. I know it bothers you, but trust me, it'll pass."

Maggie picked up the wine and tilted the bottle toward the rim of Lindy's glass.

"No, no more, I have to get going. Staff meeting in the morning. Thanks for dinner."

Lindy rose, slipped her jacket on, and put an arm over Maggie's shoulder as they walked toward the door.

"Cheer up, honey," Lindy told her with that faint hint of a New Orleans drawl, "I still think he'll be back before the week's out. And I'll be more than happy to say I told you so."

Maggie closed the door after her departing friend and locked it. She cleaned up the living room, went into the kitchen, and methodically washed glasses and plates. Returning to the living room, she turned on the television and stared mindlessly at the screen. When the news broadcast ended, she turned off the TV and picked up a magazine, which she thumbed through, scanning one article after another, none of which captured her interest. When she became too tired to avoid it any longer, she turned off the lights and went to bed.

Stretched out alone in the dark, she pulled over the pillow he'd used and placed it under her head as she had every night since he'd left. She felt her eyes burn as she gave in to melancholy. She sniffed quietly, as if to keep her sadness from being detected by anyone else, though she was alone. It embarrassed her to feel so adolescent. Guilty? Maybe. Perhaps Lindy was right, maybe her conscience was bothering her. She wondered if she'd ever see him again. And she wondered who, in whatever city he was in, had received a breathtakingly beautiful bouquet of white roses that morning.

7

"IT'S NOT EASY TO ESTABLISH A RELATIONSHIP WHEN YOU'RE TRAV-eling around so much, you know," J.D.'s voice cut through her reverie, "but I was determined not to lose her. We'd gone from Philadelphia to Charlotte, then to Louisville, all in three or four days. It was exhausting. When we finally got to Baltimore for two nights, I called her and asked her to drive down for the weekend—we were only two hours away. It had been almost a week since I'd seen her, and I'd been thinking about her every day and every night. And after the weekend in Baltimore I knew that she was the only woman in this world for me."

Maggie rolled her eyes at the statement, and he continued as if he hadn't seen.

"We spent almost every weekend together after that," he continued. "Maggie'd fly to whatever city we were playing in or I'd fly back to Philadelphia whenever we got a break. The more time I spent with her, the more I needed to be with her."

"That must have been very exciting, Maggie, all the travel, being part of the entourage," Hilary commented.

"I hate to fly," Maggie snapped peevishly, "and I was never part of his 'entourage.'"

Hilary leaned back with a smile, watching Maggie's tension build, hoping she might crack soon and do something crazy. The show needed something to spice it up.

"Maggie means we spent very little time with the band," he interjected smoothly. "Most weekends we spent investigating whatever city we were in, checking out the tourist sites. We were still getting to know each other. We'd come from very different backgrounds, you see, and there was so much to learn . . ."

The weekend in Baltimore had been wonderful, and so he invited her to join him in New York on the following Friday. His shows had been scheduled for Wednesday and Thursday evenings, and he was there at the train station waiting for her when she arrived.

They'd spent the next two days and nights exploring the city and sampling its offerings. It had been years since Maggie had been to the Metropolitan Museum of Art, and she begged him to take her on Saturday afternoon. He did so reluctantly, not being in the mood to play the tourist but later had grudgingly admitted he'd enjoyed the exhibits they'd waited in line to see. They spent one night in the Village, seeking out the small jazz clubs, another night uptown, enjoying the glitz and glitter.

He found that she was slipping quietly into his heart and was unable to let her board the train that would take her back to Philadelphia without knowing when he would see her again. So he had asked her to fly to St. Louis the following weekend. After St. Louis, there was a three-day trip to Kansas City.

The band had played next in Richmond, and Rick had surprised everyone by unexpectantly inviting Lindy to accompany Maggie on the trip. They'd split up after the concert, Rick and Lindy in search of a party, J.D. and Maggie quietly retiring to their hotel room.

"How long were you married?" he'd asked her later that night as they lay close together.

"About eight months," she replied.

"That's all?"

"It wasn't a very good match," she explained.

"What happened?" He leaned up onto one elbow, curious. He'd been curious for weeks and had resisted asking her about it, half afraid he'd find out she still had feelings for her ex-husband.

"Nothing 'happened.' It was just something I never should have done in the first place."

"Then why'd you do it?"

"It's a very long, involved, and not very interesting story," she sighed.

"Do you ever see him?"

"Mace? No, not really. He calls once in a while to see how I'm doing when he's in the city and feeling nostalgic, I guess. He's a sports writer for a magazine and travels around a lot. But I don't really see him if I can avoid it."

"Bad feelings?"

"No, not at all," she told him, then added, "at least, not as far as I'm concerned."

"Then why do you avoid him?"

"You're a persistent bugger," she laughed. "I feel guilty when I see him, okay? He didn't want the divorce, but I did, so he agreed to it. He wasn't happy about it, but he went through with it because I wanted it."

"Why'd you want a divorce? Did you fall in love with someone else?" he couldn't help but inquire.

"No, I didn't fall in love with someone else." She was becoming tired of the subject. "I just didn't love him."

"Then why did you marry him?"

"Aarrgghh . . ." She pretended to strangle him, and they both laughed.

"Come on, Maggie, I want to know."

"Look, I met Mace when I first got to college. He was a year ahead of me. He was very handsome and bright and sweet, and he was the first guy who ever fell head over heels in love with me—"

"I find that hard to believe," he interrupted with a smile.

"Mace was from a town about thirty minutes north of

where I grew up. I caught a ride home with him for Thanksgiving my freshman year. My parents adored him. He was polite and well mannered and didn't have long hair"—J.D. grimaced self-consciously and she laughed—"and he was very, very Catholic. My father immediately opened our home to him. Invited him back over the weekend to go to a football game with him—my dad teaches history at the college in the town where I grew up."

"Why didn't you go there? Why'd you go away to school?"

"And be under Frank Callahan's watchful eye every minute of every day?" she asked, wide-eyed at the very thought.

"I see." He grinned.

"You'd have to know my father to really 'see.' Anyway, to make a long story short, I dated Mace pretty much exclusively for the next three years. Everytime I stopped seeing him, he and my father would gang up on me until I went back with him. Then he graduated, and I guess I took advantage of the fact that he wasn't there and I started dating someone else. Mace waited very patiently, and when this other guy dumped me and broke my heart, Mace was there to put me back together again. He acted like nothing ever happened, just picked up where we'd left off. That's when I knew how much he really loved me. I didn't think that anyone would ever love me that much again. And I figured I owed it to him to try to love him, too. Unfortunately, I never really did. And my family was really upset about the whole thing. No one'd ever been divorced in our family. It was a hard pill for them to swallow."

"Why? Divorce isn't such a big deal these days."

"Well, you know, I was the first child, and I've always been close to my parents. Particularly my father."

"Daddy's little girl," J.D. teased.

"More or less," she admitted.

"And it's not as if you're the only child, you know, what with a brother and three sisters. And you're the only person I know who has a sister 'sister.'"

"Oh, you mean Frankie?" She grinned. "That's Sister Mary Frances Joanna to you. And she's not the only member of the family to take Holy Orders, you know. There's Aunt Cecilia, my mother's oldest sister—she's been a nun for thirty-five years or so. And my cousin Agnes and my cousin Mary Rose—they're both nuns, too. Now, as far as priests go, we have—"

"Enough," he laughed. "I'm thoroughly intimidated by a vision of a heaven peppered with Callahans, one in holy garb crouched behind every cloud. My family simply isn't in the same league with that ecclesiastic lineup."

"That's because there are so few of you and so many of us," she laughed. "It's just you and your sister, isn't it?"

He nodded.

"You never mention your father," she said, straightening the pillows and making a nest for herself.

"He died when I was seven."

"I'm sorry. That must have been rough."

"It was," he admitted. "It took my mom a long time to recover. It was maybe a bit easier on me, in some ways, because I didn't understand what it all meant. All I knew was that he'd left for work one day and never came back."

"What happened to him?"

"Heart attack. He was only thirty-eight. I remember how confusing it all was. They let me see him in the casket—I suppose so that I'd understand that he was dead. But *dead* didn't mean anything to me, and the man in the coffin didn't appear at all like my father."

She looked at him quizzically.

"My dad was always so lively, so animated," he explained patiently, speaking slowly, the emotion in his voice very evident. "Always moving, always talking, singing, laughing . . . The man in the box was silent and still. I didn't recognize him at all. So I guess I kept waiting for him to come back, and I grew more and more angry with him as time passed and he didn't return. I didn't really understand what *dead* meant until I was about twelve . . ." His voice faded.

"What happened then?" she asked in a near whisper, caught up in his tale.

"Went out one morning to feed my dog and couldn't find

him. So I went looking for him, up over the hills behind my mom's house. I found him laying on the ground, his eyes open, but he was so still . . . It was just a bundle of fur there on the ground. And I knew he was gone. And that's when I understood what being dead meant. And that's when I stopped being angry with my father and finally began to mourn him."

He sat silently for a minute or two, a pillow propped behind his back, the vision of his father's face suddenly vivid in his mind's eye. He stared long and wistfully at the image. He still missed him, still had times when he wished he could sit and talk to him, like he did when he was a very small boy. Other than Judith, his sister, he'd never discussed this painful subject with anyone, avoiding any mention of his father for years. Yet tonight the words had come to him freely, and Maggie had listened to every one. She seemed to understand his silences, and he knew that he had found in her someone who would always listen, would always understand.

He looked at her and smiled wryly. "Poor Dash, he'd just gotten caught in the wrong place at the wrong time."

"Dash? Was that your dog?" she asked.

He nodded.

"What do you mean?"

"There's a man who lives up the road; he goes a bit batty every once in a while. See, years ago, oh, maybe it's been close to twenty-five years now, his wife took off with another man. Never came back. And from time to time, old George just sort of loses it, I guess, and goes out looking for them."

"Looking for them where?"

"Up in the hills. Supposedly he'd found them together in a very compromising situation. He'd gone back to his house to get his gun, was going to do them in right then and there apparently. But by the time he got back, they were gone. Every now and again he goes out looking for them, where he'd found them before. I guess he takes his gun with him thinking next time he finds them, he'll be ready. Only, of course, he never will find them, they'll not be back—"

"You mean he goes out looking for his wife to kill her?"

Maggie leaned forward, incredulous. "I can't believe he's allowed to roam around like that, Jamey. He sounds really dangerous."

"Only to the occasional sheep that crosses his path at night. Or a dog now and then—that's what happened to Dash."

"It would give me the creeps to think someone was roaming around outside my house in the dark with a gun." She shivered. "Don't you worry about your mother or your sister?"

"Of course not. We've all known him all our lives. He'd not harm any of us. It's his wife he's looking for—"

"Jamey, anybody who would mistake a sheep or a dog for his wife probably can't be relied upon to be discriminate when he's got a gun in his hands."

"Well, for the most part, we just feel sorry for him. It's sad, in a way . . . I'd have thought you'd have more compassion."

"I'd be more inclined toward compassion if he was locked away someplace. The guy obviously needs help."

"And we obviously need to spend a little less time talking here." He reached for her, pulling her to him. "You know, I never realized just how long a week could be . . ."

The weekend had passed with incredible speed, and all too soon he found himself standing alone in the parking lot watching her drive away, feeling more lost than he'd ever felt before. Everything that made sense to him in this life, everything that made the sun warm to his skin and made food taste good and made the music come alive was behind the wheel of that car.

He walked through the lobby and took the elevator up to his floor, pushed the door open with the key, and turned on the light. He stood at the window and watched the lights from the cars in the parking lot trace bright patterns with long glowing tails in the darkness. The room was so quiet now, and he felt very much alone. He lay on the bed and felt a sadness spread through him—a sadness stronger than he'd ever experienced. He knew it was more than just missing her physical presence. It was everything that Maggie brought with her, everything she took of him when she left, that filled him with an overwhelming sense of desolation. He could not have known that night that it would be a feeling he'd come to know well over the years, one that would be with him every night he'd spend without her for the rest of his life.

8

"CORRECT ME IF I'M WRONG, BUT WASN'T IT THAT FRIEND OF yours, Linda something or other—I can't quite recall her name—who was involved with Rick Daily all those years?" Hilary directed the question to Maggie, who all but froze at the thought of discussing that particular ghost on this particular occasion.

"You mean Lindy. Lindy Burton." Even with the microphone, Maggie's voice was barely perceptible.

"That was certainly a very tragic set of circumstances," Hilary continued sympathetically, hoping one of them would elaborate. There'd always been something unsettling in Hilary's mind about that whole episode, something that had seemed not quite right, but even her sharp instincts could never quite pinpoint what it was.

"Yes, it was, for everyone involved." J.D. attempted to draw the attention from his wife, knowing how painful the subject was for her.

"You know, I met her several times some years back in London, with Rick," Hilary went on, inwardly reflecting on the image of Rick Daily that had flashed through her mind.

Now there was one exceptional man. "They were the most striking couple I'd ever seen, he so tall and handsome, and she so stunningly beautiful. Why do you suppose they never married?"

J.D. merely shrugged. "I've no idea. I've never asked him."

"There was something about her that I could just never get a handle on," continued Hilary. "I don't know. Maggie, how would you have described her?"

"Lindy was a very complex person," Maggie said evenly.

Complex? The word barely scratches the surface where Lindy was concerned. Manic-depressive was the clinical term, but screwed up more often came to mind. It hadn't been her fault, of course; she'd had it rough from the beginning. And she tried sometimes to break through that wall she'd built around herself, tried to open up and let someone else in.

Those times, Maggie recalled with a chill, were few and far between, and the glimpse that was permitted only served as a reminder that Lindy was the loneliest person she'd ever known. At times it had been so very difficult to be her friend; at times the bits of herself that she shared all but broke your heart . . .

"Lindy, come into the kitchen with me. I need to find something for us to eat. I don't know about you, but I'm starving," Maggie called to the figure reclining in the living room.

Upon arriving at Maggie's apartment after the weekend in Richmond, Lindy'd crawled onto the sofa, nursing the remnants of a fierce hangover. Lindy groaned and pushed herself up. "God, I feel like shit."

"You deserve to feel like shit, all the drinking you did this weekend," Maggie teased, then added, "I hope it was worth it."

Lindy's response was slow in coming. "Yes, it was worth it."

Maggie watched out of the corner of one eye. Lindy had

seated herself at the small kitchen table, busying herself picking at her nail polish, a nervous habit she'd had for as long as Maggie had known her.

"Well, you know, the band has almost a whole week off next week. Jamey'll be here Friday through the following Wednesday. Maybe you could ask Rick if he wants to—"

"No" was the simple, sharp reply.

Maggie turned and looked at Lindy in surprise.

"No." Lindy was still peeling her nail polish off, leaving tiny chips of dark rose dust scattered like tiny petals on the table. "I don't want to see him next weekend."

"I thought you said—"

"It doesn't mean I want to see him next weekend. Or maybe any other weekend."

"I don't understand you."

"You don't have to."

Maggie turned her back, resumed measuring coffee grounds into the white paper filter, poured the water into the coffeemaker, and removed two cups from the shelf.

"Maggie . . ." The voice was so low it was almost inaudible. "Maggie, I don't understand me, so I can't expect anyone else to. I don't even make sense to myself sometimes."

"We all feel that way from time to time, Lind. Right now, you're tired, you're hungover and hungry and, let's face it, you've spent the last few days with a mad man."

"Rick's not really that bad, you know . . ." Her voice trailed off. "We spent a lot of time fooling around, but we spent a lot of time talking, too." She looked up at Maggie. "It was nice."

"What did you talk about?"

"All kinds of things."

"Did you tell him about—"

"About the fact that I've spent two-thirds of my life visiting a shrink twice a week? No, Maggie, I did not." Lindy toyed with the spoon, stirring the coffee round and round in continuous swirls.

"Lindy, you weren't responsible for what your father

did," Maggie said gently, well aware of the burden Lindy carried in her soul.

Lindy raised her head slightly, pulling the long blond hair back with both hands, the frantic look of a lost child crossing her face for the briefest of moments, then disappearing as quickly as it came.

"Lindy, if this therapist hasn't been able to help you to understand that much, after all this time, maybe you should look for someone else who can," she suggested. It hurt deeply to see her friend in such pain, knowing she could do nothing to help heal the wounds.

"Changing doctors means that I have to sit down and start at the beginning and talk about the whole thing all over again. And I just don't want to go over it again and again. I can't deal with it anymore. I've had to do it so many times over the past seventeen years, Maggie."

"But maybe you could learn how to stop shutting people out of your life." Maggie rested an elbow on the table, her chin in her hand. "You know, you've dumped more guys than I'll ever even meet."

"Maggie, I just don't want to be in a position ever where it matters to me if someone stays or goes. And I've never had a problem attracting guys."

"That's great while you're young and gorgeous. What about when you're seventy?"

"I won't live that long, so I don't worry about it." She shrugged indifferently.

"Why do you say that? What do you think will happen to you?"

"Oh, I don't know exactly how it will happen, but I won't make it to thirty-five. I've always known it." Lindy appeared to be totally unconcerned. "It's okay, Maggie. It doesn't scare me."

The steady matter-of-factness of her voice and the cool, level, blank look in her eyes chilled Maggie all the way through.

"Everyone dies eventually, Lindy, sooner or later. Most of us just hope it's later." She tried to make a joke but was unable to muster the lightness that she'd intended.

"Sooner's okay," Lindy replied with frank nonchalance.

"Lindy, isn't there anything in your life that you feel really strongly about, anything you think is worth living for?"

Lindy was pensive. Finally, she answered, "No."

"But that doesn't mean there won't be—"

"I don't want there to be, Maggie. That's the whole point." Lindy was becoming agitated. "Look, I don't expect you to understand. You grew up in a real family, with two parents who loved you and gave you a wonderful home life and enough security that you could grow up to be a person who knows how to give and how to take." Lindy lit a cigarette, her hands shaking. "Do you have any idea what it's like for a little kid to deal with an alcoholic mother? And God forbid anyone outside the family should know that the beautiful, talented Andrea Burton had a drinking problem. How the woman ever managed to get paint onto her canvases is still the greatest mystery of my life. Other than why she had me or my brother in the first place. God knows she never wanted either of us." She paused and took a sip of her coffee, carefully replacing the cup into the saucer before continuing.

"My father took care of us and took care of her and arranged her showings and made excuses for her when she didn't show up. I hated her. I have never, in all these years, shed a tear for her. And I've never felt sorry or guilty over it either. The woman gave me life, for what that's worth, but as far as I'm concerned, she abandoned me the day I was born."

Her voice, so low and steady through her litany, had stopped. Maggie wondered if she was all right.

"And then, I guess my dad just snapped. I had never been aware of how much he must have loved her, you know, it never had occurred to me that he did. But three weeks after she died, I walked into the garage, and there he was, hanging there. No note. No explanation . . ."

"Lindy . . ." Maggie fought hard for words that would not express her horror at hearing it all, the same horror she'd felt the first time she'd heard it. How the nine-year-old Lindy had climbed onto the roof of the car and cut his body down with hedge clippers before calling the police, carefully shielding her six-year-old brother from the sight. And how she'd spent the next nine years in a clinic for mentally ill children, not speaking a word for the first twenty-three months.

"Lindy, I don't think your father made a rational decision to leave you and your brother. I think he just overloaded. People do that sometimes. They get to a point where they can't take anymore. If he hadn't been so unnerved by your mother's accident—"

"It wasn't an accident. She had every intention of driving into that wall." Lindy's voice was harsh and bitter.

"If he hadn't been so despondent over losing her, he never would have put you two in that situation. As difficult as it must have been for him to live with her, apparently he couldn't live without her. Lindy, you don't know what went on between your parents—you were a little girl. You don't know what forces were at work between them . . ."

"Well," she said, wiping the tears, "those forces will never be at work in me."

She sat motionless for a few moments, then whispered in a tiny voice, "I'm sorry, Maggie."

"Sorry? For what?"

"I always seem to dump the craziest shit on you."

"I'll always be there to listen to you as a friend, but I can't help you. I don't know the best way for you to deal with all this."

Lindy had made a pile out of the shavings of nail polish, her fingernails all bare now. "Mags?"

"What?"

"Can we eat now? I'm about to pass out."

Maggie opened a can of soup and threw a salad together. They ate quietly, both deep in their own thoughts. Finally an exhausted Lindy gathered her things to leave.

"You going to be all right tonight?" a concerned Maggie asked.

"I'll be fine. I think I just need some sleep." Lindy fished in her jacket pocket for her keys. "And thanks, Maggie. I know it's not always easy to be my friend . . ."

"I just wish I could help you."

"No one can help me, Maggie." Lindy smiled sadly, turned, and walked down the steps.

9

AND NO ONE EVER COULD, a doleful MAGGIE RECALLED. *Not me, not Rick, though God knows we both tried.* Friendship was never enough, nor was love, to ease the sorrows of Lindy's soul. She shook off the memory and attempted to tune back in to present, to chase the gloomy thoughts away.

"I'm just a bit curious," Hilary was saying, "as to why, if you and Rick had such glaring artistic differences, you remained together after Daily Times broke up. Why you formed another group together instead of going your separate ways at that time."

"That was entirely different, Hilary," J.D. explained. "We put Daily Times to rest specifically to start a new band. Daily Times had been a tremendous commercial success, but we felt we wanted to do some things that would be very different from what we'd done in the past. We decided to start from scratch, so to speak, and change the name of the band and most of the support personnel. We changed the sound, adding more jazz arrangements, some elements of blues, which is, of course, Rick's specialty. Later on, we agreed to disband Monkshood because we were both ready to pursue solo careers. Fortunately, our friendship never suffered, and of course, Maggie and Rick have remained very close."

"Yes, well, we'll get back to your wife's relationship with Rick Daily before the night is over, I'm quite sure." Hilary smiled at Maggie, using that invisible barometer to gauge her reaction. Maggie met Hilary's gaze without a blink. Being a pro, Hilary never missed a beat. "It's been rumored throughout the years that Rick and Maggie have had, shall we say, a very special sort of friendship. But right now, we have to take a commercial break, so don't go away . . ."

When the cameras were turned off, Hilary turned to her guests, instructing them with a smile, "And don't you go away" before stepping into the hallway for a word with the assistant producer.

Maggie relaxed only slightly, knowing there was still a long night ahead of her. She didn't want to talk about Rick, didn't want to discuss their friendship publicly. How to explain that she had been his confidant, his strength, through the darkest days of his life but never lovers as had been alluded to from time to time over the years in silly stories spred by shallow reporters who could not begin to fathom what bound them together. There were too many elements of pain running through that relationship, the full disclosure of which would most likely land Rick in jail for a very long time.

She realized her husband was leaning toward her, about to speak. She cut him off before he could open his mouth.

"Could we please move this interview along and some-how avoid discussing my relationship with Rick?" she hissed through clenched teeth.

"I sincerely doubt she'd let us. Just answer any question casually and keep it all very . . ." He'd thought perhaps if he sounded supportive and reassuring, she'd soften a bit. He was wrong.

"I don't need you to tell me how to react, thank you very much," she snapped, straightening her back and turning toward the window once again.

An incredible moon had begun it's ascent into the night sky. Glowing gold, it was already backlighting the hills.

Under other circumstances, on another night, she would have called his attention to it and begged him to accompany her out into the garden to enjoy it's enchantment. Tonight, she merely looked away.

The encouragement he'd felt earlier when she had appeared to have come around somewhat vanished, yet he could not help but speak to her, to make her respond to him, if only in anger.

"Maggie, calm down. If you get rattled, you're liable to say almost anything, which is exactly what the little viper wants. Just be very nonchalant—"

"Just get your ass out of the seventies, okay? I don't want to talk about the past." She crossed her legs, the foot resting on the floor tapping out her agitation.

"Maggie, the longer we talk about the past, the less opportunity there will be to discuss the present, unless, of course, that's what you want."

He paused and looked into the face that had held him captive for the past fifteen years, knowing her hold on him was as strong as it ever had been. The thought that he was losing her terrified him. Loving her had put his life together, had kept it together. To be without her was unthinkable. He wanted to grab her by the shoulders and shake her, wanted to hold her and kiss her the way he'd done countless times, but he dared not touch her.

"Maggie . . ." He leaned toward her, caressing her with the sound of her name, begging for an opening.

"Save it." She refused to give an inch.

"Maggie, listen to me, it's not what you think . . . How could you ever seriously think . . . Look, you've completely misinterpreted the situation . . ."

"Misinterpreted the situation?" she snarled sarcastically, "Well then, let's put our heads together and see if we can't come up with a somewhat more creative explanation of what two naked adults could have been doing—"

"Maggie, listen, I was in the shower—"

"Stuff it, J.D. It's you who taught me how to do it in the shower, remember?"

"Oh, for Christ's sake, Maggie, just . . . just look at me,

will you? Can you honestly tell me that you don't love me anymore?" He made no effort to mask his desolation.

"Jamey, love is not the issue." Her voice revealed more than a little exasperation. "I do not want to discuss this anymore."

"Maggie, please, I swear it's not what you think . . . ," he pleaded with her.

"Well, ready to resume here?" Hilary had seemed to come out of nowhere. How much had she heard? "Cameras, folks. And . . . we're back. Glad you stayed with us. We were discussing, I believe, the differences between the two bands —between Daily Times and Monkshood, that is—and the reasons why both had folded."

"Well, you know, Hilary, Rick is a phenomenal blues guitarist, and my taste in music is much more eclectic. It was good for both of us when we finally broke away from each other and pursued our own careers." He tried to sound confident, hoped that she nor anyone else would discern the unsteadiness of his voice. His wife had shaken him to his core, and he was trying desperately to keep his mind clear on two levels, keeping the interview going and gaining her attention.

Maybe I should just throw caution to the wind and get down on my hands and knees, right now, and blurt out the whole story. Sit on her, literally, and refuse to get up until she agrees to hear me out. It's a crude technique, but judging by the response I've had from her so far, it may come to that. Talk about a showstopper . . .

"And we had started to go our separate ways on a personal level as well, because I spent so much time at Maggie's that spring. Every free weekend, every time we got a few days off, I headed for Philadelphia. I got to know the area and grew to love it—you know, of course, that our home is in the suburbs there—and I'd bought a keyboard and installed it in Maggie's apartment, so that I could spend some time writing while Maggie was at work, so I'd be ready to go on my own."

And spent the rest of the time just falling in love with Maggie, he could have added, just loving her and riding the roller coaster of the painful separations, the joyous reunions. Looking to the future and savoring the magic of those days and nights . . .

"What's on the agenda today?" he asked with a yawn. They'd slept late and were still entwined, arms and legs.

"Well, I thought I'd take you on that tour of Philadelphia I promised you. It looks like a lovely day. It'll be fun," she coaxed him, "and you could use a little exercise as well as a change of scenery."

It was a great day for walking, sunny and warm and just slightly breezy. They played tourist all day, from Independence Hall to Old St. Joseph's Church, a particular favorite of Maggie's. They stopped for lunch at a small restaurant, then resumed their stroll through the tiny side streets of Society Hill, where block after block of homes, dating from the 1700s, were being restored. They walked into Head House Square, where new shops had opened on the site of the old open-air market place that had operated during the Colonial days.

They decided on dinner at an Italian restaurant not too far from Maggie's apartment. J.D. enjoyed the meal but noted, "This isn't exactly like the Italian food you get in Italy, you know."

"I guess it's tailored to American tastes," she said with a shrug.

"You know what we should do sometime, Maggie? We should go to Italy and rent a car, then drive up through the country into France and then down into Spain and Portugal. You'd love it. It would be a wonderful holiday. Nothing to do but eat and sleep and make love. What do you think?" He gazed lovingly at her, watching the light from the candle dance across her face.

"I think it sounds very romantic."

"It will be. I'll tell you what. We'll do it next year."

"Next year?" she asked with a smile of surprise.

"Yes. By the time I go home, I should have enough new songs for an album if I work on it while I'm on this tour, you know, when you're here and I'm traveling around. Then when I get home, I'll get the recording done and tend to the details, and by then I'll be more than ready for a long romantic holiday with the woman I love." He studied her eyes as his words registered, then said softly, "You do know that I'm hopelessly in love with you, don't you, Maggie?"

"Good" was all she said, eyes twinkling, a small teasing smile on her lips.

"'Good,'" he repeated flatly. "I pour my heart out to you and all you can say is 'good.'"

"Yes."

"Well." He leaned across the table, taking one of her hands in his. "What exactly does that mean, 'good,' in Callahanese?"

"It means I'm glad, very happy, actually, to hear you say that. I wanted you to fall hopelessly in love with me."

"You did, did you?"

"Yes, I did."

"And why is that?"

"Because then you'd always come back to me." She spoke in a hushed, emotional voice. "I want you to always come back to me."

"I always will, Maggie. You have my most solemn word on that. No matter where I go, no matter what happens, I will always come back to you. There's never been anyone else for me, Maggie. There never will be. Wherever you are is my home. And I will always come home to you."

"Good," she said again, and they both laughed softly.

"Say it." He looked directly into her eyes. "I want to hear you say it."

She played with her fork, making parallel indentations with the tines on the red tablecloth.

"I do," she replied quietly. "I do love you."

"And to think that I always thought love at first sight was an impossibility." He smiled.

"Oh, it happens," she said, grinning. "We always tease my mom and dad about it. See, he went to her house to pick up her sister for a blind date. Took one look at my mother and that was that. My dad did take Aunt Jane to the movies that night, but he brought her back by nine and by nine-fifteen had a date with my mother for the next night. They were married three months later on my mom's eighteenth birthday."

"Would you like anything else?" the waiter returned to inquire.

"Maggie? No? I guess not," J.D. replied.

When they'd returned to the apartment, she said, "Come into the kitchen with me while I make some coffee."

"Why didn't you have some at the restaurant?"

"Because I wanted to curl up on the sofa with you while I drank it. Want some?"

He declined, and she brought her cup into the living room, nestling next to him.

"And what have we planned for tomorrow?" he teased. "Another ten-mile hike?"

"Well," she paused thoughtfully, "maybe you could come for a run with me early, and then we could——"

"Forget it," he laughed. "If you're running, you'll be running alone."

"How 'bout a long walk then?" she coaxed.

He groaned. "You nearly walked the legs off me today. How much more of the city is there to see?"

"Lots. But I was thinking of a walk here, around town. There's lots of interesting old homes, lots of trees. You'll like it."

And the next day, when they walked down the wide streets, past the old Victorian houses, many of which looked as if they could use some major renovations, he found he did like it. Maggie pointed out the tiny Quaker meeting house, built in the late 1700s, and a two-hundred-year-old house that was said to be built from a ship's ballast. She pointed out elements she found interesting on a number of the old places they passed, a turret with a small porch here, unusual stonework there, spectacular stained glass on yet another. It was, she told him, much like the town where she'd grown up, a family town with a real sense of community where people spoke to strangers and no one was too busy to return a smile. She felt at home here, liked its proximity to the city and the feeling of living in the country. It was the best of both worlds.

They walked down a side street, and Maggie stopped in front of a large property, the house sitting far back from the street, the front yard sadly overgrown with a jungle of shrubs and vines. She leaned on the black wrought-iron fence that surrounded it and announced, "Someday I'm going to buy this house."

"Have you ever been inside?" he asked, stepping aside to permit a puffing jogger to pass.

"No."

"How do you know you'll like it?"

"I just do," she said, grinning.

"It's falling apart," he observed. "It's old and the outside's not in good repair. It's probably a mess inside."

"Probably," she agreed, undaunted.

They stood looking over the fence at the large pale pinkish stucco house, its four massive chimneys rising through the roof at various places. A rounded glassed room jutted off the one side, probably a conservatory added during Victorian times. The house seemed to ramble a bit in several directions, as if it had been added onto over the ages, each subsequent owner never quite knowing the course its growth should take.

"What about it appeals to you so?" He studied its angles, noting the stained glass windows staggered across the right side. *Must be the staircase there.*

"I don't know, Jamey. It just looks like a romantic place to live. All those windows and gables and curves."

"I think it looks spooky, all overgrown and secluded and neglected. It's likely to be haunted," he teased. "Is it for sale?"

"No. Not now. But someday it will be."

An elderly couple passed, arm in arm. They nodded a greeting that Maggie returned with a smile.

"Ahh, Maggie, it would be a big job to revive this place."

"I could handle it."

"No doubt you could." He chuckled and put his arm around her shoulder, leading her back to the sidewalk to resume their stroll. He turned once to look back at the tall, wide rectangular chimneys rising through the trees. "It is a nice property, I'll give you that. I like the way it slopes down a bit on the side there, and I like the wooded area in the back. Too bad it's such a mess . . ." And he promptly dismissed it from his thoughts.

10

"WELL, IT ALL SOUNDS VERY COZY AND VERY ROMANTIC." HILARY realized she'd gotten absolutely nowhere with him, had not gained a glimmer of what was going on between them. Perhaps a shift in gears was called for. Perhaps the wife . . . *If,* she thought wryly, *I can get her attention and keep it long enough to have any meaningful conversation with her. She appears to keep slipping off someplace.* "We've heard so little from you this evening, Maggie, and you've kept so much in the background all these years. I'd be remiss in my duties to my viewers if we didn't take this opportunity to get to know you a bit better."

"And what exactly would you like to know?" she asked stonily.

"Well, let's start by having you tell us what the wife of an internationally renowned performer does with her time." Hilary hoped her smile gave her the appearance of one who was truly interested.

"We travel a bit when Jamey has free time." She shrugged. "Spend our summers here, at his mother's. The rest of the time I mostly keep up with the children and their activities."

She thought of the many pleasant sunny afternoons spent

at the park or in the yard, watching the children on the swings, the little ones in the sandbox, or sitting in the grass making clover rings to grace a young daughter's hair. Maggie realized how fortunate she'd been and had never ceased being grateful that she'd been afforded the luxury of being able to enjoy every moment of their childhoods, that they'd been able to hire someone to do all the chores she could never seem to find time for. She wondered if that would change with her leaving him, if she'd have to give up the house.

"Well, I would suppose that's a full-time job," Hilary cooed. Why anyone would want to have such a brood was beyond her. "And someone has to keep the home fires burning. Keep up with all those little domestic details of everyday life . . ."

"Hilary, Maggie hasn't a domestic bone in her body," J.D. interjected, "if by domestic, you mean cleaning and laundry and cooking and that sort of thing."

"Well, certainly with such a large family, a large home, one would expect a housekeeper." Hilary thought perhaps if she appeared to come to Maggie's defense, it would pay off later in the discussion. "One could hardly be expected to raise seven children, keep a home, and cook."

"Well, we do have a wonderful housekeeper, but I'm the cook in the family, not Maggie," he announced.

"Now that we've covered my shortcomings as a wife," Maggie said, glaring, "could we move onto something else?"

"Sweetheart, you have no shortcomings as a wife." He patted her knee, knowing this patronizing gesture would arouse her ire. Any emotion he could incite in her at this point would be better than her stony silence.

"You don't do all the cooking?" Hilary ventured skeptically.

"Absolutely. Every night when I'm at home," he assured her. "I taught myself how to cook back in those early days, primarily to keep us from starving on those nights we were too lazy to go out to eat."

"Well, then, suppose you tell us what's your specialty."

93

"Oh, I don't know." He pretended to mull it over, then turned to his wife, his eyes twinkling, and said, "What'd you think, Maggie? Maybe that chicken in wine I've been doing for years now?"

Maggie started slightly, her nostrils filling suddenly with the aroma of a long-ago unexpected dinner he'd prepared to surprise her. How proud he'd been of himself that night, how pleased with his efforts . . .

As she had arrived home from work one night and opened the front door, the smell of something wonderful cooking filled the air. Max, her upstairs neighbor, must have dinner guests, she thought, and ran up the steps to her apartment.

She walked into the hallway and sniffed. Overcome with curiosity, she followed her nose into the kitchen. J.D. was at the stove and turned to greet her with a wide grin.

"I see my timing was perfect. Everything is just about ready."

He poured her a glass of wine and handed it to her where she stood riveted with shock and kissed her nonchalantly as if he did this every night, still grinning, still watching her face as she surveyed the scene.

He'd set the table, where two candles waited to be lit. There was no mess—he'd washed everything he'd used. And something smelled incredibly good.

"Jamey, I never expected this," she exclaimed, then stepped closer to inspect the contents of the pans on the stove. "What are you making?"

"Something with chicken and mushrooms and wine. And rice. And salad." His casual attitude could not disguise his satisfaction with his accomplishment nor her reaction. "Sit down, Maggie. It'll be done in two minutes."

He turned back to her, and seeing the look of disbelief on her face, meeting her eyes, he laughed, and she with him.

"How did you know to do all this?"

"I looked through one of the cookbooks on the shelf—you should dust them once in a while if you're not going to use them—till I found something I thought we'd both like. And I took the book with me to the food store so I'd know what

94

to buy—here, give me your plate." He tried to ignore her still wide-eyed stare. "So. How is it?"

"It's great. Unbelievable. Jamey, you amaze me."

"Thank you," he said smugly. "That good, is it?"

"Yes, it is. I can't believe you did this all by yourself."

"That's a somewhat chauvinistic attitude, I'd say."

"I'm sorry, Jamey, but this is a completely new experience for me. I've never had a man cook dinner for me. Come to think of it, I don't believe I even know any men who cook."

"Doesn't your father ever do the cooking?"

"Frank Callahan?" She pretended to choke at the very thought. "It would never happen. It is simply outside of his role."

"And what is his role?" J.D. looked amused.

"His role is to be waited on by my mother. And her role is to take care of everyone in the family. Including my father. Especially my father," she explained.

"Seems reasonable to me," he deadpanned across the table. "Nothing wrong with a woman knowing her place."

"If I thought for one second you were serious, I'd bounce you down the steps on your head."

"Well, then, tell me how two such traditional parents produced so independent a daughter."

"I'm afraid they're still asking themselves that question. They've tried to figure out for a long time where they went wrong with me." Her earlier teasing tone faded.

"You're joking, of course."

She shook her head. "Not really. I'm afraid I've been a bit of a disappointment to them."

"Maggie, what could your parents possibly have wanted you to be that you're not? You're a bright, charming, sweet, honest, moral, kind—did I leave anything out?—truly good and wonderful person. What do you think—Oh, wait, not that business about your husband?" He made a face.

"Sort of. But it's not just Mace. It's the whole inability to fit the mold, you know?" she told him, an uncharacteristic self-consciousness creeping into her voice.

"What mold?"

"The mold all the women in my family came out of. They get married, they have children, and they spend the rest of their lives humoring their husbands and raising their kids. The only acceptable deviation is the sisterhood. They do not have careers, they do not sleep with men they are not married to, they do not get divorced, they do not let anyone know they have brains."

"Well, I have to admit that now that I think about it, I've never met an Irish girl who fancied herself an intellectual." He tried to interject a lighter tone.

"I don't fancy myself an intellectual, Jamey, but I am smarter than a lot of the men I've met in my life and I can't see any reason to pretend that I'm not. My mother is an extremely bright woman, but she uses most of her wits finding ways to outsmart my father into thinking he always gets his own way, when in fact it's she who calls most of the shots. Subtly, of course. Most of her time is spent pampering my father's ego." She sighed. "My mother set a wonderful example for us in her own way. There is something noble about a person who can truly be selfless and honestly care more about others than they care about themselves. I just never learned that lesson very well."

"Why do you say that?"

"If I had, I would have stayed married. I would have stayed in the church," she told him.

"What's the church got to do with all this?"

"It has everything to do with it. As far as the church is concerned, one of the main purposes of a woman is to have children. Practicing birth control is frowned upon, and a good Catholic does not ask for a divorce when she realizes she does not love her husband. According to my father anyway."

"Then what does she do?"

"She offers it up."

"She what?" he asked blankly.

"Offers it up. You know, makes a sacrifice."

"I don't understand."

"Of course you don't. You weren't raised like I was."

"Enlighten me." He leaned back in his chair and folded his arms across his chest, curious.

"Whenever something happened that was unpleasant or painful or whenever you had to do something that you didn't want to do or had some hardship to face, my grandmother always said to offer it up. To see it through and not complain and accept God's will and offer your suffering to God."

He sat silently, staring at her for a long time.

"Am I to interpret this to mean that your parents expected you to stay in an unhappy marriage, living a miserable life, having children you didn't want with a man you didn't love and that it would somehow make God happy?"

She shrugged. "That's simplifying things a bit, but you have the general idea."

"How could your unhappiness make God, or anyone else for that matter, happy? That makes no bloody sense at all."

"It does if you keep in mind that marriage is a holy sacrament in the Catholic church."

"Do you honestly believe your parents wanted you to be unhappy."

"No. They wanted me to stop the foolishness and just be in love with Mace. Except I couldn't. My father even told me to go back to Mace and have a baby and I'd feel differently about the whole thing. Ironically, the only one who gave me any support at all was my sister Frankie, the one who's a nun . . ."

"Well, I'm sure they still love you, Maggie, and they want you to be happy."

"Yes, they love me. That's why it hurt them that I turned out to be something of the family renegade. Now, my sister Ellie, she's twenty-six, she's always done it all by the book, you know? Never given them problems, never stepped out of line in any way. They never felt they had to make excuses for Ellie . . ."

"Do you think they love her more than they love you?"

"Of course not."

"Do you think she's a better person than you? Or a happier one?"

"Ellie? She's a bitch."

He laughed heartily.

"She is. She's a miserable person. But she's done it all as they expected her to. She went to school there in town. Married an assistant professor. Got her degree in teaching, just like Mommy and Daddy thought she should. I'm sure she and Elliot—that's her husband, is that the cutest thing you ever heard, Ellie and Elliot?—never slept together before they were married. And she cooks dinner every night." Her good humor was returning, and she grinned.

"Unlike the elder Callahan daughter who prefers to have her men cook for her."

"Exactly. I really don't enjoy cooking all that much, to be honest with you, and I have to say that you are a much better cook than I am, at least, based on your effort tonight."

"Well, I have to admit I surprised even myself. And to tell the truth, I really enjoyed it. If my musical career ever flops, maybe I could open a restaurant."

"Not a chance of that happening." She smiled lovingly, then, glancing at the clock above the stove, said, "Criminy, look at the time, Jamey. It's seven-twenty. Your plane leaves in just about an hour. Are you packed? And I forgot to stop for gas on the way home. There's barely enough to get me to the station on the corner."

They'd arrived at the airport with a scant seven minutes to spare before he had to board, hardly enough time to say all the things that needed to be said till next time. She'd watched as the plane had backed up, then walked to the end of the hallway, up the ramp where the solid walls gave way to the glass enclosure that permitted a view of the runways on the left side of the terminal. She leaned against the glass, wondering which side of the plane he was on, if he would look back and see her there. The plane turned slowly, then gathered a bit of speed as it began to taxi down the runway, then lift effortlessly into the sky. She watched until the lights disappeared into the night, wondering if she'd ever get used to his leaving.

It had been a quiet ride home from the airport, and she

hated going back into the silence of her apartment. The scent of spring, fragrant and balmy, held her on the porch for a moment. She looked up into the sky, at the tiny lights, so far overhead, as they moved through the dark night. Another plane taking someone else's lover away or bringing him back home . . .

11.

HOME. SHE PONDERED THE WORD AND THE IMAGES IT CALLED UP. *Where is my home now? Could it ever again be here, in this house we've taken over bit by bit until it's reflective as much of me as it is of his mother? Can I go back to that house we've shared for so long in the States, the house we'd resurrected from ruin and made our own, where we greeted each new child, every one save Jesse and Lucy conceived under its roof? And how could I go back to my hometown, with seven children in tow, no longer the girl from Kelly's Mills upon whom fortune had bestowed more than anyone could ever have imagined: a storybook romance; a long and happy marriage to a well-known celebrity; beautiful, healthy children.*

The irony of it was not lost on her, that she had all but hidden J.D. from her conservative family for so long, fearful her parents—most particularly her father—would have dismissed the man she loved as a witless, shaggy-haired punk who couldn't find a real job. And now she could not face going into that house and telling them it was over, her marriage had failed, that she was once again headed for divorce court.

100

Looking back on how she had so closely guarded her relationship with him, she could all but feel that same sense of impotence that had seemed to envelope her and render her mute every time she had tried to mention his name under that roof. A rock-and-roll singer would have been her parents' dead-last choice as a son-in-law. *We are always our parents' children,* she sighed, *no matter how old we get. We always carry the same expectations within us, theirs as well as our own . . .*

Kelly's Mills, where Maggie had been born and raised, was a pleasant two-hour ride northwest of Philadelphia. Virtually unchanged since her childhood, it boasted wide boulevards, lined on both sides with tall oaks and maples and pines. The large, comfortable old clapboard houses, built toward the turn of the century or earlier, spoke proudly of its past as a well-to-do college town, made accessible by the railroad, made prosperous by its fabric mills, which were located on the outside of town and still operational. A large town green overlooked a picturesque lake surrounded by playgrounds and picnic areas. A tidy business district where the merchants sold their wares from the old brick buildings, carefully renovated, lined both sides of two blocks on Main Street. She could just as easily be driving into any one of a thousand towns, in Indiana or Massachusetts, Kentucky or Minnesota.

She loved the familiarity of it, loved seeing herself in memory's mirror skating on the frozen lake as a child, seated in one of the oak booths in the local soda shop after school, riding her bike to the little brick library by the lake, climbing the steps of the old firehouse to attend dances there on Saturday nights as a teenager. She wished she could bring J.D. there, so she could show him who she was and where she'd come from.

She turned off the main road onto her old street, driving slowly, noting all the changes in the neighborhood—a new paint job here, a new fence there—until the large pale yellow three-storied house with the dark blue shutters came into view. She couldn't wait to see her family. She'd hardly seen them since she'd met J.D., and she was embarrassed that it had taken a major family event—her cousin Kathleen's wedding—to bring her home again.

Colleen, the youngest Callahan, was watching for her, half seated on the railing around the big front porch, which wrapped clear around to the driveway side of the house. She jumped off as the car pulled into the drive and was at Maggie's door to open it and pull her sister from the car when the engine was shut off.

"You're awfully strong for a sixteen-year-old. Where'd those muscles come from?" Maggie hugged her, planting a fond kiss on her forehead. Was it her imagination, or had she had to stretch just a little higher to reach the top of that freckled face? "And why aren't you in school?"

"Lacrosse. Softball. Tennis. Swimming." Colleen rattled off her athletic pursuits proudly, then added, "I had my last final yesterday, so I didn't have to go today."

"My sister, the jock. Well, they're all good activities. Keeps you out of trouble. Less time to spend with the boys," Maggie teased.

"That's what her father's hoping for anyway." Mary Elizabeth Callahan, a tiny dumpling of a woman, walked across the grass to greet her oldest child. "Whether or not it's true is a different matter. How are you, sweetheart? You look thin. Are you eating?"

"Yes, Mother, I'm eating." Maggie laughed and hugged the small woman fondly. "What's this, do I see a few more silver threads among the gold?" She pretended to scrutinize her mother's hair.

"Yes, more and more each week, or so it seems. I'm starting to feel like old Otto here." She held the leash of the family dog. He'd been purported to have been half boxer, half spaniel when they'd gotten him fifteen years earlier. Neither breed accounted for his long shaggy gray coat, which now was showing a lot more white than Maggie'd noticed the last time she'd been home. She patted him affectionately.

"Taking Otto on walks these days, Mom?" Maggie opened the trunk to hoist a basket of laundry onto her hip.

"Well, I hate to let him run loose anymore. His vision isn't what it used to be, and since they started to build that new housing development out there on what used to be the old Shields farm, we've had so much traffic out here that I'm just afraid he'll wander into the road and get hit one of these days. So I let him out in the back most of the time, since it's fenced, but he still likes to check on the action out front, so we go for a little walk once or twice each day, depending on the weather. Does us both good."

Kevin, Maggie's only brother, pedaled up on his bike, dropping it amidst the jungle of azaleas that flanked the left side of the porch. A stern look from his mother sent him back to stand it up. He gave Maggie a brief but affectionate hug and, on instructions from his mother, removed the travel bags from the backseat of the car and carried them into the house.

"Where's Dad?" Maggie inquired, setting her purse on the counter in the kitchen and looking around. Even though it had been a year since her mother had redecorated the house, the cream-colored walls and light blue cabinets still came as a surprise to Maggie, whose mind's eye still saw the old white cabinets and green walls she'd grown up with.

"He should be along any minute now. His last morning class is at ten, so he should be rolling in any time now for lunch, then he has two classes this afternoon." Her mother removed a container of homemade soup from the refrigerator in anticipation of her husband's arrival, telling Maggie, "It's your favorite, chicken vegetable. What would you like with it?"

"Maybe just a small salad if you have some lettuce and cucumbers. I'll make it, Mom, assuming that you haven't moved things around too much over the past few months." Maggie rummaged around in the fridge until she found what she was looking for.

She sat across the table from her mother in the alcove, which was flanked with windows framed by blue and cream plaid curtains, chatting about old friends, catching up on local gossip. Mrs. Callahan rose to answer a ringing telephone just as Maggie's father came through the back door.

"There's my baby girl. Come give the old man a big hug. That's the way." Frank Callahan entered the room, and his presence filled it. He was a large bear of a man, with a full head of white hair and a muscular build. He looked more like the stereotypical Irish cop than the college history professor that he was. He could not conceal his joy at having his oldest child home again, even if it was only for a few days. He clearly adored Maggie.

"Hello, Daddy." She kissed him and let him hold her for a minute.

"Glad you could finally find some time to join us, Maggie. It's been so long since you've been home. I was starting to worry you'd been kidnapped by one of those gooney Canadians that play hockey in the arena. What have you been up to that's so important that you don't have time for your family anymore?"

"Well, we've been real busy at work, a lot of activities, you know . . ." Maggie shrugged nonchalantly.

"Sure, sure. I know how hard you work at that place. More likely a busy social schedule."

"Sometimes." She smiled.

"Well, you just watch out there, Margaret. You get a lot of weirdos coming and going around there. I don't know why you ever left that job you had with that accounting firm," he chastised as he shuffled through the morning's delivery of mail, then tossed the pile back onto the counter.

"It was boring," she told him for the ninety-fifth time, hoping that there would not be another discussion regarding her career choice.

"Accounting is supposed to be boring," he remarked dryly, disappearing into the refrigerator and emerging with an apple.

"That was Aunt Peg, dear," said her mother, reentering the room. "She's really in a tizzy over this wedding. You'd think she'd be used to it by now. Kathleen's the last of the group to get married, not the first. If she survived the other five weddings, she shouldn't be worried about this one. And she's positively beside herself that you haven't picked up your dress yet. The shop called her again this morning to tell her that one of the bridesmaid's dresses was still in the back room."

"I'll run over right after lunch. It's already been fitted. All I have to do is pick it up and pay for it," Maggie pointed out. "I don't understand what all the fuss is about. The wedding's better than twenty-four hours away."

"Everything is a big deal to Peg," her father reminded her. "Been that way all her life. Everything's a crisis. I married into a family of hysterics, and that's the simple truth."

"She's afraid the dress won't fit right, Frank," Mary Elizabeth defended her sister, adding, "and truthfully, Maggie does appear to have lost weight."

"I haven't lost weight, and the dress will fit just fine," Maggie told her mother.

"Peg ought to be more worried about the fit of Kathleen's dress," her father mumbled, then was silenced by a stern look from his wife.

"I can't wait till you get married again, Maggie, so I can be in the wedding," Colleen said, passing through on her way to the backyard, her long red curls bouncing.

"What makes you think I'll get married again?" Maggie stabbed a fork full of lettuce.

"You're too pretty not to," Colleen told her as she patted her sister's head on her way past the table.

"Thanks, baby," Maggie said with a wink.

"Colleen, I'd like to remind you that in the eyes of the church, your sister is still married. To Mason," her father called after her.

"Not now, Frank," chided his wife.

"Mary Elizabeth, they were married in the church. A civil divorce does not technically relieve them of their vows . . ."

"Enough, Frank." Turning to Maggie, she said, "If you're finished, you'd better run down and pick up that dress. Did you bring your shoes? Good. Why don't you see if Colleen wants to drive down with you?"

"What was that comment about Kathleen's dress not fitting?" Maggie asked Colleen as they drove into town.

"Oh, boy," Colleen told her, grinning with mischief. "Big scandal. Kathleen's pregnant. Can you believe it? Of course, I'm not supposed to know."

"Who told you?" Maggie tried not to register any reaction. There but for the grace of God . . .

"Aunt Eleanor," Colleen giggled.

"Aunt Eleanor?" Maggie laughed, trying to imagine their eighty-seven-year-old great-aunt delivering such news to a sixteen-year-old.

"Well, she didn't exactly tell me. I just sort of overheard her say something to Uncle Paul that they were lucky it hadn't happened sooner, what with all her running around, and that Kathleen's twenty-four and it was about time she got married anyway." Colleen confided the family gossip with a very grown-up air.

"She said that?" Maggie chuckled. "Well, looks like not too much gets past the old girl. And she's probably right— Kathleen always had a bit of a wild streak."

They walked into the dress shop, and Maggie identified herself to the saleswoman, who went into the back room and returned with the dress, insisting that Maggie try it on. Kathleen, whom Maggie'd always thought to have abominable taste, had chosen baby blue organza gowns for her attendants, scooped neck, puffy-sleeved numbers with huge bows on the side of the dropped waist. Maggie groaned and tried it on. She met Colleen's gaze as she walked back out of the dressing room.

"Cute," said Colleen, nodding with a straight face.

"And here's the headpiece," cooed the saleswoman, pinning a sort of half-cap, which also sported a huge bow, to the side of Maggie's head.

"Very cute." Colleen echoed the saleswoman's saccharin tone.

"It's a little big through the waist and hips." The saleswoman frowned, her voice fraught with accusation.

"It'll be fine," Maggie assured her as she walked back into the dressing room, anxious to take it off. *Thank God Jamey won't be here to see me in this,* she thought.

Maggie sighed deeply as they pulled back into the Callahan driveway.

"Oh happy day," grumbled Maggie, seeing the red car parked out front, "Ellie's here. My very favorite sibling."

"Maggie, good to see you finally found your way home," said Ellie Callahan Marsh, tucking a stray length of straight blond hair behind one ear and smiling unenthusiastically.

"Hello, Ellie. How's it going?" A lukewarm greeting was the best Maggie could muster. For some reason known only to God, the two eldest Callahan children had always been at each other's throats. It had been a source of pain to their mother through the years.

"Maggie, how'd you like the dress? Isn't it out of this world?" Ellie leaned back against the kitchen counter.

It figures, thought Maggie, *that Ellie would like it.* "That's one way of describing it." She looked at her mother, who'd known instinctively that Maggie would hate it.

"It's only for one day, dear," her mother said in a low voice as she peeled carrots and sliced them into a waiting pot.

"I know, Mom. I don't mind."

"That's big of you, Maggie," remarked Ellie.

"Eleanor, your sister doesn't have to like it. She only has to wear it, which she will do. So drop it, please."

Ellie made herself a cup of coffee in silence and, having appeased her mother by stopping in to see her sister, took the cup and wandered out the back door.

Her mother turned her knife to a mound of potatoes, and it occurred to Maggie, not for the first time, that she could never picture her mother's hands at rest. Cooking, cleaning, knitting, sewing, soothing a hurt or comforting an unhappy child, her mother's hands always appeared in motion in Maggie's childhood memories.

Kevin breezed through and joined them momentarily, dropping a notebook and a pile of record albums on the nearest counter as he headed straight for the cookies. Maggie smiled fondly as she took in his tall, gangly eighteen-year-old form. Kevin had lost some, but not all, of his adolescent awkwardness. His closely cropped hair was, she suspected, a concession to his father's wishes. Had he had his way, she felt certain, Kevin's hair would have well exceeded his collar line.

"So how's college, baby brother?"

"Great, Mags." He nodded, stuffing a second cookie into his mouth.

"How are your grades?"

"Great."

"Are they, Mom?" she asked.

"Actually, yes, they've been surprisingly good. Whether he's motivated by a desire for higher learning or the knowledge that his band is in jeopardy if his marks begin to slip, I'm not certain. But he's doing very well."

"If my grades go below a 3.0, I can't play the drums with my band," he explained, leaning back against the counter and brushing into the stack of records he'd slung there.

It was then that she saw it, the flat square of cardboard, purple in color, edged in black, which had slid from the top of the pile. The same album that sat on the table in her apartment. The same one she listened to every night. She casually reached a hand up and tilted it toward her. Monkshood's *Midnight Fever* album. She smiled inwardly. *This would be a good opportunity to break the ice and tell Mom about Jamey.* She tried to find an opening line.

Kevin noticed her interest and nodded toward the counter. "Great band. We—our band—does a lot of their stuff."

"Is that right?" *Okay, now is the time for me to say, Did I mention I met . . . No, no . . . Maybe something like, Oh, yes, they played at the arena some time ago. Did I tell you I've been dating . . . No, that sounds hokey . . .*

Why can't I bring myself to just tell them, she asked herself bleakly, realizing that she could not so much as utter his name. *Am I afraid they'll find him unsuitable or think that I've disappointed them again after all that with Mace, whom they thought was so wonderful? That's what Jamey thinks. He thinks I'm embarrassed by what he is, that somehow my parents will think there's something trivial or unworthy about what he does for a living and that he won't measure up to*

*Mace. It hurts him to think that what Mom and Dad think is
more important to me than what he thinks. Especially after
last week when he called his sister from my apartment and
made me speak with her. Judith was charming, of course, but
I felt odd and shy, trying to make some connection with the
faceless voice, not knowing if we'd ever meet and if we did,
what she would think of me . . .*

Colleen skipped in then and draped an arm around
Maggie's shoulder. "We've got some time before dinner.
Want to walk down to the lake?"

"Great idea." Maggie felt relieved. The moment to speak
was gone. She could put it off for now. "Where'd Ellie go?"

"She's out in the yard, talking with Tim and Marilyn next
door. Were you going to ask her to join you?" her mother
asked hopefully.

"No," replied Maggie and Colleen, both laughing.

"Oh, girls, please." Their mother rolled her eyes toward
the ceiling.

"Let's go before she comes in," Colleen said, grabbing a
carrot as she left the room.

Maggie headed upstairs to her old bedroom on the third
floor long after midnight, the evening's rehearsal for the
wedding having turned into a reunion of a dozen or so
cousins, most of whom Maggie hadn't seen since the last
family wedding over a year ago. She stripped off the dress
she had worn that night and hung it on its hanger, then went
into the bathroom across the hall to wash off her makeup.
Her reflection in the mirror above the sink startled her, the
twenty-eight-year-old face staring back at her, a reminder
that she was now a visitor in this house, no longer a youthful
occupant. Somehow, unconsciously, she always expected to
see herself in this mirror as she had looked those years ago
when she had called this house her home. How could she be
so different when so little else here had changed since the
day she left?

In the dim light from the hall, she could make out the
shapes and shadows of her old room. All the treasures of a
happy childhood were stored here, the trophies of having

grown up in middle-class America. Tennis rackets, lacrosse sticks, old ice skates. Beloved dolls, some bedraggled, some like new, their condition a silent testament of the love bestowed over the years by the little girl Maggie had been. Shelves spilled over with books, from Peter Rabbit and Golden Books to philosophy, economics, and art history. A large brown bear, presented to her by her father as she'd been wheeled into the operating room as a frightened six-year-old to have her tonsils removed, presided over a chair laden with other assorted stuffed animals. Dink, one of Otto's predecessors, had chewed off the bear's nose. Her mother had made her best effort to replace it with a big black button.

Dried corsages from long-ago proms, a gold chain hung over the dressing table mirror, the high school ring still dangling from it, a gift of sorts from a boy she'd met while on summer vacation on Cape Cod as a sixteen-year-old. He'd lived in Colorado, and they'd spent hours sitting on the sand, talking and laughing, hours more walking the long stretches of beaches. Her last night there they'd made out under the lifeguard stand, and he'd given her the ring. It was as close to going steady as she'd ever come.

She could see the outlines of the old photographs framing the mirror on the dresser that once belonged to her grandmother. Old friends, frozen in time, black-and-white images of faces no longer so young. She and Holly, her best friend all through school, tennis rackets raised in victory after winning a doubles tournament at a school match their junior year. Posing on the hood of the 1966 Mustang Holly's parents had given her when she graduated from junior college. *God, the times we had in that car,* Maggie mused sleepily. Canary yellow, like Holly's hair, the car had been . . .

Funny, she thought, *no matter how old I get, I always feel like a child when I'm under this roof. No matter that my next big birthday would be the big three-oh or that I've been married and divorced and have my own apartment, a responsible job. When I'm in this house, I'm Frank and Mary Elizabeth's biggest little girl again.*

She pulled the covers up and sought a comfortable position in her old bed, reflecting back on the rehearsal that evening in the church where she'd spent so many hours of her young life. While the priest was instructing the best man on his duties, she had wandered to the right side of the church, sliding into the sixth row, recalling vividly how it had felt to kneel on the hard wooden planks in the row of hard oak pews.

She couldn't remember ever sitting anyplace in this church but in that row, sixth from the altar, right side, nine A.M. every Sunday and holy day. The church was tiny—by city standards it would be little more than a chapel. Beautiful narrow arches of stained glass illustrated the life of St. Francis of Assisi for whom the church had been named. The small spotless altar, well-polished oak hewn by a local craftsman, the stark white marble statue of the Blessed Mother, the work of another local artisan, the handmade stations of the cross that hung on the walls, all bespoke of the devotion of the small Catholic community in this mostly Protestant town.

Maggie had marked every major milestone of her Catholic life in this church—baptism, her First Communion, confirmation, marriage. She wondered if her own children would be baptized under this roof or if she would be buried from this church.

She grimaced inwardly, knowing that certain members of her family gathered for the wedding the following afternoon would notice that only Maggie, of the entire Callahan clan, lacked the requisite state of grace to receive the sacrament of Holy Communion. Maggie tried to remember the last time she'd gone to confession. Certainly it had been long before the events of the past few months. She sighed as she turned over once again. Lindy had been right, it was all still within her and probably always would be . . .

The forecast for Saturday was dismal, the morning overcast, threatening rain for the afternoon ceremony. Kathleen was nearly hysterical that a downpour would destroy her gown. The wedding had seemed to drag on forever, the reception endless. Maggie danced with her father; all of her uncles; the groom; the groom's father; John, her partner for the wedding; and her brother, Kevin, all the while missing J.D., wishing with all her heart that she could will him to materialize, that she could be dancing with him now, his two left feet notwithstanding.

She thought back to her own wedding, hers and Mace's, in the same church, the reception at the same club, the cast of characters essentially the same. She hadn't been a happy bride, she recalled, and glanced across the room at a glowing Kathleen—if she was in fact pregnant, she was hiding it well. *That's how you're supposed to look on your wedding day,* Maggie told herself. *Why hadn't anyone noticed that I didn't?*

Finally, the happy couple having departed for their honeymoon, the guests started filtering out. Maggie'd had four glasses of champagne, way past her limit, and was feeling the effects. It was the damn toasts, she thought ruefully. First the best man, then the groom's brother, then Uncle Paul, then cousin Thomas, then . . . who? She couldn't recall. Too many toasts and too many memories. More than once she'd felt the tug of strangulation that had choked her that day six years ago, as she and Mace had stood before the priest, the suffocating knowledge that her life was ending and she was too weak to save herself. *Why was everyone so happy,* she had wondered, *when I am drowning?*

The opening strains of "The Wedding March" had sounded like a death knell in her head, the smell of lilies gagging her. She'd gotten through it by pretending that she was a mere observer of all that went on, that it had no connection to her. She'd drifted through the reception with blank eyes, watching her life slip away with every passing second, grieving for the happiness she would never have, wistfully recalling how good it had been to feel like she was falling in love, two winters ago, with that basketball player she'd dated at Penn. She had danced on leaden feet with her beaming father, thrown her bouquet to Ellie, perversely wishing her sister the same amount of joy that she had felt at that moment.

Kathleen's wedding party had been invited back to the

home of the bride's parents, along with the entire family, to continue the festivities. Maggie picked slightly at the food arranged buffet style on the dining room table, then joined her cousin Mike at the bar set up in the backyard, where he was drinking away a broken engagement. He made her a gimlet, and they sat and talked for an hour, Mike doing most of the talking, she commiserating the best she could considering she was barely listening. He made them both another drink when Madeline, Mike's sister, joined them to pour out her personal tale of woe. Mike made another round of gimlets.

Colleen strolled through the back door, holding the hand of a tall sandy-haired young man. *She's so adorable,* Maggie thought as she watched with pride and affection, those strawberry curls, blue eyes, and freckles. She looks so grown-up today, but it's hard to believe she's sixteen this year. She watched as the young couple walked to the end of the hedge that marked the property from the yard next door. The young man leaned down and kissed Colleen. Maggie arched an eyebrow. Who was this little varmint kissing her baby sister?

By the time Mike had set out the fourth round of drinks, Kevin discovered that Maggie was almost incoherent and barely able to stand up. Their mother insisted that Kevin drive her home and accompanied them, hoping to get Maggie into bed before the rest of the family, especially her father—who was having one hell of a good time—got back home.

It had taken both her mother and her brother to get her into the house. She slumped in a chair in the kitchen, giggling and half crying at the same time.

"Don't sit down, Maggie, we'll never get you back up again. Drat that phone. You just stay there one second, Maggie. Kevin, come in here and make sure your sister doesn't fall out of her seat . . . Hello? Yes, she's here, but I don't think she can come to the phone right now. Who's calling, please? . . . Well, actually, we've just come in from a family wedding and I'm afraid my daughter is, well, she's . . . she's intoxicated . . . Yes . . . I don't know, do you think it would help? Well, we'll try that. Honestly, I've never seen Maggie like this and . . . Yes, we'd best try to get her to bed. Thank you . . . I will tell her. It was nice speaking with you."

Mary Elizabeth hung up the phone and looked down at her disheveled daughter, whose arms and head rested on the kitchen table.

"Come on, Maggie, try to stand up. Kevin, help me get Maggie on her feet . . ."

"Looks like my big sister really tied one on," he said with a broad grin.

His mother shot him a look of disapproval and gestured for him to help Maggie up, which was no easy task. She was deadweight. Getting her onto her feet was one thing, getting her up the stairs was another. Halfway up she got giggly and started to sing "Midnight Special," a raunchy tune J.D. insisted had been penned solely by Rick and that had been included on their last album on a whim. Kevin rolled his eyes toward the heavens as his sister slurred one ribald verse and started into the second.

"Maggie, where'd you ever hear that song?"

"Jamey. Sings it," she confided.

"Well, whoever Jamey is, I like his taste in music."

They were almost at the top of the steps, and she nearly collapsed with laughter.

"Maggie, what's so funny?"

"You do," she gasped between peals of laughter. "You do. Like his music." She slipped down a step, and he gripped her arm to keep her from falling all the way down.

"Sure thing, Maggie. Whatever you say," he mumbled.

Having gotten her into her room and flopped onto her bed, Kevin turned his sister over to their mother. "She's all yours, Mom. Boy, old Maggie's really ripped."

"I'll thank you not to mention this to your father, Kevin."

"What, that I practically had to carry her upstairs, laughing and singing? Just kidding, Mom. My lips are sealed."

"Sit up, Maggie. Let me get the back of your dress undone." Her daughter nearly incapable of cooperating, it took Mary Elizabeth a few minutes to get Maggie undressed. She slid a nightgown over the slender shoulders. "Been many a year since I had to dress you for bed, sweetie. Oh . . . the aspirin. I'll be right back."

A few minutes later she returned with two white tablets. "Here, Maggie, sit up. Jamey said to make sure you took these."

"Jamey," she murmured. "Miss Jamey . . ."

"I'm sure you do, dear."

Maggie swallowed the aspirin and lay back on the pillow, eyes closed, crying softly, rambling on and on, unintelligibly. Finally, when the whispering stopped, Mary Elizabeth kissed her daughter's forehead and turned out the bedroom light.

Several times during the night, Maggie'd been up and to the bathroom, sicker than she'd ever been in her life. *I'll feel like shit tomorrow,* she thought as she tumbled back into her bed for the fourth time.

Even the lengthy Callahan Sunday breakfast was all but over by the time Maggie managed to struggle out of bed and into her clothes. Her stomach felt terrible, but surprisingly, her head didn't feel as badly as she'd expected. She said as much to her mother when she ambled downstairs and took a place at the table.

"Oh, good. Then the aspirin worked." Mary Elizabeth looked pleased. She met Frank's questioning gaze and explained, "Aspirin. If you take it at night when you've had too much to drink, you're less likely to have a headache the next morning."

"Mary Elizabeth, since when have you been the resident expert on the cure for hangovers?" her husband inquired with a raised eyebrow.

"Why, Maggie's friend told me last night when he called," she explained nonchalantly. "He sounded very nice, Frank, very polite and well spoken."

"What friend?" Maggie asked, taking the cup of tea her mother had poured for her.

"Why, Jamey, he said his name was. You didn't tell us you were seeing an English fellow, Maggie." Her mother began to clear plates and juice glasses from the table. "I always did like a British accent."

"Mom, when did you talk to Jamey?" Maggie had gone white.

"Maggie, don't you remember? He called last night as soon as we got home from Aunt Peg's. We had a nice chat."

"You did?" Maggie wondered what exactly J.D. had had to say.

"He asked me to tell you he'd call you this evening at your apartment." Mary Elizabeth carried the breakfast debris into the kitchen.

"And he must be cool, because he knows all the words to 'Midnight Special,'" Kevin added.

"How do you know that?" Maggie asked in a half whisper, wondering what she'd said last night. She rested her elbows on the table, chin in hands and tried frantically to remember.

"Because you were singing it while I was helping you up the steps last night. And when I asked you how you knew the words, you said Jamey sings it. So, he must be cool." Following this explanation, Kevin left the room.

"Maggie, please get your elbows off the table or move them closer together. If your chin gets any lower it'll be in your teacup," her mother instructed.

"Sounds like you had a better time at Kathleen's wedding than I thought you did," her father said with a laugh as he pushed himself away from the table. "I'll be watching the baseball game in the den, Mary Elizabeth."

Maggie looked across the table at her mother, who was removing the rest of the breakfast dishes. "Mom, what did I say last night?"

"Very little that I could understand. You were not very coherent."

Thank God.

"I did get the impression, judging from his concern, that this might be more than a casual relationship."

Maggie nodded.

"Are you serious with this man?"

Maggie admired her mother's cool demeanor, knowing

she had a lot of questions she would like to ask. Mary Elizabeth could extract secrets from a stone. It was all in her quiet, nonchalant technique.

"More serious than I've ever been in my life, Mom." Maggie put her cup down and met her mother's eyes.

"Does that include your former husband, Maggie?"

"I never felt this way about Mace, Mom."

"Then why did you marry him?" Her mother sat down next to her.

"I guess because I felt I had to," Maggie replied simply.

"Why would you have thought that? Didn't you love him?"

"Not the way I should have. Not the way that takes you through a lifetime. Not the way I love Jamey. I loved Mace, Mom, but I wasn't in love with him." There, it was out now. The truth.

"Then why did you go through with it?" Her mother took her hands in her own, deep lines of distress creasing her face.

"Because everyone would have been so disappointed. Everyone thought he was so perfect. And I didn't want to hurt him. And," she added, her voice lowering as in a confessional, "because I'd slept with him."

Mary Elizabeth silently studied her daughter's face.

"I thought it obligated me, Mom. I thought sleeping with him meant I had to marry him. I didn't know I had a choice . . . And he and Daddy were so close. And we'd gone together for so long. I didn't know how to not go through with it." Earnest tears slid from between her lids, closed against the judgment she feared she'd encounter if she opened her eyes.

"I'm so sorry, Maggie." Mary Elizabeth brushed the hair back tenderly from her daughter's face. "How could I have not known?"

"It's not your fault, Mom. In my heart I knew it wasn't right, but I went through with it. I don't blame anyone but myself."

"And Jamey? How long have you known him?"

"A couple of months." Maggie searched in her pocket for a tissue.

"And you feel this strongly about him after so short a time?"

"Right from the start. Mom, he's all I could ever want in this life."

"Why haven't you brought him home?"

"Mom, I want to. And he wants so much to meet you. But Dad might find him a bit hard to take. You know, Dad has these prejudices . . ."

"Maggie, is he a Protestant?" That could certainly account for her daughter's reluctance to bring this man home.

Maggie laughed for the first time that morning. "He might be Protestant, most likely is. I've never asked him."

"Maggie, you know how your father is about religion. That could be a problem."

"That's not the only thing he'll have a problem with." Maggie wiped her wet eyes with a tissue her mother handed her.

"Is it because of Mace? Because Dad is so keen on Mace?"

"That's part of it. I know he always hoped that we'd get back together. I don't know how to explain to him that it was a mistake. That staying in that marriage would have destroyed me."

"I'll talk to your father about that, Maggie. I feel some of the responsibility was mine."

"Mom . . ." Maggie protested.

"How could I have been so oblivious to what you were going through?" Mary Elizabeth asked herself softly, her voice apologetic, self-recriminating. "I'll talk to your father, sweetheart. Maybe he'll understand. Is there anything else that I should know about this new friend of yours?"

"Well, actually, Mom, there's one other thing." Maggie took a deep breath, grateful that it would all be out in the open and done with, for better or for worse.

As she opened her mouth to speak, Ellie walked into the room.

"So, here you are. And how hung over are we today?" she asked, grinning.

"Not too bad." Maggie wouldn't give her the satisfaction of knowing that her stomach was in chaos.

"Missed you at church." Ellie sat down with her coffee, oblivious to the fact that she had interrupted a conversation that would not be finished while she was present.

"Maggie was sick last night, Ellie," Mary Elizabeth told her.

"No doubt she was. Maggie, you threw back champagne like Uncle Paul throws back shots."

Laughing in spite of herself, Maggie replied, "That explains it then. I've never been able to drink more than a glass or two. And the way I feel today is a good reminder why I never do."

"Topping off the day with gimlets was another good idea," Ellie noted, then added, "I hope you're okay."

"Thanks, El." Maggie smiled, touched by her sister's uncharacteristic concern.

On impulse, she stood up and kissed the top of Ellie's head, and Ellie responded by reaching a hand around to touch her sister's face for the briefest moment. Maggie found herself suddenly wishing it could be this way more often, she free to reach out to Ellie, who had always seemed to be surrounded by an invisible barrier, like an opaque bubble, which made even casual physical contact with her almost unthinkable. Maggie had often wondered how Elliot ever approached her to make love. She thought of Jamey's loving touch and was swept with a feeling of sadness for Ellie, for lacking that simplest of joys, the caress of a loving hand.

Mary Elizabeth was clearly startled by the rare display of affection between her oldest children and was moved by it. The moment passed, and Maggie withdrew again to the other side of the boundary. With a wink toward her mother that promised to resume their conversation another time, she went upstairs to pack her things.

12

ELLIE HASN'T CHANGED MUCH, MAGGIE THOUGHT SADLY. SHE even seems to hold her children at a distance. I can't remember the last time I saw her cuddle with Mary Fran or hug little Danny.

". . . but as far as writing a song is concerned," Hilary was deep in conversation with J.D., "how do you actually do that? What comes first, the lyrics or the tune?"

"Sometimes one, sometimes the other," he told her, keeping his eyes on his wife's back. She'd been off in her head someplace—he'd recognized the signs and wondered where she'd been, what door within her memory had opened to her, and if what she'd seen when she'd peered inside had been a welcomed reminder of happier days or the stinging recollection of a bygone hurt.

"Have you any musical talent, Maggie?" Hilary asked.

"What? Oh, no . . . none," she replied flatly.

"Then it must be fascinating to live with someone who has written so many wonderful songs."

"Fascinating," Maggie agreed with a saccharine smile.

"Do you write all the parts for every song yourself?"

Hilary decided to ignore Maggie's sarcasm. "All the parts for all the different instruments as well?"

He nodded.

"How do you know how to do that?"

"Training and experience," he said, grinning. "An unbeatable combination."

"No, I mean with all the instruments. The guitars and drums, for example. How can you write for those instruments if you don't play them?"

"I do play them," he told her.

"What else?" Hilary leaned forward in his direction.

"Just about anything with keys or strings."

"But how do you know where to put the different instruments in the song?"

He looked at her blankly, as if it were a stupid question. "I just hear it in my head."

"You hear the whole thing, a whole song, with all its component parts, in your head?" *Hmm,* she thought, *maybe he's more than just another pretty face . . .*

"Pretty much. Sometimes I just hear part of it, then when I write it down, the rest of it just comes," he explained.

"Well, I'm impressed," she said, smiling almost flirtatiously, "but tell me, after having written so many songs, how do you keep coming up with new ones year after year? Where does the inspiration come from?"

"It comes from everywhere. The news. Everyday events. The people around you. And of course, my wife has been a continuous source of inspiration for me."

"Out of all the songs you've ever written, which was your favorite?"

"Absolutely no contest there." He smiled. "It would have to be 'Sweet, Sweet Maggie.' I'd written it while on the road that spring we'd met. It was a special surprise for her. She was there the first night the band ever performed it in public. In Atlanta." He turned to her, asking with deliberate emphasis on the name of the city, "You remember that four-day weekend in Atlanta, don't you, Maggie?"

It seemed he waited forever for her one-word whispered response.

"Yes."

Remember? My whole life changed in the aftermath of that weekend, she thought. *After Atlanta, there was no turning back . . .*

Maggie hated flying, hated the very idea of being wrapped in the belly of that metal container, strapped in and unable to escape, always dreaded the takeoffs and prayed for the landings. She wished she'd been able to get a nonstop flight. The additional wait in D.C. made her even more anxious.

She looked at her watch and realized they were due to land in twenty minutes or so. She rose from her seat and went into the bathroom, removed her makeup case from her purse, and sat it on the side of the sink. *Might as well fix this face before we land,* she thought and added some blush, reapplied some eye shadow, and was about to brush her hair when there was a knock on the door.

"I'm sorry to rush you," a woman's voice said, "but my little girl really needs to use the bathroom."

"Oh, sure. No problem." Maggie stuffed her makeup back into the case, the zipper breaking as she fumbled to close it, then tucked the open case into her purse. In her haste to vacate the room, she dropped it, it's contents spilling out onto the floor.

"Oh, damn," she muttered as she bent down and retrieved her wallet, keys, checkbook, hairbrush, makeup, all of which had scattered.

"I'm really sorry to hurry you like this, but she's only three and . . ."

Maggie opened the door and smiled sympathetically at the young woman and her small, fidgety daughter as she stepped past them and exited the room.

She returned to her seat. It was almost time to land. She fastened her belt and leaned back, anticipating the next four days. Four whole days. She couldn't wait to see him, to touch him, to love him again. He'd been right, two weeks was way too long . . .

He was there when she got off the plane, waiting for her as he'd promised. Her impulse was to run to him and throw her arms around him, but instead she walked casually to where he stood watching her approach. She dropped her bag to the ground, and they held each other for a long moment.

"Oh, Maggie, Maggie, you feel so good to me," he whispered. "God, it's so good to hold you again. I thought the plane would never get here."

"Me, too. I was afraid it would get lost or crash and then I'd never see your face again." She kissed him long and hard. "How far's the hotel?"

"Not too. Let's get your stuff and go."

Maggie's luggage was retrieved, a cab hailed. They sat in the backseat, drinking each other in.

"You look tired," she said, raising a hand to touch his face.

"The result of too much travel, too little sleep. I told you this is a rotten way to live."

When they arrived at the hotel, he asked, "Do you need lunch?"

"I ate on the plane," she said, and held her arms open to him.

They spent the rest of the afternoon trying to feed the hunger, the empty places filling up with contentment, the loneliness giving way to bliss. The intensity of their love-making rocked them both into exhaustion.

"Damn. Look at the time." He'd been laying in a half slumber for about twenty minutes or so and had glanced at the clock as he was about to turn over. "We have exactly forty minutes to dress, eat dinner, and get down to the arena for the show. What'll it be, Mags, room service or the coffee shop? Decide quickly."

"Room service," she muttered.

"Fine. Call and order for us while I'm in the shower, why don't you, and if we're lucky, dinner will be here by the time I'm dressed."

She called down and ordered veal and spaghetti, salads, wine for herself, and beer for him. She lay back on the pillow, gloriously happy for the first time in weeks. Nothing had ever felt like the joy inside when she was with him.

He came out of the bathroom, already dressed in his stage

clothes, jeans and a long-sleeved blue-and-white-striped cotton shirt, sleeves rolled to the elbow, tails out, as was his habit when he was performing.

"You planning on joining me tonight," he asked with a grin, "or were you planning on waiting right there till I get back?"

"Just too lazy to get up. It feels so good to be here."

"Well, you'd better get moving. Your dinner should be here any minute."

As if awaiting the cue, there was a knock on the door.

She grabbed her clothes and went into the bathroom, dressing as quickly as she could, knowing they were running out of time. He was halfway through dinner when she came out and sat down with him.

"I apologize for starting without you," he told her, "but we're so hurried right now as it is."

"It's okay. I'm not that hungry." She picked at the salad and the spaghetti and drank half her wine.

"You about ready?"

"Just one second. I want to put some makeup on." She picked up her purse and headed back to the bathroom and turned on the light.

"Damn," he heard her say.

"What?"

"My makeup case isn't in here. It must have fallen under something when I dropped my purse in the bathroom on the plane."

"You don't need makeup. You're adorable just as you are."

She made a face. "How irritating. Now I'll have to buy all new stuff."

"You can pick some up in the morning if you really think you need it, which I don't. I think you look fine, great, with or without it. But right now, we really have to put a move on it."

J.D. had gotten her a great seat, front row, near the stage, close enough so that she could be easily admitted backstage after the show. He handed her the pass she would need, told her where to look for Joseph, the guard whose job it would be to keep tabs on her and escort her backstage when they'd concluded. They walked into the dressing room pandemonium, where Maggie was greeted by the band and crew.

Rick took her into his arms and confided, "Good to see you, sweetheart. Maybe the old man will be his old self again now that you're here. He's been a miserable son of a bitch for the past few weeks."

Maggie laughed again, and within minutes, the band prepared to go on and J.D. asked Joseph to lead Maggie to her place before the lights went down. Soon she was into her seat, surrounded by an ocean of screaming faces. She became increasingly uncomfortable with the noise and the crowd swelling around her. The lights went down and then J.D. was on the stage twenty feet away from her, and she felt slightly less anxious. Soon the music engulfed her, and the tide of panic began to recede. When it was over, the great throbbing mass of vocal thunder surrounded her again, and she searched the crowd to her right for Joseph, who would lead her backstage and out of the madness.

"You'll be okay while I clean up? I'll be very quick, I promise," J.D. told her when she'd arrived back in the dressing room.

She nodded and walked to the table the caterer had set up. Taking an apple from a fruit basket, she eased onto a small sofa as the door opened and a hearty cheer erupted from the band members. She looked up and saw that a group of about a dozen young girls were led into the room by one of the road crew.

Rick grasped a pretty dark-haired girl by the arm, turned to Peter, the only married member of the band and said, "Hey, Petey, I think I've just found the cure for your depression. You know what they say, if you can't be with the one you love—" Rick stopped midsentence when he saw the look on Maggie's face.

She averted her eyes, got up from the sofa, and set about to find the wine bottle to fill up her glass, giving her an opportunity to turn her back on Rick and the others.

When J.D. rejoined them, still drying his hair with a

towel, she motioned to the door with her head, signaling she'd like to leave.

J.D. lay back on the pillow, exhausted and happy. "What a wonderful way to end two long, lonely weeks."

Maggie stretched lazily, arms and legs, and kissed his face before hopping out of bed.

"Where are you going?" He watched her fumble with her purse.

"To take a pill."

"You have a headache?"

"I will if I don't take the pill," she quipped. "Birth control pill."

She was still fumbling around, then took everything out of her purse and placed it on the bed.

"Damn. I know I packed them."

She took the purse into the bathroom and turned on the light. The small round pink plastic case was not there. Then it hit her, where she'd put them. She slowly walked back into the room.

"Jamey, my makeup case . . ."

"So buy some stuff in the morning. Now come back to bed and bring that unmade face here to me where I can kiss it and show you how appealing you are to me, with or without cosmetics."

She sat on the edge of the bed. *This will ruin our weekend, ruin our time together . . .*

"What's wrong, Mags? What is it? Come here and let me make it all better." He reached for her and felt her rigidity. "You can't be that upset about losing a few items that can easily be replaced."

"We can't replace the pills." The words seemed to echo in her head.

"What?"

"My pills were in my makeup case," she said quietly.

"The makeup case you lost." The import suddenly became clear to him.

She shook her head yes.

The room was very quiet.

"Well, then, I guess you'll just have to call your sister the nun and ask her to say a few extra prayers tonight, Maggie. It's been a very long two weeks," he said as he gathered her to him. "I'm not sleeping on the sofa for the next three nights."

He had awakened her with sleepy kisses early the next morning, and he was deaf to her protests that serious consequences could result. It had been too long since they had greeted a new day together, he told her, he would take his chances.

They had both fallen back to sleep, and when she awoke up some hours later, she rolled over, somewhat disoriented, looking for her watch. It was twelve-fifteen. He was still sleeping like an exhausted child, but she was starving and wanted a cup of coffee. She quietly got out of bed and slipped into a pair of jeans and a sweater and, leaving a note for J.D. on her pillow, went downstairs to find the coffee shop.

She stopped in the pharmacy on the first floor, bought eye shadow, mascara, blush, a lipstick. She headed for the counter with her selections and wondered if they sold condoms. One look at the stern-faced cashier, a woman of about sixty, and she knew she didn't have the nerve to ask. She'd just have to remind J.D. She just hoped it wasn't already too late.

She walked into the coffee shop, looking around for a table, and was surprised to see Rick sitting alone in a booth. She hesitated momentarily, then walked over.

"Is this seat reserved?" she asked. "Do you mind if I join you?"

"Maggie." She'd startled him. He'd appeared to be deep in thought.

"If you'd rather be alone, it's okay." She hesitated, not wanting to intrude if he was not in the mood for some company.

"No, no. Please. Sit down." He motioned to her. "Actually, I was just thinking about you."

"About me? Why?" She slid into the booth opposite him.

"Well, about last night, in the dressing room . . ."

The waitress stopped at the table, took Maggie's order, and returned in seconds with the requested coffee.

"It's okay." She shrugged, recalling the scene with Peter.

"It's not okay. I should have used my head before I opened my big mouth," he told her.

"I got over it," she assured him, signaling the waitress for some cream.

"That's not good enough. My words were poorly chosen, and I'm sorry. I was afraid that maybe you'd take it the wrong way, that maybe what I'd said to Pete caused you to be unnecessarily worried, maybe, about J.D. . . ." He paused, the ground becoming more unstable with every word.

"It did strike a nerve," she admitted as she tended to her coffee.

"Maggie, J.D. doesn't fool around anymore. I'm sure he's told you that."

"You'd lie for him even if he did." Given their long-standing friendship, Maggie knew this was an indisputable fact.

"Yes, I probably would," he admitted, "but I'm not."

"Do you encourage him, too, like you did Peter last night?" There was an edge to her voice now.

"Ah, Maggie, it's all in fun." He replaced his cup into the saucer and missed, sloshing some of the brown liquid onto the table. She handed him a napkin.

"Fun for whom?" she asked with some sarcasm.

"Maggie, I respect you a lot, so don't take this the wrong way. As long as it doesn't directly affect you, I don't see where you get off making a judgment." Rick put his cup down again, more carefully this time, and locked eyes with her.

"Well, we'll see just how casual you are some day when one of these young ladies rings your doorbell with a tiny bundle in her hands and you're burdened with a responsibility you may wish you didn't have to deal with." *I should bite my tongue for that,* she thought, *I hardly behaved more responsibly last night. Or this morning. Jesus, what a hypocrite I am.*

"Well, since abortion is legal in this country now, there doesn't have to be too many little burdens on anyone," he said offhandedly.

Their food had been served, and Rick was busy picking tomatoes off his sandwich when he realized she was glaring at him. "What?" he asked.

"Don't you think that's a pretty cavalier attitude?" she said stonily.

"It's better than having a child nobody wants."

"Having an abortion is nothing you do blithely, Rick. It's not like having a tooth removed."

He looked up at her, wondering if she was speaking from firsthand experience. It was none of his business and he knew it. He asked her anyway. "Did you ever have one?"

"No, but two of my friends have. It was not an easy decision for either of them. They both found the experience devastating."

"Then why'd they do it?"

"It was simply a necessity for each of them at that particular time in their lives. Both have regretted it. And I get a little upset when I hear self-centered, irresponsible men, who can simply walk away from the situation, say things like, Hey, no big deal, just get rid of it." As she spoke, she wondered what J.D. would do.

"Well, Maggie, all I can say is that I do think sometimes it's better for people to not be born at all than to be unwanted, unloved, and, yes, a burden for everyone involved. Trust me, Maggie, I'm on much more familiar ground than you are."

Maggie watched his eyes as he spoke, saw a shadow pass over his face, heard the emotion in his voice.

"What are you saying, that you think your parents didn't want you?" she heard herself ask.

"I know they didn't, Maggie." His voice was very low.

She looked up curiously.

"My mother walked out of the hospital—alone—three days after I was born and never came back. I haven't the faintest idea of who she was, who my father was. And quite frankly, I've no desire to find out at this point." He did not look at her and continued to pour ketchup on his french fries as he spoke, as if what he was saying had little importance.

Maggie sat speechless, unable to even look at him after what must have been a painful admission on his part, for all his attempts to be blasé. Finally, she said, "Rick, I'm so sorry. I had no idea."

"It's okay, Maggie, you had no way of knowing." He waved a hand as if the whole topic was irrelevant.

"Were you adopted?"

"It was right after the war, Maggie. There were many of us, children without parents, and life was more than a bit disrupted in England after the war ended. Not too many people were looking for stray babies to take in. I grew up in a home with about thirty other boys also without families. We had each other, you know, but none of us really had anyone . . ."

She fought hard to find something to say to him, sensing that he needed comfort and had probably needed comfort for many years in spite of his attitude to the contrary. She found herself at a loss and so said nothing.

Finally, to break the silence, he looked up and said, "And that's why I think abortion isn't such a bad idea some-times."

"You can't really believe it would have been better if you'd never been born, Rick. You couldn't possibly think that."

He didn't answer her.

"Rick, your boorish behavior aside"—they both smiled—"you're a very gifted musician and, I suspect, a very good person underneath that role you play. I'm sorry there wasn't anyone there for you when you were growing up. And while I know there's no consolation in it, for what it's worth you should know that there are people who care about you and who are there for you now. J.D. Me."

"Thank you, Maggie," he heard himself say softly, and at that moment, her warm sincerity and genuine sweetness left him no doubt as to why J.D.'s love for her was so deep. Rick ached for such a woman, one whose heart would never falter, in good times or in bad, through success or failure. Secretly he despaired that he neither deserved nor would ever find such a partner in this life.

J.D. strolled up to the table.

"Well," said Rick, forcing self-pity aside, "here's the sleepy old man now."

"Is there room for one more body in this booth?"

"Always." Maggie moved over to make room for him.

J.D. draped an arm over her shoulder, telling her, "I missed you being there when I woke up."

The love that shone in his face was so blatant that Rick had to look away, busying himself pushing french fries around on his plate.

"So tell me, what did you eat?" J.D. asked her.

"Hamburger."

"Any good?"

"So-so."

The waitress returned and handed J.D. a menu. He made a quick choice and ate the remaining chips from Maggie's plate while he and Rick discussed a new guitar arrangement Rick had wanted to try that night. They agreed to work on it after lunch, along with a new song J.D. mentioned he was anxious to perform that night.

"Do you mind, Mags? Would you rather sightsee or something?"

"Actually, I don't mind at all. I brought my running shoes with me and I think I'd like to jog for a while. As a matter of fact, I could run now if you'd give me the key."

He handed it over and kissed her cheek. "Be careful, please. And don't get lost."

She went back to the room and changed, then took the elevator back down to the lobby. Out on the street, she decided to head toward the right, toward a park she could see in the distance. It was a lovely May afternoon, and she found Atlanta much to her liking. She reflected as she ran on how happy she felt at this minute, feeling the concrete under her feet, sniffing the warm breeze, lightly scented with a hint of floral and new grass. Few things made her feel better than running. She ran what felt to be her normal distance and walked through the park to cool down on her way back to the hotel. She was in a mild lather and felt great.

The lobby was all but deserted when she strolled through to the elevator. She walked into the empty room and stripped off her sweaty clothes, took a shower, dried her hair, and lay down for a short nap. When J.D. got back to the room at 6:45, he woke her from a sound sleep.

"Maggie, it's late. Wake up, Maggie, we have to leave soon." He shook her shoulder insistently.

Her eyes opened slowly, obviously against their will. "What time is it?"

"Any chance you could get dressed and ready to go really quickly?"

"No, no chance," she murmured sleepily.

"Come on, Mags, move the bones."

"It was the run. I'm not used to running in the afternoon." She yawned and sat up. "Did you get your song done?"

"Yes."

"Is it good?"

"It's a dandy," he nodded, grinning mischievously as he buttoned his shirt. "You'll hear it tonight."

And a dandy it was. She'd sat on the steps that led to the stage, off to the right side, three of the crew members seated in front of her to block the way of any errant fans. The closest speaker was twenty feet away, but even at that distance the noise level was unbelievable. *It's a miracle more people don't go deaf from this,* she'd been thinking as she heard for the first time the love song he'd written just for her.

"The thought comes to me, from someplace deep within my mind,
The wonder of it—can this be real?—this dream I never thought I'd find.

Lost in you, I've found it all, all that life can be.
Sweet, sweet Maggie, can't believe you're loving me."

Maggie sat quietly on the step, attempting to maintain her composure, there in the cavernous room amid thousands of strangers, listening to his voice, watching his face. Memories of that night in Atlanta would return to her in the years to come, and she would always feel that same surge of love for him that she felt that night whenever she recalled it. It was the last city she would travel to that tour, and she would always remember Atlanta as the city where the course of her life had been set.

"That was so wonderful, so beautiful," she told him as he exited the stage at the conclusion of the performance. "I can't believe you did that for me. Hey," she asked as he swept her into the dressing room, "where's the fire?"

He pushed her through the door that led into the shower area.

"What are you doing?" She watched his face and, seeing both mirth and passion mingled there, protested, "You can't be serious. For God's sake, Jamey, what if someone wants to take a shower?"

"They'll find the door locked and they'll wait," he said, grinning.

"Well, just where are you planning on . . ." She looked around the room, which was devoid of furnishings.

"In the shower, of course," he replied, smiling into her eyes as he unbuttoned his shirt.

"In the shower?" She raised a curious eyebrow. "How do you do it in the shower?"

"Take your clothes off and I'll show you."

Maggie woke at dawn on Monday morning. Her sleep had been troubled, and she was not rested. She turned over and studied J.D.'s face as he slept, smiling as she took in the features she knew so well and loved so deeply. The dark hair tumbled onto his forehead always gave his face the appearance of a man much younger. She wanted to touch him, feel his skin, kiss his mouth. She hesitated, wondering if she should wake him so early. *This time tomorrow I'll be home in my own bed,* she reminded herself. *All alone.*

She considered the loss of her pills, acutely aware that they'd been playing Russian roulette all weekend. *Oh, God,* she thought, *please let it be all right,* then stopped, knowing that prayer as a means of birth control was an exercise in futility. Love and desire were at war with logic and reason. She was smart enough to know which would win the battle for her will.

She leaned over him and with her fingers traced the lines in his face. He smiled slightly in his sleep. She leaned closer, kissed his cheek, his chin, worked her way to his mouth, and felt his response, slow at first, then slightly more intense as he began to emerge from his slumber. Her kisses became more insistent, and he answered her need. They took their time, as if they had all the time in the world, knowing it would have to last what would seem like an eternity before they could be together again. He kissed her face, tasted the salty tears, kissing away each one as it slid down her face, holding her as closely as he could. They each searched for something to say that could hold back the gloom that was creeping in around them like a dense fog.

"Come into the shower with me," he said after they had lain in silence for what seemed to be a long time.

"You have got to be kidding," she said with raised eyebrows, "you couldn't possibly . . ."

He laughed. "You're right. I couldn't possibly. But I do need a shower. And besides," his voice softened as he cuddled her, "I still need to be near you. I want to keep the closeness as long as I can. I love you so much, Maggie. I don't have words to tell you what I feel for you."

She held him in her arms, memorizing how it felt to hold him, then, knowing time would start to run short before they would have to leave for the airport, pushed him back a bit and said, "I get to set the water temperature this time, though. You damn near froze me out in the dressing room the other night."

She got up and pulled him with her, pushing him toward the bathroom door.

"That water wasn't cold, Maggie. It was temperate," he said innocently.

"It was frigid. I'll show you temperate. And I get to wash my hair first."

"Bossy broad," he murmured. "Jesus, Maggie, this water's too damned hot."

"Shut up and pass the shampoo."

She laughed and pretended to take her time. Finally he reached over and turned the cold water faucet far enough to bring down a steady stream of cool water.

"God, that's cold!" she protested.

He laughed, picked up the soap she'd dropped when the cool water first hit her, and laughed again as she opened the door and all but jumped into a towel.

She was drying her hair when he came out. She saw the melancholy in his eyes, saw the blues settle into his face. She put her arms around him and held him, smoothed the wet hair from his forehead.

"I'm not whole without you, Maggie," he told her.

"I know, love. I'm not either." She bit her lip and held him closer.

"I don't want you to leave," he whispered, and she watched the tears form in his eyes. "Stay with me. Please, Maggie."

"I can't, Jamey. Not this time."

He pulled away from her and went into the bedroom. She finished dressing slowly, then followed him. He sat on the edge of the bed, depressed and desolate. She sat behind him and massaged his shoulders.

"Maggie, will you marry me?" she heard him say in a low voice.

She'd not anticipated the question and so sat silently.

"Maggie?"

"Jamey, that's a big commitment . . ."

"I know. And I'm more than willing to make it." He turned around and took her face in her hands, his fingers tangling the still damp strands of hair around her temple. "Are you?"

"Yes," she replied simply.

"When?"

"I don't know. What do you think?" she asked.

"Today would suit me just fine," he offered, only half joking.

"Might take a few days to get a license." She smiled, then suggested, "How about when the tour is over, when your travel's done."

"We'll still have this long, lonely month ahead of us, Maggie."

"I know, but it will take a while to get the paperwork together, my divorce papers, and I don't know what you'll need in the way of forms, since you're not a citizen. And I want my family to meet you first. And I want to get married at home, with my family . . ."

He sighed. "Well, I guess I could last four weeks if I knew for certain I'd never have to be without you again. That we'll always be together after that month's over."

"We will be." She kissed his chin.

"The minute you get back home, find a calendar and decide on a date. And then call your parents."

"Uh-uh. I want them to meet you first." You just didn't waltz into that house with a stranger and say, "This is Jamey. We're getting married."

"When can we do that? I'll be away for the next four weeks."

"I'll see what we can work out. And once the tour is over and you don't have to leave anymore, will it matter if we get married right away or if we wait a few weeks beyond that? If we're together, will it matter if we're married?"

"No, not for a little while. But keep in mind that I'll need to be going back home before too long, Maggie. And when I do, I'll be taking you with me, so you'd best get them prepared."

"I'm not certain of the best way to do that," she said as she pondered the possibilities.

"Tell them I'm a piano player," he suggested, "that should break the ice."

"No good. They'll be expecting Van Cliburn. Or Liberace."

"Then just tell them I'm with a band."

"Tommy Dorsey." She shook her head playfully.

"How 'bout just saying that I sing?"

"Frank Sinatra/Tony Bennett."

"A visiting Brit?"

"Prince Philip."

"Why don't you just tell them the truth?" he asked pointedly.

"Jamey, my father hates rock music. He's having a coronary because his only son has taken up the drums. When he finds out who you are, his mind will close like a steel trap."

"Well, sooner or later, he'll have to know. And it just seems to me the sooner you get it over with, the better it will be for everyone."

13

THE LIGHTS IN THE LIVING ROOM WERE HOT, AND MAGGIE RAISED her hands to lift what suddenly felt like a heavy veil of hair from her neck. The air felt good as it touched her back. *I should have worn my hair up,* she told herself, *instead of down the way he likes it, just to irritate him.*

She resisted the urge to tune back into the conversation. Hilary had apparently asked him about that lag he'd had a few years back, when he couldn't buy a hit record. It had been a bad time for him, she recalled. He'd been depressed and seriously considered retirement. Realizing he didn't have too many options other than music had served to depress him even more. He had no education to speak of, had never made a living doing anything else. It had been Rick who'd lit the fire under him then, prodding him to try again, which of course he had done, producing his biggest-selling album up to that time.

He'd been miserable until he'd completed that record, hanging around the house listlessly, following her and getting underfoot, looking to her to direct him somehow. She had three little ones to keep up with and had just found out she was pregnant with the fourth. It had been unex-

pected—they'd all somehow been unexpected. None, of
course, she recalled ruefully, as unexpected as the first one
had been . . .

By the beginning of the second week in June, she knew for
certain something was wrong. She was two weeks late—
never in her life had she ever fluctuated by more than three
days. She knew it was time to pay the piper for the four-day
dance in Atlanta. The doctor merely served to confirm her
own diagnosis. Her child was due the first week in February.

Numb, she'd returned to her apartment, caught in the
emotional crossfire of angrily reproaching them both for
their stupid, irresponsible behavior and sheer panic at
finding herself in such a predicament.

She reached for the phone a dozen times, each time
rehearsing a different opening line, a different conversation,
but could not bring herself to dial the number of the hotel in
Phoenix where he was staying. How would he react? Would
he be angry? Indifferent? *What if,* a tiny anxious voice
inside suggested, *he's changed his mind about you? What if
he's met someone else? What will he think about a baby?
What if he doesn't want it? What if he walks away? What if?
What if? What if?*

By two A.M. she had managed to work herself into a state
of frenzied confusion. She picked up the phone and dialed
the hotel. Rick answered. She could hear a party in full blast.

"Hey, Mags, congratulations. J.D. told us the news. We're
happy for you, baby. As a matter of fact, we're celebrating
the big event right now. And we'll celebrate again in L.A.
and in San Francisco, that is, of course, if J.D. permits us the
time to do anything besides—"

"Maggie?" J.D. had abruptly taken the phone from Rick.
"What's going on?" she asked.

"Ah, well, I made the error of telling everyone we'd
decided to get married, and it seemed like an excuse for a
party, I guess. Somehow everyone ended up back here at my
room." His voice sounded odd. Was he drunk or annoyed
that she had intruded into what sounded like a great party?

"You sound like you've been hitting the Scotch." She was

annoyed to find him enjoying himself when she was crazed with panic.

"Not really," he said somewhat impatiently. "Maggie, hold on. Let me try to redirect these people elsewhere. Give me a few minutes to get everyone out of here, and I'll call you back."

She lay in the darkness, the phone beside her on the bed, her hand on the receiver, waiting for it to ring. *Why is it taking him so long,* she wondered, *to kick a few dozen people out of the room?* When the call finally came, shattering the silence, she glanced at the clock on the table before answering. It had taken him almost an hour.

"Why are you up so late tonight, Mags?" he asked, and she pictured him in his hotel room, settled back against the bed pillows, one arm bent behind his head, legs crossed at the ankles on the bed, relaxed and unaware that she was about to drop a heavy bit of news into his unsuspecting lap. Her throat constricted and she began to lose her nerve.

"I needed to talk to you. Why didn't you call the past two nights? I've been worried." She tried to control her voice, which sounded, even to her ears, a bit shrill.

"No reason to be. It was late by the time we got back here both nights, and I know there's a difference in the time between here and there. I didn't want to wake you up in the middle of the night. And besides, I've been a bit distracted . . ."

"Distracted? By what?" She tapped the footboard of the bed with her big toe.

He hesitated. "I don't know that now's the best time to go into that."

A fog seemed to settle into her brain, jumbling her senses. Through the loud buzzing inside her head her thoughts scrambled in confusion. What was he hiding from her? Her mouth went dry, and she could not respond.

"Tell me why you called, sweetheart. Is something wrong?"

Ignoring his questions, she pressed him. "When will be the right time?"

. "When I get back there." He sighed impatiently. "Maggie, is there something you wanted to talk about?"

"No." For the first time, she felt like an unwanted intruder into his life away from her.

"Things okay at work?"

"Yes."

"Your family?"

"Fine."

"Then what, baby?" he pleaded with exasperated gentleness.

"Nothing. I'm sorry I called, Jamey. Remind me not to do so again unless there's a death in the family."

"Maggie . . ." he began, obviously alarmed by the snappish, shrewish jolt of her voice.

"We'll talk about it next week when you're here." *When you're back home and you're the man I know again.*

"Ahhh, well, about next week. There's been a slight change in plans. I'll be in L.A. a bit longer than we'd scheduled."

"What does that mean?"

"That means I'll be back between San Francisco and Toronto the following week. But unfortunately it won't be for six days, as we'd planned."

"How long?"

"Two. Maybe three days at the most."

"Why do you have to stay so long in L.A.?" A tingle of apprehension spread through her.

"There's something I have to do that's very important to me" was all the explanation he offered.

Her eyes burned. Everything was starting to fall apart. He had always been so eager to be with her, so miserable when he was away from her. Why, now of all times, when she needed him so desperately, was something else more important to him than being with her? And how dare he be so nonchalant when her life was falling apart.

"That's all you're going to tell me?" She could not believe the casual way in which he seemed to brush her off.

"Yes. I don't want to go into it right now," he again told

her. "Maggie, I'm tired. Exhausted. I've barely slept in three weeks . . ."

"Let me know when you can fit me in." She broke into a sweat and slammed the receiver into its cradle.

She knew that he would be upset when he heard the dial tone. She wanted him to be upset. She wanted him to be as crazy as she was. She wanted him to hop the next plane east and come home and tell her it would be all right, that he loved her and would love this child, this tiny being of whose existence he had not yet a clue. Her anger—toward him over his part in her predicament as well as his absence, toward herself for her inability to tell him—had taken on a life of its own and seemed to control her, instilling in her a hostility she did not wish to feel. But it was there and it grew and she had exploded with it.

Why, she asked herself as she lay alone in the dark, *do words of anger and bitterness come so easily to me now? Why can't I just tell him the truth, that I'm pregnant and terrified and I need him so desperately and that I love him more than anything in this life? Am I so afraid that I'm losing him that I'd push him the rest of the way out the door rather than confront him honestly?*

He had called again the next night, gently solicitous, but clearly bewildered by her attitude. She knew she'd been flat-out bitchy, and she had cursed the evil hormonal demon that had seemed to take over her mouth and dictated her very words. He'd sounded sad, distant, a note of frustrated resignation in his voice, but he was not coming home. The hazy, unthinkable possibility that maybe he'd found someone else took on the shape of the image of a ghost she'd seen in a bad movie when she was a child, a wisp of smoke that floated in midair without form or substance, and it terrified her. *There's someone else in his life now, and he doesn't know how to tell me . . .*

She sat in the chair by the bedroom window, huddled in the darkness and took a few deep breaths, trying to will the trembling inside and the tightness in her chest to stop. In her mind's eye, she saw herself in a boat speeding out of control toward the horizon. He stood alone on the shore, shrinking into an ever-smaller speck as she tried frantically to turn the wheel and head back to him, to keep him from fading from view completely, but the boat seemed to be powered by some force beyond her control. And so it continued to skim across the water on it's rapid course out to sea, where she was surrounded by a terrible loneliness and an endless fear.

"Lindy, I don't know if I can go through with this," Maggie said, her voice unsteady and tense.

They sat in Lindy's car, in the parking lot outside the clinic where Maggie had made the arrangements for the abortion to be performed.

"Honey, don't look at me to talk you out of it or into it. I will be supportive of any decision you make, but I won't be a party to you making it. I will tell you that I think you are absolutely one hundred percent wrong in not telling J.D. I think he would want to know, Maggie. You could at least wait until he comes back."

"I doubt he's coming back. Right now he's most likely knee-deep in Californian blondes."

"Maggie, you know that man loves you." Lindy tried to control her exasperation. Maggie had been an absolute madwoman for the past week and a half. *And they all think I'm the crazy one,* Lindy thought to herself.

"I know that I thought he did," she said sorrowfully.

"Maggie, he asked you to marry him."

"And now he's sorry that he did. He's changed his mind, Lindy, and he doesn't know how to tell me." Maggie's face was rigid. "He hasn't called in a week."

"Well, from what you told me, you were less than gracious the last few times."

"Lindy, I called him to share the big news, there's this loud party going on in his room . . . You know what those parties are like—don't tell me he was sitting there twiddling his thumbs. Then he tells me he's passing up on a week back here to do something in L.A.—something he wouldn't tell me about, some nebulous thing he's involved with. Does that sound like a man who'd be receptive to the kind of news I had to give him?"

"Maggie, you always said the traveling around got to him in a big way."

"Something's gotten to him in a big way, but I doubt it's the travel," grumbled Maggie.

"You can't really believe there's someone else, Maggie, there has to be another explanation." The thought was inconceivable to Lindy, who, though devoid of any real love in her own life, knew the real thing when she saw it. She never doubted for a second that J.D. adored this woman.

"I can't think of any," Maggie told her bluntly.

"I can't see him dumping you, Maggie. I don't think he's the type who falls out of love that fast."

"He fell in fast enough, maybe it passes just as quickly."

"I still think you should have told him."

"It would only make things worse. Then he might feel that he has to come back and go through with the wedding even though he'd already decided he didn't want to marry me. That's even worse than him leaving me now."

"You don't know that he has, Maggie."

The two women sat and looked at each other for a few moments, then Maggie opened her car door. "Come on. Let's get this over with."

The waiting room was brightly painted and filled with plants in hanging baskets in the sunny front window, someone having made a conscious effort to make the place look as cheerful as possible. Maggie checked in with the receptionist and took the clipboard that held the information sheet she was to complete. She sat down and with a shaking hand filled in the blanks. She handed it back to the woman at the desk, who told her there'd be a bit of a wait.

Terrified and heartsick, she sat in a silence so deep she could hear her heart beating, not permitting herself to think of anything—not J.D., not the reason for her presence there—except getting through this day. She glanced around the room at the others who were waiting. A young girl of about fifteen who sat with a woman Maggie suspected was her mother. On the other side of the room, a woman Maggie's age, also with a friend, cried softly, her friend's arm about her shoulder in silent comfort. A woman of forty or so sat staring at a potted plant on the floor a few feet away, her eyes never moving to so much as blink, her face totally devoid of expression.

The girl—a child, really, she couldn't have been older than Colleen—was the first of the group to be called. "Mommy," she had whispered in terror. Her mother had seemed to focus on a point slightly higher than her daughter's face, unable to meet her eyes as she helped her to her feet. The image of the girl, so young and so obviously terrified as she gripped tightly to her mother's hand, remained in Maggie's sight even as the two followed the nurse through the door and disappeared.

The only sounds were an occasional sniff from the crying woman, the rustle of pages turning as Lindy quietly flipped through a magazine, the ticking of the clock. Occasionally the phone would ring, a door would close with a muffled sound from somewhere in the building. The room began to take on the stifling atmosphere of an airless tomb.

"Who am I kidding?" Maggie said aloud to no one in particular. Every eye in the room turned as she stood up. "I need more time to think about this."

The young receptionist looked up from her paperwork and sighed. She'd seen this happen a half-dozen times a day. They think they want to do it, then they don't want to do it after they get here, so they leave and go outside for twenty minutes, recall all the reasons that brought them here in the first place, then come back in, some more reluctantly than others. She peered at Maggie over the ledge of the window that separated her desk from the waiting room and said dispassionately, "Ms. Callahan, if you want this procedure—"

"I don't know what I want." And with that she was out the door.

Maggie sat in the car, crying softly, Lindy's arms around her. "I just can't do this. It goes against everything I've ever believed in. Right at this minute I hate J.D. more than I've ever hated anyone in my life. And the thought of having to tell my family makes me physically sick. But I just can't do it."

"What will you do then?" Lindy asked with the gentlest concern.

"I don't know," she sobbed wearily. "I don't know."

14

Her face flushed scarlet at the recollection, and she fretted with her wedding ring unconsciously. What a singularly terrible day that had been. Even now, so removed from it by time, she felt the same knot of fear and uncertainty rise within her. How different it all would have been had that one day ended differently.

"Maggie?" Hilary had tapped her knee with her stack of cards. "I said, you must have been dying to take him home and show him off. After all, he was quite a catch."

"Not to my parents," Maggie replied, her reverie having been disrupted by the sound of her name. How had they gotten back onto the subject of her family? What had she missed? "As far as my father was concerned, *rock musician* was a contradiction in terms. They were all long-haired subversive drug addicts."

"Not a music lover, I take it?" Hilary looked amused.

"Oh, he loves music," J.D. chuckled, annoying his wife with his good-natured response, "what he considers music, anyway. My father-in-law is of the opinion that no music of any merit has been written since 1947. Maggie hid me from him for months, you know."

"That's not quite true," she protested.

"Of course, it's true," he said, grinning, pleased he'd gotten a visible rise out of her. "You couldn't bring yourself to tell them about me until you had absolutely no choice."

"I needed a little time to prepare them." She shrugged.

"Because your father didn't like rock music?" Hilary inquired.

"It was a little more complicated than that." Maggie squirmed uneasily.

"Maggie's parents were very fond of her first husband and were holding out for a reconciliation—" he began.

"You don't need to bring that up," she snapped.

". . . and were very disappointed when that didn't happen. So she figured that bringing me home would be one more disappointment, that maybe Daddy wouldn't love her quite so much if he knew she'd taken up with the likes of me."

"Thank you, Dr. Borders," she said, glaring.

"Sorry, Mags, but that's the truth."

"You have never understood the dynamics in my family," she told him archly.

"And I'd probably still be waiting for an opportunity to observe them firsthand if you hadn't gotten pregnant when you did." He could not resist the temptation to remind her.

"You're being a jerk," she hissed through clenched teeth.

"And you've been married how many years now?" Hilary asked, obviously amused by the exchange.

"Fifteen glorious years." He smiled sweetly, placing an arm around Maggie's shoulders. She froze, resenting the pretense.

"Well, I suppose that qualifies yours as one of the most successful shotgun marriages in the music business," Hilary noted.

Shotgun marriage. The phrase caught Maggie off guard. *I haven't heard that expression in eons. And if that's the worst that comes out tonight, I suppose we'll be fortunate.*

"Well, wait a minute, Hilary," J.D. had become unexpectedly defensive, "it's hardly the situation you seem to be implying. Maggie and I had planned to get married that summer. We've never for a moment regretted the way things turned out. Having Jesse when we did was just one more happy event that first year, one more blessing we shared. All of our children have been very much wanted. Especially Jess."

Maggie's eyebrows arched slightly, wondering what had prompted a response so openly emotional. She had no way of knowing that the topic had recently been the source of a somewhat tense discussion between J.D. and their firstborn, who had come across an old newspaper clipping, complete with a photograph of J.D. holding a pudgy five-month-old Jesse on the occasion of his parents' first anniversary. Jesse had been surprisingly upset to learn that he'd been conceived before his parents' marriage.

J.D. wanted to bite his tongue, knowing his comments were, at that moment, causing certain embarrassment to his son, upstairs in the presence of his siblings and his grandmother. He wondered if Jesse really understood how much his father loved him, how much he'd been wanted. After, of course, the initial shock had worn off. He'd never suspected that Maggie's telephone theatrics had been prompted by anything quite so dramatic . . .

J.D. was bounding up the steps that led to the front door of Maggie's building, whistling a merry tune and juggling two suitcases and a flight bag when the front door opened and Lindy appeared. She had begun to cross the front porch when she noticed his approach.

"Good timing, jerk," she said sarcastically.

"Nice to see you too, Lindy." The smile evaporated from his face.

They stood about five feet apart. Lindy glared at him, hands on her hips.

"What's this all about? Oh, let me guess, Maggie's pissed off because I stopped calling her. I stopped calling her because she was a bloody bitch every time I tried to talk to her. She'll be okay, she'll understand. I've something in my pocket that will make her forget how pissed off she was." He winked confidently.

"It's what's in your pocket that started this whole mess."

"What the hell does that mean?" he asked blankly.

"Ask Maggie." She turned, headed down off the steps, and crossed the street.

Shaking his head, he started to ring the doorbell, then realized that Lindy had left the door open. He ran up the stairs and into the hallway, set his suitcases down, and started to call to her when he saw her through the open bedroom door. She sat in the middle of the bed, Indian style, forearms resting on her thighs, fingers of both hands clasped together so that her arms formed a big O. Her stillness chilled him to his soul. He walked uncertainly into the room.

"Maggie? Maggie, what is it?"

She turned to look at him with such pain in her eyes that he could not bear the sight. Frightened, he sat down next to her, reached for her.

"What, sweetheart, what's happened?" Was she ill? Had someone died?

"Don't touch me." She leaned away from his outstretched arms, turning her head from him.

He recoiled as if he'd been slapped.

"Maggie, please, tell me what's wrong, sweetheart."

"It's none of your business. Get off my bed. And don't call me sweetheart." Her eyes, scarlet from crying, never left her hands.

He stood up and backed away, confused.

"Maggie, what's wrong with you? Maggie, you can't possibly have gotten this upset because I stayed over in L.A. a few extra days . . ."

"You can stay wherever you want," she snapped. "I don't really care what you do."

"What the bloody hell has happened here?" he exploded. "Okay, Maggie, you've had your little melodrama. You're scaring the shit out of me, all right? Now let's act like grownups and you tell me what this is all about and we'll—"

"Remember in Atlanta, when I lost my makeup case . . ."

As she spoke, his eyes fell upon the pamphlets from the

clinic on her dresser. He picked them up and looked them over. He met her eyes. He could barely find his voice.

"Sweet Jesus," he stared at her. "Did you have an abortion?"

"Not yet," she whispered.

"Not yet? Don't you think this is something we should talk about?"

"No. There's nothing to discuss." She would not look at him.

"You're pregnant with my baby and there's nothing to discuss?" He was dumbfounded, floundering in confusion. This was not the Maggie he knew. What had happened to her?

"When were you going to tell me?" he asked.

"I wasn't."

"You don't think I have a right to know?"

"I didn't think you'd care." She couldn't hold the tears back any longer.

"How can you say that to me? How could you possibly for one minute ever think—"

"No more than I could think you'd have something—or someone—more important waiting for you in L.A." The full force of her anger lashed at him.

"Oh, I get it. Because I didn't come back when you'd expected me, you decided there was another woman, is that it?" His voice was cold and harsh, his anger barely controlled, "And so you decided it was over between us. And you decided to abort our child without even telling me."

"Yes, J.D.," she replied flatly, not turning her head.

"Oh, and now it's J.D."

He reached into his jacket pocket, took something out, and held up his hand so that she could see the small plastic rectangle he held.

"This," he said, "is what I was doing in L.A. And in Miami. And Dallas. Every spare minute. It was to be a sort of engagement present."

He looked around the room and walked to the desk, dropped the cassette into the tape deck, and pushed the start button. The music began, the opening bars of "Sweet, Sweet Maggie," the first of eight songs on the tape.

He'd spent all his spare time over the past six weeks writing, working out the pieces of the musical puzzles until they all fit, driving the other members of the band crazy, making them rehearse when they'd rather party, making them record when they'd rather sleep. He could tell by the stunned look on her face that this was a possibility that had never occurred to her.

"Oh, God, Jamey," she whispered, flushed red with sudden shame, her eyes filled rapidly.

"I'm going for a walk," he said quietly as he turned his back and left the room.

He wandered aimlessly, his steps paced by fury, trying to sort out fact from emotion. He was livid that she would lack such basic trust in him, that she would make such an outrageous decision based upon an even more outrageous assumption without even telling him. *What in the name of God was going through her mind that she would think this would not matter to me? To assume that my extended stay in California meant there was another woman, as if she was interchangeable with anyone else.*

And then there's the matter of this baby—my baby. Mine and Maggie's. How could she ever think to dismiss it, to eliminate it and not even tell me? A rage stronger than he'd ever experienced washed over him, and for a long moment he was lost in it, ignited by it. How could she? . . . And the image of her tortured, swollen eyes came to him, and he knew it had been a decision born of desperation.

He found himself passing a place that looked vaguely familiar, and he paused to get his bearings. He was drawn to the house behind the fence, realizing suddenly it was the same place Maggie'd shown him once, the same one she said she'd own someday. He stepped up to the fence and leaned over, gazing at the wide expanse of overgrown grass, the ramshackle old building.

In the dying sun, the stucco took on a glow as if it was coming to life before his eyes. An image flashed before him, he and Maggie and this child walking up the long drive, hand in hand, the three of them. He blinked at the sight of them, and they were gone. He leaned his elbow on the top cross rail of the fence and wept, the anger spilling from him with the tears, and he knew with absolute certainty that if he could forgive her lack of faith, the vision would become reality.

Pulling a handkerchief from his jeans pocket, he dried his face. A calm had settled over him, and he understood she had acted from sheer terror, the fear of having to raise a child alone, a child she feared he would not want. *If I hadn't been so distracted, so exhausted from trying to tour and record at the same time,* he reproached himself, *I would have realized that something was deeply wrong, maybe I would even have guessed and spared her this agony.*

And could I forgive her if she eradicated that tiny surge of life? I could forgive her anything—anything. She is everything in this life to me, and that's the simple fact.

Following the concrete walk that led back to her apartment, he thought of the child. Son or daughter? It would not matter. It was his and it was hers, a blending of them both. Love in its purest form. He realized that not once since having heard her news had he wished it away, and it occurred to him as he crossed the old wooden porch that he wanted their baby, just as he wanted her. He needed to know if she wanted them—father and child—as much.

He came into the bedroom and sat at the bottom of the bed, not looking at her. Finally he said, "When are you scheduled for this little operation?"

"Today." She could barely utter the one-word response, her throat had suddenly become achingly dry.

"Today?" He turned toward her. "Did you just not go?"

"Oh, I went, all right," she replied, twisting the tissue in her hands, still unable to make eye contact with him. "I left. I couldn't do it."

"Why not?" He wanted her to tell him she wanted the child, needed to hear her say it.

She shook her head slowly side to side. "I was so confused. I could think of twenty good reasons not to have this baby, under the circumstances. I tried to be so rational about it. I'm not in a position to raise a child alone. My family would be absolutely shattered. Things would be too hard, both for me and for the baby. Everything told me it would be easier to just eliminate the problem and get on with my life. But in my heart, I knew it wasn't right for me. Something inside wouldn't let me go through with it."

"I still don't understand why you didn't tell me, Maggie."

"I tried to tell you. I wanted to tell you. I was so upset, Jamey, so frightened and confused, and my head was spinning. And when I did talk to you, I didn't know how to say it and we'd ended up arguing. So I thought I'd just wait till you got here last week, but you didn't come home, and when I asked you why, you were evasive and brushed me off, like it was none of my business, and everytime I talked to you, all I could think of was that things were like they were before we met, that you were doing all the things you used to do and that there was someone in L.A. that you couldn't bear to leave . . ." The jumble of words poured out, the tears she'd tried so hard to swallow back strangling her.

He moved up to sit next to her, put his arms around her, and cradled her head on his chest, his eyes stinging at the anguish of her sobs. "There's never been anyone but you, Maggie. Not in L.A., not in Houston or St. Louis or Dallas or Miami or anyplace else."

"That's what I used to think, but then you were acting so strangely and didn't come home . . ."

"I thought I'd have this great surprise for you, you know? I thought it would be great fun to come in and drop this tape in your lap and you'd be delighted to hear your song on the album." He sighed deeply. "It never occurred to me that you'd have an even bigger surprise for me." He rocked her gently in his arms. "Maggie, do you want this baby?"

She shook her head yes. "More than anything in this world."

"Did it never occur to you to ask me if I would want it, too?"

"At first it did. But last week, this week, I wasn't thinking that you'd be interested. All I could think of was that you'd

154

abandoned me and that I'd have to make the decision for myself." She seemed embarrassed by the admission.

"Did you think I'd never know? That I'd never find out?"

"I didn't think that far ahead," she conceded sheepishly. "Things seemed to be happening so quickly, and the doctor told me if I was going to do it, I should do it as soon as possible . . ."

"Don't fathers have any rights in this sort of thing?"

"No," she told him bluntly.

"Doesn't seem quite fair." He felt unexpectedly indignant at the inequity.

"How do you feel about it, now that you know?" she asked, shyly hesitant.

"Well, I was thinking about it while I was out walking about. I can't say honestly that I'd have planned it to happen now. But since it's a fact of our lives, I think we should have it." He paused somberly, then grinned a slow smile of satisfaction. "Actually, I'm quite taken with the idea of this small person growing so quietly inside you. And we were getting married anyway, so we'll just move the date up a bit."

"Maybe we should talk about that." She squirmed a little to sit up.

"You're right. When do you want to do it?"

"Jamey, I really think you should have some time to think about this. I don't ever want to feel that you married me because I was pregnant." She broke free from the circle of his arms to look at him. There was still a sadness in her eyes, an uncertainty that he could not define.

"Maggie, I wanted to marry you before you were pregnant," he reminded her.

"Yes, but that was before I was," she sniffed.

"That's what I just said." He stared at her wide-eyed, absolutely befuddled.

"Well, it changes things, Jamey." She leaned across him to reach the box of tissues on the bedside table. She took one and blew her nose, took a second and dabbed her eyes.

"Yes, it means that this time next year there'll be three of us instead of two." He did not know where this conversation was leading, and it was confusing him.

"Well, suppose you wanted to change your mind now. You'd feel that you couldn't and you'd feel obligated to do it anyway."

"I'm not going to change my mind. I never had changed my mind. It's what I wanted to do all along. How could I change my mind?" *What,* he wondered, *controlled the thought process of this woman's mind?*

"That's my point. You wouldn't even if you wanted to."

He pulled back and raised her face to look directly at him. "Let me see if I've got this straight. When you weren't pregnant, you agreed to marry me. But now that you are pregnant, you don't think we should. Is that what you've just said?"

"Yes."

"Maggie . . ." Totally bewildered, he groped for words. "That makes no bloody sense at all."

"Of course it makes sense. I'm afraid someday you'll think it was a mistake, that you were trapped."

"Jesus." He was shaking his head, not knowing whether to laugh or shout. "Maggie, I love you more than anything in this life. I always will. Baby or no baby. I wanted to marry you before I knew about the baby and I want to marry you now that I do—let me know if I'm going too fast for you."

She smiled weakly. He moved closer, laying down and bringing her near, caressing her arm.

"Do you love me, Maggie?" he asked softly.

"Yes. I love you very much," she sniffed.

"Will you marry me?" he asked with deliberate patience.

"Yes," she told him with a teary attempt to smile.

"Thank God we got that straightened out." He sighed with mock exasperation and pulled her to him, both of them laughing softly.

"You all right now, sweetheart? Come here, closer to me. I need to hold you. God, but that feels good, Maggie, it's been so long and this has all been so terrible . . ."

They talked long into the night. He told her how he'd been trying to talk the record company into letting them record

"Sweet, Sweet Maggie," but the management didn't want them to do a single. They wanted one last album out of this suddenly hot band and had tried every possible means to get the group to agree to stay together for one more twelve-month period. When that failed, they went back and forth, the bottom line being no album, no studio time. J.D. had been forced to use all the music he'd written over the past few months, all the songs he'd hoped to use for a first solo album, and had little time to complete the arrangements to his satisfaction. They finally got some recording time in several studios in the last three cities, finishing up the last four songs in L.A. The schedule had been grueling, recording day and night for a week, working excruciatingly long hours while keeping to the concert schedule in the evenings.

"Will I hear my song on the radio?" she asked, considering this for the first time.

"Quite possibly. It will be released as a single within the next month or so."

"Where will we live?" she asked, changing the subject abruptly.

"Where would you like to live?" He propped himself up on one elbow, not the least surprised when she replied, "Here."

"Here? In this apartment? Might get a bit crowded, what with a crib and a playpen . . ." He looked around skeptically.

"I meant somewhere around here. Can we afford a little house?"

"We can afford more than a little house, Maggie," he replied with some amusement, realizing that she was oblivious to his financial status. His sister Judith's husband, Ned, a broker in London, had been investing his money for him from the very beginning of his career. Even back in the Daily Times days, when he'd made practically nothing for those early performances, half went to Ned to invest. As a consequence of his prudence, which was at the insistence of his sister—it would never have occurred to the seventeen-year-old J.D.—money was not an issue.

"Maybe I could contact a realtor and have someone look around for us," she suggested.

"That's fine, but just keep in mind that we won't always be here," he cautioned.

"Where will we be?"

"I'll need to be in London a bit of the time. My record company is there. A lot of the people I'll need to work with are there. My family is nearby. And truthfully, I'm not certain that I'm ready to become a full-time Yank."

"Will we have to live there?"

"No, but we'll need a place to stay from time to time. We have lots of time to think about that, though, and you'll have plenty of time to look around to find an area you like."

"When do we have to go?"

"After the wedding . . . And don't make it sound as if this is a trip to Hades we're talking about. Why the lack of enthusiasm? Is there some reason why you don't want to make this trip?"

"Yes."

"And what's that?"

"I hate to fly," she admitted reluctantly.

"You've made a number of flights over the past few months," he reminded her.

"None of them went over the ocean. And I was desperate."

"Well, then, you'll just have to get desperate again, Maggie," he laughed, "because you'll go where I go."

"I'll have to quit my job," she thought aloud.

"I suggest you do that as soon as possible. Like first thing tomorrow morning," he instructed.

"And I guess we need to talk about another date . . ."

"Well, what did you tell your parents?"

"I didn't tell them anything. I thought I'd wait until they met you."

"You mean they'll be totally unprepared for any of this?" He pushed himself up onto an elbow, suddenly realizing there was yet another problem to be dealt with. He would have to meet her family on the same day they'd receive some unwelcome news.

"I'll have to tell them this weekend." She went white at the thought.

"This weekend is out," he told her. "I'll be in Toronto. And I want you to promise me you'll wait till I can go with you."

"No, no." She shook her head adamantly. "I have to do this by myself."

"Absolutely not. You'll wait until I can get back to go with you. We'll talk to them together."

"No." She was emphatic, and he knew she was imagining the scene that would follow her announcement.

"Don't argue with me on this, Maggie. That's the end of it. You just find out what we need to do, make whatever arrangements you like—"

"Don't you want any input into this?"

"Nope. You just tell me where and when. I'll be there."

"What about your family?"

"My mother would never fly over, not even for this. She has never set foot in a plane and probably never will. Judith will definitely be here."

"You'd better see if she's free."

"She'll be here if she has to swim." He shrugged confidently.

"What day next week will you be back?"

"I'm not certain. There was some talk of adding another date. The place where we're booked isn't too large, and the promoter was hoping to book in another show. But I should be back to go to your parents with you on the following weekend. We'll talk to them then."

She averted her eyes.

"And get that look off your face. I know what you're thinking. We will tell them together, Maggie."

"Has it occurred to you that maybe I know better than you how to deal with my family?" She had the look of someone who had the task of explaining something tedious to a small child.

"It wouldn't be right for you to have to face them with this by yourself. Maggie, you were concerned about simply bringing me home to meet them. I don't want you taking the heat for this by yourself."

"I've taken the heat under that roof many a time."

"For what it's worth, I think you're wrong. I know you'll do as you damn well please, Maggie, but I'm asking you to wait."

She lay staring at the ceiling, and he watched as a tiny smile danced ever so slightly across her lips.

"What's that for?" he inquired.

"I was just wondering what he'll look like."

"Who?"

"Jesse."

"Who's Jesse?"

"The baby." She smiled up at him.

He looked down into her eyes and then laughed out loud.

"Who told you it was a he?" he asked, amused by her nonchalant pronouncement.

"It is," she assured him.

"And who decided that his name would be Jesse?"

"Don't you like it?"

"Well, yes, I do, but you have a fifty–fifty chance of being wrong, you know," he reminded her.

She shook her head, indicating she was not.

"Jesse's a good name," he conceded, "and fortunately it will do just as well for a girl as for a boy. Just in case."

"I'm not wrong." She smiled confidently, but even she had no way of knowing that her prediction would be correct or that she'd just as accurately, uncannily, predict each of her subsequent seven pregnancies.

15

HILARY'S VOICE SEEMED TO BE DRONING ON AND ON. MAGGIE HAD tuned out and was not inclined to tune back in. She glanced over and noticed that Hilary appeared to be overtly flirting with Jamey now, though to his credit, he seemed not to notice. *He's always been good at warding off the advances of other women,* she thought, *or at least I thought he was. Maybe he's been fooling around all this time, and I was too stupid to see it. Maybe he and Glory have been doing this for years, right under my nose and I never caught on.* She flushed at the thought, her anger rising all over again.

Maybe her father had been right about him all along. From the day he found out that Maggie was pregnant, Frank wanted to break J.D.'s neck. Of course, he had blamed J.D.—God only knew what line the SOB had used to sweet-talk his daughter into his bed. *That had surely been one of the hardest things I ever had to do—telling them that I, their daughter, their beloved Maggie, was pregnant and by whom . . .*

The drive to her parents' house that weekend was the longest trip she'd ever made. She dreaded the scene she knew would take place more than she had ever dreaded anything. How in the name of God, she wondered, could she bear to break the news.

Her stomach contracted tightly as she turned onto the old familiar street, and for a fleeting minute she thought of turning back to Philadelphia. Right now, eloping sounded like a great idea. She could fly to Toronto . . .

Her heart flopped over when she pulled into the driveway and saw both parents on the front porch. By the time she'd taken a deep breath and opened the car door, they were both almost to the car. She got out and greeted them nervously, hugging first her father, then her mother, unconsciously holding her for a moment or so longer than she normally would have.

Mary Elizabeth drew back slightly, studying her daughter carefully.

"Where's Kevin?" Maggie asked, averting her eyes and swallowing hard.

"He's at Joey's." Mary Elizabeth's gaze never left Maggie's face. "He should be back by lunchtime."

Frank, oblivious to the tension, called across the street to a neighbor as mother and daughter walked into the house.

"Where's Colleen?"

"Softball practice. She'll be back later this afternoon."

Maggie sat down at the kitchen table and sipped at the coffee her mother had poured for her. Her stomach was queasy and the smell of the coffee was almost making her sick. She could feel Mary Elizabeth watching her.

"Maggie, what is it? Tell me what's wrong," she asked gently.

Maggie's eyes filled, and soon a steady stream of tears followed each other pell-mell down her face. She fought for words, though none would come. Her father walked through the back door and stood motionless as he took in the scene. Mary Elizabeth looked at him with anxious concern, stunned by Maggie's stillness. Silent tears had never been her style.

Her mother sat down next to her and took her in her arms, trying to comfort her.

"I'll be okay. I am okay. Just give me a minute. This is so hard for me. And I'm not doing it very well. I really thought I could handle this by myself, but maybe Jamey was right and this was not a good idea. But you know how I get sometimes, I always have to do things my own way but now I'm wondering . . ." she babbled.

"Maggie, for God's sake, what are you talking about?" Her mother took her by the shoulders and forced her to look up.

Maggie took a deep breath and said quietly, "Jamey and I are getting married in two weeks. Two weeks from today."

Her parents exchanged a look of surprise and puzzlement.

"Maggie, if you feel this strongly about the man, why don't you just bring him home and give us some time to get to know the fellow," her father said.

"Time is something we don't have a lot of right now . . ." Maggie looked up at her mother and could tell by Mary Elizabeth's expression that she knew.

"Oh, Maggie . . ." Her mother's hand reached toward hers but did not touch the fingers that lay splayed across the end of the table, gripping its edge.

"I'm so sorry. I know this is the last thing you'd ever have expected from me. I hate having to tell you . . ."

"Tell us what? What the hell are you talking about?" Frank was clearly losing patience with his daughter.

"Daddy, we're talking about the fact that I'm pregnant." As difficult as it was for her, she looked him in the eyes.

Frank froze for a very long moment, then began to pace back and forth slowly, as he did when he was angry to the point where he could not think unless he was moving. Maggie had seen him like this only a few times in her life.

Finally, "So. Where's the father?" he snapped through jaws that barely moved.

"He's out of town."

"He's out of town," he repeated. "How convenient. What a guy, Maggie, to leave town and hide out while you break the news to your family."

"It's not like that. And he's not hiding. He's in Toronto," Maggie explained.

"Toronto. How nice for him. Doesn't have the nerve to come here and face us, so he leaves the country." Frank's rising blood pressure was tinging his face ever more scarlet.

"Daddy, he didn't want me to do this. He told me to wait . . ."

"And I'm sure he'll be heartbroken when he finds out that he didn't have to be here when you told us. I'm sure he'll be very upset." He paced again. "Who is this person?"

"His name is Jamey Borders."

"And what does Mr. Borders do for a living?"

Knowing this wouldn't be the worst news she had that day, she said, "He's a musician. He sings and plays the piano and makes records."

"What kind of records?" Her father's face was immobile.

At that moment the back door flung open, and Kevin blew into the room with his usual exuberance.

"Maggie! Hey, Mags is home." He bent and kissed her head, oblivious to the scene into which he'd walked, and as he did so, he put the items he'd carried under his arm onto the table in front of his sister. On top of the pile was the Monkshood album he'd played the last time she was home.

Picking up the album, Maggie stared at the photograph of the five long-haired musicians on the jacket and in spite of herself started to giggle, then laughed out loud as the irony, the absurdity, of the situation became more than she could bear. Her family looked at her as if she'd lost her mind. She was absolutely out of control, crying at the same time she laughed uproariously as her emotions collided like speeding tractor trailers, pounding her fist on the table, tears in her eyes.

Kevin, who had no idea of what was going on, bent to take the album from her. She shook her head, waving him away as she slid the cardboard envelope across the table until it rested in front of her mother.

"This," she announced when she could finally sputter a word, her index finger tapping on J.D.'s image, all long hair and cocky nonchalance, "is your future son-in-law."

No one reacted.

"This is the musician, the piano player?" Her father's

voice rose slowly. "This long-haired punk is the man who's gotten you—"

"He doesn't have long hair anymore, Daddy. Mom, he doesn't look anything like this picture," she assured them, trying desperately to regain her composure.

Frank wasn't listening again. "You walk out on a perfectly good husband—for reasons I've never been able to understand—and then you walk into this house and tell us that you've been fooling around with some wimpy rock-and-roll singer who got you pregnant, who's not man enough to face your family." She started to protest and he cut her off. "What makes you think this guy is going to marry you?"

"There's no question of him wanting to get married. We'd already planned to get married in August, before, well, before I found out."

"And as soon as he found out, he hightailed it for Toronto."

"That's not fair. He's on tour. The dates were scheduled months ago."

"Another break for him. What makes you so sure he'll be back?"

"He loves me," she said simply, "and I love him. More than I ever thought it was possible to love anyone."

"And you think that's enough to justify your behavior? Margaret, to say that you've disappointed us is an understatement. I thought we'd raised you with better morals—"

"It has nothing to do with how I was raised. And it isn't a question of my morals. It happened, Daddy, it happens to lots of people."

"Lots of people are not my daughter." He slammed a large fist on the table.

All the while Kevin had stood listening to the exchange between his father and his sister, watching their faces. At first he'd thought Maggie was kidding, that it was all somehow a big, crazy joke.

"Maggie, are you serious?" he asked wide-eyed. "You really know J.D. Borders?"

"Apparently your sister knows him intimately, Kevin."

Frank had stopped pacing and glared at his daughter, making no effort to hide his fury.

"Frank, that's uncalled for." Mary Elizabeth spoke for the first time.

"Maggie, are you really, um . . ." Kevin waivered between embarrassment and curiousity.

"Yes, Kevin."

"And you're really going to marry him?"

"Yes, Kevin." She nodded.

"Wow! This is unbelievable. This is about the greatest thing that ever happened. God, J. D. Borders is going to marry my sister. That's so cool! Wait till I tell the guys." Kevin raced in the direction of the phone in the front hallway.

"Kevin, you're not to discuss this with anyone outside this room." Frank grabbed his arm, spinning him around.

"Aw, Dad, this is the most exciting thing that ever happened in this family. Probably the most exciting thing that ever happened in this whole town. This guy is the hottest singer. He has the most unbelievable band and he's—"

"Kevin, I said not one word. I'm not convinced this guy is even going to show up."

"Frank, that's enough." Mary Elizabeth rose to face him, blowing her nose with a cotton handkerchief and stuffing it into her slacks pocket. "This is hard enough for all of us, particularly Maggie."

"I suppose you think we should greet this little announcement with a toast and a pat on the back for a job well done?"

"No. Certainly not. But I don't think we need to make this any more difficult than it already is for her," she said softly.

"I can't believe what I'm hearing. You, of all people, to condone this type of—"

"I'm not condoning it, Frank. I'm saying it's done, and we can stand here and shout at each other till the moon falls from the sky and it's not going to change the situation. Maggie will marry him, Frank, whether you approve or not. She's in love with him and it's her choice. Please, Frank, this time, let her marry a man she loves."

Mary Elizabeth was breathless from the control it had taken not to shout. Husband and wife stood and glared at each other.

The phone rang, breaking the silence. Kevin removed the receiver from the wall phone in the kitchen, not wanting to leave the room and take the chance of missing something good.

"Maggie, it's him! It's J.D."

She took the phone from her brother. "Your timing couldn't be worse," she said by way of a greeting.

"What the hell are you doing there?" His voice was full of reproach. "I thought we had agreed—"

"How did you know?"

"You're so goddamned transparent. I've been calling your apartment all morning. It didn't take a genius to figure out where you'd gone. Why are you doing this?" He was clearly angry.

"Because I thought it would be easier for everyone if I got it over with." She turned her back to the room to spare herself from looking at her parents.

"Well, was it?" he demanded.

"No."

"Damn it but you're stubborn." His annoyed exasperation exploded through the telephone.

"Please don't be so angry, Jamey." She was crying again, weary tears, drained of all emotion. "Everyone's angry. Everyone's yelling at everyone else. You were right. I should have waited. I didn't, and I've made things worse . . ."

"Oh, Maggie, I'm so sorry." His anger melted away as he realized how distressed she was. "Calm down, now, sweetheart. Look, let me talk to your father."

"Have you lost your mind?" she whispered.

"Is it that bad then?"

"Yes."

"Then we don't have too many choices, do we. Book yourself onto the first flight to Toronto. We'll get married here."

"No."

"Then Philadelphia."

"Jamey, I don't want to get married in Toronto. Or in Philadelphia. I wanted to be married here, in my home, with my family." She started to break down again.

"Sweetheart," he said gently, "what is the likelihood that that will happen?"

"Not very good," she admitted sadly.

"Then we'd best make some other plans, don't you think?"

"Yes," she reluctantly agreed.

"I want you to think it over and let me know what you want. I'll do anything you want. I don't care where or when, Maggie."

"Jamey, I need to think. Can you call me back tonight at the apartment?"

"Maggie, I'm not so sure you should drive home right now. You're too upset. And I'm willing to bet you've not slept too much these last two nights and you're tired."

"I can't stay here, Jamey." Her sobs were softer now and came from someplace deep within, the rejection by her father having stung her so.

"That's quite enough, Maggie." Her mother took the phone from her with one hand and put the other arm around her daughter. "Jamey, this is Mary Elizabeth Callahan. You're not going to spirit Maggie away to Toronto or anyplace else. She will be married here if that's her choice. I'll not have this go any farther."

"Mary Elizabeth, have you lost your mind?" Frank exploded.

"Open your eyes, and take a good look at your daughter. Will you be turning your back on her, Frank?" Mary Elizabeth's lips quivered, but her voice remained firm. "I will be there on her wedding day, and she will be married in this house, Frank, with or without you. If you cannot find it in your heart to attend, you can spend the day in the hardware store with your buddies or you can go play golf. But I will be at Maggie's wedding, and the wedding will be here."

No one so much as moved. Neither Kevin nor Maggie had ever heard their mother raise her voice to her husband and had certainly never seen her defy him. Frank studied her face for a full minute and, without looking at Maggie, turned and left the room, headed, no doubt, for the sanctuary of his second-floor den.

"Jamey, I apologize for the outburst. We'd like to have a few days to get to know you before you join the family . . . That will be fine. Don't thank me, I couldn't live with myself if I hadn't . . . Yes, well, frankly, I'm not very happy with the situation either, but it's Maggie's life and yours, of course. Now say good-bye to her so that we can hang up this phone. We've a wedding to plan and we only have three weeks . . . Yes, I know Maggie said two, but I simply can't do a proper wedding in less than three . . ."

Maggie and her mother sat in the kitchen and talked for another hour, Mary Elizabeth having brought out a notebook to make some preliminary lists of guests and things to do. She was a notorious planner, and it was a family joke that she could not function without a piece of paper in one hand and a pen in the other. Mary Elizabeth watched as the light slowly returned to her daughter's eyes as she spoke of the plans she and J.D. had made, and silently she prayed, *Dear Lord, please let her be happy this time. Please let him be everything she believes him to be . . .*

Frank had retreated to his den, still in shock over the whole thing. His Maggie, his precious girl, pregnant by some faceless rogue with an overactive libido and a smooth line. He too had prayed. *God, please don't let this guy be as big a jerk as I think he is.*

Around three o'clock that afternoon, Mary Elizabeth had instructed Maggie to go upstairs and take a nap. It would give her father some time to cool down before she spoke privately with him. Tired to the very bone, Maggie had agreed. Unfolding the cotton quilt that lay across the foot of her bed, she lay down and curled up under it. Neither nausea nor emotional turmoil prevented her from falling asleep almost instantly. When she awoke hours later, the room was in shadows, the sun was setting, and she became aware of a darkly clothed figure sitting quietly on the room's other twin bed.

"Frankie," she asked drowsily, "that you?"

"Yes," a soft voice responded.

"Mom didn't tell me you were coming home." Maggie sat up and reached her arms out to her sister who had risen and seated herself on the side of Maggie's bed.

"Mom didn't know. I woke up this morning and had the urge to come home," she explained, then added, "I'm glad I did."

Maggie held onto her younger sister, searching for words. Frankie's chin rested on the top of Maggie's head.

"Your hair's getting long, Mags. It looks great," she observed.

"Thanks," Maggie whispered. "Frankie . . ."

"I know," she said simply.

"Mom told you?"

"I walked into the middle of a conversation between Mom and Dad."

"Dad's livid."

"He'll get over it."

"And Mom's being really good about it, but she's upset and I've let her down. I let everyone down."

"Let's forget about everyone else for a minute. Let's talk about Maggie. Do you love him?"

"More than I can tell you."

"Does he love you as much?"

Maggie nodded.

"Then maybe it's not so much of a disaster," Frankie said gently, removing her short dark blue veil and running long slender fingers through her straight brown hair.

"Not so much for Jamey and me as it is for the folks, I guess."

"They'll come around. You know Dad's all bluster and blunder when he gets upset."

"No lectures on chastity?" Maggie tried to smile, wondering what Frankie really thought.

"Margaret, I'm a nun, not a hermit. I know things happen between people."

"You know what I mean."

"All I really care about is that you do what's right for

you." She'd slipped her shoes off and sat cross-legged on the bed, resting her elbow on her sister's raised knees.

"The irony is that we had planned to get married in August. We were going to drive up here in a few weeks and let Mom and Dad meet Jamey and get to know him a little and then tell them," Maggie told her. "This changed our plans a little."

"When will the wedding be?"

"In three weeks. We don't have the luxury of too much more time before my condition will become very obvious. I'd like to avoid looking pregnant on my wedding day."

Frankie smiled. "Fuel for the local gossip mill."

"Well, I won't be around to deal with it, but Mom and Dad will. I'd like to spare them the embarrassment if I can. I mean, could you hear the gossip, especially coming right on the heels of Kathleen and Tom's speedy march to the altar."

"Hey, this could be the best scandal we've had around here since Mr. MacIlroney left town with his secretary nine years ago." Frankie grinned.

"Tell me the truth, Frankie. Are you upset?"

Frankie paused before answering, then said slowly, "I just don't want you to be hurt. But it's between you and him in the long run, Maggie. And between you and God. No one has the right to pass judgment on you. Not Mom. Not Dad. Certainly not me. I love you too much, Maggie."

"I love you, too," she whispered, her voice cracking as she hugged the tall lanky figure and rested her head against the thin shoulder. "Pray for me, Frankie."

"Every day, love. You can bet your life on it."

Maggie had hoped that her father would emerge from his room by dinner, but when he did not, she went up and knocked on the door tentatively. Facing each other had not been easy, each knowing how much they'd hurt the other, but in the end, he'd reluctantly agreed to give J.D. a chance, though he clearly had no intention of every liking him. He was almost as upset that Maggie would be married by a judge in a civil ceremony as he was over the circumstances. In his heart he still wasn't convinced that the groom would show for the wedding, but if Mary Elizabeth was willing to take the chance on Maggie making a fool out of herself, he could not prevent it.

"For your sake," J.D. said when he called the following evening for an update, "I'm glad your family has come around. I know how important this is to you. But you've certainly put me at a disadvantage, Maggie. Not only does your father think I seduced you, he thinks I'm a coward as well. I've got an awful lot to live down."

"He'll be okay. Just keep in mind that he's determined to dislike you, so you'll just have to prove to him what a sweet guy you are."

"Thanks for the tip," he grumbled. "Is everything set for the wedding? You and your mother get all the details worked out?"

"Pretty much. Actually, Mother has pretty much taken over. I'm still not sure who she's inviting. I gave her a short list of people I absolutely wanted, but beyond that, I told her to use her judgment, so we could have ten people or thirty or five hundred. Of course, if we let him, Kevin would invite everyone he knows, he's so excited. He still can't believe that he's going to get to meet you, and he's in an absolute tizzy over meeting Rick." She laughed. "Rick will be there, won't he?"

"Certainly. He's the best man. God, but he's been unmerciful, Maggie, ball and chain and all that."

"Well, I hope he and Lindy behave themselves. And I hope Uncle Paul doesn't get drunk and cause a scandal."

"Seems to me that it wasn't only Uncle Paul who got drunk at the last Callahan wedding," he chuckled.

Mary Elizabeth heard the car pull into the driveway and nervously peered through the kitchen window. She could tell by Maggie's body language and gestures as she exited the passenger side of the car that her daughter was giving J.D. an earful about something. She went out the side door into the driveway, smiling as she recognized the look of exasperation on Maggie's face. She hoped her future son-in-law was a man of strong character and unlimited humor.

"You told me you had a driver's license," she was shouting.

"I do. You didn't ask me if I had it with me," he replied calmly.

"Lucky for you I went to school with the officer who pulled you over after you went through that stop sign. Hello, Mom." She hugged her mother. "Mom, this is—"

"Jamey," her mother extended her hand. "I've been looking forward to this. Oh, what the heck, skip the handshake and give me a hug."

He did, gladly, welcoming the unexpected warmth. Mary Elizabeth stood back and looked him over from arm's length. Maggie smiled to herself, certain her mother was mentally comparing the man who stood before her with the photo on Kevin's album cover. She could almost hear the sigh of relief and knew exactly what was crossing Mary Elizabeth's mind at that moment. Thank heaven for small favors, she would be thinking.

They had started up the front steps when Kevin burst through the front door. He froze in his tracks, seeing J.D. on the porch.

"You must be Kevin. I'm J.D." He shook Kevin's hand, realizing the boy was awestruck. "I've been looking forward to meeting you. Maggie's told me about your band. Do you think I could hear you play sometime this week?"

Kevin nodded, speechless.

Maggie laughed. "Come on into the kitchen, Jamey. Want some tea? Mom?"

Maggie puttered a bit while J.D. and her mother made some small talk. Kevin, still speechless, hung over the back of a chair, mesmerized.

"Where's Dad?" Maggie asked.

"At the hardware store, where he has been every Saturday afternoon for the past thirty years. Here, Maggie, sit here, I'll move over. So, Jamey, is this your first visit to the States?" Mary Elizabeth had rehearsed some small talk and had decided this would be the appropriate place to start.

"No, no, I've been here several times before. I did get to do a bit more sightseeing this time, thanks to Maggie." The look in his eyes as they followed her daughter across the room dispelled any doubts Mary Elizabeth harbored. "Mags, you feeling all right?" he asked quietly.

She'd found a box of crackers and was nibbling on one as she sat back down, replying to his question by raising her eyebrows and grimacing. He rubbed the back of her neck, his gentle concern telling Mary Elizabeth all she needed to know.

Frank entered the house through the front door, slamming it behind him.

"Mr. Callahan." J.D. had risen immediately and had taken Frank off guard with his direct gaze and his extended hand. Frank accepted the hand more as a reflexive reaction than a sign of greeting or welcome. Advantage: Borders.

"So. You're J.D."

Frank took in the man who stood before him, searching this stranger's face, Maggie assumed, for a sign of weakness —something that would reaffirm his feelings about this man. Maggie knew, too, that her mother was watching him carefully, cautioning him to keep his temper in check.

As calmly as his shattered nerves and his rapidly escalating blood pressure would permit, Frank said with exaggerated pleasantry, "Why don't we two go up to the den and get acquainted."

"That would be fine." J.D. rose from his seat, ready for the confrontation he knew was coming. Frank's manner had left no doubt in J.D.'s mind that he was in for an earful.

"Daddy," Maggie protested with alarm, "wouldn't you like to sit down and have some tea with us?"

"Margaret," he replied sweetly, "I'm in no frame of mind for a tea party."

"Now, Frank," Mary Elizabeth began anxiously.

Frank ignored her.

"Come on, J.D. We've a few things to discuss, you and I."

Frank left the room with J.D., sending a reassuring wink to Maggie as he followed him up the stairs and into the den. Mary Elizabeth listened at the bottom of the stairwell and, hearing the door close quietly, marveled at the restraint

Frank was exercising, knowing he had wanted to give the door a good, hard slam. She was keeping Frank's nitroglycerin handy, just in case.

Maggie heard the back screen door squeak some twenty minutes later and came in from the living room to investigate. She found J.D. sitting on the back steps, and she sat down next to him and put her arms around him.

"Jamey, you okay?" she asked anxiously, wondering just how bad it had been.

"Fine, sweetheart," he said, nodding.

"You had 'the talk' with my father and you're fine?" she asked skeptically.

"Yes. It's okay, Maggie."

"Come on, tell me the truth." She was half tempted to scrutinize his neck for the marks her father's hands would have made had he, in fact, tried to break it the way he'd threatened.

"It wasn't too bad," he reassured her.

"Did you reach an understanding?"

"Oh, I'd say we understand each other very well."

"That sounds ominous. Did you have an argument? I was so worried that you'd get into a big row and you'd want to leave."

"No, sweetheart, that would never happen. I'm not going to get into that with him. He's your father. He loves you, and you love him. I won't come between you. He needed to blow it all off at someone, you know, and I'd decided beforehand that I'd let him yell and be done with it. And that's what I did."

"You just sat there and let him yell at you?" she asked increduously.

He nodded calmly.

"Well, what did he say?" she pressed.

"Pretty much what I'd expected him to say," he replied, "though I have to admit I was a bit amused when he got to the part about how he hadn't raised his daughter to be seduced by some Brit hooligan. I thought it best not to mention that it was you who had seduced me . . ."

175

She elbowed him in the stomach, and he laughed. They sat in silence for a moment or two, arm in arm, watching Otto chase a butterfly across the yard.

"I knew we made a mistake, that weekend in Atlanta," she sighed, leaning her head against his arm. "That's when this happened, you know."

"Most likely," he agreed.

"Not 'most likely,' that was it. I knew we'd regret it when——"

"Do you, Mags? Do you regret it?" he asked suddenly.

"Don't you?" She swung around to face him.

"No."

"You don't?" She sounded surprised.

"Not at all. Look, Mags, the way I see it, we would have gotten married in August anyway. So we're just ahead of the game by a month. We'll get back home sooner, I'll get started on my negotiations sooner, and we'll just have our little family started a little sooner."

Maggie laughed. "You're a master of rationalization, Jamey."

"You'll see how good it will all be. We'll get through this week and we'll get through the wedding and we'll be happy the way we always are when we're together. Only it won't have to end. No more sad teary good-byes, no more lonely nights staring at the ceiling, just wishing for even ten minutes together."

"The worst was when you were in L.A.," she said softly. "If you'd been another few days, if I'd have changed my mind again . . ."

"Don't, Maggie. Don't think about it. It's behind us now, sweetheart."

"Jamey, we could have lost it all."

"No, we could not have, and we never will," he said firmly.

"If I'd gone through with it, I'd have lost you. You'd never be able to love me after I——"

"Hush, sweetheart. It didn't happen. And there's nothing that you could ever do that could make me stop loving you.

Nothing. We will live happily ever after. You, me, and Jesse."

Colleen called to them from the kitchen. Ellie and Elliot had arrived, and dinner was on the table.

"You ready to take on the entire Callahan crew?" she asked, smoothing his hair back from his forehead.

"No problem. Really. The worst is over." He kissed her forehead and helped her up and took a deep breath as she led him through the doorway for his first all-Callahan family dinner.

16

FUNNY, SHE THOUGHT, *ALL THESE YEARS AND J.D. HAS NEVER told me what my father said to him that day. The one time I pressed for details, he shrugged nonchalantly and said it was between him and my father, and it never was brought up again.*

But he had, she grudgingly acknowledged, wowed the whole family that first night—all except Frank, of course, who never did come around until after Jesse had been born. After dinner he'd played a copy of the master for "Sweet, Sweet Maggie" on Kevin's tape machine and had turned her mother into a puddle. Even Ellie had been impressed.

"And this but a week before the wedding, mind you," she heard J.D. telling Hilary. "We weren't even sure if he would agree to give the bride away."

"Did he?" Hilary asked, not really caring.

"Oh, yes." J.D. nodded. "Maggie's mother saw to that. She's little, but she's mighty, Mary Elizabeth is. There'd have been hell to pay if he hadn't."

"I came across some of your wedding pictures when I was doing some background for this show," Hilary told them, "from some magazine or other. Well, there, that's a wedding picture there, isn't it, on the table next to Maggie?" Hilary pointed a manicured index finger to the small oval frame.

Earlier in the evening, as the show had begun, Maggie had turned the photograph slightly to the wall so that she wouldn't have to sit facing the happy couple for two hours. J.D. reached behind her, lifting himself half off the sofa and pressing against her as he strained to retrieve the small framed image. He could barely bring himself to glance at it as he passed it to Hilary's outstretched hand. The sight of the loving pair trapped in time and behind glass taunted him.

Hilary turned the photograph to the camera. In the photo, J.D.'s hand caressed Maggie's upturned face, her eyes shining, tiny white flowers perched behind one ear.

"A lovely photo," Hilary noted, observing that both Maggie and J.D. had turned from the sight of it, much as a creature of the night would turn from the rays of the sun. "What a lovely bride, Maggie."

"She was exceptionally beautiful," J.D. managed to say, still looking away. "It was a wonderful day."

Yes, Maggie agreed reluctantly, it had been a wonderful day. And oh, she recalled wistfully, what a wedding it had been—Everything exactly as she could ever have hoped it would be . . .

The sun had made its appearance at midmorning, and the late July day turned out to be just perfect, cooler and less humid than anyone had dared hoped it would be.

"Maggie, I think you should start getting ready. Especially if you want me to French-braid your hair." Caroline came into the kitchen, having effectively gotten the caterer's people under control, directing them to place the tables where Mary Elizabeth had indicated and to relocate the bar to a more shaded spot in the yard.

Caro had gone upstairs with Maggie, helped her into her dress, and then proceeded to arrange the bride's hair, intertwining small sprigs of baby's breath into the braid so the back of her head, from ear to ear, was a half circle of small white flowers, giving the effect of a semihalo.

"That's exactly what I had in mind." Maggie beamed, the very picture of a glowing bride.

"You look gorgeous, Maggie. Just perfect. J.D. will fall in love with you all over again." Caroline took one more spray and secured it slightly behind one ear.

Maggie walked to the mirror and took a look, then smiled at the reflection. The dress she'd selected, after several days of frantic searching, was just right. High neck and short sleeves, the palest of pink lace fluttered in graceful folds to the handkerchief hem just slightly above her ankles.

"Maggie, how do I look?" Colleen sprang into the room, her dress all muted lilacs and pinks.

"You look adorable. Beautiful." Maggie hugged her little sister.

"Time, Maggie." Ellie, whom Maggie had asked to be matron of honor at Mary Elizabeth's urging, poked her head in. "Wow, Maggie, wait till J.D. sees how gorgeous you are."

"Speaking of whom, has he arrived yet?" Maggie asked.

"He's been here for the past half hour. To say the groom is anxious to get through the ceremony would be an understatement." Ellie preened in front of the mirror, self-absorbed as always, repositioning the strand of pearls she wore around her neck, moving the clasp to the back.

"Is he nervous, do you think?" Maggie asked with the slightest hint of apprehension.

"No, not at all. He just wants to get on with it," Ellie replied, "and I suggest we do so, if you're ready."

"I guess I am." Maggie picked up her bouquet, stephanotis and roses, both pink and white, baby's breath, and lilies. "Let's do it then. Coll, go tell Mom and Dad I'm ready."

Maggie stood on the back porch, surveying the crowd gathered in the yard.

"How many people had you said you'd invited?" she whispered to her mother.

"I don't recall that I said," Mary Elizabeth replied

obliquely, straightening her hat and smoothing the folds of her light blue silk dress.

"It would appear half the town and all our relatives are out there," Maggie observed.

"More or less," her mother said, nodding calmly, and they both laughed.

"Well, I see the caterer's been busy, and the local florist, too," Maggie noted, indicating the arbor of pink roses that had been fashioned midway across the back lawn. "Come clean, Mother, are we about to witness another Callahan production?"

"Well, you know, Maggie, we've lived here all our lives. We know just about everyone in town. And the family's so large. It was so difficult to pick and choose who to invite, who not to invite, where to draw the line . . ."

"So I take it there was no line drawn and you simply invited everyone."

"More or less," Mary Elizabeth tried halfheartedly to appear contrite. "I admit it got a little out of hand, dear. You don't suppose it will upset your intended, do you? All these strangers?"

"Jamey? Nah, he's used to playing to a crowd." Maggie patted her arm.

"Well, you know, you always expect a certain number of people to decline, especially on such short notice. As it turned out, just about everyone accepted, and I can't help but wonder if it's the bride or the groom they've all come to see."

Frank joined them on the porch and looked across the wide expanse of green to where the groom waited for his bride. Next to J.D. stood Rick. Frank shook his head. He'd thought J.D. to be on the very far edge of acceptibility and had been totally unprepared for the arrival of the best man. Rick's size alone was intimidating, but his below-the-shoulder black hair and court-jester attitude made him appear to Frank to be from some distant planet.

Maggie had been adamant that there would be no wedding march, recalling her previous wedding. She wanted to simply walk without any particular fanfare with her mother and father to where J.D. would stand with Rick and Judge Donovan, an old friend of the family who was to perform the ceremony.

The judge nodded to Frank that he was ready, and as Maggie started across the backyard lawn to the rose arbor, holding her father's hand, she heard the sweet strident strains of a bagpipe as it played "Amazing Grace." She looked across the lawn and saw the solitary piper and knew J.D. had arranged this for her. She smiled at him, and he smiled back lovingly as he took two strides toward her, not waiting until her father relinquished her. Frank had backed off more graciously than anyone—particularly Frank—would have anticipated.

No one who witnessed the ceremony could have doubted their devotion to each other. They stood hand in hand, their eyes never waivered from the other's gaze, not while speaking the words that joined them nor while listening to the judge as he addressed them. Maggie's head was high, and at one point J.D. reached his right hand to her face to wipe a tear from her cheek. Other than that one gesture, neither appeared to move.

Judge Donovan instructed them to exchange rings, which Rick, in typical fashion, could not immediately locate. Mary Elizabeth and Frank were both misty as the groom leaned forward to kiss his bride, who met his lips with a look of such passion and love that revealed without question the depth of the feelings their daughter had for this man.

The simple ceremony concluded, the newly married couple turned to family and friends, and kisses and hugs and handshakes followed. Maggie sought out Frankie and presented her bouquet to her sister as she hugged her and wiped the tears from Frankie's face.

"I thought the bride normally tossed the bouquet to the unmarried gals in the crowd," Frankie said.

"Not this bride," Maggie said as she kissed her cheek.

The crowd stepped forward to greet the bride and groom, row by row, as they made their way from the arbor. They were surrounded by cousins, all anxious to meet the groom; old friends of her parents; several aunts and uncles, all of whom expressed their good wishes and took the opportunity to take a closer look at J.D.—and Maggie's waistline.

"Maggie, Aunt Eleanor wants to see you and J.D." Kevin relayed the message he'd been sent to deliver.

"When Aunt Eleanor beckons, you step lively," Maggie said and, taking J.D.'s hand, followed her brother through the crowd. "You know, Aunt Eleanor—my great-aunt who's given us the use of her house for the next few days?"

She grinned, recalling the conversation they'd had on Tuesday evening, when he'd realized they'd made no reservations for their wedding night.

"Oh," Maggie had yawned, covering her mouth with the back of her hand and snuggling into him on the sofa in the living room. "I forgot to tell you. My aunt Eleanor said we could stay at her house until Tuesday when we leave for London."

He had pushed her up to a sitting position and spun her around to look at him. "You want to spend our wedding night at your aunt's house? That should make for a real lively time."

"No, no," she'd laughed, "Aunt El will be staying with Uncle Gus's sister. Aunt El has an unbelievable old house. It's sort of like a Victorian mansion. It'll be wonderful, you'll see. And you'll love Aunt El. She's a darling. Ellie's her namesake; she's actually my father's aunt."

She led him through the throng to an elderly woman seated in the shade, a large white picture hat framing her face, her neck heavily draped with pearls. Maggie bent to kiss her cheek, and as the woman's face emerged from beneath the wide brim, J.D. found himself unexpectedly gazing into his wife's own green eyes set into the face of an eighty-seven-year-old woman.

"They named the wrong one after you, didn't they?" he acknowledged, and the old woman chuckled with obvious delight as he accepted the hand she offered.

"So, this is the one who's had my family in such an uproar for the past few weeks," she said as she greeted him. Patting the chair next to her, she silently commanded him to sit down, which he did. She waved Maggie away, wanting to have a few private words with her favorite grandniece's new husband.

Maggie wandered back toward the crowd, looking over her shoulder once to where her husband sat in animated conversation with the elderly woman. She recalled her twelth summer, when Aunt El had tried to teach her to needlepoint.

"I can't do it," a frustrated Maggie had cried.

"Of course you can," Aunt El had insisted, "and when you do, you will see how all the tiny stitches will come together to form the whole . . . There, you see the flower coming to life, all the little dots of blue will be a violet."

When an exasperated Maggie had thrown it down, her aunt had calmly picked it up and handed it back to her, saying "Margaret, it may be that you'll not learn to needle-point, but you will learn patience. With any luck, you'll learn both."

Though she had never really learned but one stitch, the memory of those summer afternoons never faded. Aunt Eleanor was a wonderful storyteller, and Maggie would sit spellbound for hours, captivated by her aunt's tales. How she, Eleanor, as a terrified nine-year-old, had crossed the ocean from Ireland accompanied only by her equally frightened sisters, Jane, who was not yet twelve, and seven-year-old Margaret, who, some fourteen years later, would become Frank's mother. Before they had boarded ship, their newly widowed mother had pressed into the hand of each of the girls something precious to take with them, sensing, correctly, that she would never see her daughters again. To Eleanor, she gave her own gold wedding ring. To Jane, she presented a tiny opal pin, and to Margaret, her youngest, a gold crucifix that was suspended from a chain as thin as a spider's web.

Having dispensed the only things that she had of value, Anne McMillan turned her back on the ship and made her way through the dirty Dublin streets to return to her two-room cottage in a crossroads hamlet, where her two baby sons were being watched by her oldest boy. This fourteen-year-old had been, since the death of his father but six months earlier, the sole support of the family. At her wit's end with no money and no job prospects, Anne had sent her middle children—her only girls—to join her brother who had found work in a mill someplace in Pennsylvania—wherever that was. With luck and God's grace, her daughters would survive. Maggie had heard the tale a thousand times, each time biting her lip and shedding a tear over her great-grandmother's sad dilemma.

She fingered the worn gold cross that lay right below the hollow of her neck, the same gold cross that had sustained a frightened little girl across a vast ocean. *I was right,* she told herself. *Eloping would have been a big mistake. These are the people who are dearest to me, the people who made me what I am. Jamey needs to know them if he is ever to really know me.*

"Maggie, this is incredible." Caroline put a hand on her elbow. "Your mother is a marvel to have organized such a beautiful wedding in so short a time. Everything's perfect."

"She is something, isn't she?" Maggie laughed. "My mother missed her true calling, Caro. She should have her own business organizing parties for those who lack her knack of pulling things together. Weddings, graduations, christenings, birthdays, you name it. Mary Elizabeth can get the job done. And you certainly appear to be having a good time. I saw you dancing with Rick."

"You know, I may have misjudged him," Caroline told her. "He's really quite an interesting person. Not nearly as boorish as I had once thought."

"He is quite a character, that's certain," Maggie laughed, "but there's really a lot beneath that wildman role he likes to play."

"That's what I was just thinking earlier." Caro's eyes narrowed somewhat, focused on something to Maggie's left. "Speaking of the devil . . ."

Maggie followed her gaze to where Rick stood, alone and fiddling with his uncooperative tie, near the arbor.

"Looks like the best man is having a bit of a problem," Caroline noted. "Maybe I should give him a hand."

Curious, Maggie watched as Caroline started across the yard. She'd taken no more than ten steps before Lindy appeared and draped an arm over Rick's shoulder. Caro stopped in her tracks as Rick began to laugh at something Lindy had whispered in his ear. Caroline turned slowly and walked in the direction of the house, a look of resignation on her face.

Oh, God, not both of them. Could both of my best friends have eyes for the same man?

Hearing her name called out, Maggie turned to find J.D.'s sister waving a camera. Judith had arrived on Thursday, embracing Maggie immediately, confiding, "My little brother is smarter than any of us had given him credit for. And he was absolutely correct. You are delightful. Mother will adore you." Maggie had known instantly that they would become lifelong friends.

Maggie was as drawn to Judith's warm smile as she had been to J.D.'s. Sister and brother were uncannily similar in mannerisms and moods, in facial expressions and speech, and shared the same droll wit. She found Ned, Judith's husband, to be charming, though he was, she thought, very British in demeanor—much more reserved than his wife and brother-in-law. They'd brought their children, sons Alex and David, who were six and four, and their daughter, Cassie, who was not quite two. The three children were positive banshees after the long flight, Judith remarked, apologizing for not leaving them home. Maggie watched with a grimace as Cassie chased Otto through the next-door neighbor's prized and pampered flower bed.

The caterer was ready to serve, and Maggie and J.D. joined Rick, Ellie, and Elliot at their table. A starstruck Colleen joined them and took her place between Rick and Elliot. Maggie winked at Colleen, knowing her little sister was the envy of all the young—and some of the not-so-young—girls in attendance. Rick had been playfully attentive to her throughout the meal and, to her unabashed delight, made a point of putting his arm around her for every photograph.

Kevin, whom J.D. found to be a decent drummer, had

carried his drums upstairs and outside to the brick patio where an impromptu trio prepared to play. Rick tuned up his guitar, and he and J.D. went over some arrangements with Kevin, who had surprised them both by knowing every drumbeat of every song they'd ever recorded, having played along with their records for the past several months with his band. J.D. sat at the piano that had been rented for the day and, removing his jacket, proceeded to roll up his shirt-sleeves.

The first song they played was, of course, "Sweet, Sweet Maggie," and she knew as she watched her little brother's face that he would never forget this day. He was so proud at that moment, not only to be playing as an equal with musicians he so idolized, but to play this special song for his sister, whom he loved so much. Maggie swore she could see a lump in his throat from ten feet away.

Even Frank had looked a bit misty, Maggie thought, and she crossed the lawn to where he sat, wrapping her arms around him from behind. His thoughts had drifted to the scene he'd walked into the previous evening as he'd come down the steps from his den and paused in the doorway to the living room, where he had seen his wife and daughter pouring over an old box of photographs. Maggie held an old high school prom picture in her hands and was laughing at her hairstyle, her youthful appearance, her dress.

"Well, young lady," Mary Elizabeth had said, "I can remember the day you found that dress. You thought it was the most beautiful thing you'd ever seen. Begged for it and, as I recall, promised to do dishes and trash duty for a month if we bought it for you."

"Did I?"

"The entire month of June."

Mother and daughter had laughed, and Frank had felt a tug at his heart as he'd watched them. It had seemed forever since they'd shared these quiet times, Mary Elizabeth and Maggie.

And later, as Maggie's headed toward the stairs for bed on that last night under their roof, she'd stopped to embrace him.

"Maggie," Frank said, clearing his throat, "Maggie, about J.D. . . ."

"Oh, Daddy, please don't say it. I know he's not what you wanted for me. I know you're disappointed in him and disappointed in me . . ."

"Maggie"—he'd had to swallow hard to get the words out—"what I wanted to say was that maybe, well, maybe he's not as bad as I thought he was."

"Thank you, Daddy." She'd put her arms around his neck, knowing the admission had taken no little effort. "Thank you. You don't know how much that means to me."

Frank had held her, stroking her long dark hair, and, for the briefest of moments, she was his little girl again.

Frank's reverie was shattered by a hard-driving song the impromptu band was playing, and he shook his head.

"Don't suppose they know 'Sunrise, Sunset,'" he said, turning around in his seat to face his daughter, and they both laughed.

The younger members of the crowd had gathered around the brick patio, clapping their hands along with the music, then later dancing as the champagne continued to flow. It was, all in all, a wonderful wedding, a memorable day for all who attended.

Maggie had gone into the house with her mother, gathered the bag she'd packed and, as she turned to leave the room, said, "Mom, I don't know if I can ever thank you. For getting Dad to come around, for the wedding, for being so good to Jamey, for giving him a chance . . ."

"He's a darling, Maggie. And even an old fool like your father can't help but see the man is head over heels in love with you. I can't remember ever seeing you happier than you look today. And that is all we want for you, sweetheart; we only want you to be happy. I know it sounds so trite—it's what every mother says to her daughter on her wedding day."

Mary Elizabeth hugged her, tears in her eyes and on her face. "Just be happy, Maggie."

17

JUST BE HAPPY.

In her mind's eye she could see her mother's sweet face—that much beloved face—and the simple blessing echoed in her ears, bringing tears to her eyes and a tug at her heart.

Mary Elizabeth had welcomed Jamey to the family with open arms and an open heart and had come to love him as she loved her own. She would be devastated by this unexpected twist in her daughter's life, Maggie knew. Strange how it goes. As difficult as it was to tell them about him all those years ago, how much more difficult it will be to tell them it's over.

Just be happy.

Oh, Mom—she swallowed hard—*I was. We were. For so very long, we were . . .*

She blinked back the tears lest they begin to run down her face, reminding herself that this was not the time to give in to the melancholy that was beginning to claim her. *There will be plenty of time for tears,* she thought, *and time enough to dwell upon the past.* She forced her attention to the present, immediately realizing she had picked the worst possible moment to tune back in.

"J.D., let's talk about your production experience, which goes back quite a few years. We could call to mind several dozens of albums you produced for other artists, the most memorable, of course"—a sly grin turned the corners of Hilary's mouth upward slightly—"being the *Fields of Glory* album with Glory Fielding. You were lovers at the time, I seem to recall."

Maggie wondered what showed on her face at that moment, hoping it wasn't the nausea she felt.

J.D. reddened slightly, all the while trying to appear casual. "Hilary, my relationship with her ended a long time ago, before I met Maggie."

"But you were in love with her at one time . . ."

"I married the only woman I ever loved," he replied softly.

Maggie's apparent indifference to his quiet declaration was not lost on Hilary, who was becoming ever more curious. She decided to continue this line of questioning to see where it might lead.

"The album you did with Glory remains a big seller. Do you have any comments on that? Or on your relationship? Any regrets?"

Out of the corner of her eye, Hilary could see a steel mask settling over Maggie's face. This was obviously a touchy subject. But why, after so many years of a supposedly blissful marriage, would the mere mention of an old lover cause such a reaction in this woman? She turned back to J.D.'s response.

"No, I have no regrets as far as the album is concerned. It was something Glory had wanted to do at the time, and she was having difficulties finding someone to work with her on it."

Because it was, he could have added, an absolute piece of shit. Regrets? God, yes, from every quarter. That was the most God-bloody awful thing he'd ever been associated with. It still embarrassed him that his name appeared on the cover. It had monopolized six months of his life, not because they were striving to create great music, but because they'd both been stoned most of the time. The recording that had resulted was an almost incoherent collection of abominable songs that Glory had written poorly and sung even worse. It had become unbelievably popular by virtue of its overt bawdiness, most of the lyrics crossing the border into the realm of the obscene. None of the commercial radio stations would air it, and many record shops refused to stock it. Consequently, Glory's career had really taken off after its release. She became a kind of cult figure in its wake. It was the biggest break she ever got and the biggest humiliation of his professional life.

"And your relationship with her?" Hilary pressed for an answer.

"Actually, Hilary, I have no relationship with her, and I haven't in many, many years." He could feel the heat from Maggie's glare as it ate a hole in the middle of his forehead.

"But surely you must see her from time to time—your paths must cross at least once in a while on a social basis, if nothing else. Come, now, J.D., when was the last time you saw her?" Hilary was a pit bull. She would not drop this bone until she was convinced there was not a shred of meat remaining on it.

J.D. felt the flush creeping up above his shirt collar. "Well, actually, I did see her a few days ago. Bumped into her unexpectantly, more or less."

"And you, Maggie, have you and Glory met?"

"Well, yes, of course we've met from time to time over the years." *Assuming of course that you'd count all those times the little bitch cornered me and made a point of telling me she was after my husband. And assuming that last Friday counts, when I caught them together in the bathroom.* Some demon within forced her to add "I could say that recently I've seen more of her than I ever had in the past. More, actually, than I'd ever had any interest in seeing."

Hilary would have given anything to have been in on whatever it was that passed between them, unable as she was to decipher J.D.'s look of chagrin, Maggie's hard, level gaze, a sardonic touch to her voice.

Terrific, Maggie told herself. *This night just keeps getting better and better. It's not bad enough that I have to sit here and talk about that woman, but now Hilary thinks that she's onto something. Because I couldn't resist a jab. Maybe she already suspected, or worse, maybe she knows. How could she possibly know? Of course. Glory. She probably has it spread all over London by now. By midweek, I'll be reading about it in the tabloids.*

Of course, I'll be gone by then. And Glory is welcome to him. God knows she waited long enough for him. Jesus, barely two weeks after we were married, she told me she'd never give up. Well, the little bitch was true to her word.

She bit her bottom lip to keep it from quivering, thinking what a blow this would be to J.D.'s mother, that dearest of ladies who had so eagerly taken her in at their first meeting. Luke Borders had totally disarmed Maggie with her unconcealed joy at their marriage. Luke had made that first trip to England such a delightful experience . . .

Maggie's heart was in her mouth, the thought of a flight across the ocean looming like a nightmare. The apprehension of the flight itself was one thing, but the anxiety that a crash would take not just herself but J.D. and her unborn child filled her with panic. J.D. spoke to her quietly, reassuring her that her dread was unfounded and the plane would most definitely get them safely to England. Soon she did relax and in fact managed a nap on the plane between lunch and dinner as well as a second one thereafter. J.D. had to wake her as they approached their destination, and she laughed when she realized she'd slept through most of the flight.

Judith was already at the airport awaiting their arrival when the plane touched down.

"You're smart to spend as little time in the city as possible," she told them as they piled their luggage into the trunk of her car.

"Why?" Maggie asked.

"The press is on to your arrival," she said, adding dryly, "Everyone wants to print the first picture of you bringing your American bride back to your homeland."

Maggie groaned, and J.D. laughed.

"Get used to it, Maggie," Judith said wryly. "My baby brother is a big deal around here. Everyone wants to see what you look like. The newspapers all want photographs of the woman who brought his bachelor days to a screeching halt."

"Well, how many people will be getting the chance to gape, as it were, at Mom's little get-together?" J.D. inquired as Judith swerved to avoid a car pulling from a side lane.

"Blind bugger," she mumbled. "I don't know for sure. Half the town, I'd imagine, all the family, and some of your old friends. Whom, I'm not really sure. But I do know that Rick checked in when he got back last night, and Mom got a list of names from him."

"Good Lord," he mumbled, "just about anyone could show up."

"If nothing else, you'll be happy to learn I was able to talk her into putting this party off till next weekend to at least give Maggie a few days to get her bearings and to get to know the family a little."

"Thank you, Judith. I appreciate that," Maggie replied. "With all that's happened the past week, Jamey and I haven't even had but a night or two to ourselves."

"Well, how much time you'll have to yourselves remains to be seen with Mother at the helm of the plans, but you should get enough time to catch your breath anyway," offered Judith with a smile.

Maggie leaned back and watched out the window as the countryside grew greener and the sky appeared to become more blue. It was a gorgeous day, and she was fascinated by the scenery, the little villages that appeared unexpectedly around a bend in the road, the occasional pub that seemed to spring from nowhere at a crossroads, the old manor houses that had been part of the landscape for centuries, the fields that spread around them like giant pieces of textured patchwork.

They rounded a curve, and Judith swerved sharply to avoid the old man who ambled along near the middle of the road.

J.D. remarked, "I see old George is still about."

Judith made a face. "And still as daft as ever."

"Still roaming about in the dark?" he asked.

"Not as much, but he shot one of the Mathers' sheep last month or so. He frightens me sometimes, J.D. Someday he's bound to hurt someone."

"I doubt it," J.D. chuckled. "I think he's harmless. Just keep the dogs locked up at night."

"Is that the man you told me about? The man who shot your dog?" Maggie asked, turning to catch a glimpse as the man wandered into a grove of trees off to the side of the road.

"Yes. I doubt he's really as dangerous as Judith would lead you to believe. I wouldn't give it a second thought."

The car left the dirt road and pulled up to the clearing next to a stone and stucco house that looked exactly as Maggie'd thought an English cottage should look. Louisa Borders—Luke to her friends and family—sprang expectantly through the gate of the ivy-covered stone wall surrounding the yard behind the house. Wordlessly, she embraced J.D., holding him for a long time before leaning back to look at him and plant a loving kiss on the face of her only son.

Maggie got out of the car slowly, not wanting to intrude upon the reunion, knowing it had been a long time since mother and son had been together. Wiping a tear, Mrs. Borders turned to her with outstretched arms.

"Come here, Maggie, and let me get a good look at the gal who's stolen my son's heart."

She smiled warmly, and Maggie went to her, taking in the slight form of the woman before her, the reddish hair streaked with gray, the wide smile, and the twinkling blue eyes.

"Well, you're every bit as pretty as my children have told

me. Lovely eyes, an odd shade of green, wouldn't you say? Now come inside and we'll have a chance to chat. I want to hear all about the wedding. Every detail. Judith's told me a bit, but I want to hear it all."

And with that she led them through the gate into the most beautiful garden Maggie had ever seen. Flowers of every color and size vied for her attention, so much so that she did not know where to look first. Neat cobbled paths meandered from bed to bed, and a stone bench shaded under an ancient apple tree was surrounded by columbine of various colors and heights. The tall spiky delphinium bloomed in the sun, not just the blues Maggie recognized from her grandmother's garden, but pinks and whites and lavenders. Along the wall grew roses, whites and reds and more shades of pink than Maggie could have imagined possible. She caught her breath and exclaimed, "Mrs. Borders, I've never seen anything so beautiful!"

"Thank you," Luke replied, clearly pleased. "It's a bit of a hobby, a good way to pass the time. My friends call me Luke, dear, and that's what I'd like you to call me. Come inside for some tea, and maybe later, if you like, we'll come back out and go through the garden. And be sure to see Judith's garden, too. She's absolutely amazing with plants."

The afternoon was spent pleasantly, with more chatter and lively conversation about the wedding and the upcoming party. A neighbor stopped by and was invited in for tea, and Maggie found herself feeling more relaxed and at home than she'd ever anticipated. When it was time to turn in for the night, she hugged Luke and thanked her for making her feel like a part of the family.

"But you are part of my family, Maggie, you and this sweet child my son has conveniently neglected to tell me about," she said forthrightly, with no apology and no sense of reproach. Maggie's jaw dropped open slightly, and J.D. laughed self-consciously.

"Ah . . . Mom . . . I, ah, that is, we, ah . . . ," J.D. sputtered and his mother laughed, turning what could have been an embarrassing moment into a light exchange.

"For goodness sake, J.D., did you think I didn't know? Did you think your sister could keep that from me?"

"Judith told you?"

"She didn't mean to, J.D.—don't be hard on her. I can't say it wasn't a shock at first, and I don't mind telling you I wasn't terribly happy. Until Judith got back, that is, and told me how absolutely lovely Maggie is and what a sweet and fine girl you'd married." She turned to Maggie. "I can't tell you what a relief you are, my dear. I was sick to heart worrying about what sort of gal he'd gotten himself involved with. He'd been involved with some, well, let's say, unsuitable girls there for a while. I was scared to death he'd be bringing one of those home some day."

"Well, Mom, I'm happy you found Maggie acceptable," J.D. laughed.

"She's more than acceptable. She's a delight."

Luke put her arm around her son and daughter-in-law as they headed toward the steps. "I'll see you two in the morning. And J.D., I've made up Judith's old room for you. I think you'll be comfortable in there."

"In Judith's old twin beds?" he blurted.

"Of course not," she chuckled. "I had Ned move them into my room. You'll find the accommodations satisfactory, trust me."

Luke returned to the sitting room, shaking her head and muttering to herself, "Twin beds, indeed."

The accommodations were just fine. Judith's old room was at the end of the hallway, a large corner room with windows on two sides and it's own bath. Luke had thoughtfully placed a vase of the varied pink roses and white delphinium on the table next to the bed, which J.D. told Maggie had been his parents. She snuggled next to him and he asked how she'd liked her first day in England.

"I loved it. I love your mother and I love your home. And I absolutely loved the garden. I want to get out there tomorrow and have her show me everything. Maybe someday I'll have one like that at home."

"Well, home is wherever we are, you know," he told her.

"Then I guess I am home," she said, moving closer, her arms encircling him.

"I guess you are," he replied and reached over and turned off the light.

"And this tall shrubby-looking plant with the white plumes is what?" Maggie was making her way around the garden with Luke the next morning after breakfast.

"Goatsbeard, it's called. For the obvious reason." The tiny white flowers on the long graceful feathery plumes did, indeed, call to mind the silky beard of a goat. *"Aruncus* is its proper name."

"These I know. These are Canterbury bells," Maggie said, moving on down the row, and Luke nodded. "What's this yellow flower?"

"They are centaurea," Luke explained, "a form of cornflower."

"Cornflowers? I thought they were blue."

"Some are. But some centaurea are yellow. And those red ones next are red valerian. The mauve ones are valerian also, as are those white and pinks. Then in the next bed we have dianthus—pinks, as you will. I'm a bit partial to them, so I grow a variety. These here, the first ones, are cottage pinks. The darker ones with the purple tinge are maiden pinks, and these with the slightly darker circle in the center, these are Allwood."

"I recognize these." Maggie had walked down the path a little farther and stopped in front of a bed of tall flowers. "Foxglove. But I've never seen these colors before."

"They come in all colors, from white and cream to dark rose and shades of pinks and purples. That's a fine old plant, but highly poisonous."

"Digitalis." Maggie was pleased she'd remembered. "They make the heart medication, digitalis, from foxglove. My grandmother had these also but only the dark pink ones. I like the cream-colored ones, I think, even better. And what's the green stuff there, the ones without flowers?"

"Aconitum. Monkshood, it's called," Luke laughed, "the

namesake for my son's band. We used to have them all around the back doorway, until the apple tree shaded them out completely and I had to move them. It's taken me quite some time to get them to come around; they dislike being shuffled about, you know. J.D. always liked the name. It didn't surprise me in the least when he used it for his band. I used to tease him that his friends would think him odd, naming his band for his mother's garden flowers. They're not quite ready to bloom, won't be for a bit yet. They also are poisonous, even the seeds."

Maggie spent a part of each day in the garden with her mother-in-law, learning the flowers and their preferences for sun or shade, moist or dry soil, their habits and care requirements. Later in the week she spent a day with Judith, whose garden was even larger and more elaborate than her mother's and filled with more flowers of more varieties than Maggie could ever have imagined. When Maggie commented on how much there was to learn and remember, Judith presented her with a small leather-bound book, it's pages blank, so that she could take notes, should she ever need a reference.

Maggie found Judith's garden to be particularly intriguing. She had managed to obtain seeds for some relatively obscure and rare plants and had nurtured them until she had clumps of many old varieties of flowers that, abundant generations ago, had fallen out of fancy and all but disappeared from modern gardens. Maggie was pleased that Judith had offered to send her seeds for some of those flowers that she had most admired, once Maggie had a garden of her own.

On Wednesday evening, Maggie had surprised J.D. by asking if there was a church nearby.

"Yes, in the village. The church we always went to. When we went that is. Why?"

"Can we see it tomorrow?"

"Sure. We can walk down if you're up to stretching your legs a bit. Or we could drive down if it rains again."

Maggie felt she needed the exercise, so in the morning

after the rain had ceased, they strolled off down the road, past Judith's house and on down the mile or so into the village proper. The church was at the edge of the tiny hamlet, set back off the road, with the requisite tower and churchyard lined unevenly with white headstones.

They walked around the side of the church into the cemetery, and Maggie followed J.D. down the path to the left of the gate, being careful not to step on the graves, many marked with only small flat stones. He walked to a grave not far in from the fence and stood silently looking down, his hands in his pockets. Maggie read the name on the stone. David James Borders.

"Your father?" Maggie asked.

"Yes." He looked back at her and said wistfully, "I wish he could have met you."

"You were named for him," she observed.

"Yes. Only he reversed the names because he didn't want me to be a junior." He appeared thoughtful for a time, then told her, "My dad was a good guy, Maggie. A great person, a lot of fun. I hope I can be as good a father to ours as he was to Jude and me."

"You will be." She rubbed his back reassuringly.

"Hello." They heard a call from the gate and turned to see a tall, thin elderly man with a round face.

"It's the old vicar. Come on, Maggie."

As they approached him, the old man smiled.

"I thought that was you, J.D. I'd heard you were back for a bit. With your bride." He greeted Maggie with an outstretched hand. "Welcome, young lady."

"Thank you." She smiled.

"This is Reverend Andrews, Maggie. He's an old friend of the family."

"Delighted, my dear." The old man patted her hand, still entwined with his own.

"Maggie wanted to see the church," J.D. explained.

"Then by all means, let's bring her inside," he said and led them around the side to the front door.

Maggie stepped into the stillness of the tiny church and

looked around. The altar was sparse, much less elaborate than the Catholic churches she'd spent so much time in, and there was none of the marble she was accustomed to. The wooden pews were highly polished as was the railing around the altar, and the interior smelled faintly of wood polish. It was lovely in it's simplicity, and she said so.

"Perhaps we'll see you some Sunday while you're visiting then," he suggested.

"Perhaps you will," she said, smiling.

On the walk back to the house, J.D. asked, "What was that all about anyway? Why the sudden interest in the church? You getting religion?"

"I've always 'had religion,'" she answered with a laugh, "though it's been quite some time since I've gone to services on Sunday. I have to admit I miss it. And it seems to me that we should agree on how we'll raise our family. Jesse should have some religious upbringing. And we should probably have a church of our own."

"Would you like to come down on Sunday for the service, Maggie? Is that what all this is leading up to?"

"Yes."

They both laughed, and she added, "And it occurred to me that it would be nice if we asked the vicar to bless our marriage. Do they do that sort of thing in England? They do in the States."

"Yes, of course they do. And I'm certain he'd be pleased to do that. When would you like to have this little blessing performed?"

"Maybe Sunday. After the service but before the party. What time was the party anyway? Two o'clock?"

"I think so."

"Maybe we should ask your mother what she thinks."

"I know what my mother will think. She'll think it's a lovely idea. Which it is," he said as he draped an arm over her shoulder. "My parents were married there, you know. As well as my grandparents. And my sister. And we were all christened there."

"Okay, okay. I get the point," she laughed.

"Want to stop at Judith's?" He pointed to the left side of the road toward his sister's house.

"Certainly." She crossed the road with him, and they walked up the path leading to the front door and knocked. Alex admitted them.

"Mom's out back."

They walked through the hall into the back of the house and out into the sunny garden where Judith was retrieving a mud-splattered Cassie from the huge puddle into which the toddler had blithely sashayed.

"There are times, Maggie, when you understand that the good Lord makes children as cute as He does merely as a means of assuring they'll survive times like this," she quipped, nodding her head toward her youngest child. "Cassandra, you're a mess. Alex, take your sister in to Mrs. Young and ask that she clean her up. Oh, bother," Judith grumbled as she rinsed her hands in her watering can, then grinned as she dried them on her brother's shirttails. "And can you believe that Ned wants another?"

"Four might be a bit much to handle, Jude," J.D. chuckled.

"Three is a handful. You'll be wise to have just the one, little brother. Remember this, Maggie, if he tries to talk you into a second . . . or a third."

Maggie laughed, and the memory of that day and Judith's words were to become a family joke over the years as both her family and Judith's multiplied.

Luke's house was bustling with activity when the small group returned from church on Sunday, following the blessing of the marriage by the vicar. Judith had arranged for a caterer from the nearest city and had pretty much taken over the party preparations from her mother, who was content to leave the planning in her daughter's able hands. There had been barely an hour to spare between the conclusion of the simple ceremony and the party's appointed hour. Luke had decided early that morning that the flower arrangements scattered here and there throughout the house lacked sufficient fragrance and would benefit greatly from the inclusion of some lavender. Maggie trailed behind her with a flat basket as her mother-in-law inspected the bed of herbs, selecting the best stems and clipping them neatly with her old garden shears.

"We have an early arrival," announced J.D. from the doorway.

A beaming Hobie Narood burst into the garden and quickly followed the cobbled path to where the two women stood.

"Mama Luke, it has been too many years." He embraced her fondly.

"Too many, indeed," Luke said, planting an affectionate kiss on his broad, brown face, "but, oh, my wandering boy, it's a delight to see you again."

"And you." He gave her another hug before turning to extend a hand to Maggie. "Ah, the little lady from the jazz club."

"You remembered." A pleased Maggie took his hand.

"Of course." He grinned. "I told you that same night, did I not, J.D., that this was a woman worth pursuing?"

"You did at that." As J.D. approached, Maggie noticed the tall woman who accompanied him. She moved like a cloud, seeming to float across the cobbled walk without a sound.

"My wife, Aden," Hobie introduced her, "you know, of course, J.D.'s mother . . ."—Luke embraced her warmly— "and this is his new wife—"

"Maggie Borders." Maggie took in the woman with fascinated eyes.

Aden was fully as tall as her husband—a good six feet—but thread-slender where he was beefy, his roundness a stark contrast to her sharp angles. Her very bones appeared to define the colorful strapless dress, a sarong of sorts, which wrapped around her body and was held fast on one side by a large, plain disk of hammered gold. Her earrings, fashioned of gold beads, fell to her shoulders. Her hair was cropped short, her eyes the palest amber, almost yellow in the midday sun, her skin a glowing deep brown, rich walnut to her husband's lighter oak. She carried herself with a natural grace, an inborn dignity. Maggie had never seen a more singularly elegant human being. Aden acknowledged Maggie's greeting with a slow smile but did not speak.

"We are early," Hobie told them, "and I apologize if we have interrupted your preparations."

"Not at all," Luke assured him. "We'll put you to work. J.D., I see Judith pulling into the drive. You and Hobie give her a hand with whatever it is she's doing there." Luke turned to Maggie and handed her the scissors, saying, "Some of the light pink phlox would be lovely, I think, Maggie. Snip some, if you would—leave the stems long, remember—while I get this lavender into some water." She bustled toward the house, a thousand unfinished details buzzing in her head.

"Please, Aden, sit and visit with me while a cut a few of these for Luke." Maggie motioned toward a stone bench. "Have you been here before? In England, I mean."

"Only once"—Aden's voice was clear, her words slightly clipped—"to visit Narood's mother before we were married. It was then that I first met your husband, his family. Narood is most fond of them, J.D. and Luke."

Maggie smiled to herself that Aden referred to Hobie by his last name only.

"This is my first trip," Maggie confided. "I was so nervous meeting J.D.'s mother for the first time, wondering what she would be like, what she would think of me . . ."

"I was also unnerved," Aden told her. "It was so strange, a new country to see, everything so different. Narood's mother did not approve. It was unpleasant . . . She had wanted Narood to marry Western, not in keeping with the traditions of his father."

"I'm sorry," Maggie offered.

"Narood's mother had much bitterness to her husband and did not wish Narood to know him, even after his death," she explained. "Narood came to Anjjoli to find his family and found also himself. Our uncle convinced him to follow Anjjolan tradition when it came time to look for a wife.'

Maggie glanced up quizzically.

"It is the custom in Anjjoli to marry first from within the family," Aden continued.

"Within the family?"

"Narood's father and my father were of the same tribe . . . cousins."

Maggie recalled J.D. telling her that Anjjolan custom also permitted more than one wife and wondered if subsequent wives had to be from the same "family" as well.

As if she'd read Maggie's mind, Aden added, "Secondary marriages may involve other tribes. In Narood's case, however, it does not matter. There will be no other wives." Her eyes twinkled as she made her proud pronouncement.

"Good for you," Maggie whispered, and Aden laughed heartily.

"That is one Western custom we agreed to follow," she told Maggie.

"Your dress is wonderful." Maggie admired the richness of the cloth, deep purple and gold in color.

"It is traditional," Aden said simply, "woven on hand looms."

"I didn't know anyone still wove fabric on hand looms. Except maybe a few leftovers from the sixties."

"It is not so difficult." Aden shrugged.

"You know how to do that?" Maggie, who could not sew a straight seam if her life depended on it, was obviously impressed.

"Of course. It is quite a relaxing pastime actually. Though this particular design"—she fingered the hem of her dress —"became a bit tedious."

"You made that? The fabric?" Maggie put her flower basket down, bending closer to inspect the cloth. "It's positively wonderful. I'm in awe. How long would something like this take?"

"Some weeks"—Aden shrugged—"you do a bit now, a bit a little later."

"But you don't make the cloth for all your clothes . . ." Maggie marveled that women still did such things. Particularly this woman, married, as she was, to a man who was certainly well-off.

"Only for special things. Like your wedding party," Aden told her. "We live very simply in Anjjoli. When last we came here, Narood bought Western clothes for me to wear, but I did not like them. Very contrived, I thought. And very uncomfortable . . . your undergarments." She shook her head at the memory.

"I know exactly what you mean." Maggie laughed and stood up, her arms loaded with flowers. "We'd better get these in to Luke, she's in a bit of a frenzy. Let's see if we can give her a hand."

Shortly before two, several cars pulled into the flat field across the road and parked. Maggie watched from a hall window as Rick alighted from a dark blue sedan and took the arm of his blond companion as they hurried toward the house. She gasped with pleasure. It was Lindy.

"What a wonderful surprise," she exclaimed as she hugged her old friend. "I had no idea you'd planned to come."

"Actually," Lindy laughed, "I didn't. Rick came home with me after the wedding, and he suggested I take a week or so off and come back with him. It sounded like fun, so I did."

Rick bear-hugged Maggie.

"So," he said, "the old man treating you okay?"

"Just fine. And I'm having the absolute time of my life here."

"You really haven't had a honeymoon, Maggie. Aren't you planning on going away for a few days?" Lindy asked.

"I feel as if we have. But we will be in London this coming week. Jamey has a few appointments, so I'll be going with him and staying for a few days. I guess that will be it until we decide what we're doing." Maggie had moved back into the hallway just as the door opened again and a group of ten or twelve entered.

"Hey, Rick, how you doing? Where's the groom? And where's the bride? We're all dying to meet her," a tall, bearded man with red hair greeted Rick.

"Don't know where the groom is, Jack, but this is the bride." Rick proceeded to introduce Maggie to the late-arriving guests, all musicians, all old friends of Rick's and J.D.'s from years past.

Maggie's attention was drawn to the last entry into the hall, a tall, spectacular woman in her early twenties, long golden hair pulled back from the most breathtakingly beautiful face she'd ever seen. Her dress swirled around her, a silvery gossamer cloud, cut very low in the front, flowing with every curve of her body to her ankles. Maggie stared in fascination at the ethereal creature, whose entrance had made the bride, in a pale cream silk dress that pulled slightly across her growing middle, suddenly feel like the resident frump.

"So, Rick," Maggie heard her say in the most honeyed of voices, "where's the boy?"

"Ah, he's about," Rick appeared to be caught off guard by this latest arrival. "It's nice to see you again, Glory. I hadn't known you'd been invited."

"Actually, I wasn't. But Tommy kindly offered to bring me along. Now, Rick, you honestly didn't think I'd let this pass without making an appearance. Do tell me where to find J.D. I've a few words for him."

Maggie's heart all but stopped in her chest. Who in the world was this woman? Her conversation with Rick made it apparent that she was more than a casual aquaintance, certainly more than just another musician friend. Maggie held her breath as J.D. walked through the front door with his sister and stopped dead in his tracks.

"Glory. What a surprise," he managed, eyebrows raised. Judith glared with open hostility.

"I'll just bet it is," she purred and walked slowly to the doorway, "maybe not as great a surprise as I got when I heard you'd been married. Nice of you to let your old friends in on the secret. Are you going to introduce me to the lucky woman?"

"Of course. Maggie . . . There's Maggie." He turned to his wife with a wink and a look of chagrin touched with amusement. "Maggie, this is Glory Fielding. I worked on Glory's last album with her. Produced it, actually. Glory, this is my wife, Maggie Borders."

The tall blonde took the longest time to look Maggie over very carefully from head to toe. Maggie stared into the woman's flint-gray eyes and willed herself not to blink.

The two women were still sizing each other up when Rick, in an attempt to avoid an exchange that could embarrass everyone, called to J.D., "Look who else is here. Andy and Harry both. How long do you think it's been, J.D., two years, three? Come introduce your bride . . ."

A collective sigh of relief seemed to escape from most of the guests gathered in the hallway. As Maggie moved through the crowd with J.D., she sensed the real confrontation with this woman was still to come. She knew she was at a disadvantage, not knowing who she was or what role she'd played in J.D.'s life. He'd never mentioned her, not one time.

An hour or so later, Maggie had been about to go into the garden when she heard J.D.'s voice from the other side of the door.

"To tell you the truth, Glory, it never occurred to me to call you. I didn't think we had that kind of relationship. Actually, I didn't think we had any relationship, other than maybe friendship."

"How can you say that to me? We lived together for six months, practically the entire six months before you left last fall."

"Glory, you know as well as I do that was a lark. Don't look at me as if I'm telling you something you didn't know. You used me to get that album produced. There was no love lost there."

"Are you telling me you didn't love me?" Maggie could almost see the woman's lips form a seductive pout.

"Are you telling me you ever thought I did?"

"J.D., you're a bastard. You know very well how I feel about you." Glory's voice was a silken purr. "You left the country without so much as a good-bye and the next thing I know, you're coming back with a wife. I'll never forgive you for this."

"Look, Glory, I'm sorry that, well, that apparently you and I had a totally different idea as to what went on between us. I never thought for a moment you took me any more seriously than I took you. And very honestly, you'll forgive me if I tend to view your theatrics as less than heartfelt. I think your pride may be a bit wounded, but I sincerely doubt if your heart's broken."

"You are a callous son of a bitch. I loved you, J.D. I still do."

"You needed me, Glory. And right now, it would appear that what you need is a little help getting a new contract, judging by your escort today."

"That was a cheap shot. Tommy adores me. He's a nice guy."

"He also owns the second largest record company in the country."

"Well, think twice if you expect them to sign you up as a solo. You'll have to get past me to get to Tommy, J.D." Her venom spewed out in the sweetest of voices.

"Well, I think Tommy's a better businessman than that. However, if I have to go to another company, I'll do it. Or I can go to the States if necessary," he replied calmly. "I'm just sorry you're talking on this way, Glory. It never occurred to me we wouldn't be friends."

"I don't want to be your friend. I want things to be the way they were."

"No chance. I am very much in love with my wife, Glory. You're wasting your time."

"We'll see. I'll always be around."

Their conversation was interrupted by Judith, who took her brother by the arm to steer him to his grandmother. Glory opened the door and all but fell on Maggie, who'd hastily taken a step or two back to make it appear that she was about to go outside. The look on Glory's face as she sized up Maggie was chilling.

"So, the little bride. You're not what I'd have expected

him to take up with—'cute' really isn't his style, you know?" Her eyes narrowed into thin slits. "Don't think for a minute that you'll be able to keep him. I don't expect it will take much to coax him from your bed back into mine, so I wouldn't go to the bother of having the sheets monogrammed."

Maggie was mesmerized—the mouse spellbound in fascination by the snake.

"I believe in being up front about things, so you might as well know. I want him back, Maggie." The words were delivered matter-of-factly, as if there could be no question that she would succeed. "And I don't easily give up when I want something."

Before Maggie could open her mouth, Glory was past her, into the dining room where she gathered up her escort, sashaying from the house with not so much as a glance over her shoulder. Maggie was still riveted to the spot when she felt a hand on her arm and turned, ashen-faced, to look up into Rick's eyes.

"Ah, I see Glory's gotten to you," he whispered. "Don't take her seriously, Maggie, not for one second. She never meant a thing to J.D. I know that for a fact."

"She's so intimidating. So gorgeous and sure of herself," Maggie said, grimacing, then confided uneasily, "I heard her tell Jamey she's in love with him."

"Rubbish," Rick laughed. "Glory doesn't know the meaning of the word. And I doubt she ever had such a notion before she'd heard he was married."

"She said she'd get him back . . ."

"She never had him to begin with." Rick put his arm around her gently.

"I never even heard him speak of her."

"I've no doubt. Look, Maggie, you should talk to J.D. I'm sure he'll reassure you that she doesn't mean a thing to him. Don't give her another thought. Trust me, there's nothing for you to be worried about as far as she's concerned. Now let's do something that will bring that smile back to your face." He fished inside his jacket pocket. "Here, take a look at the photos I took at your wedding last week. Great shot of your mother, don't you think? And here, here's the bride and groom . . . Handsome couple, wouldn't you say? And look at this one of Caroline . . . She's beautiful, isn't she?"

"Yes, she certainly is." She pushed Glory to the back of her mind as she gazed down at the photograph, at Caroline's shy smile, the hint of a blush tinting her cheeks. "Rick, you took this? It's wonderful."

"It's easy to take good photos when the subject is so lovely," he mumbled as he stuffed the packet back into his pocket. "How long have you known her?"

"Known who?" Maggie had been momentarily distracted as another small group of strangers filtered in through the front door.

"Caroline."

"Oh, gosh, ten years maybe. We roomed together at college. Why?"

"She's just a very interesting person, that's all. Smart and sweet and—"

"Oh, no, you don't, Rick Daily," she told him sternly. "Don't you be playing my two best friends against each other. If you are seeing Lindy—and evidently you are— leave Caro out of it."

"I've no intentions of playing anyone against anyone else," he said somewhat gruffly. "I was just curious about her . . . She's a very different sort of woman. Lindy's such a fireball, you know. She's so wild and sort of reckless, a good match for me, I suppose. But I always feel, I don't know, calm when I'm around Caro."

"Well, things may not be so calm if Lindy gets wind of it." She poked him in the ribs playfully. "So if you're going to continue this relationship with Lindy, I'd suggest you put Caroline on the back burner and leave her there."

"Maggie"—Judith stuck her head around the corner— "Grandmother Jennings is looking for you."

"I'm coming," Maggie told her, then turned to Rick before stepping out into the garden. "You tread very carefully where Caroline is concerned, Rick. She's not the sort of woman you play with."

* * *

Maggie could not wait to probe J.D. about Glory, and she did the moment the party had ended and they'd gone to bed.

"So, tell me about Glory."

"Not much to tell," he said, having fully expected the conversation to turn to this topic. "Glory wanted to do an album last year. It was some pretty awful stuff. She asked me to work on it with her. I went into the studio to listen one day, we ended up getting stoned, and I ended up working with her, and it took us six months to produce the most dreadful piece of trash I've ever heard. You've no idea how humiliating it is for me to hear any of it. And yes, I had an affair with her. I hate to even use that word, because it connotes some manner of emotional involvement. And there was none, not as far as I was concerned. It was one of those things that happened more or less out of proximity and convenience. But I was never in love with her, and I never pretended to be. I suspect whatever feelings she thinks she has for me surfaced after she heard I was married and after she started looking for someone to work with her again."

"That's pretty much what Rick told me," she said.

"Oh, so you checked this out already, did you?"

"He brought it up. This afternoon. After Glory advised me she hadn't quite finished with you," Maggie told him. "I hadn't asked him."

"It's okay if you did. I was trying to find some private minute or two to talk to you alone, but it seemed you were always in the midst of a conversation. And for the record, just so you never have to wonder, I am very much finished with Glory, in spite of what she might have said to you. She likes a bit of a drama, you know."

She stared over his shoulder toward the night beyond the open window.

"She called me cute," Maggie grumbled.

"Who did?" He yawned.

"Glory." She spat out the name.

"Well, you are cute," he whispered, "cute as a button."

"Oh, please," she groaned, and he laughed.

"What's wrong with cute?" he asked.

"Coming from someone who looks like Glory, cute is an insult," she told him crankily. "Puppies are cute. Small children are cute. A pregnant woman on the brink of thirty is not cute. And she knows damned well there wasn't another woman in this house as beautiful as she is."

"That's sheer nonsense." He pulled her over to him. "You're much more appealing than she is. You're the one I fell in love with, the one I married. And why this sudden concern about the way you look?"

"In case you haven't noticed, I've gained almost ten pounds. And my hair's gone stringy and my coloring's off . . ."

"All temporary conditions, sweetheart. Didn't the doctor tell you that?" he reminded her. "And your hair looks fine and your face is a constant source of joy to me. Don't give her another thought, Maggie. She simply has no meaning in our life together."

"Can she really do what she said? About making sure you don't get a contract?" she asked after several minutes had passed.

"I doubt it." He shrugged off the possibility. "She may work Tommy over a bit, but he's not stupid, you know. He's not likely to let someone walk away who could make money for his company. And I've always made money for whomever I've recorded for. I wouldn't give it a second thought. I'm having lunch with him this week in the city, so we'll have to just wait and see how it plays out."

It played out pretty much as J.D. had predicted. Tommy had been more than happy to offer J.D. a good solid contract, which called for three albums over a five-year period. To J.D.'s amusement, Glory's name never was mentioned.

"So what would you like to do now," J.D. asked Maggie over dinner in a quiet, elegant restaurant. "Would you like to take a trip? I've a little time to spare, you know. I'm employed, but I don't have to start work immediately. Would you like to go someplace? Paris? Rome?"

"What I'd like is to spend a few days here in London. Then I'd like to go back to your mother's for a bit. It's nice to have the time to get to know them, your mother and Judith and the kids. We'll be going back to the States sometime soon, I would guess, and we won't see them for a while. Paris and Rome can wait," she said. "Tomorrow I'm spending the day with Lindy. We're going shopping. In case you haven't noticed, I have exactly three articles of clothing that still fit me comfortably. It's time for me to buy some clothes specifically designed for my expanding midsection."

"Well, then, by all means, shop with Lindy tomorrow. I'll see what Rick is up to. Maybe we can get together with some of our old cronies."

"Which old cronies?" She raised an eyebrow.

He laughed. "Some of the guys we used to hang around with years ago when we started out. Harry—you met him on Sunday—has a new band and I'd like to check them out. And maybe drag Hobie along if he's still in town."

"He is," she told him. "He and Aden are staying at the Dorchester."

"Then I'll ring him up in the morning," he said, adding, "I was happy to see that you and Aden hit it off so well. I doubt she was looking forward to the trip—the only other time she'd left Anjjoli was the one time Hobie brought her here to meet his mother."

"She'd mentioned that. Mrs. Narood apparently doesn't care much for her, which is sad. Aden is wonderful."

"She is that. And she seems to have given Hobie roots, you know? I doubt he'd even realized how much he'd missed by not knowing his father until after the man died. But his mother, who raised him all those years, remember, was incensed that he had—in her opinion—turned his back on her and preferred the 'uncivilized' culture of his father."

"Does Hobie make a lot of money?" she asked.

"I would think that he should. He's highly regarded, worldwide, highly sought after. And he's slated to begin a long tour in about six weeks. I'd say he does very well. Why do you ask?"

"Aden told me she makes some of her clothes," Maggie said thoughtfully. "I mean, right down to weaving the cloth. And it struck me as odd—more than odd, actually—that she would do that. And they live very simply. She said their house has only four rooms, and Hobie and his cousins built it in a sort of family enclave."

"So?"

"You don't think it's odd that an internationally acclaimed musician would build his own house while his wife weaves the fabric for the clothes she wears?"

"Hmmm, now there's a thought," he mused. "Maybe Aden could teach you how to—"

"Don't even think about it," she laughed. "But I can't help but wonder, Jamey. Where do you suppose all Hobie's money goes?"

A week or so later, as Maggie trailed around behind Luke as she tended her garden, an unexpected call came from Mary Elizabeth. The realtor that Maggie had contacted to find them a house phoned and wanted her to call him as soon as possible. She hurried outside to tell J.D. the news.

"Jamey, guess what? You'll never believe this. I'm so excited—"

"For heavens sake, Maggie, calm down," he said, looking up from the newspaper.

"I just spoke with my mother. She got a call from Mr. Lynch. You know, Mr. Lynch, the realtor I talked to back home, the one who's looking for a house for us. He told my mother it's for sale. Jamey, can we go home? Jamey, I'm afraid someone else will buy it, and I'll never forgive myself if—"

"What the hell are you talking about?" He folded the newspaper and dropped it to the ground as he looked into her shining eyes.

"My house. My house is for sale. Oh, Jamey, please, can we—"

"What house?" He hadn't a clue.

"My house. The one I showed you, remember, with all the chimneys and—"

"And the overgrown yard and the peeling paint and the crooked front porch?"

"Yes, yes. It's for sale. Can I call him and tell him we're coming back and not to sell it to anyone until we look at it?" she begged.

"Maggie, I don't think we'll have to rush back. I doubt there'll be a long line of buyers for that old place. I can just imagine what it must be like inside. I would suspect that the realtor may get a lot of curiosity seekers, but few real prospects."

"Jamey, I don't want to take that chance. I want to call him. I want to go back. Please, Jamey."

"Call him and see what he has to say," he suggested, then said to his mother, who was pruning a rose bush, as Maggie flew into the house, "Maggie has her heart set on this house that looks as if it's about to tumble down in the next bad storm."

"If she likes it that much, maybe you'd better go in and talk to the realtor." Luke smiled.

"She hasn't even been inside this place, but she's enamored by it."

"Then you'd best go in and see what the man has to say about it, J.D."

He walked in the back door in time to hear Maggie say "Well, no, I don't know when we can get there, Mr. Lynch, it's not as if we're around the corner. I'm sure there are, but if you could just hold off showing it to anyone for a few days, I'm sure we . . . It would be absolutely criminal for someone to knock that house down and build apartments—please don't tell me that. Well, maybe by Thursday . . ." She looked at J.D. with pleading eyes. He smiled and nodded, and she hugged his neck, telling the realtor that they would, in fact, be there by Thursday. She hung up the phone and wrapped her arms around him.

"Thank you, thank you." She danced joyously.

"Just a minute, now. First we'll have to see when there's a flight. Then we'll have to see the house. Maggie, we may not want it. Maybe it needs a roof and a heater and God knows what all. It may cost more to fix it up than it will to buy it. How much are they asking anyway?"

She stepped back and looked at him sheepishly. "I forgot to ask."

He laughed.

"It can't be all that much, do you think? I mean, obviously it needs some repairs. The realtor told me it does . . ."

He shook his head, still laughing, and called the airport.

Thursday at one o'clock, they walked up the drive with the realtor. Maggie was hardly able to contain her excitement while J.D. was wishing that he was still sleeping on the plane.

"Now, keep in mind that it is being sold 'as is,'" Mr. Lynch was saying as he unlocked the front door, pushing hard to force it open. "She—Miss Whiteside, that is—didn't use this door very often . . . Here we are. Now, what about that staircase?"

It was lovely, rising from the right of the front door to the second floor, a beautiful stained glass window at the landing bringing the only light into the downstairs hallway.

Maggie turned to the left of the hall and peeked into a sitting room. The windows were heavily draped and tightly closed, the air musty and suffocating. A room opened beyond, a huge parlor crammed with furniture, and across the hall, a large dining room. Thin, uneven fingers of peeling wallpaper reached from every wall. Layers of dust covered everything with a thick gray film.

Maggie walked into the dining room and found J.D. staring up at a large hole overhead where a chandelier had hung. The chandelier was on the floor, shattered into a thousand pieces, surrounded by a good portion of the plaster ceiling. He looked from her to the ceiling, then to the floor and back to her again without comment.

"I told you it was likely to need some repairs," she said archly and, without so much as a blink, turned heel and walked into the kitchen, hearing him chuckle as she left the room.

The kitchen area, a rabbit's warren of small rooms, could have possibilities, she thought, and a large rounded conservatory, filled with withered plants long dead, opened off to the left. There was a large screened porch, or what was left of it, off the back. J.D. viewed it all with a most skeptical eye, but one look at his wife's face told him he'd never be able to talk her out of it.

He sighed deeply and said to the realtor as Maggie ran up the steps to check out the second floor, "How much are you asking for this pile?"

18

MAGGIE SIGHED, RELUCTANT NOW TO TURN HER INWARD SIGHT from the glow of the memory. *Those were the best years of my life, settling into the house, having the children, and living out those carefree days, so full of love and the tiny joys of everyday routines. Did I treasure them for what they were? Savor the sweetness of those days even as they passed? God, but we had everything . . . love and youth and time.*

She was powerless to look away from those early times, those dearest times, when the children had started to arrive in such rapid succession, each a miracle of love in his or her own right. Starting with Jesse. *God, but I'd been scared to death, that first time, but oh, how beautiful it had been. How beautiful that whole first year together had been . . .*

"I have to hand it to you, Maggie," Caroline said as they dragged the Christmas tree in through the front door. "I never would have believed this place would have been habitable this quickly."

"Maggie beat the contractor's men into a frenzy. Believe me, Caro, she was unmerciful," J.D. told her. "And just when they thought they were almost through, she made them start on the second floor."

"Amazing." Caroline shook her head in wonderment, the change in the house had been so dramatic.

"So was the bill," J.D. told her.

"It was worth it every penny, and you know it." Maggie grinned at him and again admired the finished result.

The sitting room, where they'd decided to put the Christmas tree, had been transformed from a dark, dingy cave into a cozy nest. The carpet was a thick, deep rose wool, the loveseat and sofa, both large, comfortable overstuffed pieces, had been covered with a dark green fabric sporting florals in Maggie's favorite shades of rose and lavender and cream, the walls, a gentle rose and white stripe. Two small wing chairs on either side of the fireplace had tiny checks of rose and cream, each home to a needlepoint pillow in a rose design made by Luke as a housewarming gift. Shutters painted cream covered the lower sashes of the windows, the tops draped with a simple swag of lace. Pictures found in the attic hung once again on the walls, and a collection of old hand-painted porcelain teapots, found wrapped in newspapers dated 1931 and stashed in a box in a second-floor closet, paraded across the mantle, interspersed with boughs of white pine and bunches of dried baby's breath and roses, like tiny nosegays. Maggie'd had J.D. assist her in hanging ropes of white pine around the lace-covered windows. The effect was lovely. Even Miss Whiteside would have approved.

Maggie dragged a box into the sitting room from the hallway and went back out and returned with some paper bags.

"Christmas ornaments," she said to Caroline. "These, in the boxes, were in the attic. Wait till you see."

J.D. finished putting the tree in the stand and secured it, then went into the kitchen and made coffee while Maggie showed Caroline her treasures. Maggie had found the finely blown glass ornaments, colored, sequined, and feathered, in a trunk in an attic alcove. She opened the bags of new decorations she'd bought, and they discussed where to put what. J.D. returned with three coffee mugs.

"Jamey, here," she said, handing him an object wrapped in tissue. "Be very careful, please, when you put her on the top of the tree."

He gently unwrapped the paper to find a beautiful angel, bisque face and golden hair, white satin dress, and wings like gossamer.

"She's lovely, Maggie. Where did you find her?" he asked.

"In the trunk with the other Christmas things. I took her to the dry cleaner's to have her dress and wings cleaned up. I was afraid I'd ruin her. She is perfect, isn't she?" Maggie beamed as J.D. placed the angel at the top of the tree.

"So, what do you hear from Rick?" Caroline asked as she fastened a small glass parrot onto a branch.

"Hmmm?" Maggie was digging absentmindedly in a box from which she extracted a glass Santa. "Oh, Rick. Not a whole lot. We saw him on and off last summer, but I haven't talked to him in a few months. Why do you ask?"

"No particular reason."

"Here, Caro, hang this one with the feathers up there," Maggie pointed toward the top of the tree.

"Is he still seeing Lindy?" Caro stepped onto a small stool to reach the designated branch.

"Far as I know he is, when he's here." Maggie put down the box and stole a sideward glance at Caroline. "Why the sudden interest?"

"I just haven't seen Lindy in a while and was curious, that's all," she said, shrugging casually. "How about we put those sparkly angels on the upper branches, like a heavenly choir."

"Perfect," said Maggie, beaming happily. "This will be the most perfect Christmas tree ever."

Later, when Caroline had left, J.D. put Christmas carols on the stereo and joined Maggie on the floor in front of the fireplace. The faint glow of the fire draped its soft sheen across the room. The shadows from the crèche figures on a nearby table were magically cast by the pale light onto the far wall, the dim forms of Joseph, Mary, and the shepherds looming as enormous, eerie shapes that seemed to move slightly as the flames flickered.

"So, what is it that has you so deeply wrapped in thought?" he asked.

"Christmas. The baby. The house. You," she replied. "I never knew just how good it could get."

He pulled her closer, resting her head on his shoulder.

"Do you realize," she asked, "this time last year we didn't even know each other? And now here we are, settled into our own home, our baby a little more than a month away. It's absolutely mind-boggling."

"Hmm, amazing," he agreed. "You are aware, of course, that this will be the last Christmas when things will be this tranquil, aren't you? That by this time next year, young Jesse will be crawling around and grabbing at the tree and playing havoc with the decorations? And, I'd venture, there will be a mountain of toys for the young master next year."

"This year," she laughed and reached over to the shopping bag near the chair and pulled out a large, soft brown bear, a huge red satin bow tied around its fuzzy neck. "Jesse's first bear."

She propped him under the tree, and they sat in silence for a few minutes, listening to the recorded choir.

"It's magical," he said softly. "It's a magical season and a magical night. And just think, we have your left ankle to thank for all this."

She smiled and snuggled down farther in his arms.

"And your eyes. Your emerald eyes. They're so beautiful. Especially in this light, with the fire so close," he said thoughtfully.

The words came to him in a rush and with an amused Maggie watching, he grabbed the first piece of paper he could find and wrote them down:

> Pools of fire, draw me near.
> Whisper, only I can hear.
> Green eyes shining in the night,
> Warm me with their gentle light.

Softly, softly, call my name . . .
Green eyes burning with the flame.
Dreams that hold me, in your eyes I see
Pools of fire that beckon me.

And so "Pools of Fire," his first solo hit song, was written on the back of a Christmas card envelope, a loving tribute to his wife and to the quiet night they shared as their first year together wound to a close. It had hit the charts two weeks after its release and had stayed at the number one spot for well over a month. Unfortunately, it would be his last hit record for almost three years.

An insistent pressure in her abdomen woke Maggie early on the morning of the tenth of February, 1976, and she panicked momentarily, halfheartedly praying for one more day. In spite of all her reading and the natural childbirth classes they'd attended at the local hospital, she was scared silly. She rose silently, remembering she was to time the contractions, and searched through a dresser drawer for the stopwatch she'd used when she had been serious about her running. Those days seemed so long ago. She prayed she wouldn't be in labor this time tomorrow.

As it was, she was blessed with a relatively short labor and an uncomplicated delivery. Jesse David Borders was born right before dinnertime, much to the delight of his parents. He was healthy and beautiful, vocal and alert. One of Maggie's fondest memories throughout her lifetime was the image of J.D. in the delivery room, holding the small bundle that was their first child, speaking softly to him and watching the baby follow the sound until father and son were eye to eye, baby staring intently, father with tears in his eyes and on his face.

Ravenous after the intense physical activity of the day, Maggie ate the dinner that the nurse brought her, then sent J.D. out to get her a roast beef sandwich from the local ale house. She devoured it and part of his as well.

Jesse was ravenous, too, they found, when the nurse

brought him to her for his first meal. Maggie held him to her, and his mouth sought her frantically. She jumped as he began to nurse.

"Take it easy, little boy." She laughed and looked up at J.D. "He's got a mouth like a little vacuum cleaner. Slow down, baby."

She nuzzled his soft head and watched him nurse blissfully, his eyes closed and his tiny hand clenched in a fist. A light flashed before her eyes, and she looked up to see J.D. with the camera.

"Oh, no. Don't tell me you're one of those dads who has to capture every moment with his camera."

He laughed good-naturedly. "Not every moment, Maggie, but this one is special. You look so beautiful. And he's so beautiful. It's a lovely sight, you and Jess."

"You look a bit misty-eyed, Jamey," she observed.

"No doubt," he admitted. "It's been a big day for all of us. And we have this lovely little boy. What a miracle it all is, Maggie. Watching his birth was fascinating, but it all went too quickly. I've not had time to reflect on it until now. Seeing you hold him, nursing him, he seems such a part of you. Such a part of us. It's absolutely incredible."

"Do you want to hold him?" she asked.

"Is he finished with his dinner?"

"I guess so. He's asleep." She handed the tiny infant into his father's arms.

"He's just adorable, if I do say so. Who do you think he looks like? Do you think he looks like me?"

"Maybe. I can't tell, truthfully. He reminds me a bit of Kevin when he was a baby, but I really can't tell."

She smiled as he seemed not to hear her, so lost was he in their son. When he looked back at her, she motioned to the side of the bed for him to sit down next to her. She leaned over and put her arms around his neck.

"Thank you," she said.

"For what?"

"For all of it. For loving me. And for Jesse. And for being with me all through this."

"I wouldn't have missed it for the world, are you kidding? This was the happiest, most exciting day of my life, Maggie."

"Time for the youngster to go back to the nursery," announced the nurse who appeared in the doorway.

"So soon?" Maggie was reluctant to let him go.

"He'll be back soon enough for a snack. You might want to get some rest."

"Rest? I'm high as a kite. Let's call my folks and Caroline and Lindy and your mother and Judith and Rick," she suggested, "and Frankie. I want to talk to Frankie."

By the time their first anniversary was but three weeks away, J.D. was itching to go back to London, having spent a good part of every day working steadily in his little home studio—a small outbuilding set back behind the house that had at one time served as a stable. He was working on some songs he'd offered to write for Rick, who had done absolutely nothing, workwise, since the band had split up. J.D. had hoped that the half-dozen songs he'd written for Rick would spur him back into the studio.

"Why can't you and Rick do that here?" she asked. "What's the point in spending all that money for a studio and then have to go someplace else anyway?"

"It's Rick's project. And even if he is ready to record and wanted to do it here, we'll need engineers and other musicians, Maggie. The studio's been a godsend, but he'll need live musicians. And left to his own devices, Rick may not make an effort to even look at this stuff. Besides, it's time Jesse met his other grandmother and the rest of his family."

"Well, I can't argue with that. Luke's absolutely dying to see the baby, but if Rick doesn't want to work, that's his business, don't you think?"

"Rick is lazy and irresponsible and would party his life away. Working will keep him out of trouble." *If it isn't already too late,* he told himself, disturbed by rumors passed along by mutual friends.

And so they spent the next two and a half months visiting

with Luke, who adored Jesse and was grateful for the opportunity to have the family with her. When J.D. suggested he and Maggie look for a small house to rent for the duration of their stay, Luke had bristled indignantly, and Maggie supported her, preferring her mother-in-law's company and home to a house some miles away. As long as Luke wanted them, they would stay with her. And the added bonus was that she proved to be a wonderful baby-sitter.

While J.D. stayed in London, Maggie sketched out her property back in the States, noting sunny spots and shaded areas, and Judith helped her draw up some plans for Maggie's garden. Several nights a week J.D. returned for the evening but took Maggie back into London with him in the mornings, leaving the baby with a delighted Luke. The visit had been a happy one for Maggie as well as J.D., who was well pleased with the way Rick's album turned out. J.D. had played on only two cuts but had lent his production experience to the project, which meant essentially letting Rick be Rick. The end result was a spectacular series of guitar solos that enhanced Rick's reputation as a craftsman and an innovator and earned him a platinum record and numerous assorted awards for his efforts.

Maggie and J.D. had a party to celebrate their first anniversary as well as Jesse's birth, pictures of which landed in a London newspaper. It had irked Maggie relentlessly that a photo of Glory Fielding, taken at the studio party celebrating the completion of Rick's album, had appeared on the same page. Beautiful Glory, standing between Rick and J.D., an arm around both of them, her golden blond head tilted in J.D.'s direction. He had sworn he'd barely spoken to her all night and had been on his way out when she had nabbed both him and Rick and had swung in the direction of the ever-lurking photographer.

Soon it was almost November, time for them to leave. Luke reluctantly relinquished Jesse at the airport.

"He's such a love, J.D., and ever so much more pleasant than you were as a baby," she mused, confiding to Maggie, "J.D. was an absolute terror from the day he was born until he was well past four."

"You're welcome to come back with us," Maggie told her. "It would be wonderful to have you visit."

"Oh, Maggie, I'd love to," Luke said, shaking her head, "but I'm afraid not even this darling baby could coax me across the ocean in a man-made bird."

When they were back in their own house and stretched out in their bed, she asked, "When will you be starting to work on your own album?"

"Probably right after the New Year."

"Oh, bother." She wrinkled her nose and groaned.

"Now what was that for?" he said.

"It would appear Jess is going to have a sibling," she announced, awaiting his reaction.

"What? So soon?" He sat up in surprise.

"I'd expect to hear that from my mother, but not from you," she laughed.

"When?"

"I'll have to check with the doctor to be certain, but I suspect around July."

"How did that happen?" he asked.

"The same way it happened the last time." She lowered her voice to a whisper. "I think it always happens the same way, Jamey."

"Another baby." He plopped back on the pillow, pondering the news.

"You don't mind, do you?"

"No, of course not. It's wonderful. I just hadn't expected it so soon, that's all."

"Neither did I." She propped herself up onto one elbow. "But all the symptoms are there, and I feel just like I did the last time. So I'm sure."

"Well," he said, pulling her close and snuggling her, "any guess as to what this one will be?"

"It's another boy," she said with deliberate nonchalance.

"Oh, is it now?" he mused.

"Yes. It is."

"Do I get to name this one, or does he come, as his brother did, with a name?"

"Tyler. James Tyler," she yawned, stretching out next to him.

"But what if it's a girl?"

"It isn't. But if it is, you can choose any name you like, okay?"

"I think we made this deal last time," he recalled, laughing.

The following July, James Tyler Borders arrived just in time to help his parents celebrate their second wedding anniversary.

19

"TIME FOR ANOTHER BREAK . . . WE'LL BE RIGHT BACK." HILARY reached for her water glass, found it empty, and with a bored smile went to seek a refill. *This is all very nice,* she was thinking, *but I need to get to him. There are things he knows that no one else knows—except maybe her—that I'd love to be able to drag out of him. I'll bet he knows where Daily was for those four months when he all but disappeared from the face of the earth.*

The couple on the sofa sat in an uneasy silence. J.D. turned to his wife and shuffled through the scramble in his brain for something to say, but no clever words would come.

He could tell by a look that had crossed her face from time to time that she had not been untouched by the past. He wondered what had gone through her mind. Was there a longing to go back, to relive it all again, or merely a review of events, no more than the scanning of the table of contents in a magazine?

She gave no sign; her expression, for the most part, had been as tightly controlled as his own. He had felt a breaking of his own heart with each image that had emerged from the closet of his own memories, as he had pulled each out and held it before her, searching for the right one, much as he had seen her do with dresses before an evening out.

"This one, Jamey?" she would say, holding a garment up to her body. "Or this one? Which would work best?"

Which would work best, indeed, he thought. *If I knew that, we'd be crying in each others arms by now.*

"I can't take anymore." J.D. turned to Maggie, rubbing the palm of his right hand with the fingers of his left, the tension having caused him to dig his nails into the flesh without even realizing he had done so. The massage gave him little relief.

"You brought this on yourself," she told him. "Don't start just because she's out of earshot."

"You're carrying this too far, Maggie," he pleaded. "If you'd only hear me out, you'd know it's not what you think."

"I think the circumstances speak for themselves."

"Damn you." He banged an angry fist onto the top of the coffee table. Maggie jumped, as did the cameraman and two production assistants. "You're so goddamned willing to believe the worst. Will you destroy this family without listening to the truth?"

They stared each other down. Hilary stood in the doorway and stepped into the room before either could blink. *Very interesting. Maybe before the night is over I should try to divide and conquer, as the expression goes.*

"So, let's resume here," she said, smiling, her hopes renewed. "J.D., many of your contemporaries have had serious drug problems, a few of whom did not survive. Some of those who died were close associates of yours. How were you able to avoid the involvements that afflicted some of your closest friends?"

"Well, I can't claim to have been lily-white, Hilary. There was a time, when I was younger, when I experimented a bit," he hesitated, not wanting to lie. He could not deny he had used drugs in his younger days, yet he did not wish to elaborate, knowing his children—particularly his teenage sons—were glued to the television and hanging on every word. "Of course, all that ended when I married Maggie."

"Would that Rick Daily had been so fortunate," Hilary noted, watching his eyes.

"What do you mean?" he asked cautiously.

"Well, I recall the rumors that he was heavily involved with drugs. There were all sorts of stories going around that he had a serious addiction at one time."

"Well, he may have dabbled with this or that." J.D. was not going to discuss his best friend's past problems for the sake of adding a touch of sensationalism to what he knew must be a lackluster interview.

Dabbled was the very least Rick had done, and God knows he paid dearly for it. In some ways, he's still paying the price, though no one knows that but me and Maggie. He'd been into it real deep for a while, though not, time would prove, as deeply as Lindy had been.

J.D. had completed the recording of another album—a commercial failure, though the critics had acclaimed his efforts—and immediately set off with Maggie on a belated second honeymoon. After dropping their sons off at his mother's, they spent six weeks rambling—no itinerary, no reservations—Greece, Italy, France, Spain, living an incredible, romantic, once-in-a-lifetime dream. They'd returned reluctantly to England, happy though they were to see their sons. Jesse and Tyler had run Luke into the ground, she joked, but she'd had a wonderful time.

J.D. called Rick the day after they'd arrived but was unable to get an answer at his apartment. He tried the next two days without success and happened to mention it to Judith one morning as they sat in their mother's dining room having their morning tea.

"Keep trying," Judith told him. "My sources tell me that Lindy is here with him."

"Lindy? Great! Maggie'll be delighted."

"I'm not so sure. I hear she's quit her job and come to stay with him."

"I don't understand why you think that would bother Maggie . . ."

"My sources tell me they're messing with some heavy stuff," Judith told him levelly.

"How heavy?" he asked, putting his cup down quietly.

"Big time." She nodded her head up and down very slowly, her eyebrows arched, her demeanor grave.

"Lindy, too?"

"In a very big way, or so they tell me," she stared at him intently. "And you, J.D., are you off the stuff?"

"Good God, Jude, I haven't had so much as a joint since I met Maggie."

Finally, he had to ask, "Okay, so how'd you know anyway? That I used to smoke."

Judith laughed, repinning a few stray hairs that had slid from the tight dark twist at the back of her neck. "You have to be kidding, J.D. Did you think I was stupid? Jesus. 'How did I know?'"

"Guess I wasn't as smart as I thought I was," he acknowledged.

"J.D., I know just about everything you did up until your nineteenth birthday and you went to Germany on that tour. I admit I lost track of you there for a while, but I could fill in a lot of highlights from your early days."

"How'd you hear so much?"

"Friends. Your big sister is very well connected. I heard about almost every move you made there for a while."

"Like what?" he felt compelled to test her.

"Like Lilly what's-her-name taking the train down to London that time on the pretext of visiting her girlfriend from summer camp. Only she and her girlfriend spent their long weekend in that apartment that you and Rick and Hobie had. The person who related this little tale, incidently, was scandalized, since you'd just turned eighteen. Of course, my informant didn't know you'd long since lost your virginity. Now that was a scandalous episode."

His jaw almost dropped to the floor. "You couldn't possibly know about that."

"Of course I could. I know who, where, and when."

"You're bluffing."

Judith leaned back in her chair and sighed, a sly smile on her lips as she related, "You were fifteen years old. I admit I've forgotten the girl's name, but she was eighteen or nineteen and worked in Mr. Dixon's pharmacy. Shall I continue?" she asked smugly.

He was speechless.

"Damn," he said when he'd found his voice again, "you're good, Jude."

She laughed again, then noted, "My sources are very good."

"This is your way," he told her soberly, "of telling me that those same sources are telling you about Rick."

She nodded glumly.

"And you're certain they know what they're talking about this time?"

"Absolutely certain." She hated telling him as much as she had hated hearing it herself. Rick was like family and Lindy was one of Maggie's best friends.

"Would you be insulted if I checked in with my own sources?"

"Not at all."

He went into the kitchen and called around to a number of old friends. Judith's sad news had been immediately confirmed.

"Your network is incredibly accurate," he told her, "but my God, Jude, how will I ever tell Maggie?"

"Tell me what?" Maggie had been out jogging along the four-mile trail she'd laid out for herself, and her unexpected return startled both J.D. and Judith, who exchanged a look of conspiracy. Balancing a cup of coffee in her left hand, she struggled to remove the sweatband from her forehead. "Come on, Jamey, tell me what? Why the gloomy faces on this lovely morning? First morning since we've arrived that it's not raining . . ."

"Well, Maggie . . . Lindy and Rick are in London." As the words left Judith's mouth, she became aware of the expression on her brother's face. *Don't,* it pleaded. *Too late,* she apologized.

"Great! That's wonderful. I had no idea Lindy was

considering a trip over. What a coincidence. Let's call them. Maybe they can drive up for a few days. Maybe tonight. I'm dying to see them, Jamey." She reached for the phone and looked up at him. "What's the number?"

"Maggie, put the phone down." J.D.'s voice was soft, but the seriousness was unmistakable.

She hesitated and looked across the room at her husband.

"Hang up, Maggie. They're not at Rick's."

"How do you know?"

"Because I already called there. And I checked around a bit."

"Where are they then?" She felt a bit confused.

"I'm not quite sure. Out of town was all I was told."

"By whom?"

"An old friend."

"So call someone else. Call some of your many mutual friends." She held the receiver out to him.

"I've already done that."

"And?"

"Sit down, Maggie," he said gently.

"Jamey, has something happened to them?"

"Well, yes, sort of. Maggie, I don't know how to tell you this. Judith heard the rumors, and I checked them out with a couple of people because I didn't want to believe it myself."

"What rumors? What are you talking about?"

"Maggie, it seems our good friends have developed some very unsavory habits." He wasn't sure he could get the words out.

"What kind of habits?"

"Heavy drug habits." She was wide-eyed, and he knew he had to tell her the rest. "Heroin."

"Heroin." She sat dumbfounded, the one word seeming to echo in the silence of the small room. It seemed to take forever for her to find her voice again. "Who told you?"

"Some friends."

"Who? What friends?" she demanded.

"Jason. Harry. Will."

"There has to be a mistake." Her voice trembled.

"There's no mistake, Maggie. Both J.D. and I have heard

it from a number of sources." Judith spoke up for the first time.

"How do you know the information is reliable? How do you know these guys know what they're talking about?" Maggie turned back to J.D.

"Jason has apparently been using with Rick. He's been supplying him for the past few months."

"Nice bunch of friends you have. Junkies and pushers," she spat disgustedly.

She rose and walked from the room. He heard the back door slam and saw her walking across the field, past the small barn and out toward the woods beyond. Her hands were jammed into the pockets of her jacket, her head hanging down. Judith looked up, sadness reflected in every line of her face. She watched her brother as he followed Maggie from the house and into the early morning mist.

He found her seated on a low rock, making circles in the dirt with the toe of her right foot. Her face was wet, tears spilling down onto her knees. He sat behind her, placed a handkerchief in her hands, put his arms around her, and rocked her gently in the circle of his arms.

"Don't run from me, Maggie," he whispered. "Don't run away from me when you hurt."

"I can't deal with this. I don't understand this."

He heard the anger in her voice and waited for her to explode with it.

"How could they be so goddamned stupid? Why would they get involved with something like this? They can't possibly be so ignorant that they don't know that stuff can kill them. What could they possibly be thinking of?"

"Maggie, people become addicted, and they cease to think. They go from one hit to another, and they generally don't think about too much in between."

"How can you be so blasé about this?"

"I'm not being blasé, Maggie; I'm trying to deal with the reality of the situation."

"How could Rick let this happen?" She begged J.D. for an explanation, as if he would have one to give.

"I doubt that Rick is in control of the situation at this

point. And you know how he is, Maggie; he's not a very disciplined person. He's always been one to more or less go with the flow of things. I suspect they did it for a lark, played around with it a bit, then found themselves playing around more and more. It's my guess that Rick's been using it on and off for a while, then Lindy probably wanted a try."

"I'll kill him for this," she said, weeping. "And Lindy. Of all people to get into something like this. Why would he even give the stuff to her, knowing how she is?"

"That's assuming he has some control over her, isn't it? How likely do you think that is?"

"I want to talk to them. I want to sit down with them and—"

"Maggie, don't do this to yourself." She looked at him with a puzzled expression. "Even if we knew where to find them, you can't rationalize with an addict. All you'll end up doing is berating yourself for not being able to make them stop. The best we can hope for is that one or both of them will decide it's gone too far and they want to clean up their lives."

"I can't understand your attitude. Two of our best friends are shooting heroin into their veins on a steady basis, and you're throwing up your hands and saying let them do it!"

"No, Maggie, you've missed the point entirely. I can't change the situation. Believe me, if I thought anything I could do or say would make the least bit of difference, I'd not hesitate for a second. My God, Maggie, Rick's been closer to me than a brother for years. But he's on his own with this. The fact that I understand the situation doesn't mean I like it. And I know I can't change it. Only Rick and Lindy have that power, Maggie."

"Don't they realize that people die—"

"Rick certainly knows the dangers. He knows enough people who didn't make it through."

"How could he think it could be different for him?"

"Maggie, don't we all believe the truly bad things only happen to other people? That somehow misfortune is meant for someone else. That we lead charmed lives . . ."

"Do you believe that?"

"In a way. I have everything that I could ever hope for. I'm doing it all exactly as I want. I work when I want and with whomever I choose. I'm very fortunate in that. And there's no secret that I believe I'm the luckiest man alive to have you and the boys. You're everything in this life to me, Maggie. I couldn't live without you."

"Sure you could. If I died tomorrow, you'd have to go on living."

"You won't die tomorrow. And I wouldn't let you go without me. They'll have to take us both at the same time, sort of a two-for-one deal."

"What a romantic thought. And morbid. I don't want to talk about dying anymore, Jamey. This has been the most depressing day ... ." She leaned back into him.

"It's only ten A.M.," he noted with a glance at his watch. "Want to go back to the house and collect the lads and go for a walk or maybe drive into town?" he suggested.

"Walk into town," she told him.

He groaned. "I'll have to carry Tyler. And then Jesse'll want me to carry him, too."

"I'll occupy Jess. Come on." She stood up and pulled him along with her.

He held her for a moment. "You feel better now?"

"No. But I can deal with it a little better."

They walked back across the field, headed toward the house, holding hands. Rounding a bend in the path, an old man came upon them, his approach sudden and silent. He was dressed in a tattered tweed jacket and faded black trousers, an old brown bowler covering his thin gray hair.

"Morning, George," J.D. addressed him, and the old man merely grunted a kind of greeting, his eyes darting only briefly in Maggie's direction as he scurried on his way.

"J.D., that's him, isn't it?" She tugged at his sleeve, looking over her shoulder. "That's—"

"George Brenner," he finished.

"His eyes are creepy," she whispered, "sinister. I get a chill up my spine every time I pass him. I see him all the time when I run. He scares the wits out of me."

"I think your imagination gets the best of you some-

236

times," he said. "George is hardly sinister. A bit odd, perhaps, but hardly sinister."

As they went through the garden gate, she turned and said, "I want to write Rick a letter."

"What will you say?"

"That I love him. And Lindy. And I hate what they're doing. That if they need or want help, that we're both here for them. That I think they're both stupid beyond belief and that I despise their drug habits and want to slap some sense into both of them. That if they kill themselves, I'll never forgive them. That I don't want to see or hear from either of them until they're straight or want to be. And that if I never see them again, it'll break my heart."

He looked down at her and smiled gently. "Do you think it will do any good?"

"Maybe not for them," she replied as she walked past him into the house to write the letter that would not be read by its recipients for eight months.

Arriving back home to the States, Maggie first blamed her lethargy on jet lag, then on the heartache she felt over Lindy and Rick's predicament. But when it lasted beyond two weeks, a quick look at the calendar told her she was pregnant again. J.D. was elated. So was she when she wasn't sick.

She was grateful he was home with her those first few months, when she had a queasy stomach, an endless capacity for sleep, and two very active young boys to keep up with. She napped when the boys did and often slept beyond their wake-up time. On those days, J.D. got the boys up, gave them a snack, and took them for a long walk or into the yard to play. She was relieved when the nausea ceased and she found herself more energized. J.D. insisted on her continuing her afternoon rests and each day kept the little ones occupied until she awoke.

"There's a method to your madness, and I'm on to it," she told him one night as he cuddled her.

"What's that?"

"You take the boys and let me rest in the afternoon so I have energy left at the end of the day to entertain you."

"Seems like a fair enough deal to me," he replied. "You're not complaining, are you?"

"Of course not. I just wanted you to know that I figured out your game."

"Well, I have to take good advantage of my time with you while I have it. I'll be on the road a bit more this next year. I didn't do much to promote either of those last two albums, and I've been advised to tour more after the next one, which is due toward the end of the year. And before we know it, we'll have this new little guy . . ." He stroked her rounded abdomen, loving the smooth feel of it, loved knowing that a part of him was growing inside her.

"Not a guy this time, I told you."

"Ah, yes. Louisa Elizabeth. After both our mothers."

"Lucy," she said.

"But if it's a boy . . ."

"Yes, Jamey, you get to name it." She yawned and snuggled up to him. "If I'm ever wrong, you get to choose the name."

Which of course, he never did.

"Tell me again why we're having Caroline to dinner tonight," J.D. inquired as he finished buttoning his shirt. "Not that I mind, of course."

"Caro's had a rough year." Maggie rummaged in her closet for her favorite long denim skirt, just the thing, she'd been thinking, for a casual dinner with a close friend. "David really did a job on her, you know. Sometimes I wonder if she'll ever forgive herself for letting him talk her into that abortion."

"Ah, yes, David. Smooth, charming, sophisticated, politically motivated, married David. What was it he was after, a judgeship or something? Tough to arrange those things, I suppose, when you have a wife and family in the city and a mistress and an illegitimate child in the suburbs." He watched as his wife pulled a thinly ribbed red knit shirt over her head.

"Caro did not deserve all that rubbish she had to deal with. He didn't even tell her he was married for the first three months he was taking her out. Then he told her he was getting divorced. Then it was, well, we're separating when the school year ends, don't want to upset the kids. Then it was after his father-in-law had his open-heart surgery. What a jerk that man proved to be." She stepped into her skirt and buttoned up the front. "I thought it would be good for her to be here, be around friends, since she's been a mess for the past month or so. Never wants to go anywhere . . . Have you seen my other red shoe?"

"I think one of the boys was playing with it this morning." He reached under a chair, picked up the shoe, and shook out a small herd of tiny plastic horses. He handed it to her with a grin, noting, "It's none the worse for being used as a stable."

"Thanks." She balanced on one foot while she slipped a shoe onto the other. "Besides, I haven't had much time to spend with Caroline since Lucy was born, and there's nothing more comforting for a broken heart than to be with an old and trusted friend."

"Well, there's some truth in that, though I doubt Caroline's come this far through life without having her heart broken a time or two." He sat on the edge of the bed and leaned back against the pillow.

"Umm, not so much as you'd think. Caro's always been pretty careful with the men in her life." She frowned as she added, "Up until now, anyway. She's had her share of beaux, but she's always lost interest after a while. For one reason or another none of them measured up to whatever it is she's looking for . . . Where did I put the earring that matches this?"

"What do you suppose she's looking for?" he asked.

"I don't know for sure, but I'd guess someone strong and sensitive, someone who takes her seriously and who isn't afraid to let her know that he loves her to death. Of course, Donald, the guy she dated in college, met all the criteria, but she broke off with him because when all was said and done, she really wasn't attracted to him."

"Maybe what she's looking for and what she needs are two different things," he observed.

"No"—Maggie shook her head—"she knows what she

wants, but the chemistry has to be there, too. Oops, there's the doorbell, come on, Jamey."

He descended the stairs in his wife's wake and greeted Caroline warmly. She did look like she'd been under the weather a bit, he thought as he observed the dark circles under her eyes.

Dinner had been a somewhat sedate affair. Caroline had seemed distracted and subdued. It was a relief of sorts when the doorbell rang halfway through the meal. J.D. disappeared into the foyer and returned ten long minutes later.

"Maggie," he announced, "look who's seeking shelter from the storm."

Rick stood in the doorway. She rose from her seat and embraced him, holding him for a very long time.

"How are you?" she asked simply, taking in his thin, tired appearance. The lines around his eyes were deeper, his expression almost somber. He sported a beard and a shorter haircut.

"Much better, thank you. God, you've got company, I'm so sorry . . . Oh, Caroline. Hello, darling."

He smiled with genuine pleasure, walking to her side of the table as she slid from her chair to hug him.

"Rick, what a surprise. I haven't seen hide nor hair of you for . . . gosh, it must be at least a year. You've lost weight. Have you been ill?" Caroline asked with concern.

Maggie apparently had not told her.

"Sort of. But I'm fine now." He met Maggie's gaze, and she smiled.

"Here. J.D., bring that over." Maggie motioned toward a chair against the wall. "Sit down, Rick. Have you eaten?"

"On the plane," he replied.

"Where's Lindy?" Maggie asked pointedly.

"In London." He avoided her eyes. "She wasn't up to the trip." Then he added quietly, "I'm sorry, Maggie."

She did not respond.

Rick changed the subject. "I saw Hobie last week. In Munich. He told me he'd been here for a brief visit a month back."

"Too brief," Maggie told him. "They only stayed for four

days this time because Hobie had to make some appearances in Europe. They usually spend a week or so in London—they come to see us every year, you know, and we always have the loveliest time. I adore Aden—she's great fun. And their children are precious, both of them."

"What brings you over?" J.D. asked.

Rick hesitated. "Just wanted to check in with old friends."

"We're glad you did," J.D. said. "Can you stay for a few days?"

"A few. I have to be in L.A. by Tuesday for some meetings. I'm finally getting back to work. And guess who's working with me, J.D.—Andrew Jenners."

"You're kidding. I thought he'd retired."

"He did," Rick told him, proudly adding, "but he agreed to do this one more project for me."

"Ugh. Shop talk," Maggie groaned. "Caro, want to help me clear this and get dessert?"

Rick's presence added a bit of spark to the party, and before long, he and Caroline were reminiscing about the first time they'd met.

"You were such a boor in those days, Rick," she laughed.

"I'm crushed, Caro. I thought you were so beautiful—you still are, by the way—and you totally ignored me."

"I thought you were so strange. And obnoxious. You really thought you were hot stuff."

"I was hot stuff"—he winked—"though apparently that wasn't quite the thing."

"Quite what thing?" she asked.

"Quite the thing to attract your attention." He grinned. "I always had the feeling that you never really noticed me."

"I noticed," she said shyly.

"Well, supposing you bring me up to date on all you've been doing since last we saw each other." He leaned back in his chair as Maggie poured coffee into his cup before heading toward the kitchen.

Gina, the fifteen-year-old babysitter whom Maggie had called in to watch the boys so that she could enjoy an uninterrupted evening with Caroline, came downstairs.

"Mr. Borders, do you think you could drive me home now? The children are all sound asleep, and it's getting late."

"Sure thing." He groped in his pocket for the car keys, telling his guests, "I won't be long."

Neither Rick nor Caroline appeared to notice.

J.D. returned in minutes, and Maggie motioned for him to help her clear the table.

"What was that look for?" he asked when they were in the kitchen.

"I want you to help me clean up so that we can go to bed. Lucy'll be up in about two hours for a late-night snack and I'm exhausted."

"What about Rick and Caroline?"

"Caroline can drive herself home. Or she can sleep over, too. She can sleep in Lucy's room. Rick can sleep in the guest room. Or they can sleep together. I really don't care."

J.D. raised an amused eyebrow and followed her into the dining room to say good night to their guests.

"Mommy, Uncle Rick is here," a giggling Jesse announced as he rode into the breakfast room upon Rick's shoulders the following morning. "We found him, me and Tyler found him, and we pounced on him."

"At ten minutes to six, I might add," Rick laughed.

"Boys," Maggie began her admonishment, "what have I told you about waking people up when they're sleeping."

"I didn't mind." Rick slung Jesse to the floor. "I got to play swamp thing with my favorite little guys."

"My turn," Tyler demanded, holding his arms up so that Rick could boost him skyward.

"Where's the new baby?" Rick asked, trying to sip coffee from a cup while parading Tyler around the room.

"She's been back to sleep since about five." Maggie began the breakfast preparations. "But don't worry, she'll be up again before too long and you'll get to see her."

"I see Caro's car is gone," J.D. observed.

"She left around, let's see, it must have been close to

four . . . There you go, little buddy, you can have another ride later." Rick plopped Tyler into his chair.

"Four? What on earth were you doing all that time?" Maggie removed a carton of eggs from the refrigerator.

"We don't want eggs," Jesse protested. "We want pancakes."

"Jesse, Mommy hates to make pancakes." Maggie made a face.

"I'll do it," J.D. volunteered. "You sit and have your coffee."

Maggie kissed him on the cheek. "You're a good father, J.D."

Then, as the two little boys began a duel with their spoons, Maggie suggested, "Why don't you guys go out on the swings until your pancakes are ready? We'll call you as soon as they're done."

She closed the back door and leaned upon it after the two tiny tornadoes had passed through it.

"Now for ten minutes of peace," she laughed, then said pointedly to Rick, "so, you were about to tell me what you and Caroline had been doing till four A.M."

"Talking," he told her.

"What about?" She sat down at the table across from him.

"Everything," Rick poured himself a glass of orange juice. "My work, her work. We traded our tales of woe . . . the plans we'd each dreamed up as children to escape from where we were . . ."

"Rick, I can understand why you'd have wanted to run away," J.D. said as he measured pancake mix into a large pottery bowl, "but I thought Caroline had come from a nice, solid family."

"She did," Maggie interjected. "She grew up on a farm in Iowa. Her family raised beef cattle."

"Doesn't sound so terrible," J.D. commented.

"Every spring her father would let her raise a calf for the county fair," Maggie explained, "and after the fair, the calf would be sold along with the others for slaughter. She couldn't stand it . . . She told me once that she picked Penn out of all the schools she'd applied to because it was the farthest from Iowa. She still can't bring herself to eat beef or veal in any form. To this day, the very thought of it makes her physically sick."

"I guess that explains why we always have chicken or fish when she's here," observed J.D. wryly.

"And we talked about that son-of-a-bitch ex-boyfriend of hers. I'd give a king's ransom for the privilege of pounding that bugger senseless," Rick said as his face darkened, "for what he did to her."

"You mean David?" Maggie asked.

"Whatever his name was." Rick frowned. "Thank God she had you to comfort her."

"I don't know how much comfort I was," Maggie told him, "since Lucy was born very shortly after Caroline had the . . . Did she tell you everything?"

"About the abortion?" He nodded glumly. "Yes, she told me. She cried for almost an hour last night. Broke my heart . . . She's so wonderful, such a sensitive and sweet woman . . . She's having a terrible time forgiving herself."

"Well, let's hope the future holds some happiness for her," J.D. said.

"I would like to think so." Rick looked pensive. "I'd like to think that maybe someday . . . after we've both sorted out our own sorrows, maybe someday when things are less complicated, when I've gotten Lindy straightened out—"

"Is that likely?" Maggie asked bluntly.

"Who knows?" he sighed, pulling a restless hand through his hair. "But I have to stick it out with her."

"That could take forever," Maggie said quietly.

"That may be, but I cannot abandon her." He rested his chin in the palm of his hand. "I got her into this. I have to pull her out."

"That could be a very long and unhappy road for you, Rick," J.D. reminded him.

"How happy do you think Lindy is right now?" asked Rick cynically.

"Where is she?" Maggie rose to set plates upon the table.

"Well, she should be at my apartment, hopefully making

her best effort to kick her habit. I have someone there with her, a hypnotist who helped me."

"Where have you been all these months?" J.D. asked. "We've been really worried. No one seemed to know."

"No one did," Rick admitted, "I was in Scotland. A tiny crossroads hamlet outside of Edinburgh. That's what he— the hypnotist—insisted upon. That I get out of London and go someplace where no one could find me until the treatment had been successfully completed."

"Do you think it will work for Lindy?" Maggie felt some surge of hope. After all, it had obviously worked for Rick.

"I don't truthfully know if she really wants to go off the heroin. But I did get her to agree to try." He paused, then continued. "Lindy had been staying with someone else for a few months. When that little novelty wore off and she wanted to come back to the apartment, I agreed, on the condition that she straighten out."

"You mean she was staying with another man?"

"Yes."

Although her actions were never logical, this behavior of Lindy's visibly upset Maggie. While it had been accepted that Rick and Lindy were never in love, each had seemed to give the other what they needed. There had been a time, early on, when Maggie thought they seemed to stabilize each other. It had been no secret that Rick had always had other women. And it would have been no surprise to learn Lindy had been seeing someone else from time to time. But for her to leave Rick and drift off for a few months with another man was out of character. Rick had been the only man Lindy had ever tolerated on a long-term basis. She had once said that apart from Maggie, Rick was the only real friend she'd ever had.

A few days after Rick had left to go to California, Maggie mentioned to J.D. that she thought Lindy's behavior more than a bit curious and wondered who this new man was, what their relationship was like. J.D. had merely shrugged and had offered no comment at all.

He could not bring himself to tell her that the "relationship" was little more than a barter between Lindy and her supplier. The dealer was more than happy to keep Lindy supplied with heroin in exchange for sex. At first, he had furnished her with what she needed free of charge, but after a few weeks, he cashed in. The fact that Lindy was so gorgeous was a real incentive, and the fact that she had been Rick Daily's lady for the past few years made it even better.

After a month or so the creep started getting a bit rough with Lindy, and about two weeks ago, she had showed up at Rick's apartment, battered and sick. Rick let her stay, of course, but only after she agreed to give up the stuff. She had a rough time of it, Rick had said, and he had called in the hypnotist who'd worked with him to try to straighten her out.

Rick told the story to J.D. late one night after Maggie had gone to bed. He didn't want her to know, he'd told J.D., not ever, that Lindy had, in effect, prostituted herself for the sake of her habit. Rick's guilt ran deep for having been the one who started her on the heroin in the first place, and he was having a harder time dealing with her addiction and its repercussions than he had had with his own. The sense of responsibility he felt for her would lead them all down a very twisted path over the next several years.

20

THEY ARE THE ODDEST PAIR, HILARY REFLECTED, *BOTH PERCHED
like plaster mannequins on the edge of that sofa, she devoid of
any expression, and he in obvious despair, both red-eyed and
pale. He looks the worst of the two—whatever has happened
between them must have been his doing. Though he doesn't
look guilty, just sad. He's been tough, though, I'll give him
that. Hasn't missed a beat all night.*

*She's been a snippy little shit when she's condescended to
say a word or two. Snippy and unpleasant and distracted, as if
she couldn't wait to get out of here, as if this is all a waste of
her precious time. Now what,* Hilary's eyes narrowed, *is at
the bottom of all this? I simply can't get a handle on them.*

"One of your best-selling early albums from the eighties
was *Shadows on the Moon.* What made that recording so
special for you?" Hilary had glanced at her notes, having
decided to attempt to ease back into a relaxed atmosphere
again before she nailed Borders on Narood. She gave in on
the Daily issue but would not back down on Narood. She'd
invested better than an hour in these two, and they were
boring her silly. She would lull him to sleep, then hit him
hard.

"Well," he was saying, "that was the first album I'd recorded one hundred percent solo, you know, playing all the instruments myself, doing the background vocals . . ."

"Now how could you do all that alone?" she asked him coyly.

"It was quite simple, actually, given all the new equipment."

"I thought somehow that Rick Daily worked on that album with you." She frowned, looking at her notes.

"Only on one song," J.D. pointed out, wryly pondering the irony that he, J.D., recognized as a great vocalist, acclaimed as a songwriter, never once in his career had a hit record on which Rick had not backed him on guitar. The only cut from the album under discussion to reach number one status had been the title track—the only one Rick had played on.

"Well, he'd certainly been a busy boy that year," Hilary commented, "after having recorded that album that was so big—"

"Daily Blues," J.D. said, nodding, "won every conceivable award that year and is still looked upon as his best work ever. It was a phenomenal collection of music, no question about it."

My guess is that she's the weaker of the two, Hilary mused. *She'll break first, though she's been off someplace most of the night, that's been plain. Odd how she rallied though, when Narood's name came up. And there's something there about her and Daily that she's guarding with her life, but what?*

"Had Rick been inspired, do you think, by his impending fatherhood?" Hilary addressed Maggie directly.

"I don't know," she half whispered, the unexpected query kick-starting the knot in her stomach.

As difficult as it was to think back on it all when she was alone, now, under the heat of the lights, she was suddenly suffocating. Those days had taught her that no one can really understand the devastating effects of addiction until they have loved an addict. It had been a terrible lesson to learn.

* * *

Five months had passed since Rick had stopped unexpectantly at the Borders' home. The next time he appeared at their door, it was with a much subdued Lindy in tow. Maggie cried tears of joy to see her again, then was struck dumb to discover Lindy was seven months' pregnant.

"So how do you feel, about the baby, I mean?" Maggie asked when they were finally alone.

"I don't want it, Maggie. If I'd found out about it sooner than I had, it would have been gone, believe me," she said flatly. "But I was almost six months when I realized it, and it was too late to do anything about it."

"Well, how does Rick feel?"

"He knows there's a very good chance it isn't his. Then again," she said, shrugging, "it could be."

Maggie studied the lines that had appeared in her friend's face since she'd last seen her. A pain grew inside her as she pondered Lindy's dilemma.

"Rick's been so good, Maggie," she said slowly. "He wants me to marry him—can you imagine? He doesn't love me and he knows I don't love him and he doesn't even know if he's the father. But he wants to marry me."

"Why?" Maggie heard herself ask.

"I don't know. Maybe it's because he never had a father or a mother, and he feels sorry for the baby. Maybe he thinks it's his and he doesn't want his own child to grow up alone like he did. Maybe he feels responsible for me somehow. I don't know."

"What did you tell him?"

"I told him no. The best compromise we could come to was to agree to have his name shown on the birth certificate as the father instead of 'unknown.'"

"That's pretty big of him," Maggie commented.

"That's an understatement. I wish I could be in love with him, Maggie. I really do. But I'm not. The best I can say is that if I could ever love anyone, it would be him. He has spent more time and more money and gone through more aggravation trying to hold my head above water this past year or so . . ." She paused and shook her head slowly. "You just don't know."

"Do you want to tell me?"

"No. If you knew how bad things had gotten, you'd never speak to me again."

"That's ridiculous," Maggie protested.

"No, it's not. I was in way over my head. A lot of stuff happened that, well, that's better left alone. It's been a long, dark tunnel, Maggie, and I don't know if I'll ever be out of it."

"Why do you say that? You're not still using, are you?"

"No, Rick would kill me. But it doesn't mean I don't want to. Right now I have to get through this and have this baby, and then . . . I don't know what then."

"Maybe you'll change your mind after it's born."

"That's a nice thought, Maggie, but unlikely. I never wanted a child, never. I have absolutely no maternal feelings, no emotional attachment to it. I wish it hadn't happened, but I have to see it through. For two cents I'd . . ." The flat detached voice had sent a chill up Maggie's spine.

"You'd what?"

Lindy did not reply.

"You'd what, Lindy?" Maggie repeated and found herself growing frightened.

Lindy broke down and wept uncontrollably. Maggie let her cry, sensing that the tears had been a long time coming, that the fear and despondency behind them needed to be released.

"Just for your peace of mind," she said when the tidal wave began to recede, "just so that you know, I tried to want this baby, thinking maybe it would give purpose to my life, a direction. I mean, I haven't even been working the past few years. I've lived off Rick like a parasite. And I haven't even been able to love him for it. But there's something in me, Maggie . . . All the things I tried to tell myself about this baby aren't real and never will be. It would have been better if I'd been able to have an abortion. That's the solemn truth. I wish I could be different, but I'm not. I wish I could love it, but I know I won't." Lindy looked up at Maggie, pleading, "Please don't hate me."

"I don't hate you," Maggie said softly. "I don't always understand you, but I could never hate you. We've been friends for too long, Lindy. And you know I'll help you in any way I can. If you want to come and stay here with the baby after it's born, you're welcome to."

"Thanks, Maggie. I don't know what I'm going to do with it."

"If it gets to be too much for you, bring him or her here," Maggie offered.

"You mean just plunk it on your doorstep?"

"If that's necessary, yes."

"You're still the best person I've ever known, Maggie. It helps knowing I could do that. I'd be lying if I said it wasn't a possibility."

"Wait and see how you feel after the baby's born. You might surprise yourself."

They heard Rick and J.D. in the hallway, heard their laughter as they walked through the kitchen and into the sunroom.

"Mags, you've got to listen to this," J.D. was saying. "Wait till you hear."

"What is it? What have you two been up to?"

"We were down at the studio, fooling around, and listen to what Rick added here." J.D. was plugging a tape recorder into an outlet. "Wait till you hear how great this sounds."

The tape began, the master for "Shadows on the Moon," which J.D. had recorded in his small stable-studio over the past four weeks. Rick had recorded over J.D.'s original tape, and the sweet, sad notes from Rick's guitar seemed to be weeping, a dramatic underscore to the vocals:

"I feel the darkness closing in on me.
Is it just a shadow on the moon?
Light is fading, sun is slipping away,
Night always comes too soon.
No promise made can't be broken,
Every dawn fades into the day.
The seasons so quickly pass by us,

Is there anything ever can stay?
So bring me your love and dream me a dream
And make me believe it won't die,
And I'll sing you a song to hold in your heart
Till the silent shadows pass by."

"Well," he said, turning off the recorder, "what do you think, Maggie?"

"Rick, you're the only person I know who can make a guitar actually cry like that," she said. "It's beautiful. Absolutely beautiful."

"I think it sounds morbid," Lindy mumbled.

"Why do you say that?" Maggie asked.

"I don't know, it just sounds so . . . hopeless. But I like it. I like it a lot. It is beautiful, J.D."

Rick sat beside her. "Legs," he said quietly, "nothing is ever hopeless."

"Of course, it is. We're all going to die someday, you know, Rick. Even you."

"Everyone except me," he quipped, trying to lighten the suddenly gloomy mood. "The rest of you may be willing to throw in the towel when the time comes, but not me."

"I refuse to engage in a heavy conversation tonight," Maggie announced and left the room. She returned with a bottle of Perrier and some tall glasses filled with shaved ice and bits of lime. "It's been so long since we've been together, the four of us, and I refuse to not enjoy this reunion. Lindy, if you have any other unpleasant thoughts, I'll thank you to keep them to yourself."

She filled the glasses and passed them around. "Here's to us," she said, "and to those who will come after us. To Rick's million-selling album and to Jamey's, which hopefully will do as well. To our friendship."

"And to the past five years," Rick proposed.

"And to the next five," added Maggie.

Only Lindy did not raise her glass.

Maggie got the call from Rick on a day in late February. Lindy had delivered a baby girl, Sophia Margaret, the night before. Lindy had expressed no interest in the baby, Rick told her unhappily, not even wanting Sophie brought into her room at feeding times. She was fed in the nursery by the staff or by Rick in the dayroom.

"She's a pretty little thing, Maggie. Golden hair, pretty little features," he told her, awed by the child, "and so tiny."

"Any baby of Lindy's would be a beauty, Rick."

"Right now she doesn't really look much like her mother."

"Who does she look like?" As soon as the words were out of her mouth, she wanted to bite her tongue.

There was a long pause on the phone.

"I don't know. I wish I did," he said. "I've never met anyone in Lindy's family, and I've no idea what my parents looked like. That's assuming, of course, that she's my daughter."

"Rick, you know, if it bothers you, you can have a blood test done—"

"No. I don't want to do that," he said, cutting her off abruptly.

"Why not? At least you'd know."

"Part of me doesn't want to know, Maggie. This way, there's a chance she's mine. And my name is on her birth certificate. That's all she'll ever need to know, do you understand? At least she'll have one parent around for her."

"Where do you think Lindy's going?"

"After this dies down, I don't know where she'll go or what she'll end up doing."

"You sound as if you expect Lindy to abandon her."

"Don't you?" he snapped gruffly.

"Give her a chance, Rick."

"I'll give her all the chances she needs. But you have to admit that her track record is extremely poor, Maggie."

"Look, Rick, I've told Lindy that if she has problems or needs some help, to bring the baby here for a while. The offer still stands. Anytime."

She repeated the conversation to J.D. later that night while they lay in bed.

"I just can't get over Rick's concern for this child. It's

almost unnatural. I mean, considering the fact that she may not be his and considering the fact that Rick has always been one of the most irresponsible people I've ever known, I just can't understand it," he said.

"Well, maybe he doesn't want history to repeat itself. If there's any chance at all that Sophie is his, I think he wants to protect her from going through what he went through. Or, maybe he just feels guilty about getting Lindy involved with the drug thing. I told him he could bring the baby here if he had to."

"Did you also tell him the stork would be paying us another visit in a few months?"

"No. If he really needed help, he wouldn't come if he knew I was pregnant. But it'll be okay if he shows up with her. Having Mrs. Price here all the time has been a godsend. I didn't realize how desperately I needed live-in help until I got it. I don't know how I functioned without her. And besides, Sophie could be a playmate for the little girl-to-be," she said.

"Ah, yes. Emma," he mused.

"Emma Kate," she corrected him and repositioned herself inside the circle of his left arm. "You know, this time you didn't say 'If you're wrong, can I name the baby?' like you always do."

"I've given up. You've not been wrong one time. That's a hell of an average, you know."

Emma Kate was born just one short hour before the televised music awards show announced that *Shadows on the Moon* had been selected as Album of the Year. The baby's father watched with one eye as his manager accepted for him, the other eye focused on Emma, who was, at the moment his name was announced, anxiously awaiting her first meal.

"It'll only be for three days, Maggie, I promise," Rick was saying, "just until I finish these three shows in New York and can find someone to watch Sophie full-time."

"You've found someone. You can leave her here."

"Thanks, Maggie, but the last thing you need right now is another baby on your hands."

"She'll be no problem. Mrs. Price is here so I have extra hands."

"Do you think Mrs. Price might like to go on tour with me?"

"No. And I'm not certain Sophie should either."

"She'll be fine. As soon as we find a nanny who likes to travel, Sophie will learn to love it."

"Well, just make sure the references you check on this nanny are specifics other than her measurements."

"Not to worry, Maggie," he laughed, "when it comes to Sophie, it's strictly business. I don't want some bimbo looking after her. She's such a good little girl, Maggie, she really is. She looks more and more like her mother—"

"Who is where, Rick?"

He was silent for a moment or two, then said, "The last time I saw her was at the house. I told you I'd bought a house just outside of London? It was right before the tour started at the end of November. The last few times I called home she wasn't there and the housekeeper wasn't sure where she'd gone."

"I'm so sorry, Rick," Maggie said softly.

"I'm sorry for Sophie. You know, I've always tried to understand Lindy, always tried to just go along with her antics and let her just go her own way when she needed to and let her come back when she wanted to. I've never judged her. But I simply can't understand how she could be so disinterested in her own child."

"If it helps, I think Lindy really wanted to love her. Deep inside, maybe she does. I don't think she'd know how to express it if she did. And maybe she's scared."

"Well, that's fine for Lindy to keep herself safely locked away, but how do you think Sophie will feel when she gets older and realizes that her mother flat out wants nothing to do with her? I know that feeling very well, Maggie. It can come very close to destroying you. Sophie doesn't deserve that."

"At least she has you, Rick. And I can't wait to see her. We'll see you tomorrow night." Maggie hung up the phone.

She went into the kitchen and made herself some coffee. The house was gloriously quiet. The three oldest children were at school, Jess a big first grader, Tyler in kindergarten, Lucy at nursery school for another hour. Emma was napping, and Mrs. Price was upstairs watching her morning television shows. Maggie took her cup into the sunroom.

She shook her head, reflecting on the irony of it all. There's Caroline, who'd give the world to be able to go back in time and have that baby she'd aborted three years ago and it's breaking her heart. And here's Lindy, with a child she can't bring herself to look at and that she'd never wanted. And then there's Rick, who has to be the world's most unlikely candidate for father of the year, trying hard to protect the tiny girl from the pain he'd known as a child, changing his life to raise a baby that may not even be his.

Sophie was an angel, with a golden halo of curls and the biggest blue eyes Maggie had ever seen.

"She's a darling, Rick. I'm so happy you brought her to us," Maggie told him as she lifted the child from his arms the next evening. The child adored her father, and it was clear that the love was greatly returned.

"Well, I promise not to impose on you any longer than I need to," he assured her. "An agency I contacted in New York has several potential nannies lined up for me to meet this week. If all goes well, I can come back for her by Thursday or Friday."

"No way are you taking her from us with her birthday just a week away," Maggie protested. "She has to have a proper first birthday with all the requisite hoopla."

Rick had been a little late getting in from the airport the night of the party and had been pleased to walk into the house in time to see the entire group gathered in the dining room. Miss Sophia Margaret Daily sat regally in the high chair, reveling in the attention, not understanding the nature of it, but fully aware that she was at its center. Caroline walked in behind Maggie, carrying Sophie's birthday cake. She set it down on the table and hugged Rick, happy to see him again.

"I'm absolutely in love with Sophie," she told him. "If I'd known you were looking for a nanny, I'd have applied for the job myself. She's a doll, Rick."

"Well, had I known you'd be interested," he laughed, "I'd have been more than happy to hire you on."

At the sound of her father's voice, the guest of honor clammered to be released from her high chair. Rick lifted Sophie out and planted a loud kiss on her face. She wrapped her pudgy arms around his neck and pulled his hair so that they were nose to nose. Maggie looked carefully, but try as she might, could see no resemblance between the two.

As the party began to wind down, a sleepy birthday girl climbed into Caroline's lap, a cloth doll dressed in gingham, a gift from Lucy, clutched in her arms. She lay her golden head against Caro's shoulder and closed her eyes as Caroline lovingly stroked her back. Rick had watched, a wistful expression on his face, as Caroline gently rocked his tiny daughter to sleep. The three of them appeared, Maggie thought, as pieces of the same puzzle.

257

21

MAGGIE COULD SEE THE IMAGE STILL, CAROLINE'S BLACK HAIR spilling over her face as she had helped the little girl with the cornsilk curls onto her lap, Sophie snuggling into her body, eyes closing sleepily. Rick had stood ten feet away, though the smile he had exchanged with the dark-haired woman who cradled his child seemed to lessen the distance. A casual observer would have thought them a family, Maggie recalled.

She had always wondered about them, Caroline and Rick, so easy with each other on the occasions they were together at Maggie's house. They had always seemed to fit somehow, and yet Rick had been caught up with Lindy and all the complications of that relationship, and Caroline over the years had been involved with one man or another. It was, she thought, as if fate had brought the wrong people together. Two more opposite women were unlikely to be found, Caroline so full of love and warmth, so gentle in her nature, and Lindy, so much drawn to the darkness, so dominated by her own needs.

Maggie's head shook involuntarily, recalling the roller coaster Lindy had kept them on for so long . . .

* * *

As soon as the school year concluded, Maggie and J.D. packed up their brood and left for ten weeks in London with Luke. But the crowded quarters soon wore on J.D.'s nerves, and so Luke suggested they hire an architect to design an addition that would expand the living quarters to accommodate the expanding family. The plans for the new addition kept the style of the old section of the house and included a new, much larger living room and sitting room downstairs along with an extension of the kitchen and three additional bedrooms and two bathrooms on the second floor. With luck, it would be completed by the time Maggie and J.D. returned for the Christmas holiday.

They visited with Rick and Sophie for a few days, but Lindy was nowhere to be seen.

"I don't think she can face you, Maggie," Rick had told her. "Truthfully, there are days when she can't face herself. Or me. She spends very little time here."

"Where does she stay?"

"In London. With friends." He looked away. "She's into the junk again, Maggie."

"Oh, God, no . . ."

"I'm sorry. I debated telling you about it. But there's little reason not to at this point. I kept hoping, you know, that she'd straighten out"—his voice held a sadness deeper than anything she'd ever heard—"but it won't happen. The last time she was here, she kept out of my way and out of Sophie's sight."

"What's she living on? What's she using for money?"

"I guess the money she got when her mother's paintings were sold last year," he said with a shrug. "They sold them all off, she and her brother. They made a small fortune."

"Any chance I might catch up with her this trip?"

"You don't want to."

"Yes, I do." Maggie was angry to her soul that Lindy had so carelessly tossed aside the people in her life who'd truly cared for her.

She tried her best to track Lindy down, but even Judith's circle of friends and acquaintances could not locate her. It wasn't until they'd returned for Christmas that their paths crossed.

She and J.D. had gone to a holiday party at a hotel in London given by J.D.'s record company, delighted to find Hobie and Aden in attendance. Maggie and Aden stood at the bar and watched Glory Fielding flit through the crowd, flirting with all the men. It was amusing until Glory had pulled J.D. onto the dance floor and wrapped her arms around his neck. J.D. made light of the situation by making faces behind Glory's back to his wife, who was watching him like a hawk. She and Aden giggled behind their hands like schoolgirls along with the others at the bar who were entertained by J.D.'s antics at the expense of his unsuspecting dance partner. When the song had ended, Glory had turned to give Maggie a smug smile, unaware she'd been mocked by the man she was stubbornly determined to win.

The large room soon grew crowded and hot, and Maggie, five months' pregnant and not nearly as unaffected by Glory's proximity to J.D. as she had pretended to be, excused herself and sought the ladies' room.

As she opened the door, a tall, lanky figure stepped past her. Maggie smiled absentmindedly, then turned in shock.

"Lindy." The name escaped unconsciously from her lips in a whisper, then again, "Lindy."

The woman did not turn around, but had simply kept walking down the hallway. Maggie turned rapidly, caught up with her, grabbed her by the arm, and spun her around.

The two women stood and stared at each other for a very long minute. Lindy looked terrible, her cheeks sunken in, her once beautiful face devoid of expression.

"Why'd you walk away from me?" Maggie demanded.

After a long, pause came the reply. "Because there's nothing I can say to you, Maggie."

"Why not?"

"Maggie, please." She attempted to turn to walk away, but Maggie refused to let her pass.

"Don't you walk away from me, damn you," Maggie

hissed. "How could you, Lindy, how could you do this again?"

"I don't want to talk about it, Maggie."

"Well, that's just too damned bad." Maggie forced the thin frame against the wall as a group of people from the party passed by, glancing with curiosity at the scene. "I have plenty to say, and you're going to listen to every word."

"Okay, Maggie, go ahead. Tell me how spoiled and selfish I am. Tell me what a terrible person I am for leaving my baby. Tell me what a fool I am and that I deserve the worst out of this. Tell me how disappointed you are in me, how you always believed there was something better in me . . . Does that about cover it?" She looked at Maggie with hollow eyes that had not a spark of light left in them.

"That's pretty damn close. You are the most self-centered, unfeeling, uncaring, stupid person I've ever known. And yes, let's start with your baby."

Lindy turned her face.

"I told you I didn't want that baby, Maggie. I told you what would happen."

"Lindy, Sophie is a darling baby, she deserves—"

"A mother whose head is screwed on tightly," Lindy shot back with more emotion than her tired face had appeared to be capable of. "A mother who can love her. A mother who can read her stories and braid her hair and patch up her wounds. That's not me, Mags. I can't patch up my own wounds."

"Then let's talk about Rick."

"I've nothing to say about Rick," she said, turning her head.

"Lindy, that man's done more for you than anyone should ever be expected to do for anyone."

"I know that, Maggie. I just can't face him anymore. I've let him down so many times. He looks at me, and I see the resentment and the disappointment and I know he's disgusted with me and with what I am. But I can't change it, Maggie."

"For God's sake, Lindy, you could get help."

"There's no help for me." Lindy looked her in the eyes for

the first time. "It only works when you're committed to it, when you believe in yourself and know there's something better for you than the next hit. Now me, I know that's not true, Maggie. I know it's too late."

"Why is it too late?"

"Because I know that this is all there is for me. Sophie's better off not knowing me, and Rick's doing a better job with her than I could ever do. He does love her," she said, adding casually, "He's not her father, by the way."

"You knew?" Maggie's jaw dropped.

"Of course, I knew."

"Why did you let him think he could be?"

"Because I was desperate and needed him to help me," she replied bluntly.

"This is the worst thing you've ever done in your life, Lindy." Maggie backed away from her slowly, horrified at such despicable an act. "Letting him think Sophie's his, telling him she could be when you know he's not . . ."

"Why? It's worked out perfectly for both of them. He gets a chance to make things right for her, and somehow he's releasing himself in the process. Don't tell me you haven't seen the change in him. And she gets to grow up loved and cared for and secure. She's Rick Daily's daughter, Maggie. She'll have everything. She'll have a chance to be happy. Much happier than if she'd been raised by her junkie mother and her pusher father."

"I will never forgive you if you tell him, do you understand me?" Maggie had gone white with rage, clenching Lindy's pencil-thin arm in a tight grasp.

"Maggie, stop." Lindy tried to twist away. "You're hurting me."

"Promise me. Swear you'll never tell anyone."

"I promise. I wouldn't have anyway. I'd never hurt Rick like that. Despite what you think, I do care about him," she whispered, "and her and you."

Maggie released her hold on Lindy's arm and backed away, taking a long look at her old friend. Tears sprung to her eyes, and she was unable to stop them, unable to speak.

"Please, Maggie, don't cry. I'm not worth it. Don't think

that all those years don't mean anything to me. It's just that things have gone too far now . . . I'm sorry Maggie." She turned and walked away.

Maggie stood leaning with her back against the wall, her knees too weak to support her shaking body, watching Lindy disappear, ghostlike, through a doorway. Aden started into the hallway and, seeing Maggie standing there with an ashen face, sobbing, ran to find J.D.

"I want to go home," Maggie cried as J.D. held her trembling form tightly in his arms, bewildered, not knowing what was wrong. "Please, Jamey, take me home.

On a cold, stormy early March morning, Maggie stood in her kitchen, surveying the mess of mixing bowls and baking paraphernalia the kids had left for her to clean. There had been no school that day due to the snow, and Maggie had decided to let the kids bake cookies to ease their boredom. *This had always seemed such a lark when we did this at home,* she thought ruefully as she began to clean up. *My mother always made this look so easy.* She recalled many a snowy afternoon when she, Ellie, and Frankie sat at the big kitchen table, each with their own bowl, as Mary Elizabeth went from one to the other, measuring out ingredients. *Vanilla and nutmeg and ginger,* she mused, *the smells of a winter day.*

She delivered a plate of still-warm cookies to the room where the children sat before the television, engrossed in a movie, and returned to the kitchen to begin the cleanup. Stacking the dough-encrusted bowls in the sink, she filled them with water and cleaned off the table, pausing to turn on the kettle to make herself a much needed cup of tea. The whistle's shrill cry began just as she completed her chores, and she took her cup into the sunroom for a few moments of peace.

Easing herself into a big wicker chair, she shifted the pillow behind her to comfort her aching back and raised her legs onto the ottoman. The masses of daffodil bulbs she had forced into bloom lined the windowsills, giving the room the appearance of full-blown spring, though outside the storm continued to swirl the snow about in a blur of white. She sipped at the tea and closed her eyes, rubbing her greatly swollen abdomen.

Twins this time, and any day now, her doctor had told her, though the official due date wasn't for another six weeks. Take it easy, he had cautioned, they will be premature as it is.

The sound of a ringing telephone startled her from an unexpected slumber. She blinked her eyes to rally herself, sighing deeply as she prepared to lift herself from the chair when the ringing stopped. *Good, someone else got it,* she smiled, sinking back into her cushions, hoping the call wasn't for her.

"Daddy," she heard Jesse call up the steps, "Uncle Rick wants to talk to you."

Wonder what Rick's up to these days, she thought, half tempted to pick up the extension in the kitchen, then abandoned the thought. She was too comfortable, too weary to rise, and she closed her eyes and drifted back to sleep.

The day had grown darker, more gray than white, by the time the first pains had awakened her. She started to sit up, then realized that J.D. was seated next to her feet on the ottoman.

"Maggie," he said somewhat hoarsely as she stirred.

"Oh, shit, Jamey, I think this is it." He could not mistake the alarm in her voice. "Of all days for these two to pick . . ."

"You're in labor?" His head shot up.

"Yes, I'm in labor," she replied crankily. "How in the hell will we make it to the hospital in this mess?"

An anxious glance out the windows told her the storm had intensified.

"I can call an ambulance." He rose quickly. "It'll be safer. Be right back."

It had been a full twenty minutes before the ambulance pulled into the drive and another thirty to make the one-mile trip to the hospital. The babies, however, thankfully held off for another hour. They were tiny bundles, neither of them much over five pounds, both jaundiced, but essentially healthy.

"By the way, what did Rick have to say when he called this morning?" Maggie asked J.D. as she traded babies with the nurse, handing over just-fed Susannah and cuddling Molly for the first time.

"Rick?" J.D.'s head, bent over his newborn daughter, snapped up with a jerk.

"Rick. Rick Daily," she repeated, adding cheerfully, "You remember, tall guy, dark hair, plays guitar . . ."

"Oh, nothing we need to go into now," he brushed her off nonchalantly. "Let's just concentrate on these new young ones. Maggie, however will we tell them apart? They're absolute mirror images."

It had seemed to her, in retrospect, that there had been some underlying tension in J.D. over the next two weeks, something that went beyond the disruption created by having to run constantly back and forth to the hospital to tend to the babies who had been kept behind due to their prematurity. But the days had been hectic, and Maggie was exhausted by the strain of dealing with four small children at home and the two tiny ones in their isolettes a mile down the road. Her mother's arrival helped immensely, but Maggie was greatly relieved when first Molly, then Susannah, were sent home with a clean bill of health. It had been emotionally draining to have left the hospital without them, and she was delighted to have them both in their own cribs, under their roof.

"It's such an empty feeling to give birth and leave the hospital without the babies," she told J.D. the night the second twin had been released, "I worried about them the whole time I was here and worried about the others when I was there."

"Hmmm? Oh, yes, well, they're both fine," he agreed absentmindedly.

"Okay, what is it?" She sat up in bed and turned the light on.

"What is what?" he asked with some caution.

"What's on your mind? What's distracting you?"

When he failed to reply, she said more pointedly, "What's going on that you don't want to tell me?"

"Lindy . . ." he began, stopped, then began again, "Lindy's had an accident. She was driving too fast and ran the car down an embankment."

"When? How bad?" The chill traveling down her spine sat her straight up.

"Actually, it was the day the twins were born," he admitted. "Rick had called, and before I could tell you, you told me you were in labor and it seemed not the best time—"

"How bad?" she repeated.

He took a deep breath, then said softly, "Her spinal cord is severed, Maggie. She's paralyzed from the shoulders down."

"And you waited two weeks to tell me?" She began to cry, pushing his hands away as he sought to comfort her.

"Maggie, you've had more than your share to deal with these past few weeks. I thought I'd wait until things settled down a bit for you. And it's not like there's anything you can do."

"I could call her, talk to her—"

"She's not talking to anyone, hardly speaks to Rick, he tells me. She's in a terrible state of depression."

"Jamey, we have to go . . ."

"Maggie, you're not ready to go on a trip and neither are the babies. We just brought Susannah home today—there's no way you can travel with them right now. Are you willing to leave them behind after having waited two weeks to bring them home?"

She knew he was right; she could not separate herself from her newborn daughters. She leaned against him.

"Is it permanent?" she asked. "Lindy's condition?"

"I'm afraid so," he told her softly. "Rick has called in every specialist he could find."

"She'd rather be dead," Maggie whispered.

"Apparently that's true," he nodded, "from what Rick's told me."

"As soon as we can all travel, can we go?"

"Of course," he assured her, "as soon as we can."

Maggie insisted on calling Rick the next day at the hospital number he'd given to J.D. Lindy refused to speak to her when Rick had placed the phone to her ear, shaking her head to tell him to take the phone away. It had been another ten days before Lindy would respond to her and then only to say yes, no, or uh-huh.

"We'll be there next week, Lindy," Maggie told her one day.

"Don't," Lindy replied and, breaking her habit of mono-syllables, added, "Maggie, I don't want to see anyone. I wish I was dead."

"Lindy, don't think that way," Maggie pleaded.

"You've no idea what hell this is, Maggie," she sobbed. "I can't stay like this."

"Lindy, if there was anything I could do to help you . . ."

"You can help me"—her voice lowered—"you can tell him to help me. He would do it if you told him to . . ."

"Told who to do what? Lindy, what are you talking about?"

"She's upset, Maggie, I think she's had enough for one day." Rick's voice drowned out Lindy's sobs.

Over the next several days her conversations with Lindy had reverted to the dull yesses and noes, so Maggie was totally unprepared when Lindy got on the phone a week later and said, "You must think I'm a terrible friend . . . I never even asked about your new babies."

"What? Oh, they're fine," Maggie managed to respond, jarred by the light tone in the voice on the other end of the line.

"I guess I should have inquired earlier," Lindy said apologetically, "but I've been preoccupied . . ."

"It's okay." Confused by Lindy's suddenly buoyant mood, Maggie asked, "Has there been a change, Lind, any improvement?"

"Nope. Never will be. I will spend the rest of my days right here, flat on my back," Lindy assured her, a bit of the old sassiness breaking through. "Can't even snap my fingers or tap my toes to the music anymore. Ain't much happening among us undead."

There was a silence then, Maggie not knowing what to say.

"Look, Maggie," Lindy said, breaking the awkward void, "I know I've done a lot of things that have hurt you these past few years, and I want you to know I'm sorry. And I want to thank you for all the times you cared when there was absolutely no reason why you should have. You were a better friend than I ever deserved. You're what I'd have chosen to be, had I had a choice . . ."

She had paused to take a deep breath before adding, "Keep an eye on Sophie as she's growing up, Maggie, you'll be a better influence on her than I would."

"Lindy, maybe in time—"

"Time won't change what is, Maggie. I never want her to see me like this. Not ever. I don't want anyone to see me like this, I can't bear it. Look, you take care, okay? And tell J.D. I said good-bye. Here's Rick . . ."

"Rick, is she okay?" Maggie asked tentatively. "Are they drugging her or something?"

"She's fine," he replied somewhat stiffly. "Look, the nurse is here, we'll talk soon . . ."

Maggie was still standing next to the phone when J.D. came in through the back door.

"What's wrong?" he asked, noting the look of confusion on her face.

"I just had the most bizarre conversation with Lindy," she told him. "She was pleasant and talkative, almost like the old Lindy."

"Maybe she's finally come to terms with her condition," he said with a shrug.

"She'll never come to terms with that," she said, "and she went on and on, thanking me for being her friend—"

"She should thank you," he said, nodding. "You've been a better friend than she ever deserved."

"That's exactly what she said. And before she hung up, she told me to tell you good-bye."

"People normally say that at the end of a conversation, Maggie, I don't see where that's so odd."

"Well, it was odd," she insisted uneasily.

"For the past weeks you've been upset because she's been depressed and wouldn't speak to you, now, when she finally engages in a conversation, you're upset." He reached behind her to lift an apple from a wooden bowl, rinsed it off, and bit into it, chiding her playfully, "There's no pleasing some people."

She gave him a dirty look.

"Look, sweetheart, we'll be there in five days. You'll see her and have more time to talk. And I think you'll probably find that she's just come to accept that she can't change what's happened and is just trying to make the best of it."

"That's not her style," she insisted.

"Then what do you think it is?"

"I don't know." She shook her head. "I just don't know."

There was a bustle of activity for the next several days, trying to pack and make arrangements for the dogs, cats, parakeets, and other assorted family pets. Two days before they were to depart, Rick called, his voice a weary whisper. "It's all over," he told Maggie tearfully.

"What's all over?" She froze where she stood.

"Lindy's gone," he said simply.

"Gone?" she asked uncertainly. "Gone where?"

"She's dead, Maggie." He seemed to choke on the words.

"Dead?" She caught her breath and stumbled into the nearest chair as her legs began to shake uncontrollably. "How could she be dead? Three days ago she was fine . . ."

"A lot has happened since then," he said sadly. "When will you be here? I want you to be here for the funeral."

"I don't understand," she cried. "How could she be dead?"

"She passed in her sleep." He seemed to choose his words carefully.

"Were you with her?"

"Yes," he replied after the briefest of pauses, "yes, I was there."

The memorial service, brief and to the point, had been arranged so that J.D. and Maggie could attend and was held on the day after their arrival in England. They returned with

Rick to his home and barely got beyond the vast foyer when he immediately disappeared into his study. An hour passed, then two, and still he did not emerge.

Tentatively knocking on the door with a cup of coffee in her hand, Maggie hesitated before she called to him. "Rick?" She knocked again lightly on the heavy mahogany door. "Rick?"

When he did not reply, she opened the door cautiously. The room was in semidarkness, the glow of the setting sun through the far window and the tidy fire burning at the hearth the only light. He was seated on the small brown leather sofa, staring blankly into the fire that had been made earlier to dispel the chill. She sat the coffee before him on the table, and he nodded his thanks, looking up at her with haunted eyes.

"Can I sit with you for a few minutes?" she asked.

"Of course," he said, clearing his throat.

"Rick, did you ever wonder if she did it on purpose? The accident?" she asked quietly.

He shook his head. "I don't know. I suspected it, though she denied it . . . said if she'd planned it she would have driven into a wall at full speed. Like her mother did."

"I still don't understand why she died. I thought she had stabilized. How could she have taken such a turn? Did something just give out? Her heart? Her kidneys?"

"Her will," he replied. "Her will gave out. She wanted to die."

"Rick, as terrible as the situation was, as crazy as it made her, people don't die just because they want to."

"She did," he said with a nod. "She was in complete control."

"In control of what?"

"Me," he said simply. "She was in total control of me."

"Rick, you're not making a bit of sense."

"She made me do it," he said as he turned to face her. "She was relentless, Maggie. Every day, every night, pleading, crying, begging . . ."

"Oh, God, Rick," she whispered in horror. "What did you do?"

270

"Exactly what she wanted me to do," he told her. "I acquired a certain amount of morphine and put it into her IV that night . . . that last night . . ."

"Jesus, Rick, you—"

"Killed her." He spared her the agony of accusing him. "Yes, I did. I did not want to, but I felt I had no choice. There's no question in my mind that she wanted to die. If she'd had the means, she'd have done it herself. But she could barely turn her head, you know, and it was driving her mad. And I finally gave in. She was so much happier, knowing it would end soon, Maggie, she was happier than I'd seen her in years."

"What if you'd been caught?"

"Little chance of that. They'd been giving her morphine every night to help her to sleep, and we figured that if they ever checked, they'd think that they had overprescribed her dosage. There was no autopsy, Maggie, and it seemed worth the risk for her to finally be at peace."

Maggie sat in stunned silence, absorbing the shock of Rick's revelation.

"What would you have done?" he asked.

Mrs. Gaines, the housekeeper, knocked on the door and entered to inquire about their plans for dinner. Rick gave abbreviated instructions, and after she'd closed the door behind her, he repeated the question, "What would you have done, Maggie?"

She walked to the fireplace and stood directly in front of it's blazing warmth, seeking to shake off the chill that had spread through her, pondering his dilemma, recalling her last conversation with Lindy. There was no question that Lindy would have worked him over unceasingly. She had never feared death.

"I most likely would have done the same thing," she said as she turned to him, tears clinging to her dark lashes.

He nodded slowly, and they locked eyes.

"Maggie?" J.D. poked his head through the door. "Everything all right in here?"

The two in the room had frozen at the intrusion, and J.D.

sensed immediately that his sudden appearance had interrupted something of importance.

"What is it?" he asked, apprehension washing over him as his wife and his best friend exchanged a long look of conspiracy.

"Come in and close the door," Rick instructed him. "I have something to tell you . . ."

22

WOULDN'T HILARY LOVE TO BE READING MY MIND RIGHT NOW,
Maggie thought. *What a coup for her to uncover that little
item.*

For months she had had nightmares that Rick had somehow been found out, awakening with a chill at the headlines
that had appeared in her dreams: From Guitar Great to
Mercy Killer. Rock Idol Murders Lover. She shuddered at
the very thought of what the press could do with a story like
that, the consequences to Rick, to Sophie . . .

Had he done the right thing? There had never been a
question in Maggie's mind that Lindy had been one hundred percent certain that she'd wanted to die. Maggie had
never ceased to pray that Lindy had found, in death, the
peace that had eluded her all her life and that Rick would
not be judged harshly on his own final reckoning day for his
part in her passing.

What was it Hilary was discussing now? Oh, that stuff
about three of J.D.'s former bandmates suing him a few
years back for a greater portion of the rights to some of the
old Monkshood albums that were newly issued on CD. J.D.

had been incensed when they had sued him directly rather than the record company, which had control of the funds. She knew he'd be pretty testy on that issue. Not the money—he'd never been one to keep close tabs on the cash—but the publicity—the implication that he had not treated his friends fairly—had made him crazy.

She glanced at Hilary from the corner of one eye. *She's enjoying this,* Maggie realized. *She thinks she's getting some hot scoop because Jamey had declined to be interviewed on the subject.* Personal anger aside, J.D. thought that the matter was trivial, not of any lasting importance to him. He had let the lawyers hash it out. It wasn't the type of thing that really touched his life in the long run.

Barely listening, she crossed her legs and nudged her foot from her shoe, wiggling her toes as they were gratefully released from the bondage of the tight black leather pumps. The dangling shoe slipped from her toes, and she tried to spear it back onto her foot without making too much show of it. Hilary was still grilling J.D. about that legal issue. Old news. That must have been, what, 1984?

What a crazy year that had been. The twins were born and Lindy died. Luke made her first trip ever to the States to spend the holidays with us, and we'd had a full gathering of the clans for Christmas. The year had started with a bang and never let up. There was one big event after another, right through to New Year's Eve . . .

Luke finally made her first transatlantic flight at the insistence of both her son and her daughter. She boarded the plane with Judith and Ned and their children—five of them at that point—and by the time the plane had landed in New York, she was berating herself for having resisted the trip for so long. She'd spent all week engaged in activities with her grandchildren, baking cookies and making special treats for them to share, helping them to shop for little surprises for their parents—with her money, of course—and tending to her new granddaughters while Maggie shopped and wrapped presents.

Near midnight on Christmas Eve, as Maggie fitted the last

of the children's presents under the tree, the doorbell rang. Being alone downstairs, she went into the hallway to see who the late arrival might be.

"Caroline!" Maggie exclaimed. "I'd given up on you. Where have you been? Hello, Allen. I see Caro's dragging you around for the Christmas Eve visits."

"I know it's late, Mags, but the lights were still on . . ." Caroline began her apology.

"Don't be silly," Maggie laughed. "This is Christmas Eve in a house with six children . . . eleven, actually, Judith and Ned are here."

J.D. came down the steps, carrying boxes of presents he'd squirreled away in the back of his closet to surprise his wife.

"Good to see you both," he greeted as he dropped the pile of gaily wrapped packages beside a chair. "Can I get you some holiday cheer?"

"We brought our own," Caroline said, handing him a bottle. "All we need are some glasses."

"Champagne? What's the occasion?"

"Well." Caroline took a deep breath and seated herself on the sofa. "Allen and I are getting married."

"What?" Maggie dropped the handful of tiny packages she'd been stuffing into the children's stockings that hung from the large oak mantle.

"I said, Allen and I are getting married," she repeated, her words seeming to echo in the room, which had become embarrassingly quiet in the wake of her announcement. Her eyes held Maggie's for a long moment.

"Why . . . what a surprise. I'd had no idea . . . You caught me off guard." Maggie attempted to recover. "I guess this is a cause for champagne. Have you decided when you're going to do this?"

"Well," Allen replied, "we were thinking of New Year's Eve."

"You mean next week?" Maggie's jaw dropped. "Next week?"

Caroline nodded as Allen explained, "All of my children will be home by then. My two sons are in college, you know, and my daughter and her husband and my little grandson

275

will be here, so it seemed like the most convenient time. I need to be back in Washington by the fifth, so I figured, what the heck, why wait? We can get married by a justice of the peace, and Caroline can make the trip back to D.C. with me."

Maggie sat on the floor, looking up at the couple on the sofa, Caroline so beautiful with her dark hair pulled back, Allen handsome and distinguished and a full twenty-five years older than his fiancée.

"I'm in shock, I'm sorry." Maggie giggled self-consciously. "I wish you every happiness, Caro, you know I do, but I hadn't expected it."

"I know it's a surprise," Caroline replied, avoiding the questions she read so clearly in Maggie's eyes.

J.D. brought in a tray of glasses, which he passed out to those assembled, and proposed a toast in honor of the forthcoming wedding. The champagne was soon depleted, and Maggie retreated to the kitchen in search of a bottle of wine. A moment later, Caroline joined her.

"So . . . what do you think?" Caroline asked her hesitantly.

"I think I'd like to hear a little more," she replied candidly.

"He's a nice guy, Maggie. And he loves me very much. I'll be okay."

"Yes, he's a nice guy. And it's obvious he loves you very much. But is 'okay' the best you can do?"

Caroline shrugged. "What would you like to hear?"

"How about 'I'm madly in love and can't live without him'?"

Caroline did not immediately reply.

"It'll be okay Maggie," she said with a sigh. "I'm not going to sit here and tell you I'm madly in love with him. Because I'm obviously not."

"Does Allen know that?"

"I think so."

"Why are you doing this?"

"I guess I'm just tired of waiting for . . . for something . . . a handsome dragonslayer, a Prince Charming. I don't know what I was waiting for, Maggie," she sighed deeply, "but I've given up. It's not coming . . . whatever it was I once thought I'd find . . ."

"Caroline . . ." Maggie whispered, her heart all but breaking.

"Anyway, it seems like the best thing to do."

"Best thing for who? Caro, have you thought this through completely? How does Allen feel about starting another family at his age?"

"Well, he really doesn't want to. You know, Edie, his daughter, has a son who's only two—"

"For crying out loud, Caroline, you're not even thirty-five years old. And you always wanted a family."

"It'll be okay," she said again, averting her gaze.

"Caroline, don't you think you deserve more than—" She stopped abruptly as Allen walked into the room, and they were unable to complete the conversation.

By the time the evening had ended, Maggie couldn't wait to get J.D. alone to bend his ear.

"Why in the name of God did you offer to have the wedding here?" she glared.

"Maggie, I thought you'd be pleased. Caroline's your oldest and dearest friend, isn't she?"

"Well, yes, but—"

"So what is the problem?" he asked.

"The problem is that Caro's making a terrible mistake, Jamey. She shouldn't marry him."

"Maggie, that is not your decision to make."

"He is absolutely the wrong man for her," protested Maggie.

"What's wrong with him? He seems like a nice enough sort."

"He is nice," she sighed with exasperation, "but that's not the point. She doesn't love him, Jamey. And he's better than twenty-five years her senior. He has grown children. And he doesn't want anymore. You know how Caro always wanted children. She's making a big mistake."

"That may or may not be so. But it's not your place to tell her that. You could be very wrong, Maggie, so my advice to you is don't give any advice to her. It's Caro's choice. Maybe they'll be very happy."

"They won't be," she grumbled.

"Well, I remember when people very close to you thought our marriage was a mistake. And they were people who thought they knew you well and knew what was best for you. And look how wrong they were. I know you're concerned about Caroline because you care for her, but even if it is a mistake, you can't prevent her from making it."

"What should I do?"

"Be a happy matron of honor and pray she knows what she's doing."

Caroline's elderly parents did not attend because her mother was recuperating from recent heart surgery, but her brother Thomas, ten years older than she, made the trip from Iowa to give the bride away. Thomas and his wife, Betty, both quiet, reserved midwesterners, seemed overwhelmed by the Borders crew, the presence of the many young children, Judith's family, the Callahans, and assorted friends of Caroline's and Allen's and, of course, Allen's children.

The ceremony, presided over by the local justice of the peace, was held in the parlor and was brief and to the point. Allen's eldest son served as best man, and Maggie, as the bride's only attendant. J.D. broke out the champagne after the vows had been exchanged, and the judge, anxious to get on with his evening, had asked for his overcoat as soon as he'd toasted the bride.

"Rushing the New Year a bit, don't you think?" rang a cheery voice from the doorway. "It's only ten past eight, a bit early for a New Year's toast."

The gathering turned to see a smiling Rick holding a squirming Sophie in his arms. He set her down and put his arms out to a very surprised Maggie.

"Sorry for dropping in like this, but we've just wound up what turned out to be the longest tour of my life. We've been everywhere—Japan, Australia, you name it, we played there. So Sophie and I thought we'd celebrate and surprise you. I was hoping you'd be having a party tonight." He grinned broadly.

"Well, actually, Rick—" Maggie was interrupted as Rick spotted her mother.

"Mrs. Callahan, what a pleasure to see you. Sophie, this is Aunt Maggie's mother, do you remember?" He turned his attention to his daughter who was struggling out of her coat, assisted by Lucy. "Oh, and there's Caro . . . Hello, darling. I was praying you'd be here. Can't think of anyone I'd rather see in the New Year with." He put his arms around her and before she could utter a word, impulsively kissed her on the lips, leaned back and looked at her face. Mistaking her dismay for compliance, he kissed her again.

"Ah . . . Rick," she pushed back from him. "Rick, there is someone I'd like you to meet . . ."

"Oh, no, you've got a date. Of course, you would. Any chance you can ditch him a bit early," he teased, only half joking, "and we can sit up all night and talk, like we did the last time. We've got lots to discuss, you and I—"

"Rick," she said, blushing crimson and extricating herself from his arms as Allen approached, forced humor in his forced smile. He placed a hand firmly on her elbow. "Rick, this is Allen Fisher. My husband."

There was a long embarrassed silence. Rick was dumbstruck.

"Allen, this is Rick Daily, an old friend."

Recovering as quickly as he could, Rick quipped, "Well, looks like I'm a day late and a dollar short. Caro, I had no idea . . ."

"We only decided very recently, Rick," she explained as calmly as she could, wishing that Allen would release his grip on her arm and that the sudden, unexplainable ache in her stomach would vanish. "Maggie and J.D. offered to let us get married here tonight."

"Tonight? You mean you just, just now . . ." His jaw dropped and his skin went ashen.

"Yes. About twenty minutes ago," she told him, unable to look away from his stunned face.

A day late indeed.

"Well, then, I guess congratulations are in order for you both," he said softly, shaking Allen's hand with an obvious lack of enthusiasm, a hollow space opening up inside him.

23

Maggie's muscles were aching, the result of holding her body so stiffly in one position for such a long time. She was pressed tightly against the arm of the sofa. If she shifted her weight, she'd be touching him, and she did not wish any physical contact whatsoever. Emotionally drained, she could not even look at his face. "The woods are full of ghosts tonight . . ." Where had she read that? The specters from the past leaned heavily upon her. She could bear to see no more of them.

The TV lights had heated up the room unmercifully, and the air was stuffy. At the next commercial break, she'd open the French doors, maybe step outside for a moment or two and breath in some fresh air. She glanced at her watch, noting the lateness of the hour and relaxed slightly. Not too much time left.

Hilary had seen Maggie steal a peek at the time. *I need to get this woman to react,* she told herself. *She's like a damned dummy sitting there and just about as responsive. I need to draw her back into this. I need to get her talking. Maybe I'll stumble upon a clue as to what's going on.*

"It's an interesting collection of portraits, there on the wall." Hilary pointed to the row of paintings. "They're all your children?"

"Yes," Maggie nodded.

"Well, then, introduce us to them." Hilary rose and walked toward the wall, indicating that both Maggie and the cameraman should follow, J.D. remaining on the sofa.

"Lovely children." Hilary smiled, hoping that she looked warmly, sincerely interested. "Point them out to us, oldest to youngest."

"Well, this is Jesse."

"He looks so much like his father," Hilary commented.

"Yes," Maggie went on, "and this is Tyler, he's thirteen this year. Very athletic, very much the all-American boy."

"Hardly 'all' American," her husband's voice from the sofa reminded her.

She ignored him. "And Lucy's next. She's eleven—"

"A redhead. How charming," Hilary cooed.

"And Emma is nine." She touched the frame of the portrait of the dark-haired child, eyes seemingly too large for her tiny face.

"But she's the very image of you, Maggie." Hilary could not miss the striking resemblance, the green eyes, the smile.

"She is very much like me," Maggie said with a nod, "but certainly much sweeter in disposition. More trusting, more naive than I."

Hilary and Maggie locked eyes, and Hilary knew that Maggie had seen through her expressed interest in her children as a ploy to coax Maggie into letting her guard down. *Very good, Maggie,* Hilary acknowledged silently.

"These are the twins, Molly and Susannah. They're six," Smiling, Maggie moved smoothly to the next painting, pleased she'd made her point and confident that she'd be able to survive the next thirty minutes with no further anxiety. "And this is Spencer. The baby."

"And he's how old now?" Hilary inquired.

"Two," Maggie told her, gazing with love upon the darling baby boy with the blond curls who grinned impishly from the canvas.

"A beautiful family, Maggie, and I'm sure our viewers at home are just as taken with their adorable little faces as I am." She smiled broadly and turned as if she were preparing to walk back toward their seats. Maggie was about to take a step toward the sofa when Hilary hesitated and said, "There seems to be an uncharacteristic gap of about four years there, between the twins and the last one." She frowned slightly, then added, somewhat absentmindedly, "Oh, of course, you lost a child, didn't you?"

"Yes," Maggie's jaunty confidence, so newly gained, evaporated in an instant as her throat began to close rapidly.

"Would you like to tell us—"

"No," Maggie cut her off, "no, I would not."

Light-headed and weak, she turned her back on the camera, achingly aware that one child was missing. She'd have given anything to have seen Hallie there, among the others. Even now, when she thought of that baby, she saw only a blank, featureless face. It had never ceased to haunt her.

She felt strong hands grip her elbows from behind, holding her weight. He'd felt her pain from across the room, felt the stab of her anguish as clearly as if it had been his own. Without a thought he had gone to her. She leaned back against him slightly, touching him for the first time in days, and he felt her sharp intake of breath as she attempted to recover from the sudden unwanted memory of that saddest of times, waiting for her to pull away from him. She did not.

He looked beyond her to the wall of portraits. They had not needed Hilary to point out that there were seven, rather than eight faces, displayed there . . .

"Well, Maggie, looks as if my talk on birth control fell on deaf ears," Dr. Bernard said following his examination. "All kidding aside, you really should slow down."

She laughed. "I feel fine."

"You always 'feel fine,'" he said, a serious tone in his voice, "but let's face it, Maggie, your body is not what it was ten years ago, you know."

"Is something wrong?"

"No, not that I can see. But five pregnancies back to back will take a toll. And now this one . . ."

"As long as the baby's all right, I'm all right. I'm tired, as usual, and my appetite's off, as it always is. But I'll skate through this like I always do."

And for the most part, she did, up until the beginning of the seventh month, when backaches and leg pain kept her almost completely inactive. She'd insisted that they keep to their summer schedule, and although her doctor hadn't been supportive of her decision to travel, she assured him she'd be back in a month with a month to spare before delivery.

They'd been at Luke's for three weeks when she'd awakened one night drenched with perspiration, her heart pounding, an odd, excruciating pain in her side. She lay quietly, afraid to move, until it subsided. An hour later, it returned, and she was frightened. She shook her husband.

"Jamey. Jamey," she whispered. "Please wake up. Wake up."

"What?" he mumbled.

"I said wake up."

"Why?" he made a halfhearted attempt to open his eyes.

"Because . . . because . . . ," she sputtered uncertainly. The pain was gone.

"What is it?" He turned over sleepily.

"I don't know," she replied hesitantly. "I had a pain. Two sharp pains. But they're gone now."

"Come here, Mags. Lay back down now. Do you feel all right? Want me to call Judith's doctor? I can call her and get his number."

"No. No, I guess maybe it's okay. I feel a little shaky inside, but the pain is gone."

"Maybe it was just a cramp. Remember how you used to get those cramps sometimes with Emma?"

"This was different. Sharper. And in my abdomen . . . but it's gone."

"Are you sure you don't want me to call Jude? She won't mind."

"No. But if it happens again, maybe we should. Maybe it was just a cramp." She lay back and took a deep breath and tried to relax. She lay awake long after J.D.'s even breathing told her he'd fallen back to sleep.

Several evenings later she'd been about to start down the steps after having tucked the children in when she experienced the same pain, sharper, more insistent, and she began to bleed. She stared dumbly at the bright scarlet river that flowed with horrific speed down her leg and onto the floor. Within minutes, J.D. was speeding to the hospital, eighteen miles away, where Judith's doctor would be waiting for them. Thirty minutes later, bleeding profusely and in severe pain, Maggie was helped onto an examining table.

Her previous experiences with childbirth had all been relatively easy, uneventful experiences, labor and delivery of short duration. This time the contractions were erratic and hard and had lasted for hours. She knew it was too soon for the baby to be born, and she was terrified. They'd offered her sedatives repeatedly, and repeatedly she'd refused. Ashen and shaken, J.D. bent over her bed, kissed her face, and brushed back her hair minutes before the decision was made to move her into the delivery room.

There seemed to be an inordinate number of nurses waiting in the harshly lit room. Another doctor came in, then a third. She began to panic. Over her protests, she was given a shot 'to calm her down,' J.D. was told. The medication hadn't had time to take effect before the baby's birth.

"Oh, no." The nurse's whisper cut to Maggie's heart, and she tried to sit up, tried to see J.D.'s face.

"Quickly," the doctor said, "see if we can bring her around."

There was a flurry of activity as a tiny form was wrapped hastily in a blanket and shuttled to another table.

"What's wrong?" Maggie cried. "What is it? Let me see her . . ."

She was attempting to rise but could not, strong arms sheathed in white holding her down. She knew J.D. was speaking to her, but she couldn't comprehend his words through the fog of fear and confusion surrounding her. A nurse appeared with a syringe and injected something into her arm.

"No!" she screamed. "No! Let me up! Jamey, please. Please. Make them let go," she pleaded wildly. "Don't let them put me out. Don't let them. I want to see my baby . . ." She felt her body begin to relax involuntarily, and though she tried to fight against it, her will failed her, and she faded away as she was wheeled from the room.

"I'm sorry, Mr. Borders. There's nothing we can do for her," the doctor said somberly. "The cord was wrapped around her neck. She was stillborn. I'm so sorry."

Burning tears filled his eyes and streamed down his face. He walked to the table where the tiny girl lay, half covered by a white blanket. The nurse was preparing to take her as he approached and pushed her firmly out of the way. She looked quickly to the doctor for direction, and when he nodded, she stepped back.

J.D. reached down and wrapped the perfect little girl in the blanket, folding it over her motionless chest. The nurses stood stunned as he gently lifted her to his shoulder and held her close, whispering words they could not hear as he nuzzled the still bundle. Finally, the doctor put his hand on J.D.'s shoulder.

"Mr. Borders, you need to hand her over now."

J.D. nodded and lowered the baby to look at her face, studying her carefully, noting the blond hair, the blond lashes, the tiny ears. *Maggie will want to know,* he thought. He passed the bundle into the hands of the nurse and asked, "Where's my wife?"

"Room 316."

He walked out into the hall and located the room several doors down. He sat on the bed while she slept.

Several hours later, Maggie awoke and was sedated again quickly, over J.D.'s protests, when she became hysterical. The same scene was almost repeated when she woke up the second time, but J.D. refused to permit another sedative.

"You can't keep doing this to her," he said quietly. "She has to know, and she has to be given a chance to deal with it. Leave us alone, please. She'll be all right."

He knew perfectly well she wouldn't be all right. He knew

her heart would break, but he also knew that no amount of medication could prevent the inevitable. And so he sat and held her for the rest of the night while she cried quietly for the baby she hadn't been permitted to hold. The baby's death devasted her, but the fact that Maggie had not been allowed to see her, to hold her, would haunt her forever.

Maggie could not face the trip back home with the tiny coffin on the plane and so reluctantly agreed to J.D.'s suggestion that they bury Hallie, as Maggie had planned to name the baby, along side his father in the peaceful church-yard down the road from Luke's house.

Maggie recovered slowly from the loss and in the aftermath seemed to retreat into a deep depression. It was close to the beginning of the school year, and J.D. was mindful that they would have to get back to the States before the first week in September. Maggie was avoiding the trip and kept putting off their departure.

"We'll go next Tuesday," she'd say on Thursday, then on Monday morning, she'd ask, "Could we please stay until Saturday?"

Finally, they were out of time.

"No, Maggie. We can't stay till Friday. The children have to start school Tuesday. It's time to go back. We have to leave, sweetheart," he told her gently.

Her eyes filled with tears, and J.D. held her tightly, hoping she'd finally cry it out. He'd become alarmed by her long silences, her solitary walks, her distance. He did not know how to help her.

"Jamey, I can't leave here. I can't leave my baby alone . . ." she told him.

"She's not alone, sweetheart. My mom's here. And Judith. She's not alone." He tried his best to comfort her. "But we have to go home."

He cradled her and whispered reassurances, but even when the tears had subsided, he doubted he'd reached her, and he worried.

Even the frantic scurry of school activities did little to distract her. He grew increasingly concerned and suggested to her one night that they both go for counseling. She'd declined, telling him she had to work it out herself. He disagreed but could not change her mind. And so he watched her as she grew more distant, more distracted, slipping more frequently into a silence even he could not pierce.

One day in late October he looked out a back window and saw her seated on the ground in the garden. He walked outside and sat next to her. The trowel she was using to dig in the dirt was in her right hand, and he watched as she stabbed fiercely into the soil.

"What are you planting?" he asked casually.

"Daffodils."

"Isn't it late to plant them? It'll be cold soon."

"You plant spring bulbs in the fall," she explained with a flat voice. "Daffodils bloom in the spring."

"Oh," he said. She did not look up at him.

"Maggie," he said after a few minutes had passed.

"What?"

"We have to put it behind us, Maggie."

"I can't." She dug another hole.

"You have to. I have to—"

"You already have," she spoke harshly, pulling away from his attempt to touch her. "I can't understand how you could so easily forget—"

"I haven't forgotten. I never will. But we have to get on with living, sweetheart." She did not reply, and he continued, "Maggie, we can't change what happened. Please, Maggie, talk to me . . ."

She shook her head as the tears welled and flooded her face. He moved closer and took the trowel from her hand, holding her as the tears gave way to heartbreaking sobs.

"I never saw her face, Jamey, I never held her. They took her from me and put me to sleep and the next thing I knew, they were putting her in the ground," her voice broke harshly. "I wanted to hold her, Jamey."

He rocked her shaking form gently, letting her cry, hoping that by voicing her pain, she would be released of its grip on her soul. "I wanted that baby, Jamey," she said quietly, "and maybe if I'd stayed home, maybe if I'd gone to the hospital the first night I had that pain, if I'd gotten to the hospital sooner—"

"Don't do this to yourself, Maggie. Nothing would have made a difference," he told her. "I spoke with the doctor. The cord had been wrapped around her neck. There was no heartbeat when you first got to the hospital, Maggie. It was already too late."

"Why didn't they tell me? Why did they let me go through that?"

"Maggie, stillborn or not, you had to deliver her. Would it have helped you to have known?"

"Did you know? Did they tell you?" she demanded in an accusatory tone.

"They told me there were serious complications," he admitted. "I do know that nothing that you did or didn't do was responsible for what happened, Maggie. It's not your fault or the doctor's or anyone else's. It happens sometimes. This time it happened to us. I know it hurts you terribly, sweetheart; it hurts me, too. But we have to put it behind us and go on, do you understand?"

She nodded her head slowly, a reluctant acknowledgment that she did. "There's been so much sadness these past few years, Jamey. There's been so much pain. Lindy. The baby."

"Lindy is finally at peace, sweetheart. And we have six beautiful, healthy, wonderful children. Be grateful for them. They need you, Maggie, and so do I," he told her as he dried her face. "Please come back to us. Put Hallie to rest, sweetheart."

They sat close together in the fading sunlight, and watched the shadows stretch across the grass. She remained wrapped in his arms, and he knew she was far away, lost in her thoughts. An occasional tear slid from her face, but she did not speak. Dusk began to close in, and she turned to him.

"I guess we should see about dinner," she said, and he stood up, helping her to her feet.

They walked hand in hand to the house, and he wondered if he'd gotten through to her. He couldn't tell for sure. But later that night when he got into bed as quietly as possible, thinking that she was asleep, she had nudged into his arms, kissing him with her old passion very much in evidence. As he fell asleep hours later, he knew that his wife had come back to him.

J.D. went on tour for two months the following spring, and when it was over, he and Maggie packed up the family and traveled for three weeks as soon as school was out, taking all six children to France and Germany for a family holiday. They spent the rest of the summer in England. Every morning Maggie took a walk to the churchyard to visit the tiny grave. Sometimes he accompanied her, sometimes she preferred to be alone. He feared she'd become depressed again, but when it was time to leave, she did not resist the trip home and had asked him to walk with her that last morning.

They entered the quiet cemetery, and he studied her face carefully, trying to read her thoughts as she placed a handful of flowers near the white headstone that bore the simple inscription Margaret Hallie Borders, August 1, 1986.

"I've come to the conclusion that the saddest thing in this life is burying a child, Jamey. There simply couldn't be any pain like it. I can't imagine anything that could do greater damage to your soul," she told him as they turned to leave. "It's a hurt that never goes away. And no other child can make up for one you've lost. I love each of our children so deeply, Jamey, but I'll never stop wanting her."

A lump had grown in his throat and he could not speak, and so he just nodded and took her hand as they walked back down the road to his mother's home. Once there, they rushed to get all the bags and all the children into the car and to the airport on time. The flight was chaotic, as always, the children restless and bored at first, then tired and cranky as they neared their destination. After they'd arrived home and the last child had been kissed good night, Maggie climbed wearily into their bed and turned to him.

"It was a good trip. I'm glad we stayed the summer. I was scared at first—scared I'd get crazy again and not want to leave. But your mom goes down to the cemetery several times a week, and that's a comfort to me. I know that Hallie will always be with us, inside. It took me a whole year to understand that, but I can live with it now."

24

"THANK YOU," MAGGIE WHISPERED AS SHE TURNED TO FACE him, not looking away when he looked into her eyes. "I'm all right."

J.D. followed her as she walked to the sofa and quietly seated herself.

"Maggie, I'm so sorry." Hilary was acutely aware that her audience, while loving her when she made people crazy with her innuendoes, would not look kindly upon her for flaunting a dead child in its mother's face. "It was absolutely thoughtless of me . . ."

"Life goes on," Maggie said quietly, raising her chin slightly. *Life always goes on. People die and pieces of us die with them, but it all still goes on. Days pass and we build our lives around the void.*

It can all be so unfair sometimes, Maggie thought darkly. *And yet it goes on. Always a new crisis or a new joy. Since Hallie, we've survived my dad's open-heart surgery, my mother's mastectomy. The nightmare of Anjjoli and dealing with its aftermath. Caroline's been divorced and Colleen's been married and Kevin and Jenny have had a child. And of course, there's Spencer. Blessed Spencer . . .*

* * *

It had been a hectic year, another album for J.D., another baby on the way, much to Dr. Bernard's concern.

"Maggie, I'm very worried about you, and I think you should give some consideration to, well, maybe you should think twice this time," he told her. "It could be risky for both of you."

"Then tell me how to minimize the risks," she replied, "and I'll do whatever I have to do. But I *will* have this baby, and we will both be fine."

She spent most of her time in bed for the following months, much to her frustration, but she was determined that nothing would go wrong. She tearfully acknowledged to J.D. that this would be the last one, and when he offered to have a vasectomy, she agreed it would probably be a good idea.

Spencer Thomas Borders was born the following spring—the last of their children.

On a lazy midsummer day shortly after their arrival at Luke's for their annual visit, the entire family packed into the car and headed toward Rick's to spend the afternoon.

"Sophie's growing so tall, Rick," Maggie observed as she watched the lanky blond girl run across the grass, concentrating on the soccer game she was playing with Emma and Lucy and Judith's daughter Pamela.

They sat on the veranda, overlooking the huge expanse of lawn behind Rick's palatial home.

"Didn't call her mom Legs for nothing," he said. "She's a pretty thing, don't you think?"

"A true natural beauty," Maggie readily agreed, "she looks so much like Lindy."

"Gratefully, she lacks her mother's moodiness, her melancholy."

"That's your influence on her." Maggie smiled.

"Well, I certainly didn't have such a great influence on her mother, that's for certain," he said grimly, watching his daughter as she ran to retrieve the ball, which had blasted through the hedge following a hard kick by Lucy.

"You still harboring some guilt?" Maggie asked.

"Always. I took her life."

"You did what she asked you to do. As you always did."

"Do you think I did the right thing?" He looked at her with eyes that were still haunted.

"I don't know." Maggie sighed deeply. "You did what she thought was right for her. Would she be better off had she lived these past years, flat on her back? The decision was hers, Rick."

"I got her into the drug thing. That's what did her in," he said flatly.

"Rick, Lindy spent a lot of time looking for a way to shut it all out. She'd have found it sooner or later, with or without you. At least you didn't abandon her; you did everything a person could do to try to help her get away from it." She put her hand gently on his arm, then added, "She had something inside her that we couldn't see and couldn't understand. It's haunted me since it happened, but I've come to the conclusion that it couldn't have ended any other way for her."

"And what do I tell Sophie? She's asked a million questions about her mother. I hate to keep lying to her, but I can't tell her the truth."

"What purpose would the truth serve in that child's life? It's hard enough for her to grow up without a mother without burdening that little soul with all the gory details."

"I just want to do what's right for my daughter," he said, "if in fact she is my daughter. If Lindy knew for certain, she took that secret with her."

"Do you really need to know?" Lindy's blunt confession rang in Maggie's ears, gnawing at her conscience.

"No," he sighed. "Whether she's my flesh and blood doesn't matter. She's my little girl and she always will be. She may not have a mother, but she'll always have me. And I'll always love her. That's about the only sure thing I know in this life, Maggie."

"Well, that's a lot." She grinned, praying a silent thanks to

Lindy for having given him this most precious of gifts. Not flesh of his flesh, but undeniably, Sophie was his heart.

"Look at them." His focus was on the four young girls as they lounged on the grass, taking a breather from their game. "They all look so grown up. I'm not ready for them to grow up quite yet."

"Neither am I. You know Jesse turned thirteen this year? And already starting to look at the girls."

"With any luck he'll have his father's good taste in women, and you won't have to worry about it. Of course, his father wasn't quite as selective as a young man," he teased, "but he grew smarter as he grew older."

"What about you? Are you seeing anyone special these days?"

"Not really. I've been busy. New album, an international tour. Sophie," he said, somewhat self-satisfied. "It's such a kick, Maggie. Do you realize that now that I'm an old man, I'm a 'legendary guitar great'? I guess that happens to you, once you pass forty. It's amusing, don't you think?"

"There's nothing amusing about passing forty, Rick," she grimaced.

"You don't look a day over thirty, Maggie. You never really change very much. Neither does J.D."

"I think it has something to do with being happy all these years," she told him. "I wish you could find someone to share your life with. I imagine you get lonely sometimes."

"I do," he admitted, "though there's never a lack of female companionship."

"It's not the same as being with someone you love."

"I've only loved one woman in my life, Maggie," he said very quietly, "and I've given up hope of ever—"

J.D. called to them as he rounded the side of the terrace and began to ascend the steps to where they sat.

"So, how was the hike? And where are your sons?" Maggie asked, disappointed that the conversation had been interrupted.

"Down by the duck pond," he said. "Young Spencer here is soggy and could probably use a nap."

"Well, since I've been sitting here relaxing all day while

you've been dragging the boys all over the countryside, I'll take him in and clean him up and get him a drink."

She took her blond, curly-haired little boy from the backpack in which he'd been riding. He was such a joy to her, this last child, and his pleasant ways and sweet disposition filled her heart every time she held him. He was a cuddler, and now as she walked into the cool of the old brick house, she felt him snuggle into her neck as she carried him. Knowing he would be her last baby made him extra special to her, just as Jesse, being the first, was special. She hoped the others didn't sense it and think she loved them any less.

Three days later, Rick had dropped Sophie off at Luke's, which had become more and more Maggie and J.D.'s house. They had expanded again two years ago, and at Luke's suggestion, Maggie had redecorated the entire house. Even the garden bore Maggie's mark, with the newly built wall enclosing an even greater space that housed those flowers to which she was partial. All along one side she'd planted dozens of her favorite roses, an ashy lavender color with the sweetest of fragrances. She filled every room of the house with them when they were in season, in vases and bowls, the aroma everywhere.

Maggie was placing a newly cut bouquet in her bedroom when Emma and Sophie trailed in, bored and looking for something to do. Maggie made a few suggestions and wasn't the least surprised that all were immediately rejected, eight- and ten-year-olds being as they are. She caught the movement out of the corner of her eye as Sophie drifted toward her bedside table and picked up a photograph, studying intently.

"Is this my mother?" she asked, touching the glass reverently with a small finger, wanting to touch the face of the woman she'd never known.

"Yes," Maggie said, walking toward her slowly. "That picture was taken a long, long time ago. Before I met J.D. and before she met your daddy."

"Where was this?"

"In Philadelphia. After a bike race we were in." She smiled, thinking back to that day so very long ago.

"Did you win?" she asked.

"Not by a long shot," Maggie laughed, "but we didn't expect to. We did it for fun."

Sophie smiled up at her, a light in her eyes. "Was it fun? Was she fun?"

"Oh, yes. She was a lot of fun. She had a great sense of humor, and she was, as you can see, very beautiful. We had many good times together back in those days, your mother and I."

Sophie looked wistfully at the photograph of the mother who had never hummed a lullaby to her sleepy child nor rewarded a handful of clover with a kiss. "How old was she when this picture was taken?"

"Well, let me think. This must have been, um, 1973? The spring of 1973, I think. So Lindy would have been about twenty-five."

"I never saw a picture of her when she was this young. In the few Dad has, she was older."

"Well, if you'd like, I'll have that one copied for you. And I have a few back home that I think you should have. I'd give you this one, but I don't have the negative, and it's one that I particularly like."

"Why?" Sophie asked.

"Oh, because it makes me remember the day, and it makes me think of your mom and how we were back then. And that day was special to me. See, after the race, we went out for some dinner, and we sat and talked for a long, long time. That was the day we started to get to know each other, the day that marked the beginning of our real friendship." Maggie's throat tightened as she recalled that night, as Lindy, sensing that Maggie was a person she could trust, slowly told her the story of her life and all it's tragic twists and turns.

Seeing Lindy's daughter holding the photograph, the tragedy was real to her again, and she was saddened for the little girl who looked so much like the mother she'd never known. In some ways she was a bit like Lindy, sassy and bright and beautiful but, gratefully, lacking the darkness that had pervaded her mother's nature. She was, in this respect, truly Rick Daily's daughter, lighthearted and jovial, casual in her approach to things with that same seemingly boundless energy and enthusiasm.

When they'd returned home to the States, Maggie spent a morning going through boxes of old photographs, selecting those she thought Sophie would most appreciate. She had them all copied, and several she had enlarged and framed. She packed the box carefully, enclosing a note that told the story behind each picture. Sophie called her the night the package had arrived to thank her, but as she began to speak, she broke into tears.

"Oh, Sophie, I'm sorry. I never for a minute thought it would upset you," Maggie apologized.

"I'm not upset," Sophie replied. "They are beautiful pictures, Aunt Maggie. It's the best present anyone ever gave me. I'll always keep them."

"Which one did you like the best?" Maggie asked when Sophie had settled down.

"I like them all, but I love the one on the beach. The one with you and my mother sitting back to back, and her hair is long over one shoulder and you are laughing. The camera was real close to you, and your faces are big in the picture. I have that one next to my bed, on the table . . . Oh, Daddy wants to talk to you."

"That was a lovely gift, Maggie. Thank you. You have no idea what it's meant to her, to see her mother smiling and looking happy. The few pictures I have mostly make her appear morose, as she tended to get those last few years. It's been wonderful for Sophie to see Lindy in less complicated times."

"It was my pleasure, Rick. I'm glad they were well received." She paused and looked out the window as Caroline's car pulled up the drive. "Well, I see my dinner guest is here. Caro just arrived."

"Caro and her old man? No pun intended," he said dryly.

"No. Just Caro. She left Allen."

"When?"

"A few weeks ago. I don't know exactly why. I suppose I'll hear about it tonight. Jamey's in L.A. for some award thing

so I'll have the whole night to sit and listen and commiser-
ate."

"Well, tell her . . . tell her I've been thinking about her.
And give her my love."

"It was a mismatch, and I told you it wouldn't last,"
Maggie said smugly to her husband as she poured his coffee
on the morning of his return from his trip. "Not that I'm
glad it didn't work out, but I knew she wouldn't be happy
with him. And I'm glad she realized it as soon as she did,
before she spent ten or fifteen years in misery."

"So what is Caroline planning on doing?" J.D. asked as he
flipped through his mail.

"She's going back to work and is getting her life back on
track. Actually, she seems relieved. She didn't cry or accuse
Allen of mistreating her or say anything negative about him.
Just that she didn't love him, wasn't happy, shouldn't have
done it, and she was filing for divorce this week. Period. All
very matter-of-fact."

She looked out the window into the woods behind the
house, staring blankly into space. "I hope she'll be happy
with someone someday. I always wondered if someday
maybe she and . . ." Her voice trailed away.

"She and who?"

"Rick," she said over one shoulder.

"Rick? Rick Daily? You think so?"

She nodded. "I think they would be good for each other. I
don't know that it will ever happen—it seems they've
missed each other at every turn—but I think they could be
very happy together."

"Well, don't be playing matchmaker with your two best
friends. That rarely works out. And besides, they've known
each other for years. I'd think if either of them had any
serious interest, they'd have made it known by now."

"I'm not so sure they haven't."

"Well, you keep out of it, Maggie. Do not go poking
around in other people's lives."

"Oh, speaking of poking around in other peoples lives, we
got a phone call today from Geoff Fox."

"Who?"

"Geoff Fox. Remember we met him and his wife at that benefit auction back in July, in London? The guy who produces that TV show with that snoopy woman who tries to get people pissed off on the air when she's interviewing them so that they'll say something stupid and make fools out of themselves?"

"Oh," he laughed, "you mean Hilary Gates."

"Yes."

"I do remember him. Nice chap. What did he want?"

"He wanted us to go on her show."

"Forget it."

"That's pretty much what I told him."

"I hate stuff like that. I hate giving interviews. Why anyone would want to know that much about anyone else's life is beyond me." He slid the letter he'd been scanning back into its envelope. "Of course, if my mom finds out we've been asked, there'll be hell to pay if we turn it down. She loves that show."

"That's the rest of the story," she continued, pulling out a chair and seating herself across from him.

"What do you mean?"

"Well, it seems Geoff called your mother for our number here in the States."

"Oh, no," he groaned, knowing what was coming next.

"Oh, yes. She called not ten minutes after Geoff, proud as a peacock and wanting to know when the show would be. She's enthralled."

"Oh, God," he grumbled, "how do we get out of this one? That woman is notorious for digging up the most outlandish dirt."

"Jamey, we've nothing to hide. What in our past could possibly qualify for the type of junk she likes to talk about?"

"Well, I can't think of much," he conceded.

"I can't think of anything. The closest she could come would be to poke at my relationship with Rick, you know, the way the newspapers did there for a time when Lindy would go off and I'd be at the house with him or when he'd visit here when you were elsewhere, that sort of thing. But no one ever took any of that seriously. At least, no one with any sense."

"Glory. She could talk about Glory."

"What about her? That she throws herself at you every chance she gets? That she's been throwing herself at you for fifteen years? That she's a sarcastic bitch who is going to get her face slapped someday?"

"Whoa, Maggie," he laughed again. "Still touchy, I see."

"She makes me more than touchy. If I had a dime for every time she has cornered me over the years to inform me that she was still on the case, if I ever thought for one minute that you'd—"

"I wouldn't. I have the sweetest, sexiest, most loving woman in the world. Why on earth would I want Glory Fielding or anyone else, for that matter, when I have you?"

"Haven't you ever gotten tired of the same old lady after all these years? You know, in July, next year, we'll be talking fifteen big ones, Jamey. That's a long time."

"Not long enough," he told her quietly, "and no, I've never gotten tired of you. Never wanted anyone else. I love you more than I ever thought it would be possible to love anyone, Maggie, and I will until the day I die."

"Which hopefully won't be for a long, long time. It's all been so good for us, Jamey. We've taken a lump or two from time to time, but our life together's been wonderful. It's been so right." She had gotten up and walked around the table to where he sat, and at her approach he had pushed back his chair and opened his arms to her. She sat on his lap and snuggled close. "I wish sometimes that it would never end."

"It never will, sweetheart," he told her solemnly, "it never will."

"Geoff Fox called again this morning," he told her several weeks later.

"What did you tell him?"

"I told him no. Twice. He told me to talk it over with you and call him back toward the end of the week."

"Do you want to do it?"

He shrugged.

"We'll be boring as hell," she said.

"Probably. I'll tell him no."

Geoff had not agreed that they'd be boring. He loved J.D.'s music and thought Maggie was adorable. After three more conversations, J.D. gave in on the condition that the interview wait until the following summer when the family would be in England for their annual holiday.

"That gives us plenty of time to change our minds," he told Maggie.

They pretty much forgot about the commitment until May when Hilary called them to confirm a date in mid-August. Maggie shrugged it off, unconcerned about it. If Hilary thought she could find a skeleton in their closet, she was welcomed to try. She wasn't about to waste any time worrying about it. There were dance recitals to plan for, the boys were busy with their softball games, and the end of the school year was fast approaching. Life was full and good and busy—too busy to look ahead to August. What was the worst thing that could happen?

25

AND SO IT GOES ON . . . FROM THAT DAY ON THE PARKWAY TO THE present. *And here we sit,* Maggie thought, *not speaking, not touching. Has the last memory been made, and is it this, this silence, this pain? Is this then the sum of fifteen years?*

She tilted her head so that she could look at J.D., and he met her stare with sadly resigned eyes, conceding defeat. He seemed all but dazed, no longer able to make any further effort to appeal to her, but the evidence of his submission brought her no sense of triumph. Rather it stabbed at her someplace deep within, and she felt the depth of his anguish. She recalled the strength of his hands as they had held her up moments before, how he had come to her when he had known she needed him, no longer concerned with keeping score in this senseless game they'd played all evening. Jamey had always been there when she needed him, she acknowledged, and with that admission, the distance between them seemed to narrow.

Maybe, a tiny voice inside suggested, *you could at least listen to what he has to say. Maybe,* it continued cautiously, *one indiscretion, in the context of a lifetime, isn't enough to negate everything that's come before. Maybe it's not too late to put it back together again.*

Hilary announced a brief commercial break, the last of the evening and, with an abbreviated nod in the direction of the sofa, walked out of the room. She had to regroup her thoughts, to plan her final onslaught.

J.D. wanted to weep; his frustration and the sheer exercise of his will to hold on had left him exhausted. He had given it his best shot, but he had not succeeded. He had not found the key, and so it was done. The show would conclude, and Maggie would leave him. The entire evening had come down to these last few minutes, and he had run out of time, out of memories.

Maggie shifted slightly to face him, was about to speak when he turned to her, unbearable sadness in his eyes.

"Maggie, I know this has been rough on you, and I'm sorry. I want you to know it was never my intention to bring back the pain." He swallowed hard and cleared his throat, then continued. "I thought maybe if I brought back the good times, made you think about how good our life together has been, that you'd give me a chance to explain. All I wanted was to make you see how much there is between us, how happy we've been. And it would seem I've failed miserably, that all I've managed to do is to resurrect those things that have been our greatest sources of sorrow over the years. And I'm so sorry, Maggie."

"Jamey, I . . . ," she whispered, but the words that could ease his suffering and hers died in her throat. All of the emotion of the past few days, the past few hours, seemed to choke her.

"Well, then, last segment." Hilary signaled to the cameraman, glancing at the couple briefly as she sat down, then glancing back again. What had happened in her short absence? What had she missed?

They sat in exactly the same place, J.D.'s arm still rested on the back of the sofa behind his wife. But where she had previously leaned forward and away from him, she now leaned back, her neck pressed against his forearm. As Hilary watched, Maggie slid her right hand behind her to rest upon his, and he touched her neck with the side of his thumb. She did not pull away as she had done earlier in the show, and some unspoken communication passed between them, her to him, as they locked eyes. Gone was the hostility, the bitterness, the anger.

Well, goddamn it, what the hell is going on? Hilary glared at the both of them, neither seeming to notice. In the remaining ten seconds Hilary made the decision to go for the jugular. They had been the worst guests she'd ever had. These people had been uncooperative all evening, shutting every door she'd tried to open. J.D. had directed the course of the interview as if it had been his show, boring her half to death with the boring little snippets of their boring little life, so artfully steering away from the areas of his life he wished to avoid. *I've had enough,* Hilary told herself angrily. *I'm going to finish this show with a bang.*

"Well, we're winding down tonight's show," Hilary smiled. "You know, J.D., all things considered, you've shown us a very ordinary life tonight."

"We're very ordinary people, Hilary," he said simply. "We've always tried to keep things very low key."

"Why is that so important to you?"

"Because it's what we are. Small-town people, both of us. We enjoy our family and have always made our children, our homelife, our priority. And because we never wanted our children to think they were special simply by virtue of what their father does for a living."

"How very admirable," she said dryly. "So tell us, what does the coming year hold for you? Any new music we should watch for?"

He relaxed, anticipating the show's conclusion.

"Well, I've been playing around with some songs I wrote over the years for the children, lullabies and such, and I'd thought maybe I'd record them and release those next year."

"How charming. A kiddie album." She smiled acerbically, then added innocently, "Any political causes you're supporting these days? Any superstar benefit concerts you'll be participating in?"

He froze, realizing how prematurely he'd dismissed her.

That's why she's played along all night, why she let me ramble about the unimportant things. She was waiting . . .

"J.D.?" she said his name to tell him she expected a response.

"I do not get involved in political issues, Hilary." He was suddenly sweating, his head pounding as if some tiny drummer had moved into the space between his ears. "And I do not participate in benefit concerts."

"Not since 1988." She deliberately held it before him. "Since Anjjoli."

"I have nothing to say," he told her flatly.

"Come now, J.D." She smiled her sweetest, giving a little coaxing one last chance.

"I have nothing to say," he repeated, making eye contact with her but refusing to blink.

"Look here, J.D., I've been uncommonly kind to you this evening." Her voice rose slightly, the patience forced, an exasperated mother veiling her anger as she reprimanded her child in a public place. "You didn't want to discuss Lindy Burton? We didn't discuss Lindy Burton. Maggie doesn't want to talk about the child she lost? We let it drop. Rick Daily's drug abuse—which you know as well as I do was more than rumor—I let that slide. But not this, J.D. The concert at Anjjoli became an international incident. Twenty-two of the most prominent musicians from eight different countries were held hostage by terrorists. The entire world held its breath for twenty-four hours to see who would walk out alive. Every other survivor, including your buddy, Mr. Daily, has spoken publicly about the experience. So when J.D. Borders—and only J.D. Borders—continues to say 'No comment,' one has to ask why."

She spoke rapidly, firing off the barrage of words, which he met with the blankest of expressions.

"It is none of your business." And with no further explanation, J.D. rose from the sofa, turned his back on the room, and walked through the French doors into the garden.

Hilary sat in shock, absorbing the fact that he had, in fact, walked off the show before its conclusion. She regrouped quickly and turned to Maggie, who, to Hilary's horror, was herself rising, a faraway look on her face as she searched through the darkness outside for a glimpse of her husband.

"Sit down," growled Hilary, no longer concerned with appearances. "This interview is not over."

"It would appear that it is," Maggie told her absently as she started toward the open doors.

Hilary signaled frantically for a commercial break.

"You agreed to a two-hour interview," Hilary screamed at Maggie's back, "and the two hours are not over. You may not walk off this show. You have no right—" Hilary stamped her foot like a child in the throes of a tantrum.

"You have no right," Maggie spun to face her, "to open wounds that took a very long time to heal." Her calm was the starkest of contrasts to Hilary's furor. "You may remove your equipment and your people and yourself from our home."

Maggie passed from the brightly lit and now chaotic scene into the warmth and fragrance of the night. She stopped at the end of the first row of roses, acclimating herself to the dark. She scanned the garden, then sighed with relief as she saw him seated on a bench in the shadow of the far wall. He was leaning slightly forward, his head in his hands.

She knew with absolute certainty that he was reliving it all over again . . .

The concert at Anjjoli had been organized by Artists for International Relief, a group comprised of recording artists who performed annually to raise funds for Third World countries that were experiencing undue hardship, whether due to famine, drought, or other devastating acts of nature. The organization was in its fourth year, and upon the suggestion of the current president, Hobie Narood, Anjjoli would be the proud host of the prestigious event.

It had been the most heavily publicized concert in history, and the tickets, priced outrageously high, had sold like hotcakes. The new luxury stadium in the capital city was completely sold out. The Anjjolan president, Makubo, was delighted. What better way to show off their new city with its fine hotels and gourmet restaurants? The international crowd would discover that Anjjoli had indeed come into the twentieth century, its new resort areas as glamorous as Monte Carlo and Rio.

The chartered plane from London carrying musicians and their wives and equipment had a carnivallike atmosphere. Rick had suggested a full Daily Times reunion onstage, and it had been billed as a headline act, eagerly awaited both by longtime fans who had loved the group in its heyday as well as the younger rock aficionados. The video that was to be taped promised to be a best-seller.

J.D. and Maggie found their hotel accomodations to be heaven. The huge suite overlooked the beach, the deep blue ocean a stone's throw from the balcony. J.D. had thought it would be good for both of them to have some time away together, the past year having been hectic and emotionally trying. Maggie, in particular, had had a rough time of it; both of her parents had been hospitalized for life-threatening conditions. Now J.D. hoped Maggie would be able to relax and have some fun, see some old friends, and forget her worries for a bit.

They ran into Hobie at rehearsal on the morning of the concert. Oddly, he seemed surprised to see her.

"I had not realized you would attend," he said stiffly.

"Now, how could I pass up the opportunity to see my three favorite guys perform together?" she said with a grin as she embraced him. "The one and only Daily Times reunion. And of course, I'm dying to see Aden."

"Aden is not here," he told her.

"Not here? How could she not be here?" Maggie was genuinely disappointed at the unexpected news.

"My wife left the city this morning." He appeared preoccupied all of a sudden. "A sickness in the family, an aunt. Aden is tending to her."

"Will she be back in time for the concert tonight?" Maggie asked hopefully.

"I fear she will not, but I will, of course, tell her you had asked for her." Kissing her cheek, Hobie excused himself.

"Well, honestly, Jamey, did you ever . . ." She stood in shock at the brusque departure.

"He was a bit abrupt," he muttered, then added, "but I'm sure it's just the pressure, Maggie. Hobie's organized this thing; he's responsible for pulling it off. There are probably a million things on his mind right now. He'll be his old self once this is over. Look, maybe we can hang around for a few extra days, maybe Aden will be back in the city by Monday and you can have a nice visit."

Hobie's odd behavior was dismissed.

The concert, which lasted almost sixteen hours, was an incredible success, both musically and as a fund-raiser. The finale, which brought all the performers together for a series of all-star encores, went on for a full thirty minutes. When the last note had been played, all those onstage were escorted onto a bus that would return them to the city for a party that promised to last all night.

What a night this has been, J.D. thought as he settled back into his seat. *What fun to be performing all those old songs again with the original group. Wasn't sure I could still hit those high notes in "Thief in the Night," but it was all right. Actually, it had sounded great. Makes me wonder why I resisted it all these years, every time Jack or Colin had suggested we all get together again. And I hadn't realized that neither of them had fared quite so well as Rick or Hobie or I had. Well, maybe their luck will change.*

He closed his eyes, thinking about the evening ahead. He'd arranged to meet Maggie back at the hotel, where he'd take a quick shower, then they would spend the rest of the evening dancing in the moonlight. Maggie had hitched a ride back to the hotel with Maura, Colin's wife, and hopefully was already there, waiting for him.

The bus lurched suddenly to one side, catching everyone off guard, as the tires had seemed to leave the roadway and embark upon bumpy terrain. Seconds later, the interior lights, which had blazed festively as the jubilant group had begun their celebration en route, were extinguished. The passengers became awkwardly silent in the unexpected darkness.

"Okay, okay, very funny. Now turn 'em back on," someone called out with exaggerated patience.

"Someone ask the driver what the hell he's doing," a second voice called. "He's gone off the goddamned road!"

Angry voices were hushed as the lights flashed back on. Eyes readjusted, then focused without comprehension on the three men who stood across the front of the bus. Dressed in identical khaki, the security guards who had boarded with the performers were silhouetted against the broad windshield. The green bandanas previously worn around their necks were now tied around their foreheads like sweatbands. Each was armed with an American-made semi-automatic weapon.

"What the bloody hell . . . ," someone hissed to break the silence.

"Ladies and gentlemen"—one of the men stepped forward slightly, speaking perfect English in the deepest voice imaginable—"we are pleased to tell you that you are now guests of the Anjjolan Liberation Coalition."

The twenty-two passengers on board each scrambled to process the words.

Steve McEntee, an American seated toward the front, called out cautiously, "What does that mean, 'a guest'?"

"I think it's another term for hostage, mate," Rick answered from somewhere behind J.D.

"Very good, Mr. Daily," the spokesman said, nodding in Rick's direction.

For a moment no one moved or spoke, then chaos erupted as several in the group rose from their seats and started toward the front of the bus. Three shots rang out from behind, and almost as one, the entire group turned to face the rear. Four more men, green bandanas around their heads, stood side by side, a solid wall of khaki, their guns prominently displayed.

"I would suggest that this is not to be a night for heroes, gentlemen. Please be seated, and remain so," instructed the man who stood directly behind the driver. "We will reach our destination soon enough."

"Where's that?" someone asked in a voice that trembled mightily.

"Soon enough" was the abrupt reply.

The crowd was hushed, each individual trying desperately to understand the implausible twist their lives had just taken.

Holy mother, J.D. thought, *how can this be happening? Sweet Jesus, let it be a dream . . .*

He felt a slight change in the motion of the bus. It no longer rocked as it had moments before as it had navigated what he had assumed to be the ruts of a dirt road. A smooth surface was now underwheel, he felt certain of it, and up ahead in the distance were lights. He watched as a structure of glass and steel rose before them out of the darkness. From somewhere in the distance he heard the engines of a plane. *Of course,* he thought, *the airport.*

The bus drove onto the runway and stopped directly behind a plane that looked as if it was being prepared for takeoff. The four men who had stood silently in the back of the bus now marched wordlessly up the aisle and disembarked. They converged about the steps to the waiting plane, then boarded.

The passengers on the bus waited in terror. Were they to be flown someplace with these fanatics?

Several long minutes passed before the instruction was given for them to leave the bus, single file, and walk directly to the plane. They were herded on legs wobbly with fear and ushered rapidly aboard the plane, taking the first seat available to them as they had been commanded to do.

"You are wondering, of course, what is happening here," the spokesman addressed them when all had been seated, "and quite naturally, you are concerned for your welfare." He lit a cigarette and inhaled deeply, taking his time, knowing the terror would grow along with the suspense. "Your fate is now in the hands of President Makubo. Whether you walk off this plane to your freedom within a few hours is up to him."

"What does that mean? What's this all about?" a voice inquired. "What is it you want?"

"The release of the nine Anjjolan Federation elders who now rot in Makubo's prisons. When they are set free, so too shall you be."

"And what if they're not?" someone asked tentatively.

The spokesman frowned, as if pondering the possibility for the first time, then replied with considered nonchalance, "That would be most unfortunate. This plane will take off in precisely twenty-four hours, its destination the bottom of the Atlantic."

"Why us?" The question, a sob, hung in the air.

"Why indeed. You are all internationally famous. Would the Americans risk your demise, Mr. McEntee? And Mr. Daily, it is said that you have inspired a generation of guitarists. Would not the British government intervene on your behalf? And you, Mr. Narood, our own pride and joy. Would Makubo turn his back on the most well-known Anjjolan of all time? I think not." He grinned with satisfaction, then added darkly, "For all of our sakes, I hope not."

Their captor turned and walked into the cabin where the pilot sat in terror, a gun held to his head, ensuring he would make no valiant attempt to use the radio.

It had seemed to J.D. that the man's brief speech had lasted a lifetime. He sat enveloped in his own dread, heart pounding loudly and furiously, wondering how in the name of God he could have been caught in so absurd a predicament. No one dared speak, each man or woman having escaped into his own private world of fear.

Several hours of bleak and desperate silence had passed before the spokesman appeared before them to announce that the women on the plane—seven of them, a Swede, two Brits, and four Americans—would be released immediately. A buzz of relief filled the plane as the grateful women rushed toward the doorway, none of them meeting the eyes of those left behind. They were directed toward a doorway, some sixty feet from the plane, in which stood an Anjjolan soldier. The remaining hostages held their breaths, praying their colleagues would make it across the runway, that it was not a trick.

And so they sat through a night of terror, frozen with the unvoiced fear of what was still to be.

The sun rose and soon the interior of the plane began to heat up in its increasingly warming rays. Water and food had been distributed, but no news of the negotiations for their release was forthcoming. The anxiety increased as the day progressed, but there was no communication from their captors. By the end of the day, eighteen hours into their ordeal, the unwilling passengers were beginning to fall apart, little by little.

The onset of dusk brought some small relief as the air inside the plane cooled slightly. Food and water were once again offered, and the hostages were told to walk to the front of the plane in order of their seats to receive their evening rations.

J.D., seated toward the rear, was among the last to make his way to the simple concession. As he walked back down the aisle with his bottle of water, sandwich, and fruit, he noticed Hobie, sitting alone and staring out the window. He slid into the vacant seat next to his old friend.

"Aren't you going to eat?" he asked, unwrapping the sandwich, which was two thick slices of bread with some type of thick yellow substance between. "You don't know when they'll feed us again."

Hobie did not respond.

"Look, Hobie," J.D. whispered, "if you're feeling somehow responsible for this mess, I mean, because you organized the show . . ."

Hobie turned his head wordlessly.

"Are you scared then? Is that what it is?" J.D. leaned over and put his hand on the man's shoulder. "Look, Hobie, I'm scared witless. I'm scared I'm going to die in this bloody plane and all I can think of is Maggie, my children . . ."

He choked up unexpectantly, his wife's face filling his inner vision. He needed to see that face there, to feel her with him. He was terrified to his very soul that the worst would happen.

"So if that's it, Hobie, if you're scared—shit, you'd have to be a moron not to be . . ."

"I never meant for it to go this far." Hobie's words were uttered in a tortured whisper. "I am so sorry."

Certain he'd not heard correctly, J.D. leaned forward.

"What did you say?"

"It wasn't supposed to happen like this." Enormous tears rolled down the big man's face.

"What are you talking about?" J.D. hissed.

"It was only supposed to be the bus." Hobie spoke as if only to himself. "They said they'd hold everyone on the bus, that was all, until Makubo let the prisoners go . . ."

"You knew about this?" J.D. was incredulous. "And you didn't try to stop them?"

"It wasn't supposed to happen like this," he repeated. "They promised no one would be hurt. And by the end of the evening, they'd all be free . . . Ebbu, the others, would all be free."

"Ebbu?"

"My brother. Of my father's second wife. He was one of the elders of the Federation of Tribes. He was arrested last year."

"Why?"

"The federation was banned fifteen years ago by Makubo. He wanted to force the tribes' allegiance to him, but his actions only made them more defiant."

"What's your role in all this?" J.D. demanded heatedly.

"My father was an elder, J.D., and now my brother. My loyalties are with the federation."

"Did you plan this? Is this some kind of twisted revenge for your father's assassination?"

He shook his head. "No, J.D. I've been funding the organization for years, but I had no hand in planning this."

"Have you any influence with them? Can you stop it?" J.D.'s hand gripped the larger man's arm like the jaws of an angry dog.

"I don't know." Hobie shook his head uncertainly. "It may have gone too far . . ."

"Try, goddamn you." J.D. rose angrily and stormed down the aisle, finding an empty seat and plopping into it, and turned his face to the window, gazing into the darkness as the evening spread, thick as an oil slick, around the plane.

Goddamn him, he thought. *Jesus, if we survive this madness, I swear I'll break Narood's neck with my own bare hands. I should have been able to live out the years with*

Maggie. He felt self-pity wash over him. *I should have been able to watch our children grow up and grow old with Maggie, making jokes about our failing eyesight and our arthritic joints.*

Rick moved into the seat next to him. "You all right, mate?" he asked. "I mean, I saw you talking to Hobie."

"Did you hear the conversation?"

"No, but it looked pretty intense." Rick was incredibly composed, as if they were seated in his own living room.

"It was." J.D. fought the urge to tell him about Hobie's involvement but could not resist asking "How can you be so calm in the face of all this?"

"I have no one to leave behind but Sophie," he said with a shrug, "and I know Maggie will take care of her."

"And if you make it and I don't, will you take care of Maggie?" he heard himself ask.

"You'll make it. We'll both make it," he said confidently.

"What do you know that I don't?" J.D. asked bleakly.

"I've felt death breath down the back of my neck on several occasions, old friend, but I don't feel him there now. Maybe for others, but not for me. Nor you," Rick told him solemnly as his eyes drifted toward the front of the plane. "Now what do you suppose he's doing?"

Hobie had made his way up the aisle and was attempting to speak with the man in the doorway, who appeared to be ignoring him. Another terrorist emerged from the cockpit, and Hobie took several steps toward him. The man raised his hands as if to push him back when suddenly a blaze of gunfire erupted. The door of the plane was blown open and, with it, the gates of hell.

The hostages hit the floor as the incessant, thunderous barrage continued. They covered their ears against the unholy fury exploding around them, but it was useless. The noise level inside the plane was deafening. J.D. lay shaking long after the gunfire had ceased.

"Up! Get up!" Someone, his accent distinctly American, prodded him. "You hit? No? If you can walk, go quickly. We're not sure of just what we hit or if this sucker will blow."

J.D. didn't need to be told twice.

Making his way out, climbing over bodies without consciously realizing it, he searched the rapidly moving line as it snaked forward. There was Rick just disappearing through the doorway and Colin, he'd located him several feet in front of him. Where was Hobie? He had a score to settle with him.

He was almost to the door when he saw, amid a pile of unmoving bodies, the bright blue shirt Narood had worn, now running rivers of red like water pouring from pinholes in a balloon. He stopped abruptly, then was pushed from behind.

"Move, damn it!"

"Oh, Jesus," J.D. muttered, feeling sick to his stomach but unable to look away.

"Move!" the voice behind demanded, two firm fists slamming into him roughly, propelling him toward the doorway, out into the night.

The entire airport was now flooded with light and there was a sudden convergence of people and vehicles. Army personnel rushed into the plane he'd just fled, looking for survivors among the heap of bodies. Medics were everywhere, as were members of the press.

"Are you hurt?" someone asked.

"What?" he replied dumbly.

"Are you hurt?"

"No."

"This way, please, sir. We've an ambulance waiting."

He pushed past the medic and wandered through the sea of reporters and film equipment. The same cameras that only a short twenty-four hours earlier had taped his performance now filmed his staggered steps. Microphones were shoved in his face from a dozen different directions.

"J.D., can you tell us what happened?"

"J.D., what was it like?"

He walked past them, bewildered and barely hearing, and made no response. In the midst of the noise and confusion he saw Maggie's face and thought he was hallucinating. He knew he must be suffering from shock and told himself it could not be her. But when she reached him and gathered him into her arms, he knew she was real, that the nightmare was over. Ignoring the chaos that swarmed around them, she led him through the airport and to a waiting car.

"Take us to the nearest hospital," she told the driver.

"No," he whispered, "the hotel."

"You should see a doctor, Jamey, the shock . . ."

"The hotel," he insisted, and she nodded to the driver to do as he asked.

He had lain awake all night, shivering as from cold though he lay wrapped in the warmth of Maggie's arms, overwhelmed by the events of the past day and night. He could neither speak of it nor could he close his eyes.

It was midmorning before he slept and early evening before he awoke. Maggie had watched the televised accounts all day, the same scenes played over and over, the endless commentary. The same pictures of the plane on the darkened runway, the films of the rescue efforts by a multinational SWAT team, were repeated until she had memorized them.

And each time it was rerun, the resolution was the same. All of the terrorists and four of the performers on board, most prominent among them being Hobie Narood, had been killed. The eyewitness accounts from his fellow hostages indicated that just moments before the rescuers broke through the door, Narood had gone to the front of the plane and engaged their captors in conversation. The speculation was that Narood had seen the SWAT team moving toward the plane from his window and had deliberately distracted the terrorists. By the time J.D. had awaken, Narood had been declared an international hero.

"Jesus, I can't believe it," he all but shouted.

"I should have turned it off," she said through her tears, "and told you about Hobie myself, instead of letting you find out from the TV. Oh, Jamey, I can't believe he's dead."

"Better him than me," he grumbled, sitting down beside her, eyes fastened to the screen.

It took a moment for her to react. His remark was so out of character.

"Jamey, I know this has been a terrible ordeal; every

minute of it must have been hell," she told him, "and I know how you must feel about Hobie . . ."

"Bloody stupid bastard," he muttered, "could have gotten us all killed."

"What are you talking about?" She wiped the tears away with a tissue, confused by the harshness of his reaction when she'd expected tears of grief for his old friend. "You mean when he went to distract the terrorists they could have turned on the rest of you?"

"Distract them, my ass," he growled. "He went to try to call it off."

"Call what off?"

"The whole goddamned thing." He could tell she hadn't a clue.

"I don't understand," she told him.

"Maggie, Hobie was in on it. He knew about it, he agreed to it. He was a member of the organization, has been financing their efforts for years."

"What?!" She sat back in shock. "You mean—"

"I mean our boy Hobie, our good best-buddy Hobie, was in on the whole bloody thing right from the start."

"Jamey, I can't believe it." She shook her head, "Are you sure?"

"He told me, Maggie. He bloody apologized to me. And now they're calling him a hero. Well, I'll set them straight on that, you can bet your life on it."

She sat stunned and speechless, then slowly turned to him.

"Jamey, you can't," she whispered.

"What do you mean, I can't?" he glared. "I can and I will."

"No, Jamey, please." Her eyes had grown wide with fright.

"Maggie, are you asking me to cover up for him? After what happened over the past two days? Maggie, had I not moved to the back of the plane when I did, I could bloody well be in a body bag right now," he all but shouted at her, "not to mention that he was partially responsible for the most hellish hours of my life." He rose and began to pace with aggravation.

"But he's dead, Jamey," she said.

"Yes, he's dead, but he's no dead hero."

"But, Jamey," she pleaded, "Aden and the children. What will Makubo do to them if he finds out? He's already rounded up the families of the other terrorists for an 'indefinite detainment' . . ."

He sat back down on the nearest chair and exhaled deeply. It had never occurred to him . . .

"How do you know she didn't know, that she wasn't in on it, too?"

"Aden did not know." Maggie shook her head adamantly. "She called late yesterday afternoon after you left. She was infuriated with Hobie for sending her out of the city. It seemed his aunt was neither expecting her, nor was she ill. She didn't know, Jamey, I'm certain of it. As long as Makubo continues to think Hobie's a hero, she and the children will be safe."

He hung his head down, elbows on his knees, head in his hands.

"Jamey, it's been terrible—God, I can't even begin to imagine what you and the others went through—but Hobie's dead, Jamey. Aden and her sons shouldn't have to suffer because of what he did, and she shouldn't suffer more than she has. She's lost her husband—you know how much in love they were. God, Jamey, if I lost you and then had to face the kind of consequences she'll face if the truth gets out—"

The soft knock at the door interrupted her impassioned plea, and J.D. walked slowly to the door, his mind a swirling whirlpool. Four men stood in the hallway. British Intelligence. American CIA. Two members of Makubo's own internal intelligence agency.

Maggie excused herself to take a shower, backing out of the room, her eyes begging for his silence.

The interrogation had lasted two hours, and he was exhausted by the time the delegation had departed. He found his wife on the balcony, reclining on a lounge and staring into the vastness of the sea beyond. He sat down next to her and took her hands in his.

"Is it over?" she asked without looking at him.

"Yes," he nodded.

"Did you tell them?"

"No," he sighed deeply, "I did not."

She pulled him slowly to her and rested his head on her chest.

"I know how difficult it must have been for you." She very gently massaged the back of his neck.

"But you were right. Hobie is beyond retribution, and his family would pay the price for his actions. As much as I despise what he did, causing his wife and sons to suffer would not change what happened. I would only hope that if I ever did something as ungodly stupid as he did, that someone would care as much for you and our children."

"How will you handle the press?" she asked.

"With a very firm 'No comment.'"

"Do you think they'll let you get away with that?"

"They'll have to," he said resolutely. "No one can force me to make a statement. I've given my report to the authorities and I am not obligated to discuss it publicly with anyone else. And I won't."

And for two years, despite the nightmares in which he had relived every second of the ordeal, he had held his silence. Arriving in Philadelphia, they had found the airport jammed with press, but he had walked past them stonily as if he did not see or hear.

Once back at their home, he had immersed himself in his family. It had been weeks before he'd set foot beyond the fence that ran the length of the property and months before Maggie could convince him to leave the sanctuary of their home, even to visit his in-laws, so deep within him remained the fear of never seeing his wife or his children again.

26

"AH, SO HERE YOU ARE!" LUKE EXCLAIMED FROM THE DOORWAY. "What a spectacle that was! Hilary left in a fine snit. You'll be hearing from her lawyers, J.D., she did tell me to relate that to you. Rude, she was, about it, too, when she stormed out. Good for you, son, sticking to your guns . . . None of anybody's business but yours, I say. But it was certainly an odd gamut you ran tonight. Lord knows you lost me for a time or two, what with your odd behavior. You feeling all right, you two?"

"We're fine, Mother," he replied.

"Well, the children are in their beds, Maggie, sleeping like angels, no need for you to tuck them in." Luke had turned toward the door. "But I would ask you, J.D., to give a minute to Jesse if you would. He seems a bit out of sorts."

"I'll be up in a minute," he told her, and as his mother disappeared into the house, he turned to his wife, a thousand questions in his eyes and on his face.

"Go tend to Jess," she said softly, "then come back down and we'll talk."

He nodded uneasily, afraid to speculate upon the outcome of the conversation yet to come.

Maggie stood in the dark alone for a few long minutes, then walked into the room that only a brief time earlier had bustled with activity as the television crews had dismantled their equipment. She took off the high heels that had been bothering her all night and slipped into a pair of well-worn flats and walked through the quiet hallway into the dining room. She snapped on the lights and went to a small cabinet and lifted out first one, then a second goblet, and searched a drawer for a corkscrew. Opening a cupboard that was built into the wall, she removed a bottle of wine and passed back into the living room and through the still-opened doors. Seating herself on the top step of the patio, she carefully set the crystal goblets next to her on the bricks and proceeded to open the bottle.

Surely it had been an emotion-filled night, the ceaseless stream of visual images flowing past her inner eye, each following the other so effortlessly in their passing. The bright, shining moments of past joys had danced through her mind on gossamer feet, like fairy children in the night, specks of golden dust sprinkled in their wake.

Yet it had been the dark moments that had held her gaze the longest, as if she had lifted the rock that had hidden each one from her consciousness and gazed in horror on the dark, writhing thing that had lay beneath it. *At what point,* she reflected as she poured some of the sparkling liquid into her glass, *had it occurred to me that I cannot live without him?*

As she had poked and prodded each moment of pain, she had seen his face emerge to absorb her sorrows. It had been his arms that had held her through sleepless nights, his strength that had enabled her to rise each morning after. How could she conceive of a life without him? What life could there be for her if he was not a part of it?

She mindlessly turned the glass around and around in her hands, watching the pale yellow liquid swirl closer and closer to the rim, but she did not raise the glass to her lips. She had been so resolute when she had arrived this evening, so positive that nothing could reach her. Yet every memory had left its mark.

How can I forgive him, she asked herself wearily, *and yet how can I leave?*

"Maggie," he said from the doorway.

She watched over her shoulder as he approached, gesturing to him to join her. As he lowered himself to sit, she poured wine into his glass and handed it to him. He, too, played with it but did not drink. They sat together for a very long, quiet time.

"Thank you," he said, breaking the awkward silence, "for jumping in there at the end . . ."

"Thank you," she replied, "for pitching in when you did. I mean, about Hallie . . ."

"That was a bit of a cheap shot on Hilary's part," he told her.

"I'd say Hilary wasn't the only one to throw a cheap shot tonight," she said, "what with every bell and whistle from our past being rung."

"I'm sorry, Maggie." He was sincerely contrite. "I was at my wit's end. I thought if maybe I could make you see how much we have had together, how much we stand to lose—"

"You should have thought about that on Friday," she snapped.

"Oh, Jesus, are we back to that again?" He ran his fingers through his hair. "Will you, once and for all, listen to the truth so we can be done with it?"

"All right, Jamey," she sighed, knowing that sooner or later she'd have to hear it, "suppose you tell me why you decided to entertain Blondie in the shower."

"I swear to you, I don't know where she came from or how she got in. I opened the shower door, stepped out, grabbed a towel, opened my eyes, and there she stood. And then you walked in immediately thereafter." He shook his head. "I swear to you that's exactly how it happened, preposterous as it sounds. Any chance you'd left the door unlocked when you left?"

She thought for a minute.

"I don't remember. I was a little distracted, I remember, thinking about all the things I wanted to accomplish. Your mom's birthday present, a dress for the garden party next week, and then I walked past this shop and there was a wonderful old writing desk in the window. I went in and looked at it and thought it would be perfect in the hallway, you know, that bare spot along the one wall? The more I looked at it, the more I liked it, and I decided to come back and get you and see what you thought of it—"

"And there stood Glory in the all-together," he said, finishing the thought for her.

"And that was it?" she asked sheepishly.

"That was it." He shook his head. "I swear it, Maggie, on my life."

"Oh, God, do I feel stupid," she moaned, burying her face in his shoulder. "To think I was ready to pack up the kids and—"

"Well, it didn't come to that." He stroked her hair lovingly, relieved to his soul, knowing it was all still there between them.

"How did she even know we were there?" She lifted her head to ask. "How'd she know what room we were in or that I was gone?"

"The only thing I can think of is that she saw you leave the hotel; either she was in the lobby or walking past and asked at the desk. Maggie, I swear I didn't ask her to come." He studied her face. "Do you believe me?"

Instead of answering, she said slowly, "You should know that was the thing I have feared most. I was always afraid she'd come between us, all the years she threatened she'd get you back."

"It could never happen, Maggie," he reassured her.

"But she's so beautiful, Jamey."

"Ah, but there's no comparison." He put his arm over her shoulder and pulled her to him. "She can't hold a candle to you, sweetheart. I had a choice a long time ago, and I've never regretted the choice I made. Not for a second. You are absolutely the single best thing that ever happened to me . . . my heart and my soul. I love you more than anything in this life, and I always will. Do you believe me?" he asked again.

"Oh, yes. I love you, too, Jamey. How could I have been so foolish . . . to think that I could go on through this life without you."

He stood up, pulling her up with him, embracing her, kissing her to welcome her back, to tell her all the things for which he could find no words.

The air was warm and balmy, fragrant as the breeze drifted toward them, and they looked out over the fields beyond the garden, beyond the small barn. The moon was most splendid—full, golden, and bright enough to illumine the gently sloped hills.

"Look at it." Maggie was mesmerized by its glow. "Have you ever seen anything like it in your life?"

"Um, no, it is spectacular." He kissed her neck, then said suddenly, "Wait right here. I've an idea."

He disappeared into the house and returned a minute later with a blanket over his arm, a large black dog trailing behind.

"Come on, love. Let's take a walk." He took her arm and started to lead her through the gate, telling the dog, "You, Duff, may stay here."

"Where are we going at this hour?" she laughed.

"Ah, Maggie, the moonlight is irresistible. You're irresistible." He kissed her. "Humor your old man, sweetheart, this has been so dreadful an evening."

"Jamey, if you're feeling amorous—and it's obvious that you are—why don't we just go back inside and—"

"And waste a night like this? Come on, Maggie, we may never see a moon like this again. Besides, it's been a long time since we slept under the stars. Come and take a walk up over the hill with me and we'll make love in the moonlight. What better way to celebrate?"

With a reluctance she couldn't have explained, she took his hand and they walked together toward the hills.

George Brenner was just closing up his cottage for the night when he looked out the kitchen window and saw the lovers as they ascended the hill, dark images against the golden sphere, the light from which flooded the valley. He froze and watched as the figures disappeared.

"Ruthann," he murmured to the darkness. "Ruthann."

He took down his gun and walked through the door into the night, a determined smile spreading slowly across his face.

"What are you thinking about?" he asked, tracing her features with the index finger of his right hand.

"How grateful I am that you did what you did tonight and brought me back to reality. How good it's been, our life together."

"It always will be, I promise."

"And God, when I think about how close I came to leaving you." She shuddered.

"You wouldn't have gotten very far," he told her, his humor having returned. "I would never have let you walk out of my life without a fight. Of course, I hadn't reckoned on having to do that on national TV."

"It was a nerve-wracking evening, wasn't it?" She kissed his chin, grateful to be back in his arms, where she knew she belonged.

"The worst night of my life, Maggie. Fearing I'd lost you was more devastating than anything I've ever experienced. Even Anjjoli," he whispered, adding with a sigh of relief, "but it's over now, and we're together and we'll stay together, always. There's nothing that can separate us again, sweetheart."

George had stopped but once on his ascent up the hill to catch his breath. He was an old man now, and the anticipation of the confrontation after all these years was making him light-headed. At this moment, in his own mind, he was twenty-five again, and he was giddy with the knowledge that he'd now have the chance to do what he should have done the last time he'd found them together.

* * *

Maggie lay quietly in his arms, peace at last settled around her heart. She stroked his face, then asked, "And Jesse? What was Jesse's problem tonight?"

"What makes you think there was a problem with Jesse tonight?"

"You were up there with him for so long. And when you came back outside, your jaw was still clenched. So tell me . . ."

"Well, it seems Jess was terribly embarrassed by our publicly discussing his premature conception," he began, "and was feeling a bit sorry for himself, thinking now that perhaps he's illegitimate."

"That's silly, Jamey."

"That's what I told him, but he seems terribly sensitive about the fact that you were pregnant when we got married. And since he knows all his friends were watching tonight, he knows that they all know and I guess he's a bit old-fashioned in that respect."

"How did you handle it?"

"Not very well, I'm afraid. I owe him an apology, which I will give him in the morning."

"Why do you need to apologize?"

"Because I called him a brat, among other things."

"Sometimes Jesse is a brat. Sometimes they all are."

"I didn't have to say it. He was feeling confused, I would think. And I just sort of lost my temper with him. But we'll talk it out in the morning . . ."

He'd leaned down to kiss her again and heard a rustle behind him. As he turned and lifted himself slightly, a shadow seemed to glide over them. He looked over his shoulder, and before either he or Maggie could react, the first blast struck her in the left shoulder. He flung himself over her, his instinct being to protect her, placing himself directly in the line of fire. He fell forward heavily onto her as the second shot was fired.

"No!" she screamed as yet another blast shook the night and his body seemed to jolt.

"Ruthann." The single word, spoken softly, seemed to

327

come from nowhere. She froze at the sound and looked toward its source.

Oh, God.

"Not so smart now, are you, Ruthie." The old man grinned with malicious satisfaction. "Not so smart at all. And you—" He discharged another shot into J.D.'s back. "You never should've taken her from me. I always knew you'd be back, Ruthie. Didn't know when, but I knew you would come back. All these years, I've waited for you, Ruthann."

"George," she pleaded, wondering if she could reach him through this nightmare that had begun to play out. "I'm not Ruthann. I'm Maggie . . ."

"I've had to wait so long," he said, a blissful smile appearing as he realized his quest had ended.

"Please listen. I'm Maggie. Maggie Borders," she sobbed, but he seemed not to hear. He was lost in his vision of what had been, and reality was now only of his making. Maggie had become Ruthann, and J.D., her lover. And now George would right the wrong as he'd waited to do for twenty-seven years.

He lowered the gun so that the barrel was directly in line with her face. From somewhere in the dark she heard what sounded like the faint rumble of thunder from some unseen cloud. With each slow step he took toward her, the rumble swelled slightly. Behind him a black shape stalked, half crouched.

"Duffy," she whispered, then screamed, "Duffy!"

The huge dog leaped with such ferocity that Brenner smashed face first into the hillside. Struggling to release herself from J.D.'s limp form, she crawled to where the gun had fallen and groped for the cold hard object with shaking hands. She flung it into the night as Brenner shrieked in agony as the dog attacked viciously.

"Duffy," she panted, "guard. Guard, Duff. Good boy."

Brenner moaned and tried to rise. Duffy growled menacingly, baring his teeth as the figure on the ground stirred, telling Brenner in the clearest of terms that further movement would be the signal for further attack. The old man slumped forward and remained facedown on the ground.

Light-headed, weak, and sobbing, Maggie turned back to her still, silent husband. In the dark she could not tell if his eyes were opened or closed.

"Jamey, please," she whispered a cry, "please don't die, Jamey. You can't die. You can't. Not after all this, Jamey."

On her knees, she tried vainly to lift him, becoming aware for the first time of the pain where her neck met her collarbone. Her left arm was useless. Crying, she tried to gather him up in her right arm, and it was then that she saw the blood. It had poured from him as easily as liquid from an open jar as she tried to lift him, covering them both in a warm, dark flood.

"No, no," she pleaded, "don't do this to me. Don't be dead, Jamey. Please don't be dead . . ."

With an effort greater than she had ever realized she'd be capable of, she slid her good arm under him and lifted, raising herself to her knees, then to her feet. She stumbled, bent from his weight and the awkwardness of the angle at which he leaned upon her. Step by slow step she dragged him, talking to him in a fierce whisper, begging him not to die.

The pain had become unbearable and her body shook with fear, but she continued dragging him, inching down the slope of the hill with single-minded purpose. It was becoming increasingly difficult to breath, and she stumbled repeatedly, forcing her to readjust her grip, her good arm now numb from the effort to hang on. In the distance she could see the lights from the first floor of the house, and she struggled toward them until she reached the bottom of the hill.

"Hold on, Jamey. Just hold on."

She rested him on the grass in the darkness, sinking to her knees, not knowing if he was dead or alive. Unable to take another step, knowing she would not make it to the house, she forced herself to think, to find a way to get attention from the house.

Her right arm now nearly as useless as the left, she attempted to toss a stone to Jesse's window on the second floor just forty feet away. The stone hit well below the window ledge. She sought to compose herself, her breathing coming in quick, sharp gasps as she fumbled through the grass for another stone.

"One hit," she mumbled to herself, "just one good hit."

She pitched the second stone and heard it bounce off the side of the wall.

"S'matter with you, girl?" she chided herself. "Former ace pitcher of the Kelly's Mills girls club lost her touch? Try again . . . You can do it."

She sought out another stone, larger this time, and in her mind her father's voice echoed, coaching her as a twelve-year-old, determined to make the team.

"Come on, Maggie. You can do better," Frank had encouraged her. "Underhand. Throw this one underhand."

"Underhand." She repeated the words from her memory as she struggled to her feet. "Throw this one underhand."

The underhanded pitch shattered the window.

"Jess," she sobbed, "Jess . . ."

"Mom?" He leaned out the window, groggy with sleep and confused by the sight of her, half lying, half sitting on the ground. "Mom, what the hell are you doing out there?"

"Jesse," she called hoarsely, unable to find words to tell him what had happened.

Within seconds he was there, shouting over his shoulder to Tyler, who had followed, to call for help. The last thing she remembered was her son's horror-filled eyes as he looked down into her own.

Awakening in the tiny hospital room, it had seemed to have taken tremendous effort to focus clearly enough to identify the woman who sat at the side of her bed, the gray head bent as if in prayer.

"Luke," she whispered, and in speaking, the nightmare returned vividly. She tried to raise herself on her elbows but could not. "Jamey . . ." Her voice rose in panic, her eyes widened in terror at the memory.

"Hush, Maggie." Luke's gentle hands forced her back onto the pillow.

"But Luke, Jamey . . ." Her face flooded with tears.

"The doctors are with him, dear." Luke seemed to hesitate, as if to say something further but did not.

"Will he die?" she mumbled, eyes closing against her will.

"We will not let him die, Maggie," Luke told her resolutely. "Our love will bring him through this. We will not let him die."

As her daughter-in-law drifted back off, Luke patted the sleeping hands and wearily walked to the window. Looking out she sent a prayer to her husband, long since dead, to send their son back to her and to the woman who loved him so desperately.

Will he die? The question still hung in the air. She turned to the doorway as Judith passed quietly into the room.

"He needs more blood." Judith could not make eye contact with her mother, could not bear to see the questions there.

"Isn't that dangerous, blood transfusions?" Luke asked, adding, "I've been reading in the papers about contaminated blood . . ."

"They've taken mine. Right now they're taking some from Jesse. Good thing there's so many of us who match."

Judith moved a chair closer to the bed and directed her mother into it, gently rubbing the soft, papery skin beneath the thin dress that covered the stooped shoulders. Luke seemed to have been transformed from a spry senior to a fragile old woman in a matter of hours.

"Why don't you let Ned drive you home? Or to a hotel? Get a little rest and then—" Judith suggested.

"While my boy lays dying?"

"He's fighting, Mom. He may make it yet."

Judith swallowed back the tears, not wanting her mother to realize they'd already lost him twice, first in the ambulance, then later on the operating table. She had tried to corner first one doctor, then a second, as they had emerged from that brightly lit room wherein others struggled to mend her brother's wounded body. Both had shrugged, looking away as they muttered, "We don't know yet."

Mother and daughter sat in a long, tense silence, both fixed on a heavily sedated Maggie, grateful that she, at least, would recover fully. The bullet that had passed through between the neck and collarbone had broken the bone but had caused no permanent damage.

J.D., however, had been shot three times. One bullet had struck him in the back, passing under his shoulder blade and through his right lung; a second had grazed the back of his head. The third, and most worrisome, should he survive the tremendous loss of blood and the resulting shock, completely shattered his right shoulder, turning bone and muscle to ribbons.

He won't be playing the piano anymore, Judith thought sadly. *No amount of therapy will bring that arm back. Listen to me, now, mourning the loss of an arm when we'll be lucky if that's all he loses . . .*

"What do you suppose they'll do with George?" Luke asked.

"He's in custody. Under observation, they said."

The silence returned, Maggie's breathing the only discernible sound.

"They do not deserve this," Luke said to break the stillness.

"No one ever does," Judith replied quietly.

27

THE LONG, BLACK LIMOUSINE SLOWLY TURNED THE CORNER, THE occupants of the backseat silently gazing out the window. The car came to a stop, and the driver exited momentarily.

"The gate needs oiling." Maggie rolled the window down and leaned her head out slightly. "It looks as if the lawn people have been on holiday since we've been gone, the grass is so high. But, oh, Jamey"—she turned to him with tears in her eyes—"doesn't it look glorious?"

He leaned over stiffly, propping his left shoulder against her to peer through the window, taking it all in.

"Your garden looks awful," he observed wryly, "but given the fact that for a goodly portion of the past nine weeks it was unlikely that I'd ever lay eyes upon the place again, I'd say 'glorious' was a bit of an understatement."

The driver opened the door and leaned down to assist their exit. J.D. waved him away.

"Thanks, mate, but I'm okay."

Leaning over with some effort, he offered his good left hand to his wife. They walked slowly up the drive, drinking in the sights of home, the house partially hidden by the yellows, reds, and oranges of the changing leaves. The delicate fragrance of the sweet autumn clematis that wound its way around a trellis near the back door floated toward them, borne by the soft early afternoon breeze.

"Ah," he breathed deeply, "I love the sights and smells of a Pennsylvania fall. Oh, God, but it's good to be home. There is no place on this earth that I love more than these few little acres and this house, Maggie."

A few last roses—blush pink and wine red—stubbornly bloomed, despite the recent frost, near the back porch. Maggie touched their petals gently as she ascended the steps and pushed open the door.

"Looks like your dad got a new car." J.D. paused on the top step, nodding toward the shiny black automobile parked near the garage.

"Funny Mom didn't mention it. I guess with all the confusion these past few months—her having to bring the children back for school—it slipped her mind." Maggie walked slowly through the back entry and into her kitchen. "Oh, Jamey, isn't it heaven to be here?"

"As close to heaven as I've ever been," he agreed. "I've missed this place more than I can say."

"Mom? Dad?" she called into the front foyer. "Anyone here?"

The only sound was the ticking of the grandfather clock in the hallway.

"I wonder where everyone is." She ran up the steps, then back down, telling him with a frown. "There's no one here."

"Your parents probably took Spencer for a walk. The other kids would be in school," he noted.

She wandered from one room to the next, touching things, talking to things, savoring the blessed familiarity of the home she so dearly loved. She was openly weeping by the time he found her in the kitchen.

"It's all right . . . It's all right," he murmured, embracing her with his good left arm. "We're home now and everything's all right."

"It's been such a nightmare," she sobbed.

"The nightmare is over, Maggie. We're home and everything is okay now." He kissed the tears from her chin. "And look, new artwork on the refrigerator gallery . . ."

He nodded toward the eclectic display of the children's work that completely covered the large, white appliance.

"Oh, Jamey, look at this one," she managed to laugh through her tears, "Molly did a picture of Spencer."

Molly's uneven printing announced the subject, "My Baby Brother," clearly depicting a howling little boy seated on the grass.

"I'd say she captured his spirit quite accurately," he mused.

"I can't wait to see him." Her eyes began to mist again. "I can't wait to hold him."

"Looks like the wait is over." He pointed out the side window.

"Oh, my God, it's Caroline. And Rick! And Spencer!" She ran out the back door and down the drive to meet the threesome as they meandered up the long drive.

Caroline held the tiny boy's hand while Rick pushed the stroller, which was loaded with bags.

"Mommy . . . Mommy . . ." The little boy broke free from a startled Caroline.

"Oh, my baby." Maggie gathered him up and held him tightly. "My beautiful boy . . . and Caro . . ." With one arm she reached to hug her friend.

"What are you two doing here?" she said as she cried happy tears. "Where are my folks?"

"Your brother's baby decided to come early," Caroline explained as she pushed a wayward strand of Maggie's hair from her beloved friend's face, "so your mom called on Sunday to see if I could fill in for her till you got home since she'd promised Kevin and Jenny she'd watch the other three while Jenny was in the hospital . . . God, it's good to see you."

"It most certainly is." Rick engulfed her with a bear hug. "And you, mate, you're a true sight for sore eyes."

J.D. approached with an outstretched hand that Rick ignored as he hugged him as well.

"I'm delighted to see you, too." J.D. patted Rick's back. "But, ah, what are you doing here?"

"Giving the fair Caroline a hand," he said with a wide grin.

"All week?" Maggie asked, looking from Caroline to Rick then back to Caroline again.

"Certainly all week." Rick put an arm over Caroline's shoulder. "You don't think I'd make her try to handle this mob of yours unassisted."

"Oh, I see." Maggie tried vainly to repress a smile. "So you've been here all week. Together."

"Yes." A red flush crept up Caroline's neck as she nodded.

"Well," Rick said, trying to act nonchalant, as if the two of them being there—together all week—was the most natural thing in the world. "I think we should get our groceries into the house . . ."

Rick parked the stroller by the back steps and began to load his arms with bags.

"Here, let me give you a hand," J.D. told him, then quipped, "one hand being all I have to work with these days."

"What's the prognosis on that?" Rick asked, nodding toward J.D.'s arm.

"It's pretty much gone," J.D. admitted grimly.

"No surgery, no therapy?" Caroline ventured.

"Nah. Bone's healing a bit, but the nerves, the muscles, are pretty well shot, no pun intended. Maybe in time they'll come up with something." Noting the shadow that crossed his wife's face, he attempted to lighten the mood, adding, "You wouldn't know anyone who's looking for a one-armed piano player?"

"Well, I'm looking for some new material . . . when you're up to it, of course," Rick hastened to add.

"I'm up to tossing some things around," J.D. said with a nod. "Maybe tomorrow morning or so we can play around in the studio a bit."

"I apologize, Maggie," Caroline said as they entered the kitchen, "that the house isn't in better order. Your mother had things in pretty good shape by the time we got here, but I'm afraid she's much better at keeping track of things than either Rick or I."

"You want to tell me what is going on?" Maggie asked when the two men had headed back to the drive to gather the luggage that had been left there earlier. "Since when have you and Rick—"

"Since the night you were . . . since your accident." Caroline busied herself filling a coffee pot with water. "He was in New York when he heard it on the news and took a taxi—a taxi, can you believe it?—all the way down here. Rang my doorbell just after midnight. And you want to know the craziest thing? It was as if I was waiting for him, as if I knew that he would come."

"And then what?"

"Then the next day we flew to London. That's why I was there when they finally started letting you have visitors."

"I don't remember too much." Maggie frowned. "I remember you were there and that Rick was there, but I don't recall that I knew you were there together."

"I think you had other things on your mind at the time."

Maggie digested this new turn of events, then grinned with satisfaction. "I knew that someday you'd find each other."

"Took us long enough." Caroline shook her head. "God, if you look back over the years, how many times we missed each other. First Lindy, then Lindy's baby, then my marriage to Allen. It just seemed the time was never right."

"I guess this is the happy ending you've been waiting for," Maggie said, smiling.

"The happy beginning, you mean," Caroline corrected her, "and yes, we are very happy."

"I'm so glad. I love you both so much, and I can't wait to tell Jamey 'I told you so.'" She laughed. "I can't tell you how much I appreciate the two of you taking care of the children for us these past few days. I know they can be overwhelming, especially if you're not accustomed to living under the same roof with so many."

"It's been a pleasure. The kids have been fine," she assured her, "but I don't know how you keep it all straight. This one has ballet this day, that one has tap the next, three of them have soccer on Tuesday, two on Wednesday. I can't imagine how much longer I could have kept everyone's schedules straight."

"They will keep you running," Maggie laughed, running her hand lovingly up the back of her son who still clung to his mother's neck like a little monkey.

"Let me see that boy." J.D. set the bag he carried on the floor and reached his arm out for the boy, planting a fond kiss on his son's cheek.

The grandfather clock in the front hallway began to chime three o'clock.

"It's almost time for the school bus," Maggie noted. "Maybe I'll walk down to the bus stop. I can't wait to see their faces. Do they know we're coming home today?"

"We didn't tell them in case something happened with the flight schedule." Rick poured himself a cup of coffee.

"I'll go with you." J.D. put Spencer onto the floor.

"Want a piggy ride," the little boy told him, holding upreached arms to his father.

"Spence, Daddy can't carry you on his shoulders anymore," he told him, his voice cracking just slightly. "Would it be all right if I held your hand and you walked with Mommy and me?"

"Want a ride," Spencer insisted.

"How about a ride on Uncle Rick?" Caroline suggested to the pouting boy. "He's much taller than your daddy, you'll be much higher up."

"Okay." The child flung himself onto Rick.

"Come on, Caro, we'll all go." Rick anchored Spencer firmly on his shoulders as the little parade moved toward the front door.

"Are you sure you can?" Maggie asked J.D., fearful the walk might be too much for him.

"Positive," he told her firmly. "I can't wait to see them."

"It might be a good idea, Maggie. The kids have been

really anxious," Caroline agreed, wondering if she should tell them about the nightmares several of the children had been having. Maybe now that their parents were safe and at home the terrible dreams would end.

There was absolute chaos following the dinner hour, the children so delighted to have their parents home with them again that they resisted bedtime for as long as possible. Finally, toward ten o'clock, Maggie managed to usher them all up the steps. While the four girls readied for bed, she rocked her youngest in her arms, tears of happiness streaming down her face as she prayed her thanks.

She laid Spencer quietly in his crib and closed the door slightly, then followed the hallway to the girls' rooms. Peeking into the room shared by Lucy and Emma, she found them both frantically searching under one bed.

"I knew you'd lose it," Lucy was grumbling. "You're such a dummy."

"I am not." Gentle Emma stood up, small fists clenched in frustration. "I put it in a secret place to keep it safe."

"Yeah, so secret even you don't know where it is," taunted Lucy. "So safe we can't find it."

"What is going on?" Some things, Maggie told herself with an inner smile, will never change.

"I can't find *The Secret Garden*," Emma wailed, burying her face in her mother's midsection. "I tried to remember where we put it so we could read the next chapter, like we used to before——"

"And she lost it." Lucy, always anxious to cut to the chase, summed up the situation for her mother.

"Lucy, be nice and apologize to Emma while I get the book. I know exactly where it is."

A moment later, Maggie returned, the treasured book in hand. She'd found it on her bedside table where they'd left it, months ago. The two girls climbed happily into their beds while their mother, almost choked by tears yet again, read softly, savoring the joy of sharing this small nighttime ritual.

The young ones all sleeping soundly, she turned off the

light and followed the steps to the third floor to the boys' rooms.

"My heroes," she said as she kissed her nearly grown-up sons.

"Mom, Dad's all right, isn't he?" Jesse asked with the greatest of concern.

"As all right as he'll ever be," she told him honestly.

"But his arm . . ." Tyler frowned.

"The doctors did the best they could," she told them.

"He almost died, didn't he?" Jesse said softly. "I heard Gramma . . . We were so scared, Mom."

"So was I, Jess," she admitted.

"We prayed every night, all of us did," Tyler told her.

"I've no doubt that's what pulled him through." She was near tears again.

"We're glad you're home, Mom." Jesse leaned back, permitting her for the first time in years to pull the covers up and tuck him in.

"So are we." She leaned over and kissed them both before turning out the light.

Rick and Caroline were just preparing to turn in, as she descended to the bottom of the steps. She hugged them, thanking them for sharing their homecoming, then walked into the kitchen to lock up the back of the house.

J.D. had just turned off the outside lights.

"Think we should turn in, too," she told him. "It's been an exhausting day. Won't it be lovely to sleep in our own bed tonight . . . What is it? What is that grin for?"

"That's just how you looked the day I met you, your hair pulled back like that. Even had on the same color sweatshirt."

"Probably is the same sweatshirt." She pulled at the front of the red fleece top and laughed.

"You've barely changed all these years, you know that?" He reached out for her with his good hand and wrapped his arm around her, kissing her soundly.

"Well, you haven't changed all that much either, you know. Except, of course, for that bald spot." Her fingers searched the back of his head for the spot that had been shaved in the hospital when the slight nick from the bullet had been treated. The hair had, for some reason, stubbornly refused to grow back.

She wiggled out of his arms and turned off the rest of the lights, then took his hand and led him toward the front hallway.

"Come on, Jamey, let's go to bed," she coaxed. "I want to see if what they say about bald men is true."

"And what would that be?" he chuckled, pausing as she locked the front door.

"That bald men make better lovers."

"They say that, do they?"

"Umm-hmm."

She had reached the landing and stopped suddenly. A large orange harvest moon hung above the trees beyond the house. She turned from it, shivering at the sight.

"Ah, but you can't go through the rest of your life hiding from a full moon, Maggie." He caressed her face. "It happened and it's done and we move on in spite of it. We're fine, sweetheart. We're home with our children and we're fine."

"You're not fine, Jamey. You can't use your arm. You can't play an instrument." The angry words spilled from her.

"That's all I can't do, Maggie. Yes, I lost the use of my arm. No, I will never play the piano again, not like I did. But I can still write my music. I can still sing. And the most important thing is that we are alive. We have each other, we have our precious family, our wonderful home, our friends. Compared to what I have, I'd say what I've lost is insignificant."

"How can you be so rational? We came very close to being murdered."

"Close but no cigar." He winked and fluttered an invisible cigar, doing his best Groucho Marx.

"Don't make jokes about it, Jamey."

"Look at it, Maggie, look." He gently tilted her face,

forcing her to gaze out the window. "It's beautiful, isn't it? Big and round and golden. Just as it's always been, as it always will be."

She stared at it numbly, then nodded, "Yes, it's a beautiful moon . . ."

"Now come along and we'll see if a one-armed bald man can put your fears to rest once and for all."

Later, when he had fallen asleep, she silently crept from the bed and crossed the carpeted floor. Raising the curtain to one side, she looked out with some trepidation, intent upon facing the night and the fears that haunted her.

It was a beautiful night, a beautiful moon. For the briefest moment, the terror she had known that terrible night washed over her, reminding her that he had almost been lost to her forever. As the fear slowly ebbed, she took a deep breath and looked over her shoulder to where he slept bathed in moonlight. She knew then with absolute certainty that he was right. They had the things that mattered most. They had cheated Brenner, had cheated death. They would live to watch their children grow, see each other through the trials of the coming years, grow old together, just as they had always planned.

What more, she asked herself as she turned her back on the night sky, *did anyone have the right to ask?*

A fresh and captivating
behind-the-scenes novel about the
creation of a hit sit-com and the
near destruction of its stars.

SHOW
AND
TELL

by Margaret Bard

Available
from

POCKET
B O O K S

1050

New York Times
Bestselling Author

Elizabeth Gage

presents

INTIMATE

Available in Hardcover
mid-March from

POCKET
B O O K S